Brett Battles lives In Los Angeles and is the author of three acclaimed novels in the Jonathan Quinn series — *The Cleaner*, *The Deceived* and *The Unwanted*.

For more information visit: www.brettbattles.com

THE SILENCED

Professional 'cleaner' Jonathan Quinn has a new client and a strange job: find and remove the remains of a body hidden over twenty years ago inside the walls of a London building, before the building is demolished. But Quinn and his team are being watched. Suddenly caught in the crossfire between two dangerous rivals, Quinn must unravel the identity of the body and why it still poses so great a threat even in death. Because a plot stretching from the former Soviet Union to Hong Kong, from Paris to London, from Los Angeles to Maine is rapidly falling apart. And Quinn hasn't just been hired to tie up loose ends — he *is* one.

Books by Brett Battles
Published by The House of Ulverscroft:

THE CLEANER
THE DECEIVED
THE UNWANTED

BRETT BATTLES

◆

THE SILENCED

Complete and Unabridged

CHARNWOOD
Leicester

First published in Great Britain in 2011 by
Preface
An imprint of
The Random House Group Limited
London

First Charnwood Edition
published 2012
by arrangement with
The Random House Group Limited
London

British Library CIP Data

Battles, Brett.
  The silenced.
  1. Quinn, Jonathan (Fictitious character)- -Fiction.
  2. Suspense fiction. 3. Large type books.
  I. Title
  813.6–dc23

  ISBN 978–1–4448–1152–0

Published by
F. A. Thorpe (Publishing)
Anstey, Leicestershire

Set by Words & Graphics Ltd.
Anstey, Leicestershire
Printed and bound in Great Britain by
T. J. International Ltd., Padstow, Cornwall

This book is printed on acid-free paper

With immeasurable thanks
to Mr. Kubik and Mrs. Bernhardi,
two of the best teachers I ever had

1

Petra glanced at her watch.

4:15 p.m.

Her lips tightened as she held in the curse she so desperately wanted to mutter.

The Cathay Pacific flight to New York was only fifteen minutes from boarding, and there was still no sign of Kolya.

If it had been Mikhail who had not yet arrived, she wouldn't have been so worried. But it wasn't Mikhail. He'd already been sitting in the waiting area when she walked up.

No, of course it was Kolya. She had known from the beginning that he was too young, too inexperienced to take with them. But what choice did she have?

Maybe an officer at Passport Control had scrutinized his documents. They were expertly done, but fake, so there was always a chance something had been missed. Maybe Kolya had begun to sweat and look nervous. Maybe Hong Kong security had him in a back room right that very moment, questioning him about his identity and trying to find out whom he might be traveling with.

Maybe the police were even now heading toward the gate where Petra and Mikhail waited, intending to take them into custody.

Petra looked down the concourse toward the main part of the terminal. But there were no uniformed men marching in her direction, only other passengers toting carry-ons and wasting time until their flights departed.

There was also no Kolya.

She glanced over at Mikhail two rows away. Though she couldn't see his face, she knew he had to be as tense as she was. Their operation could afford zero complications, especially after having experienced another setback, this time right there in Hong Kong, the former British colony where it had all begun so long ago.

Another possibility hit her. What if Kolya hadn't even arrived at the airport yet? They had each traveled separately. Mikhail had taken the Airport Express train, while Kolya and Petra had each hailed taxis. What if Kolya's cab had broken down? What if the driver had misunderstood Kolya's destination? Doubtful, she knew. Airport was airport. Even with Kolya's limited English, he should have been able to communicate where he needed to go.

'Ladies and gentlemen,' a voice blared over the public address system, 'at this time we will begin preboarding Cathay Pacific flight 840 to New York's John F. Kennedy Airport. Passengers traveling with small children or those who need additional assistance may board the aircraft now. Once we are done preboarding, we will start boarding all our first-class and business-class passengers, Marco Polo Club members, and . . .'

Petra pushed herself up, unable to sit still any longer. *Where was he?*

Her hand slipped into her shoulder bag as she scanned the terminal, her fingertips quickly

2

searching through its contents. They found what they were looking for. Touching it made her relax, if only just a little.

At the far end of the terminal, dozens of people wearing identical blue sweatshirts moved almost as one toward a gate. Elsewhere, individuals and couples, some using the automated sidewalks, some walking beside them, moved between shops and waiting areas and restrooms. But none of them, *none of them*, was Kolya.

'Excuse me,' a voice said into her ear. 'Did you drop this?'

Petra turned quickly, surprised to find Mikhail standing right behind her, holding a pen out. She hadn't even heard him walk up.

'What are you doing?' he whispered through his smile.

'You shouldn't be talking to me,' she whispered back. They were each supposed to be solo travelers with no knowledge of the others. It was another safety precaution. One they had used since they started on the mission. In a louder voice, she said, 'Yes, I did. Thank you.'

As he handed her the pen, he said, 'You need to get control of yourself.'

She glanced at him. 'What are you talking about?'

He held her eyes for a moment, then looked down. As she followed his gaze, her breath suddenly caught in her throat. In her other hand was the photograph. She had actually pulled it out of her purse and was holding it in front of her.

Anyone who glanced at it probably wouldn't

have given it a second thought. But to have it out in the open was tempting fate. This was their map, the only reason they were in Hong Kong and the only reason they were heading to the East Coast of the United States. If someone *was* tailing them and figured out what the photograph was, all could be lost.

'Thank you for waiting, ladies and gentlemen,' the voice on the overhead speaker announced. 'At this time we will begin boarding our first-class . . . '

'Put it away,' Mikhail whispered.

Petra slipped the photo back in her bag, then hunted around for her ticket. 'Kolya?' she whispered.

Mikhail glanced past her for a moment. 'Have a nice flight,' he said, then dipped his head and walked away.

Once he was gone, Petra stretched, then re-adjusted herself so that she was facing the direction Mikhail had been looking. Sure enough, standing on one of the moving sidewalks was Kolya. He was letting the system do all the work while he leaned against the handrail and sipped at a can of soda.

'At this time we will begin boarding seats in rows thirty-one through forty-four. Rows thirty-one through forty-four.'

Petra watched their young companion a moment longer. Then, with a final mental pull of an imaginary trigger, she retrieved her boarding pass and got into line.

2

Late September

'At this time, Harold's son, Jake Oliver, would like to say a few words.'

The old wooden pews creaked as people used the break between speakers to reposition themselves. When no one immediately stood, necks craned and heads turned, looking toward the first row of the chapel.

Jonathan Quinn felt something poke him in his side. But he continued to stare forward, lost in his own thoughts. When it happened again, this time harder than the first, he pulled himself out of his head and looked over. Orlando was staring at him. Before he could ask what she wanted, she motioned toward the front of the room with her eyes.

He looked over and saw Reverend Hollis gazing at him, smiling.

'Jake, whenever you're ready.'

Quinn closed his eyes for a second. *Oh, God.* He'd been hoping this moment would somehow never come.

Despite the dead bodies he dealt with on a regular basis, attending funerals was something he'd been able to avoid for the most part. His reason was simple. It was the grieving. Death marked the living more than it marked the dead, and Quinn was never sure how to deal with

5

those who mourned. Plus, seeing that grief made him think too much about what he did for a living. And that was something that was becoming more difficult to do.

Slowly, he rose. This funeral was different. The man lying in the open casket at the front of the room wasn't some casual acquaintance, and the grieving weren't friends of the deceased he had never met.

The mourners here in the Lakeside Mortuary Chapel in Warroad, Minnesota, were people he'd known for a long time. And the man in the box? He was the person Quinn had called his father.

He took a step away from the pew and glanced back at his mother. Her red-rimmed eyes were firmly fixed on the casket several feet away, her face not quite accepting, but resigned now.

Two days before, as they'd sat in the mortuary office, her face had been covered in shock and disbelief. Because of this, Quinn had ended up answering many of the questions the funeral director had asked. After a while he had put a hand over hers. 'Mom, would you rather we finish this later?'

Nothing for several seconds, then she looked at him. 'I'm okay,' she said, failing at an attempted smile. 'I don't want to come back and do this again. Let's finish it now.'

Quinn held her eyes for a moment, still unsure.

'Sweetheart, I'm fine. I'm just glad you're here to help me.'

They had talked caskets and hymns and Bible passages and who would deliver a eulogy.

'I'd like both you and Liz to say something,' she'd told him.

He had been caught off guard by the request. Speak at his father's funeral? What would he say that didn't sound insincere or made up? It would be much better if his sister was the only speaker. He started to say as much, but the look in his mother's eyes stopped him.

'Of course. If that's what you want.'

And now here he was, slowly making his way to the podium, a piece of paper with some random scribbled notes in his pocket, but really having no idea what he was going to say.

'Just think of your mother,' Orlando had told him a few hours earlier as they were getting ready.

'I've been doing nothing *but* thinking of her.'

'You've been doing nothing but worrying about her, and, even more than that, worrying about screwing up in front of her.'

'Exactly.'

'You're thinking too much,' she'd said, then kissed him on the cheek. 'You'll know what to say when the time comes.'

He'd pulled her into his arms and held on tight, needing the energy she was feeding him. So naturally, just as some of his tension was starting to ease, his phone had rung.

'Who is it?' Orlando had asked.

'David Wills.'

'Don't answer it.'

He frowned. 'You know I have to.'

Wills was a client who worked out of London. A week before Quinn's father had died, he had

7

put Quinn on standby for an upcoming project. With very few exceptions, if Quinn agreed to do a project, he'd do it.

He flipped the phone open. 'Hello, David.'

'Quinn. How are you?'

'What can I do for you?'

'I'm calling about the project we discussed. We're officially on,' Wills said, his British accent clipped and proper. 'I need you to get on a flight tonight to — '

And there it was, one of those exceptions. 'Let me stop you. I can't do tonight.'

'Okay,' Wills said, not sounding particularly happy. 'Then first thing tomorrow morning — '

'David, I'm sorry, but the next few days are out. If you need to find someone else, I completely understand.'

Orlando leaned through the bathroom door. 'He'd *better* understand.'

'Have you taken another job?' Wills asked.

'No, of course not. It's just . . . a personal issue.'

'How personal?'

Quinn, annoyed, said, 'Very.'

A few seconds of silence.

'Right, then, sorry. Didn't mean to push. How long will you be tied up?'

'Could be up to five or six days.'

'Five or six days?' Wills said, surprised. 'Hold on.' There was half a minute of silence, then Wills came back. 'There is some flexibility with this project. I think I can arrange things so that the early operations are covered. Then you can take over and finish everything off.'

8

''Operations' plural? How big is this?'

'It involves several related assignments,' Wills said.

'That could get expensive,' Quinn said.

Quinn was a cleaner, the guy you went to when you needed a body — or in Wills's case, apparently, bodies — to disappear. His rate was simple: $30,000 a week, with a two-week minimum for each project. If someone had two jobs for him, and each took a day, it was still $120,000 total. He'd explained all that to Wills before the first job he'd done for the Englishman.

'I realize that, but I thought maybe we could work out a flat rate.'

'I don't do flat rates.'

'Quinn,' the Englishman said quickly, 'please, just hear me out first. Given your scheduling conflicts, I anticipate only needing your services on three separate operations. Four, tops. Time-wise, we're talking no more than three weeks. What I'm proposing is a flat rate of one hundred and ninety thousand.'

Quinn paused. He didn't like making exceptions to his rules, but given what he was dealing with at the moment, getting back to work would be a nice diversion.

'Make it two-ten and we have a deal.'

'Can I count on you being available to start by October first?'

That was a little over a week away. 'Depending on where you need me, I should be able to do that.'

'Your first assignment will be in the States.'

'I'd say that's doable.'

'Great,' Wills said. 'Then we have a deal.'

As Quinn neared the podium he almost wished he'd told Wills he would fly out that night. It would have meant he and Orlando would've already been on the road to Minneapolis, a six-hour drive away. He could have avoided the whole ceremony. But the reality was he could never have done that.

He caught sight of his sister, Liz, sitting next to their mom. Predictably, she didn't return his gaze.

When he and Orlando had arrived a couple of days before, he had thought that maybe their father's death would spark a reconciliation between Liz and himself. Maybe not full on at first, but at least start things moving in the right direction.

But because of her school schedule in Paris and the long transatlantic flight, Liz hadn't arrived in Warroad until right before the service. Quinn had been in the lobby greeting mourners when she came rushing in, still wearing jeans and a sweater.

'Liz,' he said, surprised.

'I'm not too late, am I?' She seemed to be all motion: fidgeting with the shoulder strap of her bag, one foot tapping, and her head swiveling side to side as she took in everything in the lobby except her brother.

'You've still got thirty minutes.'

She nodded, her face neutral. 'Where's Mom?'

'She's in back with Reverend Hollis. She should be out in — '

Liz started walking toward the chapel doors.

10

'She's through here?'

'Liz, it's probably not a good idea to interrupt them right now.'

'I don't care what you think. I want to see Mom.'

'Liz, wait.'

But before he could say anything else, she had disappeared into the chapel.

The podium was right before him now. There was no backing out.

With a deep breath, he stepped behind it, then looked out at the room full of his parents' friends and relatives. Everyone watched him, waiting.

Everyone except Liz. Her eyes were riveted on the flower display behind the casket, her jaw tense. Quinn couldn't feel mad at her. He knew, like his mother, she was hurting. She'd lost her father. If anyone in the room had ever understood Harold Oliver well, it would have been Liz.

Quinn pulled the notes he'd written out of his pocket and set them on the podium. After another deep breath, he smiled at his mom, then looked again at the people gathered before him.

'What I remember most about my father . . . what I . . . '

He stopped and glanced at his notes, but there was nothing there that could help him.

I remember his coldness. I remember his distance.

He had written down things he thought people would want to hear. Lies about a relationship with his father he had never experienced. Feelings he had never had.

11

I remember his anger. I remember his inability to love. Me, anyway.

If he tried to say any of the things he'd prepared, everyone would see right through him.

He glanced up at his mom again. She was looking back, her eyes soft, streaks of tears on her cheeks. He wanted to tell her he was sorry, that the right words just weren't coming. But then, as he looked at her, he realized there was something he could say, something that wouldn't be false.

'What I remember most about my father is the way he loved my mother,' he said. 'You could tell in the way he looked at her, and the way he always waited to eat until she was at the table. And the way he waited for her, and didn't give up hope before they were married.' He told stories of life on the farm, of family trips, of Fourth of July picnics all from the perspective of the relationship between his father and his mother.

'He loved her,' Quinn finished. 'And that was enough.'

3

No one who came to the Olivers' farm that afternoon arrived empty-handed. There were casseroles and sandwiches and baked chicken and pans of Jell-O and cakes and pies and cookies and almost anything you would want to drink.

Quinn guessed that at least twice as many people had jammed into his mother's house as had come to the chapel. When it got to the point where he couldn't turn around without bumping into someone, he caught Orlando's eye and motioned to the back door.

The yard was considerably less crowded than inside the house, but it was something equally annoying to Quinn.

Cold.

He shivered as they walked down the steps. Anything below sixty degrees just felt wrong, and the current temperature was definitely well south of that mark. If this had been Los Angeles, the day would have been considered full-on winter. But here in northern Minnesota, it was merely typical fall. And, as if to emphasize that point, several of the dozen or so people who had also opted for the outside weren't even wearing jackets.

Quinn shivered again, then pointed at a couple of empty chairs. After he and Orlando were seated, he began picking at his food, but nothing looked appetizing. After only a few minutes, Orlando set her equally untouched plate on the ground and said, 'I should check on Garrett.'

She had left her son at home in San Francisco under the watchful care of Mr. and Mrs. Vo. Orlando and Quinn had agreed that this was not the time for Garrett to be introduced to Quinn's family. Perhaps the following summer.

Before she could retrieve her phone, though, several women approached them.

'Jake, that was just lovely — what you said about your father,' one of the women said.

'Thank you,' Quinn replied. He remembered her as the mother of someone he'd gone to school with, but her name escaped him.

'Yes,' one of the other women said.

'Absolutely lovely,' the last told him.

'Thank you.'

'I can't believe how grown up you are now. And who is this beautiful woman you're with?' the first asked.

Quinn could feel Orlando tense beside him. 'Oh, I'm sorry,' he said. 'This is my girlfriend, Claire.'

The first woman smiled. 'Nice to meet you, Claire. I'm Mrs. Patterson.'

'How nice you could come with Jake,' the third said. 'I'm Mrs. Moore.'

'Claire? I wouldn't have expected that name,' the second one said.

Quinn frowned, annoyed, but Orlando immediately put a calming hand on his thigh and said, 'My father was part Irish.' It wasn't a lie. Her father was half-Irish, but her father had also

14

been half-Thai, and her mother one hundred percent Korean. When someone looked at Orlando, her Irish ancestry was the last thing she saw.

'What name do you want my family to call you?' Quinn had asked Orlando before they'd left for Minnesota. 'Your real name?' Orlando was not the name she'd been born with. Like most in the secret world, she'd taken on a new identity, burying who she had been.

She scoffed. 'I hate my real name.' She was silent for a moment. This would be the name Quinn's family would always know her by, so it wasn't something to be taken lightly. 'Claire was one of my father's favorite names. He always said he wished it had been mine.'

'Then that's what it is now.'

After the women left, Quinn said, 'Sorry.'

Orlando smiled. 'It's fine.'

Quinn was just raising his beer to his lips when the back door to the house swung open and Liz stepped out. She looked around at those milling outside, then spotted Quinn. With sudden determination, she began walking toward him.

'Uh-oh,' he said.

'It's okay,' Orlando murmured. 'She's not going to cause a scene. Not here.'

As he watched his sister approach, Quinn couldn't help but be amazed at how the little tomboy he used to know had grown into such a beautiful woman. Not model beautiful, not put-together beautiful. Naturally beautiful, the kind of beauty not everyone noticed right away,

15

but once they did, they would never forget. Liz could just roll out of bed, throw on a T-shirt, a pair of jeans, and a baseball cap, and she'd still be more attractive than most women.

Of course, the half scowl on her face wasn't particularly helping her looks at the moment.

'Would you mind if I borrowed my brother for a few minutes?' she asked Orlando once she reached them.

'Not at all.' Orlando started to stand. 'I have a call I need to make anyway.'

'No need to get up. I feel like a walk. Thought maybe Jake could go with me.'

They both looked at Quinn.

'Sure,' he said. 'Here.' He handed his plate to Orlando, grabbed his bottle of beer, and stood up. 'Let's go.'

They walked in silence, Liz striding out a few feet ahead of him. She guided him down the dirt road that led to the barn. The building was big and white and in need of a new coat of paint. It had been at least six years since their father had stopped actively farming, so after the animals had been sold off and the fields on either side of the house had been leased to a neighbor, maintenance of the barn had no longer been a priority.

Liz turned onto the path leading around the left side of the barn and into the woods.

Once they were among the trees, the trail narrowed, much of it overgrown from disuse. For several years when Quinn had been a kid, he had taken the path every day. When his sister, eight years younger than him, had been old enough, she had done the same.

They walked for ten minutes before Liz finally stopped exactly where he knew she would — the site of the old fort he'd built for himself. It wasn't long after he outgrew it that Liz had made it her own. Only the fort was gone now, reclaimed by nature, the wooden walls rotted and turned to mulch. Quinn could see a few rusty nails protruding from the surrounding trees, but that was about all that was left.

'I used to think you made this for me,' Liz said.

Quinn took a couple of steps forward. The ground was covered in brush and saplings, just like it had been when he'd first chosen the spot. Back then he had cleared it, and built a wooden floor that sat a foot above the soil on two-by-four beams and old bricks.

'I guess maybe I built it for both of us,' he said.

Something caught his eye. It was black and half-buried next to a tree. He knelt down and tugged on it until it came free. It was a license plate. Black background with faded orange-yellow letters. The three upper quarters were taken up with the number, while below was a single line:

19   CALIFORNIA   54

He had found it in a neighbor's barn and had taken it when no one was home. It had been in a dusty pile with several other plates from various states. He didn't think it would be missed.

It was the only one he took, though.

California. It had seemed exotic and exciting and, most of all, far from Minnesota. He remembered staring at it for hours, dreaming about escaping to San Francisco or Los Angeles or San Diego. He smiled at the realization he'd actually achieved the dream.

'What?' Liz asked.

'Huh? Oh.' Quinn tossed the plate on the ground. 'Nothing. Just . . . nothing.'

She stared at it for a moment. 'Mom's going to need help,' she finally blurted out.

'Is that what you wanted to talk about?'

'I have to go back to Paris tomorrow. I'm already missing too many classes as it is.'

'I can stay for a couple more days,' he told her. 'But after that, I have to return to work.'

As far as Liz and his mother knew, Quinn was an international banker. It was a cover he often used on the job, too. It helped explain his extensive travel.

'So I'm supposed to just stay? I'd have to take the term off.'

'Relax,' Quinn said. 'Of course you should go back. Uncle Mark and Aunt Carole are going to check on Mom every day. And I've spoken to Reverend Hollis. He's going to have some of the ladies from the congregation help her out until she's feeling better.'

'That's your solution? Get others to do it for us? Great.'

'Liz, come on. It's going to be fine. I'll be here for — '

Quinn's phone buzzed. Instinctively he pulled it out and looked at the screen.

18

David Wills again.

Liz rolled her eyes. 'Work, right?'

Quinn sent the call to voicemail and shoved the phone back in his pocket.

'You're going to have to leave sooner than you thought, aren't you?'

'I said I'd stay for a couple more days, and that's what I'm going to do.'

She took a step away, looking deep into the forest. 'You know, I used to think . . . I used to think that maybe . . . ' She paused for several seconds. 'You know, never mind, Jake. Just . . . never mind.'

She turned and started walking back down the path.

'Liz,' he called out.

She didn't stop.

'Liz!'

But she had already disappeared among the trees.

Quinn ached at the distance between them, but didn't know what to do about it.

Despite their age gap, they had been close once. Right up until he'd left home. She'd been nine then, and he knew she'd been at an impressionable point. But he'd had no choice.

He had hoped one day she'd understand. One day she'd realize he'd done it for her, and would forgive him. But so far, that day had yet to come.

His phone buzzed again, notifying him he had a message. He listened to it.

'Good news,' Wills's recorded voice said. 'I won't need you until October third. We're still firming up your first op location, but at the

19

moment it looks like Los Angeles. I'll call with more details in a couple days.'

Quinn erased the message, then stuffed the phone back in his pocket.

At least he hadn't lied to Liz about how long he could stay.

4

October

Their flight out of Newark International Airport, just outside of New York, had been delayed on the tarmac because of bad weather. So by the time they touched down in Los Angeles, Petra was ready to rush down the aisle and rip the aircraft's door open herself to get out.

The minutes they'd lost had been more than just the hundred and twenty they'd spent sitting on the ground. The delay had caused them to arrive in the late afternoon, when the freeways of Los Angeles turned into parking lots.

She swore under her breath.

'What is it?' Kolya asked from the window seat next to her.

'Not important.'

Because of the near debacle in Hong Kong, and contrary to the precautions they'd taken since they'd left home on their mission, she had decided to keep Kolya close. At least this way he was with her at all times.

She knew it was a huge risk. Dombrovski had been very adamant during their training. 'Never give him any means to know who you are. Constantly change your identities. Travel alone. And always assume he is looking for you.'

And looking for them he was. If Dombrovski's

own murder back home hadn't been enough proof, losing Luka in Bangkok was. Luka had been closing in on one of their targets, Petra just ten minutes behind him. But by the time she reached his position, he was dead. Their team of four suddenly down to three.

She sent up a silent prayer that this break in protocol didn't lead to a similar disaster.

Taxiing to the terminal at LAX seemed to take as long as the flight, but finally the plane slowed, then stopped. A second before the engines died and the seat-belt tone went off, Petra was up and moving down the aisle, bag in hand. She got to within two rows of the front door before an overweight man in an ugly brown suit stood to open one of the overhead luggage compartments, blocking her way.

She glanced over her shoulder. Kolya hadn't done as well as she had. The boy was strong and had some useful talents, but, like in Hong Kong, his youth often denied him the experience she desperately needed him to have.

A minute later Petra was walking rapidly through the concourse. Kolya caught up to her just as she reached the escalator to the baggage claim area. As they rode down, they both scanned the crowd standing near the bottom.

'There,' Kolya whispered, looking toward a man holding a sign that read PEGGY ROBERTS.

'You know what to do,' she said.

He nodded, then moved off the escalator in the direction of the nearest carousel.

Petra went to the left through the crowd, her eyes searching for any signs of trouble. They were so close. This had to be it. Here they would uncover the information they needed. She was sure of it.

She found a spot near a group of French tourists. They were slowly gathering their luggage and arguing about the location of the bus to their hotel. She watched as the throngs of recently arrived struggled with one another in attempts to locate their appropriate carousels, then secure spots where they could wait and silently hope their luggage would be the first to come down the chute.

Despite the size of the crowd, Petra did her best to check every face, sometimes taking in several people in one quick scan, sometimes lingering several seconds on a person who, for any number of reasons, required more attention.

The driver holding the ROBERTS sign continued to stand near the base of the escalators, his gaze flicking from one person to the next as passengers descended from the terminals above. He had the bored look of someone who had done this a thousand times before.

Kolya, on the other hand, looked anything but bored or inconspicuous. He had done as instructed, and was standing near one of the carousels, but he seemed more interested in the man with the ROBERTS sign than in the bags circling on the never-ending conveyor belt. The luggage was where his focus should have been, creating the illusion that he was just another generic member of the masses.

Petra swore under her breath, but knew there

was little she could do. Kolya had not received the several years' worth of training that she and Mikhail had. He was new to the art of deception, his only education coming sporadically when Petra or Mikhail found time for a little instruction.

Because of this, she had tried to minimize Kolya's involvement, keeping him busy with the things he was good at, or at least could handle. Like driving or acting as communications point. Bringing him along on this trip to Los Angeles was taking a chance, she knew, but the alternative would have been to leave him with Mikhail in New York. And while Mikhail liked the kid well enough, his patience level with Kolya had dipped even lower than hers. If things got too involved, she could just stick Kolya in a motel room somewhere, as she had done when she and Mikhail had gone on their unsatisfying hunt for David Thomas.

No, not unsatisfying. Bitterly disappointing.

Mikhail had tracked down Thomas's last known address to a house in Clifton, New Jersey. But they arrived to find the Englishman had been missing for a week.

And they all knew 'missing' in this case could mean only one thing. The man was dead.

Just like Freddy Chang in Hong Kong, or Stacy McKitrick in Bangkok.

Chang's body had been fished out of the East Lamma Channel the day after Petra and her small team had arrived in Hong Kong. And in Bangkok they had at first lost Luka, then McKitrick herself had turned up dead on a walkway along one of the old city canals.

So close.

Perhaps Thomas would turn up in the Atlantic at some point, but even if he did, it didn't matter. Dead was dead, and of no use to her. She needed at least one person from her photograph to be alive. She couldn't question a corpse.

But now with Thomas sharing the same fate as most of the others, the list of possibilities had been reduced to two names: Kenneth Moody, last known location Philadelphia, and Ryan Winters, last known location Los Angeles.

At least one of their two targets had to still be alive. If not . . .

Petra wouldn't even let herself think about it. She and Kolya were here in Los Angeles pursuing Winters, and Mikhail was back on the East Coast hunting down Moody. They were doing everything they could. Thinking more was just wasting energy.

She did another quick sweep of the baggage area, decided their arrival had gone unnoticed, then walked over to carousel number two and tapped Kolya on the shoulder. Without waiting for a response, she walked over to the man with the sign.

'Ms. Roberts?' the man asked.

'Yes,' Petra said with a slight Southern twang. 'I'm Ms. Roberts.' She had worked very hard at perfecting an American accent, and had done well enough to fool most people.

'Great,' the man said, his smile more functional than earnest. 'My name is Frank. No bags?'

'Just what we're carrying.'

This didn't seem to surprise him. He'd undoubtedly seen it all in his job. 'Would you like to wait here while I get the car?'

'We'll come with you.'

★ ★ ★

Frank drove them to the San Fernando Valley and dropped them off at the Days Inn in Studio City. Kolya and Petra found the dark gray Buick Lucerne that Mikhail had arranged for them parked near the back. No paperwork, no way to trace the vehicle to them. If they were being tracked, the trail would end at the motel.

'Keep to the speed limit,' Petra instructed, not wanting to draw the attention of the police.

Once they were back on Ventura Boulevard, she entered their destination into the GPS mounted in the dash, then examined the route. Laurel Canyon Boulevard was a mile to the east. From there it would be a quick drive into the hills to Winters's house. She guessed ten minutes tops.

Above them, the sky had turned a deep blue, but few stars were visible through the haze of the city lights. *Just like Moscow*, Petra thought.

The pay-as-you-go cell phone she'd acquired in New York buzzed in her bag. 'What happened?' Mikhail asked before she could say anything. 'You were supposed to call hours ago.'

'Our flight was delayed after we'd already boarded. If you had checked our status online, you would have known that.'

26

Mikhail was silent for a moment. When he spoke again, his tone had softened. 'Where are you?'

'We just retrieved the car from the motel.'

'No problems?'

'None. Anything on Moody yet?'

'I found someone who remembered him. A neighbor. Said he thinks Moody moved to New York, but he wasn't sure.'

Petra frowned. 'Keep looking.'

'What do you think I'm doing? Sitting in a bar getting drunk?'

Petra closed her eyes. 'Of course not. I know you're doing your best. But we can't afford to lose another chance.'

'We'll find them.'

'We found Chang and McKitrick and Thomas, too,' she reminded him.

'I meant alive.'

'Have you heard from Stepka?' Petra asked.

'No. You want me to call him?'

'I'll do it.'

She hung up. Stepka's role in the operation was that of technical support. Dombrovski himself had ensured that Stepka got the best training available. Something the young man would undoubtedly use to make millions once their mission was finished. He was based out of a Moscow apartment. A significant amount of their funds had been used to equip the space with the best computers and communications gear.

Petra calculated the time difference. Moscow would just be waking up, which, knowing

Stepka, meant he was starting to think about going to bed. She made the call.

'Yes?' Stepka said in typical hurried fashion.

'It's me,' Petra said.

'Hold on.' The delay was only a few seconds long. 'Where are you?'

'Los Angeles. Heading to the address you found for Winters.'

'Excellent.'

'Have you made any progress on the other matter?' she asked.

She had tasked Stepka with trying to find out who had been hired to erase the people she and her team had been trying to find. If they could figure that out, they might be able to get one step ahead of them. That could very well be the difference between failure and success.

'I'm still working on it.'

'Work faster,' she told him. 'We need to know.'

'I'm doing what I can,' he insisted.

'If Winters and Moody are dead, too, then the only lead we'll have left is whoever's doing the killing.'

'I know!'

'We can't afford to — '

'Petra,' Kolya interrupted.

She put her hand over the phone. 'What?'

'We're almost there.'

★ ★ ★

Winters was home.

Unfortunately, he wasn't alone.

His house was located where Laurel Canyon

28

began its rise into the Hollywood Hills, several blocks south of Ventura Boulevard. It was one level, and impressive: a dark wooden roof, outer walls painted creamy yellow, window frames and front door a bright, glossy white, and a wide grassy front lawn. Back in Moscow it would have been something only the very rich could afford, but by American standards, she had no idea where it fell on the monetary status scale. In the driveway were two sedans, a Mercedes and an Infiniti.

As Kolya drove the sedan leisurely down the street, Petra took another glance at the house. Through the front window, she could see the dark shapes of several people. She told Kolya to keep driving, then instructed him to turn down the next street and park. She opened the glove compartment, but it was empty. A bit more anxious, she slipped her hand under her seat and dug around until her fingers touched a hard object wrapped in what felt like cloth. She pulled it out.

It was a canvas bag, the kind someone would use at a grocery store. From within she pulled out the Baby Glock subcompact pistol Mikhail had arranged to be waiting with the car.

'You think you're going to need that?' Kolya asked.

'I hope not,' she said, then slipped the gun into her bag and climbed out of the car. 'Keep the lights off and the engine running. I'll be back soon.' She closed the door silently behind her.

Night had descended in full over Los Angeles. But while the lights along Ventura Boulevard had

29

been bright enough to leave little hidden, up here in the hills the streetlamps only cut ineffectual holes in the darkness. Despite this, Petra proceeded with caution, taking the relaxed pace of someone out for an evening stroll. She noted lights on in most of the houses she passed, but she was the only one out.

Then, two houses down and across the street from Winters's place, she spotted a man leaning against a tree.

He wasn't exactly hiding, but close enough. He had positioned himself in such a way that the tree blocked the light from the nearest streetlamp, creating a dark shadow that all but enveloped him. His short height made her think that he might be a teenager, but her gut said no. In her mind, a giant sign hung above him, reading DOESN'T BELONG.

Without missing a step, she continued down the sidewalk, one arm wrapped around her chest as if she was fighting off the cool night, the other draped at her side, her hand resting near the opening of her bag inches from the grip of the Glock.

When she'd closed to within ten feet of the man, she glanced at the ground pretending to check her footing. She stayed that way until she was abreast of him, then looked back up, her gaze swinging to the left like one might naturally do. She stopped abruptly, her eyes wide, staring at the man.

'My God, you scared me,' she said.

'Sorry,' the man said, not moving from the shadow.

Up close, the darkness did not mask him completely, and she could see he must have spent a lot of time in the weight room. No doubt, she guessed, to compensate for his lack of stature.

'It's okay.' Petra let out a nervous laugh. 'It's just you're kind of hidden there.'

The man smiled without showing his teeth, but remained otherwise silent. His attention seemed to be focused more on the house across the street than on her.

'Nice night, huh?' Petra said.

He responded the same way he had before.

After a moment, she smiled and started walking off. 'Have a good evening.'

At the next block she turned left. As soon as she was out of sight, she stopped and turned around. She almost expected to see him standing behind her, but the sidewalk was empty.

He was a watcher, not a local. And by the bulge Petra noticed under his jacket, an *armed* watcher. But was he watching to make sure no one got in, or that no one got out?

Or was he *with* the group inside? Standing guard in case . . .

In case someone like me shows up, she thought. She closed her eyes and swore under her breath. Like the others, Winters would soon be a dead end. If they hadn't been delayed in New York, they wouldn't have gotten stuck in traffic, and it was possible they would have been able to get to the house first. Winters would have been theirs.

She pulled out her phone and called Mikhail.

'We're too late,' she said.

'What happened?'

She told him what she'd found.

'He's still alive, though,' Mikhail said. 'There's still a chance.'

'The only chance I see involves a high percentage of bullets aimed at my head. Is that what you want me to try?' When he didn't answer, she said, 'Have you made progress on Moody?'

'A little. I traced him from Philadelphia to an address in Manhattan, but he's not there anymore, either. I'm trying to figure out where he went next.'

Petra wanted to scream, but instead she said, 'Get us on a flight back tonight.'

She disconnected the call, then stood there for several moments thinking. Maybe Mikhail was right, and Winters wasn't yet a lost cause. At the very least, pictures of those who had him could be very useful in identifying who the killers were.

She traded her phone for the palm-size digital camera in her bag, then, keeping low, moved back onto Winters's street, crouching behind a parked car to mask her return. She was only there a few moments before the watcher stepped away from the tree and started crossing the street. He was tilting his head the way a person did when he was listening to a receiver in his ear.

She shot off a couple of pictures, then turned the camera on the house. The front door was now open, and standing just inside was a large man in a suit that did little to hide his bulk. He stepped aside so that another man, this one only slightly smaller than the first, could pass

32

through. Two others appeared in the doorway. Neither was in the same size class as the two behemoths. One looked to be in his late thirties or early forties. He was thin, but walked with a confidence that made Petra think he was in charge. The other man looked pale and nervous. Petra estimated that he was in his mid to late sixties, the right age to be Winters.

The one in charge had a hold of the other guy's arm and was helping to keep him from collapsing. Once they were outside, one of the big men took over, lifting the man so that his feet barely touched the ground as he walked him toward the Mercedes in the driveway.

When the car door opened, the dome light came on, illuminating the older man's face.

Winters. Definitely.

Even from this distance, she could see fear on the man's face. She touched the zoom, took one more picture, then slipped the camera back into her bag.

Once Winters was shoved into the back of the silver sedan, Petra retreated to the next street down, then sprinted back to the Buick.

'Go!' she yelled as she jumped back into the car. 'We have to follow them.'

Kolya pulled the car onto the road. 'Follow who?'

'A silver Mercedes. They have Winters.'

Kolya turned onto Winters's street just in time to see the taillights of the Mercedes turning two blocks away.

'Hurry,' Petra said. 'But for God's sake, don't let them know we're here.'

33

★ ★ ★

They followed the Mercedes south on the 101 freeway into Hollywood and then downtown. There it finally exited onto a side street.

'Not too close,' Petra said. Unlike on the freeway, they could be easily spotted now.

'I know,' Kolya shot back. 'But I don't want to lose them, either.'

They were surrounded first by skyscrapers, then by squat storefronts with signs mostly in Spanish. After a while, these gave way to warehouses and manufacturing plants, most with no identification at all.

It was quiet here, almost deserted. The buildings that didn't look abandoned were shut down for the night. But it wasn't only the buildings that looked abandoned. The roads, too, were nearly deserted. Petra was sure they would be spotted at any moment.

'Slow down,' she said.

'Trust me,' Kolya told her.

He immediately turned right onto a side street. As soon as they were out of sight of the Mercedes, he flipped the Buick's headlights off, then executed a quick one-eighty. A moment later they were back on the main road, the Mercedes's taillights fading in the distance.

'Don't lose them,' she said urgently.

'Which is it? Don't lose them or slow down?'

Petra didn't answer.

They raced forward, closing the gap by a third before Kolya eased back on the accelerator. Ahead, red brake lights shone brightly in the otherwise dark, empty night. Kolya let the Buick coast to a halt in the darkness near the curb.

After half a minute, the brake lights dimmed as the Mercedes crept forward several feet, then turned off the road. A second later it slipped behind a building, but it didn't completely disappear. The brake lights had come on again, and the red glow leaked back to the street. It stayed like that for half a minute, then everything went dark.

'There was a parking lot about half a block back,' Petra said.

'I saw it,' Kolya said.

'Take the car there and wait. If the Mercedes comes back out, duck down and make sure they don't see you.' Petra opened the door and climbed out.

'How long do I wait?'

'You have something better to do?'

'No. I was just . . . I mean, what if you need help?'

'I won't.' Petra hesitated in the opening. 'If I'm not back in two hours, go to the airport and call Mikhail.'

'What about you?'

'If I'm not back by then, I'm dead.'

5

Quinn and his apprentice, Nate, had been waiting for almost two hours. But waiting was part of the job, and they were both experts at it. They sat quietly, saying very little, their minds wandering but their senses alert. When their handheld radio came to life, neither of them even flinched.

'Give us five to clear out, then you're on,' a male voice said on the other end.

Quinn clicked the Talk button. 'Copy.'

He had no idea who the prime op was on this job. Wills had supplied Quinn with all the instructions he would need, so there had been no face-to-face with the other team. Sometimes you knew who you were working with, sometimes you didn't. It was the world they lived in.

As far as his own team was concerned, after reading through the job specs, Quinn had determined there would be no need for more than the two people. So after Minnesota, Orlando had gone home to San Francisco to be with Garrett.

'Be careful,' she'd said. 'If you need me, I can be there in a couple hours.'

'We won't need you.'

'That warms my heart.'

'I need you, but not for this. Is that better?' he asked.

'It's a start.'

Quinn and Nate waited quietly for five

minutes to pass. The room they were in had served as an office at one time, but it had been years since it was last used. They had brought two folding chairs, a thermos of coffee, and a couple Styrofoam cups, but otherwise the room was empty.

'Time,' Quinn said without looking at his watch.

He tossed the walkie-talkie to Nate, who bagged it up with the thermos and cups. They then folded the chairs and set everything in the hallway to be picked up on their way out.

A wipe-down was unnecessary. They'd been wearing gloves since before they'd gotten out of the van. They'd also taken the additional steps of wearing hairnets and garments that covered everything except their faces. Unless their DNA could be pulled out of the air, no one would ever know they'd been there. Quinn was always careful, but the fact they were doing this job in the same city he and Nate called home made him want to cut the risks down even more.

The op room was on the other side of the building, one floor down. Nate walked past the door and continued on toward the nearest building exit to make sure that the others had left and no one else had shown up.

While Nate did that, Quinn approached the op room door and pushed it open. A mixed odor of gunpowder and blood wafted out. Both were familiar smells, so were no more than background noise to him. There, but easy to tune out.

The floor revealed what he expected to see. One body. Male.

The man was on his back, a bullet hole just a little off center in his forehead.

Quinn frowned. The shooter had used a 9mm by the looks of it. A .22 would have been better. It was a close-in job, so no need for more power than a .22 could provide, and, most important to Quinn, a .22 would have left less mess.

But being prepared was something he took very seriously. So, from the start, Quinn assumed the ops team wouldn't care about what they left behind. That's why he and Nate had draped the entire room in a double layer of plastic when they first arrived. Just in case. As expected, the sheeting had contained the blood splatter. Now all they had to do was wrap everything up, carry the package out to the van, account for the bullet, then do a final sweep to make sure they hadn't missed anything.

Ten minutes tops.

Nate walked up behind Quinn. 'Building's secure.'

'Good.' Quinn motioned into the room. 'After you.'

The dead man looked to be in his mid-sixties. He had a bit of a spread around the waist, but was otherwise in decent shape. His hair was more salt than pepper. Visually, there was nothing particularly remarkable about him. Whatever sins had necessitated his removal ran deeper than his appearance.

It wasn't Quinn's job to stand in judgment. He was only there to make the condemned disappear. It wasn't that he was amoral, but he'd learned over the years that it was often hard to tell where the line between right and wrong was drawn, and sometimes there didn't seem to be a line at all. The best Quinn could do was align himself with organizations he trusted, whose work was usually on the up-and-up.

That had become harder after an organization known as the Office had been dismantled. They'd been his de facto employer for years, and for the most part he had always been confident where they stood. He felt he could trust them, and not constantly question their motives. Up until the end, they had given Quinn a steady stream of work, which meant he seldom had to deal with other clients.

Now it was different. In a span of several weeks, he could work with multiple organizations whose motivations were often harder to discern. He did his best, doing what front-end investigation he could and trusting his gut when he had to. It kept things interesting, and made him realize just how easy he used to have it.

In less than five minutes, they had the body wrapped and ready to go. At Quinn's direction, Nate was probing the small bullet hole in the exterior wall. 'Went all the way through,' he said.

'We'll make a quick sweep of the perimeter. If we can't find it right away, we'll forget it.'

Their van was parked in back next to an old loading dock. The dock itself was sealed off by a chain-link fence, but a few feet away was an unimpeded double door.

The first thing they did was load their equipment and the stuff they'd left upstairs into the vehicle. Once that was done, they only had the plastic-wrapped body left.

They expertly carried the package out of the room and down the hall. At the exit, Nate had to lean it against his chest as he opened the door so they could pass through.

'Hold on,' Quinn said, then moved his hands to get a better grip on the body. 'All right.'

As they stepped outside, Quinn registered a quick, sudden movement in his peripheral vision. But when he turned to look, nothing was there.

They maneuvered the body into the back of the van, then Quinn leaned over to Nate and whispered, 'I think we have company.'

Nate kept his focus on securing the body so it wouldn't roll around. 'Where?'

'At the end of the building. I'm going to slip back inside. If we do this right, he won't see me. What I want you to do is get in the van and drive off. Take the body to Bernie's like we planned. I want to keep on schedule.'

'And you?'

'I'll meet you at home.'

'What about the bullet?'

'Don't worry about it. Even if someone finds it, they won't have anything to tie it to.'

'Got it.'

Quinn used the open doors of the van to cover his retreat back into the building. Without being told, Nate completed the ruse by closing the van's doors from inside, and crawling through to the front instead of walking around and getting in through the driver's side door. There was no way for anyone watching to know that Quinn hadn't been with him. Quality, intuitive work that emphasized it wouldn't be long before Quinn would have to either make Nate a full partner or set him free to pursue his own projects.

Another year, tops. Probably less.

The crunch of loose gravel as the van pulled away was soon replaced by an eerie silence cut only by the distant drone of the 101 freeway. Most people would have been surprised by the lack of activity so close to downtown. But the warehouse district was one of the most under-populated parts of Los Angeles. After several quiet minutes passed, Quinn began to consider the possibility that the motion he'd seen had been nothing more than one of the homeless looking for a warm place to sleep.

More silence.

Then a sound — no more than a single pebble skipping over the ground.

There was no second pebble, no sound of footsteps on the gravel. Just that one moment of disturbance in an otherwise deathly still night.

Quinn eased down the hallway until he reached the doorway of the large open space that had once been the main storage area. He stood in the threshold looking back toward the rear entrance.

Click.

A sound that almost wasn't a sound at all.

But he'd been waiting for it. The doorknob had been turned.

Quinn stepped all the way back into the storage room, then leaned forward just enough so he could still see the back door. Nothing

41

happened for thirty seconds.

Cautious, Quinn thought. *Definitely not a street person*.

Then, almost in slow motion, the door began to swing open.

Quinn pulled completely back into the storage room, then took a quick look around. There was nothing he could hide behind except the door itself. But he knew he didn't actually need to hide behind anything. If he went far enough in and kept near the wall, the darkness would be enough to conceal his presence. He began moving away from the door, careful not to step on any of the trash that was scattered around. As he did, he lowered the zipper on his coveralls enough to pull his gun from its shoulder holster. It was his standard SIG Sauer P226. From one of the pockets, he removed a suppressor, and attached it to the end of the barrel.

After he'd gone twenty feet, he stepped against the wall and stopped.

He could hear footsteps. Soft, with no pattern. Whoever was in the hallway was taking a step or two, stopping, then starting again. Cautious.

Quinn rested his gun against his thigh as he tried to picture what the other person was doing. Whoever it was had to have at least seen Quinn and Nate put the package into the back of the van. There was a good chance he had seen the operations team leave, too.

If this person was not here by chance, then the only way he could have found the warehouse was by following the ops team in. Quinn was the one who had secured the building, the one who had

42

informed the operations team where it was after they were already en route. No one other than Nate knew about the location, and they had arrived together, without being followed.

But whatever the reason the intruder was here, he was only one thing to Quinn — a problem.

Quinn's job was to cover up the crime scene, and make it so no one would know what had gone down. Sometimes that meant misdirecting someone who'd strayed dangerously close to the job site.

But this was different. Here was a person who obviously knew that something had happened. By now the still-potent smells emanating from the op room were acting as a guide, drawing the intruder forward. The question was, what should Quinn do about it? Killing was not a normal component of his job.

In the hallway, the steps stopped right outside the door to the big room.

Quinn raised his gun and aimed it along the wall.

A dark shape leaned through the doorway into the room.

Not a man, Quinn realized. A woman.

She was maybe five-five or five-six. Age, hair, skin tone, all impossible to tell due to the lack of light.

She hung in the doorway, unmoving and patient. She was good. If someone other than Quinn had been the one hiding, he might have made a move by now, alerting the woman to his presence.

So was she a direct threat or not? If yes, all he

43

had to do was pull the trigger and she would be dead. But that would create another mess that would need to be cleaned up, this one without the benefit of any preplaced plastic. And for all Quinn knew, she might not be alone. A successful cleanup was obtained through knowledge and planning. He had neither with this woman. Who knew what chain of events her death would set off?

Until he saw a gun in her hand moving in his direction, he would wait and observe. Without shifting the SIG, he removed his finger from the trigger.

The woman stood in the doorway a few seconds longer, then disappeared back into the hallway. As Quinn lowered his gun, he could hear her steps moving toward the op room.

Quietly, he made his way back to the door, stopping just short of the jamb. The woman continued down the hall away from him, still unaware of his presence. As soon as he was sure she'd entered the op room, he headed for the rear exit.

When he reached it, he checked back down the hallway, then stepped outside.

★ ★ ★

It was another ten minutes before the intruder exited the building. Quinn watched her from behind a couple of old weather-beaten signs. She moved with caution, but not as much as she'd used entering the building. Quinn could now see she was Caucasian, in decent shape, and

44

probably about ten years older than he was.

He waited until she had rounded the side of the building out of sight, then crept out from behind the signs. The woman only had two choices: return to the back of the building or head toward the main road. Of the two, the latter made the most sense.

Instead of following her, Quinn cut over to the other side of the building and made his way to the street, paralleling the path she would be taking on the far side.

He stopped at the corner, tight to the wall, and did a quick visual sweep. The areas in front of the warehouse and off to the right were deserted. The building next door, a dingy two-story monstrosity with more windows broken than intact, was dark and dead.

Quinn turned to the wall, then eased his head out just enough to clear the corner. In the distance, the lights of downtown glimmered against the night sky. Closer, but still about a hundred yards away, a solitary streetlamp provided the only illumination for blocks.

He searched for any sign of the woman, but all was still. He then focused on the far corner of the building and waited.

It wasn't long before a shadow took a step away from the warehouse, paused, then took several more. He gave her a head start, then followed. She must have a car stashed somewhere. His goal now was to get a plate number. He stuck as close as possible to the empty buildings that lined the street, and kept a good fifty feet between himself and the woman as she walked along the curb.

About sixty feet shy of the feeble streetlight, she turned into a small warehouse parking lot. Quinn slowed, then dropped to a crouch and continued forward another twenty feet. There he used the bushes growing at the base of a useless chain-link fence as cover. He pulled his phone out of his pocket, accessed the camera, and switched to night vision mode.

Ahead he heard a car door open, then voices. One voice was muffled and indiscernible, while the other was clearer and female. The words they spoke weren't from any of the several languages Quinn was either fluent in or familiar with. But that didn't mean he didn't have a pretty good idea what language they had used.

Russian. Or, at the very least, some derivative.

Quinn slid around the chain-link fence and shimmied in as close as he could get, then watched the woman climb into the car and pull the door closed. He took four pictures before they pulled away: one of the car, a close-up of the license plate, and one each of the young guy behind the wheel and the woman. The intruder.

Whoever she was, Quinn had never seen her before.

6

'I'm not a killer,' Quinn said.

He was walking toward Little Tokyo, a more populated part of downtown Los Angeles, where he'd be able to arrange for a taxi. Under his left arm he carried the folded-up coveralls he'd been wearing over his clothes at the warehouse. His first call had been to Nate to make sure everything was going as planned.

It was.

He'd then put in the call to David Wills.

'I know you're not a killer, but aren't you supposed to take care of loose ends?' Wills said, irritated. 'Aren't you supposed to make sure no one finds anything?'

'And she didn't,' Quinn said. 'We were finished by the time she entered the building.'

'Did she see you carry the body outside? Did she see the vehicle that took it away?'

Instead of answering, Quinn tried to change the focus. 'Whoever she was, she had to have followed the ops team in. She waited for them to leave before nosing around.'

'So you're saying she didn't see you remove the body? Didn't maybe take a picture of your vehicle's license like you did of hers?'

'If she did, it's not going to lead her anywhere.' As always, he and Nate had taken the proper precautions. 'And in case you forgot, my standard procedure when something like this

47

happens is to follow, identify, and report. It's one of the conditions we discussed when we first started working together. Or don't you recall that?'

'What if she was a police officer?'

'Even better reason not to shoot her,' Quinn said, then added, 'She wasn't police.'

'How the hell do you know that?'

'Because the cops in L.A. don't usually speak Russian.'

Silence. Then, 'What do you mean?'

'I heard her say something to her partner.'

'In Russian?' The Englishman sounded troubled, but not surprised.

'If it wasn't, it was pretty damn close. Does that mean something to you?'

'You're sure she wasn't waiting there the whole time?' Wills asked.

'Yes, David. I'm sure. I was the only one who knew about the location ahead of time. When I called your ops team, I was already there, and had done several area checks. We were clean at that point. The only possibility is that she followed the others. Unless you have some other theory.'

Wills said nothing.

'I don't like the fact someone showed up on one of my jobs any more than you do,' Quinn said. 'But I did everything according to my rules. I even got you pictures.' Around him traffic was starting to pick up. 'Sorry you're not happy, but that's not my problem. Gotta go.'

'Wait,' Wills said. 'Look, I apologize. You're right. You did exactly what you should have. I'm just feeling a lot of pressure on this one. But that's not an excuse.'

Quinn took a moment, letting his own agitation ebb. So far Wills had been a decent client, fair even. No sense in damaging a good relationship.

'It's fine, David. It happens.'

'I seem to be staying just a step or two ahead on this one, when I'd rather it be a mile,' Wills said. 'We need to talk about the next assignment.'

Quinn looked around. Though there were more cars on the street, he was still the only one on the sidewalk. 'All right.'

'After what happened tonight, I don't want to take any chances, so I'm moving up the next phase. I need you and your team on the East Coast by tomorrow morning.'

Quinn didn't need to check his watch to know it was almost 10 p.m. 'Not possible. By the time we could get to the airport, there won't be any flights.'

'You won't go commercial,' Wills said. 'I'm chartering a plane for you. I'll email the details within the next thirty minutes.'

'Where exactly are we going?'

'Maine.'

* * *

Petra had told Kolya to drive straight to the airport. After leaving the car in one of the long-term lots, they grabbed a free shuttle to the terminals, taking seats in the back as far from

49

the handful of other passengers as possible. The bus was nearing Terminal 1 when her phone began to ring. She didn't need to look at the display. Only Mikhail and Kolya had the number.

'Where the hell have you been?' she asked. She'd been trying to reach him for the last half hour with no luck.

'Busy,' he said.

Petra frowned. 'We're at the airport. Did you get us a flight or not?'

'Winters?' he asked.

'Dead.'

Mikhail paused for a moment, then, 'Continental Airlines 634. You leave at eleven-thirty.'

'Okay,' Petra said. 'Have a car meet us when we arrive. We'll see you at the hotel.'

'You're not flying to New York.'

That caused her a moment's pause. 'You've found him?'

'I've narrowed it down,' he said.

'Where?'

'You switch planes in Cleveland, Ohio, then fly on to Boston. I'll be waiting for you.'

'You'd better be.'

7

The private jet could have easily fit twenty passengers, but besides the two pilots up front and a single attendant, Nate and Quinn had the plane to themselves.

As soon as they were in the air, Quinn announced that he was going to get some sleep.

Nate knew this was more than just information; it was a suggestion that he do the same. With seats that reclined to a fully horizontal position, and the eye-shades and earplugs that had been on the seat cushions when they came aboard, sleep should have been easy.

Nate removed the prosthetic that served as his lower right leg, tilted his own seat back, and tried to get comfortable. But an ache in his missing ankle kept sleep from finding him. Phantom memories, the physical therapist had explained. 'You'll have them the rest of your life.'

Great.

Like he often did, he began to wonder why he could remember his leg, but couldn't remember the moment it had been crushed. It had happened in Singapore outside a hawker center. Arriving at the center with Quinn and Orlando — yes, he remembered that. Racing into position to back up his boss, that too. But the moment the car had intentionally rammed into him? Nothing.

When he woke up a day later in a private

51

hospital, his right leg had already been amputated below the knee. Doctors and nurses had come in and out in no apparent pattern, some looking at his stump, some checking his charts, but few talking to him. The ones who did told him he would be fine. That artificial limbs had come a long way from the plastic and metal boat anchors they'd once been.

At the time Nate had barely listened. Part of it was the shock, but mostly it was the almost-certain knowledge that his career as a cleaner was over. What awaited him was a return to normal life, to a life devoid of the challenges and the excitement and the sense of truly being alive that he'd had as Quinn's apprentice. When he realized this, he almost wished the car had killed him, because he knew the boredom he was facing surely would.

But then, two nights after the accident, Orlando came to see him. It was her second visit of the day. Earlier she'd come with Quinn, who'd hardly been able to say anything.

Pity, that's what Nate thought his boss was feeling. It had been enough to drive Nate deeper into depression.

As soon as Orlando walked back in, Nate looked to the door expecting Quinn to follow.

'I'm alone,' she said as she approached his bed. 'I wanted to say goodbye.'

Nate nodded, the look on his face neutral. 'Okay.'

On the table that hovered above his waist was his untouched dinner. He picked up the fork and pushed some of the rice around.

'I need to get back to Garrett,' she said. Her son was still living in Vietnam at that point.

'Sure, I get it.' He squeezed his eyes closed as pain spiked up his leg into his torso.

'Are you okay?'

'I'm fine.'

'I could get the nurse. Get you some pain-killers.'

'I'm fine!' His voice leaped from his throat, harsh and loud.

Neither of them said anything for several seconds.

'Sorry,' Nate said. 'I just . . . I . . . '

'You should eat,' she said.

'I'm not hungry.'

'What are you talking about? This looks great.'

'You can eat it, then.'

She picked up the spoon from the tray and scooped up some vegetables, a piece of chicken, and some rice, then held them in the air. 'You sure?'

'Be my guest.'

She slipped the food into her mouth, then smiled. 'This isn't bad.' She sat on the edge of his bed.

'I thought you were leaving?' he said.

'In a few minutes.'

He shrugged.

She filled up the spoon again, but this time held it out to him.

'I'm not hungry,' he told her.

'Just try it.'

'No.'

She moved the spoon to his lips. 'Come on.'

'I said I'm not hu — '

53

She slipped the spoon into his mouth.

Having no choice, he started chewing the food. 'I wouldn't even let my mother do that.'

She filled the spoon again and held it back up.

'I can feed myself,' he said.

'Yeah, but will you?'

He scowled at her for a moment, then picked up the fork and stabbed a piece of chicken.

Smiling, Orlando redirected the spoon into her own mouth. 'Could use a little spice. But this is a hospital, so I guess bland makes sense.'

They both chewed in silence for a moment.

Finally Nate said, 'Where's Quinn?'

'Back at the hotel.'

Probably either sleeping or having a beer in the bar, Nate thought. Moving on, no doubt. Maybe even thinking about getting a new apprentice.

'He's trying to arrange appointments for you back in California,' Orlando said, like she was reading his mind.

'Appointments?'

She helped herself to another spoonful. 'Doctors. Physical therapy. Prosthesis fittings.'

'Oh. Great,' Nate said with no enthusiasm.

'Are you going to take another forkful, or am I going to have to feed you again?'

Reluctantly, he got some more food and put it in his mouth.

Orlando watched him eat for a moment. 'Look. You can just take this, go home, and live out your life thinking what could have been, or — '

'Or?' Nate said. 'Seems to me there's no 'or.''

54

'You're still in shock. Your system is full of drugs.' She paused. 'You lost your leg, for God's sake. Of course that's all you can see.' She worked a piece of broccoli away from everything else, then picked it up and popped it between her teeth. 'But it's not the only choice.'

'What then? I'm done being a cleaner.'

'Why? Because you don't want it anymore?'

'No! I want it. I want it more than anything.'

'So what's the problem?' she asked.

'I lost part of my leg. Or hadn't you noticed?' he said. 'Being a cleaner is a physical job. How the hell am I going to be able to keep up?'

'You're good, Nate. You have the skills. You know that. Quinn knows that, too.'

'Quinn thinks I'm done. I could see it in his face when you guys were here earlier. He could barely look at me. He was like one of those people in the movies standing around the bed of someone dying. Great knowing you, good luck on the other side.'

'You're right,' she said. 'He does think you're done. But he's not feeling sorry for you.'

'What then? He's already written me off?'

'Guilt,' she said. 'He's the one who had to make the decision to amputate your leg. And don't forget, he's the reason we're here in Singapore in the first place. This wasn't a job. This was a personal mission for him. And now he feels responsible.'

Nate looked away. 'Well, you can tell him I don't blame him. I wouldn't have been here if I hadn't wanted to be. That should get rid of his guilt.'

Orlando scooped up some more food and held it in the air between them. 'You or me?'

Nate picked up his fork again. As he shoved it under the vegetables, he knocked a piece of chicken off the plate and onto the tray.

Orlando smiled. 'It's good that you're angry.'

'Go to hell.'

'I mean it. You can use that.'

He put the food in his mouth, chewed it, then said, 'Use it for what?'

'For your rehab. So that when you come back to work, you'll be even better than before.'

'As a cleaner? I already told you I physically couldn't do it anymore.'

'There's no way you can know that. Prosthetic devices are pretty amazing these days.'

'So the doctors have told me,' Nate said.

'I was reading on the Internet today about a guy from South Africa who's missing parts of *both* of his legs. But because of the prostheses he has, a couple years ago he almost made the Olympic team.'

'As what? A mascot?'

'Track and field. He's a runner.'

That made him pause. 'A runner?'

She nodded. 'How much do you want this?'

'It's all I want.'

'Then make it happen,' she said. 'Work your ass off. Use the time to study and learn everything you can. Throw yourself into your rehab and your training.'

He wanted to believe her, but then he thought about his mentor. 'Quinn won't go for it.'

'He might think you won't be able to do it, but

he'll give you the chance to prove him wrong.' She smiled. 'And I might have a little influence over him.'

She stood up. 'Are you going to finish eating everything?'

He smiled a little.

'Oh, progress,' she said.

'Have I told you to go to hell yet?'

'So are you going to finish?'

'I'm going to finish.'

She took a step toward the door, then turned back. 'I'm not just talking about the food.'

'I know.'

A whole year had passed since his injury, and he had used the time well. He had done exactly as Orlando had suggested. He'd studied the subjects he was going to need for the job: learning how to fly a plane, perfecting the French he'd taken in high school, expanding his knowledge of chemistry, memorizing the makes and particulars of over a hundred types of trucks and cars, getting a start on Spanish and dozens of other topics large and small. He'd also pushed himself hard in his rehab, surprising his physical therapist and even himself.

Quinn had paid for everything, even purchasing a whole set of prosthetics that could be used under various conditions. First Nate relearned to walk, then to run. By the time Orlando had talked Quinn into taking him out on a job again, Nate was running several miles a day and hiking a couple of times a week in the hills that ran through the middle of Los Angeles.

Quinn's skepticism had soon disappeared.

And Nate's own belief that he would one day become a full-fledged cleaner had returned.

'I told you you could do it,' Orlando said to him a few months earlier.

'Did you?' he said. 'I don't remember that.'

She eyed him critically. 'You know, you're still Quinn's apprentice. I could make sure you get some pretty lousy assignments.'

'You really think you have that much influence over him?'

She huffed. 'Excuse me?'

Nate smiled.

'Excuse me. Sir, excuse me.' The voice was female, both distant and close at the same time.

Nate pushed the eyeshades up. The flight attendant was leaning down next to him, haloed by sunlight seeping in through the windows.

Morning, he thought. He'd fallen asleep after all.

He pulled the earplugs from his ears. 'Yes?'

'Your friend thought you might like to have some breakfast before we land,' she said. 'But you'll have to eat fast. We'll be on the ground in forty minutes.'

Nate glanced over to where Quinn had been sleeping. His mentor was now sitting upright, a plate of food on a table in front of him, a cup of coffee in his hand.

'I'll have a cup of that. Black.' Nate paused. 'Better make it two.'

8

There was a blue Toyota Camry waiting for them at the airport. Quinn climbed behind the wheel and popped the trunk so Nate could throw their bags in back, then he reached under the seat. There he found a thin manila envelope.

Inside were three sheets of paper and a hotel keycard. He glanced through the papers. Two of the sheets were maps. The first covered an area that included Portland, Maine, in the east and a small town called Gorham about ten miles to the west. Someone had marked the map with one blue X in the vicinity of Gorham, and a smaller black X closer to Portland, just north of the airport. The second map was a detailed close-up of Gorham showing a couple of dozen streets — a single blue X on this one corresponding to the blue one on the wider map.

The third page was an info sheet.

```
BLACK Holiday Inn
Timothy Garner, Room 211

BLUE 23 Main Street, Gorham
1:30 p.m.
```

The passenger door opened, and Nate climbed in.

'What do we got?' he asked.

59

Quinn handed him the papers, then started the engine.

The black X indicated the location of the hotel they would use as their base. They had already been checked in to room 211 under the name Timothy Garner. The key card would allow them to avoid contact with the hotel office. The blue X was the meeting site. Where the actual job was to take place had not been indicated.

'Not giving us a lot of time to relax and see the sights,' Nate said.

Per the info sheet, they would need to be at 23 Main Street in a little less than five hours to meet with a man named Donovan.

'We're not here on vacation,' Quinn said.

'Speak for yourself. First time I've ever been to Maine. Isn't this where they're supposed to have the good lobster?'

Quinn rolled his eyes, then pulled out his phone and tossed it to Nate.

'Check in with Orlando.'

It was always smart to have a point person who knew what they were up to, especially when the location was an unfamiliar one. Quinn's go-to in these situations was always Orlando. It was more at her insistence than his request, but he wasn't complaining.

'No, it's Nate,' Nate said into the phone. 'We're here.' He listened for a moment. 'No. All smooth.' A pause, then he looked at the papers Quinn had given him. 'The Holiday Inn on . . . um . . . Riverside Street. West side of Portland.' Again he listened, then looked back at the papers. 'The rendezvous is in the town of

60

Gorham. Twenty-three Main Street. We're expected to arrive by one-thirty . . . Yeah, this afternoon . . . He's driving . . . Okay, I will.'

He hung up.

'I'm supposed to give you a kiss,' Nate said.

'You come near me and I'll cut off your other leg.'

A moment of stunned silence, then Nate laughed. 'Look at you making a joke about my leg. I think that's a first.'

'Shut up and look at the map.' Quinn gave his apprentice a rare smile.

★ ★ ★

Quinn took a shower, then checked the kit that had been waiting for them in the room.

It was a dark blue backpack containing two 9mm guns — a Glock for Nate and the preferred SIG for Quinn — a box of fifty rounds and suppressors and two extra mags for each weapon. There was also a box of disposable rubber gloves and a small first aid kit that included sutures, gauze, and antibiotics. Tucked into a compartment at the back of the bag were copies of the papers that had been waiting for them in the car, and an additional map that showed a more detailed layout of the pertinent part of Main Street in Gorham.

Quinn spent twenty minutes memorizing the map before allowing himself to relax on one of the beds. Nate had turned on the TV and found an old movie on TCM. *The Bad and the Beautiful* with Kirk Douglas.

'A classic,' Nate said. 'One of the best movies about Hollywood ever.'

Quinn had grunted noncommittally. Movies were Nate's thing.

He had to admit, though, Nate wasn't wrong about the movie. It was definitely absorbing and helped to pass the time. Once the film was over, they left the Holiday Inn and headed to Gorham.

Back home in Los Angeles it still felt like summer, but here in Maine, not so much.

The state had fully embraced the two-week-old fall with cooler temperatures, browning ground cover, and leaves that had turned beautiful shades of yellow and orange and red.

They came at Gorham from the east on State Route 25. At some arbitrary point Route 25 became Main Street, and before long they were entering the outer regions of Gorham. Homes here were separated by acres, not feet. Most were set back from the road, many down long driveways and hidden by trees and brush.

As they drew nearer to the center of the small town, the homes began to cozy up to one another and draw closer to the road. Still, compared with a big city, the lot sizes were huge. The predominant house color was white, and the common theme seemed to be colonial clapboard. But these weren't emulating a popular style. These were actual colonial homes, many a couple hundred years old.

As they passed a Burger King on their right, Nate began reading off the addresses, then nodded ahead. 'Should be right up there.'

Twenty-three Main Street turned out to be an

empty store in one half of a two-story-tall brick building on the south side of the street. The windows were covered on the inside by white butcher paper on which someone had written in large letters:

ALISON'S BOUTIQUE COMING SOON!

The other half was occupied by a café.

Quinn turned right on Cross Street and parked behind a small office building.

'Security cameras?' Quinn asked.

Nate took a quick look around. 'None.'

Quinn nodded, then opened his door. Chances were they could leave the Toyota there all day and no one would question it.

'What about the gear?' Nate asked once he joined him outside.

'We'll come back for it once we know what's up,' Quinn said.

They walked to Main Street, waited for traffic to clear, then crossed to the other side.

'They can't want us coming in through the front,' Nate said. 'Gotta be a rear entrance.'

'Check it out,' Quinn said.

While Quinn examined the menu posted in the window of the café, Nate walked around to the back of the building.

When he returned, he nodded. 'Three doors. Two for the café and one for the empty shop.'

Quinn looked at his watch. They were ten minutes early.

'Let's get a coffee first,' he said.

'And a sandwich?'

Quinn frowned. 'Fine. But to go.'

'It would probably draw less attention if you order something, too.'

'Oh, for God's sake.' But the untimely growl from his stomach belied his tone.

★ ★ ★

The man who greeted them at the back door of Alison's Boutique was small only in height. Quinn guessed he wasn't more than five foot five. He wasn't fat, though. Muscles bulged, large and menacing and almost, but not quite, obscene. Steroids for sure, and about a million hours in the gym. If his muscle mass had been toned down even ten percent, he would have been more intimidating. Small guys could be wiry and unpredictable. But with this guy's bulk, speed and agility were no longer options.

'You're late,' he said as he moved out of the way to let them in.

Quinn and Nate crossed inside.

'You Donovan?' Quinn asked, once he and Nate were inside.

The man shook his head. 'He'll be back in a bit.' He nodded toward a rectangular table in the center of the room surrounded by folding chairs. There was no one else present. 'You can make yourself comfortable there.'

'So who are you?'

'I'm Mr. Edgar.'

Quinn cocked his head. 'We've worked together before, haven't we?' He stared at the man for a moment. 'Not Edgar. It's . . . ' He thought for a moment. 'It's Mercer, isn't it?'

'Not bad,' Mercer said. 'And you're Quinn.'

Mercer had been a background player on a job three years earlier. A gig for the Office.

'You were a courier, weren't you?' Quinn asked.

'Was. But haven't been for a long time.'

Without another word, Mercer turned and walked out of the room, leaving Quinn and Nate alone.

Nate, who was already sitting down, sandwich in hand, said, 'Friend of yours?'

'Barely know him,' Quinn said as he took a seat across the table from his apprentice.

'Friendly type.'

Quinn shrugged. You met all kinds in this business.

★ ★ ★

At five minutes after two, the back door to the shop opened again, and four men walked in. They were all somewhere between thirty and forty years old and were casually dressed: jeans, button-down shirts, light jackets.

'Quinn?' the one with thinning hair asked.

Quinn stood up and held out his hand. 'Are you Donovan?'

'Yep,' Donovan said. 'Shall we get down to it?'

A moment later everyone was seated around the table looking at a map. It showed property lines and accurate footprints of each structure in the area. There were also circles of various sizes indicating the locations of trees and other vegetation. At the street end of each property was the

65

corresponding address. Donovan pointed to a block of Main Street not in the town center area, but further out in the direction of Mosher Corner.

'Here's the target house,' Donovan said.

He circled an upside-down, reversed L in the center of a parcel on the north side of the street. The home was set back a couple of hundred feet from the road.

'We're doing it in the target's home?' Quinn asked.

Donovan nodded. 'Not ideal, I know. But he lives alone, and seldom goes out. The report I have says the only visitors he gets are the mailman and a weekly delivery of groceries.'

'Bedridden?' Nate asked.

'No. Just private,' Donovan replied. 'We arrived yesterday morning. Since then I've had one of my men keeping an eye on the place using thermal-scanning gear. We're sure someone is inside, but whoever it is hasn't stepped through the front door yet.'

Quinn thought for a moment, then said, 'How positive are you that you'll need me?'

Donovan paused, then said, 'Let's you and I take a walk.'

* * *

They headed up Main Street, then south along Elm. As soon as it was apparent no one was interested in them, Donovan removed an envelope from his pocket and handed it to Quinn. A file listed Kenneth Moody's name, his address, and the letter *T*.

Terminate.

'So what does the rest of your team think?' Quinn asked.

'Per instructions, they know the mission, but not the target's ID.'

Quinn nodded. Wills had given him the same instructions. But Quinn had long ago decided that whatever he knew about a job, Nate and Orlando would know also.

'Any chance this guy realizes what's coming?' Quinn asked.

'From what I understand, he's paranoid, so he probably always thinks something's coming.'

'And you're positive he's there alone?'

'My man's been doing hourly thermal scans since yesterday. So far he's only logged one person.'

'What about a basement? I assume this house has one. Your equipment can't see down.'

Donovan smiled. 'Wills got some satellite time last night. Took ten overhead thermal images at just after two-thirty a.m. local. It confirmed our findings. Only one person.'

'What if it's not him?'

'Then we don't term.'

They walked silently for a moment. 'So what's the plan?' Quinn asked.

'The property is surrounded by a thick layer of trees and enough distance between houses that we shouldn't run into any problems with neighbors. We've ID'd weak points and will be inside the house less than two minutes from mission start.'

'Tonight?'

Donovan nodded. 'In position at nine p.m.,

67

then get things going at ten. Your designation will be team four. When we get back, make sure you get comm gear for you and your assistant.'

'Will do,' Quinn said.

'When we're ready for you, you'll get a 'Team four go.' But if I say 'Abort,' get the hell out of there.'

'Vehicle?' Quinn asked. His rental car was not body-removal-friendly.

'Parked two blocks away. A black Lincoln MKZ.' He gave Quinn the plate number.

'Gear?' Quinn asked.

'Everything on the list we got is in the trunk, less what was waiting for you at the motel.'

'Okay,' Quinn said. 'Then we're set on my end.'

It was a straightforward op, the kind that should go off flawlessly. Only the job in L.A. was supposed to have been the same kind of thing.

Quinn couldn't help wondering how this one was going to get screwed up, too.

9

'If we're too late . . . ' Petra let the sentence hang, not wanting to give voice to her biggest fear.

So much time wasted.

Bangkok. Hong Kong. New Jersey. And yesterday Los Angeles.

All a waste of time.

In each case they'd been too late. The only positive Petra could take from any of it was that they seemed to be getting closer. While McKitrick, Chang, and Thomas had been dead or missing before she had arrived, Winters had at least still been alive. For a while, anyway.

That left Moody. If they didn't find him, then the promise she and the others had made to those who had died would go unfulfilled, the justice they sought rendered permanently unfinished.

But Moody had proved frustrating in his own way. Mikhail's search for him had led from Philadelphia to Manhattan to Boston.

Only Boston wasn't the end, either. It was just another stop on Moody's trail. He *had* been there, but had again moved. It took until early evening before Mikhail was able to pinpoint Portland, Maine, as Moody's next destination.

It was a 112-mile drive north to Portland, but traffic made it seem twice as far. They were already past the two-hour mark, but only halfway there. If it was possible, the traffic here was even worse than it had been in Los Angeles.

'We'll get him,' Mikhail reassured her.

Petra glanced at him, surprised that he could read her so well. They were in the back seat of a Nissan Maxima, Mikhail with his laptop propped on his lap and a cell phone in his hand, and Petra holding nothing but her fear that they would fail again. Kolya was up front driving.

'Hello?' Mikhail said into his phone. '*Da . . . da . . .* ' He sandwiched it between his ear and his shoulder, then typed something on his computer. '*Spasibo.*'

He hung up the phone and looked at Petra.

'What?' she asked.

'Stepka got an address,' Mikhail said.

'How old?' she asked.

He shook his head. 'Not old.' He smiled. 'Current.'

★   ★   ★

They reached Portland at nine-thirty, and twenty minutes later entered the small town of Gorham.

'There,' Mikhail said, pointing at a house on the left, set back from the street.

'I don't see any lights,' Kolya said. 'Maybe he's not home.'

They drove past, continuing down the road another hundred yards before Petra told Kolya to pull to the side.

'What now?' Mikhail asked.

Petra considered their options. They could get out of the car here and work their way back in the darkness. Take some time to observe the house, make sure nothing was amiss before making a move. That would be the cautious approach.

But so far the cautious approach hadn't worked for them.

'We go knock on the door,' she said.

* * *

While the day had been cool, the night was bordering on damn cold. Quinn was wearing two T-shirts, a thick sweater, and a wool jacket. He'd even put thermals on under his jeans. Still, he swore he could feel his body temperature lowering.

Nate was similarly attired. But if he was as miserable as Quinn, he wasn't saying anything. They'd been waiting in the woods for an hour, having worked their way in from a half mile away.

They'd found a suitable hiding place between some trees and bushes, a small area that had been flattened by either kids or an animal. Not quite the fort Quinn had had in his youth, but it would do.

They were behind the garage, and from that angle could see only part of the back of the house and none of the front yard. The windows on this side were all dark. Perhaps the target had turned in early.

Donovan's voice came over their comm gear. 'Position check.'

'Set,' five voices replied, one after the other in a prearranged order.

71

Quinn and Nate remained silent. Donovan was only interested in his ops team at the moment, not the cleaning crew.

Quinn checked his watch. Seven minutes until showtime.

'How long do you think it'll take them?' Nate whispered.

Quinn kept his eyes on the dark house. 'We'll get the call at 10:05.'

'My money's on 10:07,' Nate said.

'Hundred bucks?' Quinn asked.

'Works for me.'

Quinn flexed his feet to keep his muscles warm as he wondered for the millionth time in the last hour how he could work a 'minimum temperature' clause into his job requirements.

'Car on slow approach,' a voice said over the radio. Not Donovan, one of his men.

'Which direction?' Donovan asked.

'From the east. Same car passed by a few minutes ago . . . still slowing . . . okay, stopping at the end of the driveway.'

'Everyone hold position,' Donovan said.

'Turning onto the driveway,' the voice said.

'Do you have a visual on who's inside?' Donovan asked tersely, unable to keep the growing annoyance from his voice.

'Man up front, man and woman in the back.'

'We're moving,' Quinn whispered to Nate.

His apprentice nodded, then stepped back so Quinn could take the lead. They headed twenty feet deeper into the woods, then west toward the corner of the property. There they hunched down again, this time in a spot with a view of the

72

front yard and the entrance to the house.

The car slowly rolled up the driveway. The driver had turned off the headlights, but the running lights were still on. As it neared the house, it slowed to a crawl.

'They're stopping,' one of Donovan's men said.

The car came to rest twenty feet from the house's front door.

'I've got movement inside the building,' another voice said. It had to be Dailey. He was the one set up across the street, monitoring the thermal readings coming from inside the house. 'Subject is descending from second floor . . . holding at bottom of stairs . . . okay, moving again, toward the front door.'

Just then the two back passenger doors of the sedan opened.

'Subject has stopped again,' Dailey said.

Must have heard his visitors, Quinn thought.

'Okay, he's moving to the window north of the door. Two bodies out of the car. Driver still inside.'

'Everyone continue to hold,' Donovan instructed. 'But be ready to move. If we have to, we take them all. Team four, you guys might have a little more work than planned.'

Quinn keyed his mic on and off, creating an electronic click indicating he understood.

Understood, yes. But he hoped to God that Donovan was wrong. The more people involved, the more chances things would go wrong, and getting caught with several bodies in a small town in Maine was kind of hard to talk your way out of.

73

The two from the car gathered together near the front of the sedan.

'Binoculars,' Quinn whispered.

Nate pulled a set of binoculars out of his backpack and handed them to Quinn. By touch, Quinn flipped the night vision switch, then raised them to his eyes. As he peered through the lenses, he felt his phone vibrate once in his pocket. A text message. It would have to wait.

He focused in on the car. As reported, the driver had remained behind the wheel. He was young, with short hair. And though Quinn couldn't really see his face, he could tell the kid was annoyed. *Probably doesn't like being left out.*

Quinn moved his attention to the driver's two friends. The man had broad shoulders and a hard face and looked to be in his late forties. Short for a guy, maybe five-six tops, but with the vibe of someone who could get things done.

Quinn tried to get a look at the woman, but she was turned toward the house.

He followed the duo as they approached the small porch. Then he got what he'd been waiting for. The woman began to turn, unknowingly offering her profile to him. Just as her face came into view, everything went bright white.

Quinn pulled the binoculars from his eyes and blinked rapidly.

'Dammit,' he said.

He tried to look around, but all he could see was the afterimage of the flash.

'Are you okay?' Nate asked.

'Someone turned on a light,' Quinn said. 'On the porch.'

74

'I can't see a goddamn thing.' He held the binoculars out in Nate's direction. 'See what's going on.'

The binoculars were good enough for most pedestrian uses, but as a professional tool they didn't cut it. Quinn would have gone with a model that automatically adjusted as incoming light sources increased. This was what happened when someone else took care of your equipment needs.

'The door's still closed,' Nate said. 'The two from the car are standing a few feet away, looking at it. The guy has his hand behind his back under his jacket.'

'Armed?'

'Hasn't pulled anything yet, but I'm guessing he is.'

Quinn continued to blink. 'And they're just standing there?'

'Yeah,' Nate said. 'Wait. The woman just took a step toward the door. Looks like she's saying something.'

The voice of one of Donovan's men came over the radio again. 'They've made contact.'

'Continue holding,' Donovan said. 'He may turn them away.'

Quinn blinked again, then shut his eyes and concentrated on the split second he saw the woman's profile before the flash.

The moment he reopened his eyes, he keyed his mic. 'Donovan. They're not friendlies. The woman showed up at the last assignment I had for Wills. They also appear to be armed. I repeat, they're armed.'

75

10

From the corner of her eye, Petra saw Mikhail reach for his gun when the light came on.

'No,' she whispered, not moving her lips. 'Not yet.'

Mikhail left his hand behind his back, empty, but ready to grab his weapon if needed.

'Motion sensor?' he asked.

Petra shook her head. If there was a sensor, the light would have come on as they walked up, not after they'd stopped. Someone inside had flipped a switch.

A muffled voice called out from behind the door. 'Go away!'

Petra took a step forward. 'Mr. Moody?'

'Go away! Leave me alone!'

She arched an eyebrow at Mikhail. *Not a denial.*

'Mr. Moody, we just want to talk to you.'

'Get the hell out of here or I'm calling the police.'

His accent was not strong, no doubt tempered by years in the States, but there was still a trace of British roots. *Just like Moody would have.* It had to be him. Moody was alive. For the first time, she could sense a glimmer of hope. They had gotten to him first. Finally, someone would be able to point them to the Ghost.

'We're here to help you, not hurt you. We just want to talk. Can we come in, please?'

'No.'

'Mr. Moody. Did you know a man named Ryan Winters?'

A slight hesitation. 'I don't 'know anyone by that name. Now leave.'

'How about Stacy McKitrick? Or David Thomas?'

Nothing for a second, then the latch clicked and the door opened an inch. It was dark inside, but the light from the porch was enough to see the shadowy form of someone standing a few feet back from the gap.

'What do you want?'

Petra focused on where she thought Moody's eyes were. 'They're dead, Mr. Moody.'

It was as if all the wind had been knocked out of him. 'Dead? All of them?'

'Yes. And if you don't let us help you, you'll be dead, too.'

★　★　★

'Positions?' Donovan asked over the walkie-talkie.

One by one, each of his men replied 'Set' in the same order they had answered earlier. And again, Quinn and Nate remained silent.

'Close in.'

★　★　★

'Leave me alone,' Moody said. 'I don't need your help.' He paused. 'Maybe *you're* the ones who killed them, and you've come to kill me, too!'

77

'We're not here to hurt you.' Petra put her hand on the door. 'We're here to help.'

'You're lying. Get the hell off — '

There was a faint *thup* followed by the crunch of glass. Mikhail spun back toward the car, but Petra grabbed his arm and pulled him forward just as something whizzed through the air and smashed into the side of the house.

'Inside! Inside!' she said.

Moody tried to shut them out, but Petra jammed her foot into the opening before he could. Half a second later Mikhail drove his shoulder into the door, sending Moody flying back into the house.

They raced inside. Moody was sprawled on the floor, a look of bewilderment on his face.

'Gunshots,' Mikhail said.

Petra kicked the door closed. 'I think the first hit the car.'

Mikhail gave her a look that told her they were both thinking the same thing. *Kolya*. In the driver's seat. Nowhere to hide.

From outside they heard the shattering of glass as the porch light went out. But Petra ignored it. They had come for information. She couldn't chance blowing it this time, worrying about something she could do nothing about. Reaching down, she grabbed the old man by the front of his sweatshirt and pulled him to his feet. She pulled the picture from her pocket and held it in front of his face.

'Have you seen this before?'

Moody stared at her like he couldn't understand what she was saying. He looked scared and old and frail.

'Look at the picture, dammit!'

Moody held Petra's gaze, fear in his eyes, then looked at the picture and gasped. 'Where did you get that?'

'So that's a yes?'

Moody gave her a single, shocked nod. 'Where . . . how . . . ?'

The shot had been taken in what looked like a small restaurant. There were two tables on either side of the image, and a bar that ran almost the entire length of the background, with plates of sandwiches sitting on top that looked untouched. Scattered around the room were fourteen people, nine men and five women, some sitting at the tables, some standing near the bar. All but one looked like they were between seventeen and twenty-two. The one who didn't was a man who had to be at least forty. They were dressed comfortably for the time, button-down shirts and slacks for the men, blouses and skirts for the women. Several of the men and one of the women had glasses of beer in front of them, though none were drinking at the time the image was snapped. And though they had all been looking at the camera, not one of them had been smiling. 'You're in this photo, aren't you?' she asked.

Hesitation, then another nod.

She pointed at one of the men near the bar. Young and smiling and completely average, his hand curved around a glass. 'You, correct?'

'So long ago.'

'And this one,' she said pointing at a man at the left table, leaning back casually. 'David Thomas, yes?'

79

'Yes.'

'And this is — '

'Ryan Winters.'

Petra could feel the hair at the back of her neck tingle. Finally, they had their key. Moody. He would be able to point them toward the Ghost, toward closure.

'We know most of the names of the people in the photo,' she said. 'What I need is for you to tell us who — '

The shatter of glass cut her off.

Petra pushed Moody back to the floor as a second windowpane blew inward.

She glanced at Mikhail. 'We've got to get out of here.'

'The garage,' he said.

'Is there a car there?' Petra asked Moody.

'Please, leave me alone,' Moody pleaded.

She grabbed him by the arms and rolled him onto his back. 'I am *not* here to kill you. But the people outside are. So if you want to live, you will help us get out of here.'

He nervously licked his lips.

'Is there a car in your garage?'

'Yes,' Moody said. 'A pickup.'

'Where are the keys?'

'In the kitchen. On a hook by the door.' Moody motioned toward the back of the house.

'Come on,' Petra said.

'Take my truck. I don't care,' he said. 'But I'm staying here.'

'I already told you, they will kill you if you stay.'

'You'll kill me if I go.'

'You misunderstand the situation, Mr. Moody. You're more valuable to me alive than dead.'

★ ★ ★

The glass on one of the Maxima's windows imploded.

'What was that?' Donovan shouted over the radio link.

In the moment of silence that followed, something smacked into the side of the house. A voice crackled over the walkie-talkie, one of Donovan's men. 'Someone's shooting. They hit the car and just hit the house. I think that first shot might have got the driver.'

'Who the hell fired?'

'It looked like it came from the southeast.'

'Mercer,' Donovan said, 'did you see anything?'

A slight pause. 'Nothing.'

'That's your area! Check it out! There must be someone else out there.'

'Copy that,' Mercer said.

'What about the two in front of the house?' Donovan asked.

'They've gone inside,' one of the men said.

'Son of a bitch,' Donovan said. 'Someone take out the porch light.'

'Copy that.'

A second later the lamp above the door shattered, and the yard went dark.

'Light's disabled.'

Donovan took a deep, audible breath. 'All right. Everyone but Mercer, move in. But

81

carefully. There's a sniper out there somewhere. Mercer, you find that shooter.'

'Copy,' Mercer replied.

With Mercer hunting for the sniper and Dailey monitoring the thermal scanner, Donovan's six-man team was down to four.

'Well, this is exciting,' Nate said.

'Exciting' was not a word any cleaner wanted associated with the job he was working on. Routine, dull, uneventful. Those were the descriptions most desired.

'You hear even the hint of a siren, that's an automatic abort,' Quinn said.

'Good by me.'

So far there had been no signs that any of the neighbors had noticed anything wrong. The trees and the distance appeared to be working in their favor.

Just then two men slipped out of the cover of the woods. The first crept to the tree that was near the front door of the house. The other headed toward the Maxima.

'In position across from the door,' a voice said on the radio.

'We have a problem,' a second voice said.

'Like I hadn't noticed that,' Donovan said.

'More of a problem. I'm at the Maxima. The driver is dead. Bullet caught him right below the ear. Doesn't look like a random shot to me. He was definitely targeted.'

Quinn blew out a breath. A bad situation had just gotten worse.

'Fine,' Donovan said. 'We are still on mission. Dailey, what do you see?'

82

'The heat signatures are all together, not far inside the house.'

'Is anyone looking out the window?'

'No one's near any window.'

'Good. Able, you and Cox move in close. See what you can hear.'

'Copy that,' Abel responded.

The man at the car and the one behind the tree began running in a crouch toward the front door.

'I think I jinxed us with that 'exciting' comment,' Nate said to Quinn.

'Yeah. I wasn't going to point that out,' Quinn said.

'Thanks for your consideration.'

There was a sudden movement from the far side of the car. A third man was heading quickly across the front lawn toward the house.

'Donovan, is that you?' Abel said.

'What are you talking about?' Donovan said.

'There's someone about thirty feet to my right. He looks like one — '

A muzzle flashed. It was followed almost immediately by the disintegration of one of the windows next to the front door. Another flash. Another window shattered. Quinn saw Abel and Cox dive for cover. When he looked back at the front yard, the third man was gone.

'Shooter! Shooter!' Abel yelled as he and Cox sprinted toward the Maxima.

'Correct me if I'm wrong, but this is going bad fast,' Nate said to Quinn. 'Someone's got to be calling the cops by now, don't you think?'

Quinn nodded. 'We'll hold our position so we

can act as eyes for the others. But if there are any bodies, we're leaving them.'

Abel and Cox circled the Maxima.

'He's gone,' one of them said.

'Dailey, scan the yard,' Donovan said. 'See if you can pick up something.'

'I can't reposition that quickly,' Dailey said.

'Fine. Stay on the house. Mercer, anything?'

'No.' Mercer sounded winded. 'Someone was just running through the trees, but I lost him.'

'Goddamn it. The rest of you, into the house. Now. I don't care how you do it. They already know we're coming.'

The phone in Quinn's pocket buzzed again, reminding him he had a text waiting. The vibration was loud enough for Nate to hear. He looked at Quinn, eyebrows raised.

Quinn ignored both his apprentice and the phone.

Abel and Cox darted to the front door. Without pausing, Abel kicked out with his right, connecting with the door just below the knob.

Quinn could hear the sound of the wood cracking. More noise pollution. He had seldom seen a job go this bad this fast.

Abel kicked again. This time the door flew inward, then rebounded toward them. Cox took up position against the jamb, aiming his gun into the darkness. Abel nodded, then rushed forward, keeping low.

'We're in,' Abel announced as Cox slipped inside as well.

'He's done something to his windows so we're having a problem getting in at the back,'

Donovan said. 'Looking for an alternative. Dailey, what's going on with the targets?'

Targets now, Quinn registered. *What a mess.*

'They're at the back of the house, west side.'

Over the radio, Quinn could hear the spit of bullets passing through suppressors.

'We're receiving fire,' Abel grunted.

'We're coming around to your side,' Donovan said.

'They're moving again,' Dailey broke in.

Three more muffled gunshots.

'Into the garage,' Dailey continued.

Several seconds of nothing, then the roar of an engine ripped through the night.

Quinn keyed his mic. 'They've got a car in the garage. Engine just started.'

'Everyone out front. Now!' Donovan said.

Again, Quinn and Nate held their position. This wasn't their fight.

Tires screeched, then a tremendous crash filled the air as a large pickup truck exploded through the garage door. Quinn looked at the truck's crew cab, but couldn't see anyone. They all must have been hunkered down below the dash.

As the vehicle weaved through the debris, Abel and Cox ran out the front door. A second later Donovan and Beech appeared around the corner of the house.

All four opened fire on the truck. The Ford sped up. As it reached the parked sedan, it swerved to the right, scraping against the Maxima but not slowing down.

'Abort! Abort!' Donovan shouted as the truck

raced down the driveway toward Main Street.

'What about the dead man in the car? Shouldn't we check for ID?' Cox asked.

Good idea, Quinn thought.

'Abort now,' Donovan repeated. 'No time. Team four, you're released.'

'Copy that,' Quinn said. But he held his position as the others disappeared into the woods.

So did Nate.

After ten seconds, Quinn's apprentice said, 'You want the ID, don't you?'

'The woman was the same woman who watched us in L.A. Wills is going to want to know who these people are.'

'Not our job to get an ID,' Nate observed. It wasn't an admonishment, just information.

'*I* want to know who these people are, too.'

Nate rose out of his crouch and tossed the binoculars to Quinn. 'Be right back.'

'My idea. I'll get it,' Quinn said.

'I'm already on my way,' Nate said, but before he could take a step, something moved near the bushes in front of Moody's house. Nate knelt back down. 'The shooter?'

Quinn raised the binoculars. A man skulked around the yard, holding a gun that glowed bright with the heat of a recent discharge. As he took a few steps forward, Quinn was able to focus in on his face.

'It's Mercer,' Quinn whispered. He must have come back for the attack on the truck.

Mercer snuck his way toward the car, his gun ready at his side. Then, very faint in the distance, Quinn heard a siren. Mercer's head shot up.

86

After a second, he glanced at the car, hesitated, then he whipped around and ran east toward the woods at the edge of the property. A moment later he was gone. Nate stood again.

'Where are you going?'

'The ID, remember?'

'Police are coming.'

'So I guess I'd better be fast, huh?'

Nate stepped out of the trees, then sprinted to the sedan. Quinn watched as his apprentice opened the driver's door and leaned in over the corpse. Fifteen seconds later he was up again and running back.

'Find anything?' Quinn asked once Nate had rejoined him.

Nate held up a thin wallet. 'This was it.'

The sirens were getting closer now.

'Time to go,' Quinn said, then let Nate lead them through the woods back to their car.

11

'Stay down!' Petra yelled at Moody as the truck raced over the remains of the garage door.

Mikhail was behind the wheel, keeping his own head low, aiming the truck toward the street.

Before they'd gone ten feet, a staccato *whap-whap-whap* of bullets hit the side of the pickup.

'Faster,' Petra said.

'What about Kolya?' Mikhail yelled.

'He'll have to take care of himself,' she said.

Mikhail lifted his head enough to peek out the window as they passed the Maxima. When he crouched back down, his face was white.

'What is it?' Petra asked.

His only answer was to shake his head and press down on the accelerator. Kolya had to be dead.

The truck tossed them around as they sped across the front lawn. After a moment, Mikhail looked up again.

'Hold on,' he said, then whipped the wheel to the right.

The tires squealed as the truck fought against inertia. Petra braced herself, expecting to flip over. But a moment later the rocky ride ended, and they were racing away along the main road. She glanced into the crew seat behind them. Moody was still tucked in the space between the seats.

'Who were they?' Mikhail asked.

'The same people we've been up against since we started,' Petra said.

All of a sudden the truck began to slow.

'What are you doing?' Petra asked.

'Police.'

She sat up and saw the lights in the distance coming toward them fast. 'We can't let them see us,' she said. The truck was riddled with bullet holes. 'There.' She pointed at a gravel road several yards ahead on the left.

Mikhail eased off the accelerator and turned. Once they were on the side road, he doused the lights, took the engine out of gear, and let the truck roll to a stop on its own.

They both looked over their shoulders out the back window. To the left a halo of flashing lights began to dominate the night as a siren grew louder. Then a single police cruiser rushed by, its lights quickly fading into the black.

Mikhail started to put the truck back into gear, but Petra stopped him. 'Wait,' she said.

Three minutes later, more lights appeared on the horizon. Two more police cars and an ambulance.

As soon as they passed, Petra said, 'Okay, go.'

Mikhail turned the truck around and got them back onto the highway.

'We can't stay in this,' Petra said. 'It'll draw too much attention. We need to find something else.'

Mikhail nodded, then glanced toward the back. 'How's our passenger?'

Petra peered over the seat. 'He's still hiding on

the floor.' She reached back and tapped Moody on the shoulder. 'You can get up,' she said in English. 'We're safe now.'

He didn't move.

'Mr. Moody. It's okay. It's over.'

Again nothing. She exchanged a look with Mikhail.

'You want me to pull over?' he asked.

'No. Keep going.'

She climbed into the back and leaned down next to Moody.

'Are you all right?'

There was no movement at all.

As she reached underneath to pull him up, she touched something sticky and wet.

'He's been hit.' She manhandled him onto the seat, then reached up and flipped on the dome light. The front of Moody's shirt was dark with blood.

'No,' she whispered.

She put her fingers against the man's neck. There was a pulse, though faint.

'He's still alive,' she said.

She unbuttoned Moody's shirt and peeled it back. More blood, but no entry wound.

She moved her hand over his torso, slipping it around the man's side, then stopped.

'Bullet hole,' she said. 'Right side. Near his kidney.'

She ripped off part of his shirt and pressed it against the wound. But even as she applied pressure, she realized it was too late. Moody's chest barely moved as he took a breath. It rose once more. The third time was even fainter.

There was no fourth.

'Should I find a hospital?' Mikhail asked.

She shook her head. 'No.'

'Is he . . . ?'

She locked eyes with Mikhail in the rearview mirror. He took a deep breath, then nodded.

'What now?'

'Find us another car. We'll leave the body here.'

Mikhail turned at the next street, then said, 'I meant, what are we going to do now?'

'I know what you meant.'

She only wished she knew the answer.

★   ★   ★

'I assume we're going to avoid Portland,' Nate said once they were back in the car.

Quinn nodded. 'Head south.'

Nate pulled out into the street. 'Boston?'

'New York.'

It would take a few hours longer, but as a place to disappear, New York couldn't be beat.

Quinn stayed tense as they worked their way through southern Maine. He wasn't worried about getting caught. He was disturbed by the presence of the Russian woman. Unlike in L.A., here she had actually blown the operation. How could she have known? Was Wills's organization compromised? If so, that was a huge problem. The Englishman had paid for three weeks of Quinn's time, which meant that potentially there were still over two to go. That was a lot of time for something even worse to happen.

Quinn looked out the window and stared at the

sky, trying not to think about the job anymore.

The Milky Way punched millions of holes in the dark night, the stars twinkling their ancient brilliance. In the distance, a single light moved to the west, a plane flying from one unknown point to another. Along the road, trees that were no more than dark shadows rushed by solo and in groups with no discernible pattern.

A memory hit him, unexpected and hard.

He was in the back seat of his family's car. Beside him, his sister.

Liz was probably six at the time, which would have made him fourteen. In the front his mother sat in the passenger seat and, as usual, his father was behind the wheel. Outside, it was night, and the trees of Minnesota, much like the trees of Maine, flew by the window like a dark, silent army.

Liz yawned, then leaned over and laid her head in his lap. Automatically, his hand went to the side of her head, stroking her long hair so that she'd fall asleep.

'Good night, Jake,' she said groggily.

'Good night, sweet pea,' he replied.

Quinn's phone buzzed in his pocket again, jerking him out of the past.

It was a text from Orlando, sent when they were in position outside Moody's house. He had forgotten about it.

Call Me

This was no simple request to touch base. Orlando wasn't like that. If she'd been thinking

92

about him, and wanted him to know, that's what she would have said. If she had something to talk about, but could wait, she would have said that, too. A simple CALL ME meant do it now. Urgency in her simplicity.

The phone began to vibrate in his hand. He looked down. A call this time, not a text. On his screen was a single word: WILLS.

'David,' Quinn said.

'I just got off the phone with Donovan,' Wills said. 'What a disaster!'

'Yeah,' Quinn said. 'Pretty much.'

'He told me you recognized the people who showed up.'

'Just one of them. Not the whole group. It was the woman from L.A. The Russian.'

'Are you sure?'

'No question.'

Silence.

'And the target?' Wills asked. 'Donovan thinks he left with the others.'

'That would be my guess, but we don't know for sure. They could have killed him and left him in the house.'

'Didn't anyone check?'

'There wasn't time,' Quinn pointed out. 'Donovan gave the order to abort, and we all scattered. Good thing he did — the police arrived just as I was leaving.'

'Donovan didn't say anything about the police.'

'We delayed our departure for a few minutes.' Quinn explained about the wallet Nate had taken from the victim.

'That was good thinking,' Wills said.

'We weren't the only ones with the idea. One of Donovan's men hung back to grab it, but got scared off by the police.'

'Really? Which one?'

'A guy named Mercer.'

There was just the slightest of pauses before Wills spoke again. 'Well, I'm just glad somebody got it. What did you find?'

'Hold on.' Quinn held out his hand. 'Wallet.'

Keeping his eyes on the road, Nate dug the wallet out of his pocket and handed it over. Quinn flipped it open and found a driver's license tucked behind a clear plastic cover.

'According to this his name is William Burke. B-U-R-K-E. Address in Manhattan.'

'Burke?' Wills questioned to himself.

Quinn looked through the rest of the wallet. 'He's got a credit card and an ATM card. Wait, here's something interesting.'

'What is it?'

'Several business cards. They all have the same name, but the companies are different. Comcast Cable, Faye Construction, Triple A. There's one here that says he's with the FBI. They all have the same address. Some place in Manhattan.' Quinn paused. 'No chance William Burke is this guy's real name.' Quinn looked at the guy's picture again. 'Something else.'

'What?'

'Hold on.' Quinn held the driver's license out on the dashboard so Nate could see it. 'This *is* the dead guy, right?'

Nate glanced quickly at the picture. 'Yeah. That's him.'

Quinn put the phone back to his ear. 'I'll check this guy's ID against the pictures I took in L.A., but I'm pretty sure he was behind the wheel of the car at the warehouse the other night, too.'

Wills said nothing for a moment, then, 'The client isn't going to like this.'

That wasn't Quinn's problem. Even if the job was canceled, Quinn had already been paid, and per his standard arrangement, the money would stay with him.

'Given all that's been going on,' Wills said, 'I want to meet with you in person. Today. Well, tomorrow for you. It's not even midnight there yet, is it?'

'Not quite yet,' Quinn said.

'I'll fly over. Not Portland, but maybe Boston.'

'New York,' Quinn said. 'The Grand Hyatt. There's a bar beyond the elevators on the main floor. Text me what time you'll be there.'

'Bar at the Grand Hyatt,' Wills said. 'Okay. I should be over there in time for lunch. And Quinn. Thanks again. You haven't disappointed me yet.'

'You say 'yet' like you're expecting me to.'

'Actually, I'm not.'

'Good.' Quinn disconnected the call.

He was about to slip the phone back into his pocket when he remembered he needed to call Orlando.

She answered after only one ring. 'Finally done?' she asked.

'That's one way of phrasing it,' Quinn said. He filled her in on what had happened.

95

'You've got to be kidding me,' she said.

'Wish I was.'

'You know you took a chance with the ID.'

'Not a big one,' he said.

'Bigger than you should have.'

'I made Nate do it.'

'Well, that's reassuring,' she said.

Quinn smiled. 'So what's up?'

When she spoke again, all the playfulness that had been in her voice was gone. 'Somebody tripped one of my flags.'

Orlando knew her way around computers better than most people knew how to walk. One of the things she had done was set up electronic tripwires throughout cyberspace that would notify her when someone looked at whatever it was she'd flagged.

'Okay,' he said. 'Is this something we need to worry about?'

'It got me to check some of the other related flags I'd set up,' she went on, ignoring his question. 'There are at least five that should have sent me a message, but didn't. Someone bypassed them.'

Quinn started to feel uneasy. 'What does that mean?'

'It means someone's been poking around where they shouldn't. It's been going on for over a week. The only reason I found out is that there was a dual flag set up this time. They got around the first, but missed the second.'

'What exactly are we talking about?'

'You, Quinn,' she said. 'Someone's been trying to find out all they can about you.'

12

The Past.

It was something Quinn had tried to cover up and, in many ways, tried to convince himself had never happened in the first place, convince himself he'd been born Jonathan Quinn.

The awkwardness with his father — his *stepfather* — his estrangement from his sister, and then, of course, his brother.

From early on, Harold Oliver had shown no more than an uneasy tolerance toward him. It had confused him. Especially so after his brother was born, and then his sister, neither of whom received the same disdain from their father as young Jake did. And now that his father was dead, it was too late to try and mend that wound.

Liz was still around, of course, but the wall that had grown between them when he'd left home had become as wide and as insurmountable as the Himalayas. Even if he did try to explain, she wouldn't even listen.

And then there was Davey . . .

'I just want to see it,' Davey said. He was five, strapped in his child's seat in the back, behind their father.

'No,' Jake told him. 'You should have brought your own.'

'Just for a minute. Please, Jakey.'

He leaned over in front of their one-year-old

sister, Liz, who was asleep in her car seat between the brothers. Jake flipped the page of the comic book, and turned so Davey couldn't see.

'Mom, Jake's not sharing!'

'It's mine,' Jake pleaded. 'I don't have to share with him.'

'Jake, just let him look with you,' their mother said. 'He doesn't have to touch it.'

Jake looked pained. 'Do I have to? He's got plenty at home. He should have brought one of them.'

'I've looked at all those!' Davey said.

'Boys, you're going to wake your sister. Just share, okay?'

'Fine,' Jake said, then turned just enough so that at the right angle his brother could see half a page.

'Mom!' Davey cried.

'What?' she asked, sounding weary.

'He's not really doing it.'

'Jake, honey. I told you, you need to — '

'Right now,' Harold Oliver's voice cut through from the driver's seat. 'Give it to him.'

'What?' Jake asked. 'Why?'

Davey reached toward Jake, but Jake leaned away from him.

'Give your brother the comic,' his father ordered.

'But it's mine.'

'I said give it to him!'

Jake glanced at his mother. She looked for a moment at her husband, then turned to her oldest son. The expression on her face told him all he needed to know. 'Just do it,' she mouthed.

Jake narrowed his eyes, and grunted in frustration. 'Whatever,' he said. He flapped out his hand and tossed the comic in Davey's general direction.

But the comic hit the front seat instead and ricocheted into the side of Liz's face.

Liz stared wailing as Davey grabbed for the book. She pushed at the comic, knocking it from Davey's hands and onto the floor.

'Mom!' Davey screamed. 'He did that on purpose!'

Liz's cries grew louder.

'I did not!' Jake said.

More crying.

'Liz, honey, it's okay,' their mother said, turning to the back seat.

'He threw it at me!'

'I was holding it out to you, not my fault you can't catch.'

'Liz, sweetie, it's okay,' their mother said. She slipped her shoulder strap off, leaned between the seats, then rubbed her daughter's cheek as Liz continued to sob.

'I can't reach it!' Davey wailed louder than Liz. He was stretched out as far as he could go, but the comic book was still beyond his grasp.

'Jake, please pick it up and hand it to your brother.'

'He's the one who dropped it,' Jake said. 'He should — '

'Enough!' Harold Oliver roared.

Jake looked up. The side of their father's face was red with anger.

99

'I'll get it,' Davey said quietly. He unbuckled his car seat and leaned down to the floor.

'I tried to give it — ' Jake muttered.

'I said *enough*!' Harold yelled. Only this time he turned and looked back.

The police later said that it could have been a rock in the road. But the more Jake thought about it, the more he suspected his father accidentally turned the steering wheel a few degrees to the left as he looked back at his kids.

Whatever the reason, the car changed direction just enough so that when Harold looked back, there was no chance of avoiding the deep drainage ditch that paralleled the opposite side of the highway. The best he could do was to keep the car from going straight in. It slammed down on the driver's side before coming to rest against the slope of the ditch, flipped partially on its roof.

A broken leg, a broken clavicle, a gash on the side of a head.

And one dead son.

That was the tally.

The only one to come out of it basically unscathed was Jake. Bruises from the impact, a few cuts and abrasions, that was all. If only he'd been hurt worse . . .

Though his father had never openly placed the blame on him, Jake was sure that's how he felt. Because, deep down, that's how Jake felt, too.

They laid Davey to rest five days later, Harold on crutches and Jake's mother with her left arm strapped across her chest. Liz sported a bald

100

patch on the side of her head covered with a bandage. Beneath was the gash that would form a scar that would be with her the rest of her life.

The scar Jake bore — that Quinn bore — was invisible, but just as permanent.

13

Petra and Mikhail found a motel 6 outside of Lowell, Massachusetts. Petra dragged herself to her room, then tried to sleep, but it just wasn't happening. At 4:30 a.m. she gave up.

Kolya, like Luka, was dead.

She had known at the start of their mission that death was always a possibility. But she had expected any bullet would have hit her, not one of her team members. But twice now, it had happened. At least, unlike with Luka, she wouldn't have to tell Kolya's family. They had all died when he'd been just a child. It was why Kolya had joined the search for the Ghost in the first place. If he had any family at all, she and Mikhail and the others in their group were it.

She tried to push him from her mind, but what filled the void was just as devastating. All of them, every person on her list, was dead. Chang, McKitrick, Thomas, Winters, the others before them. And now Moody.

His death was the hardest to take. They had found him alive. They had even talked to him. He knew people in the photograph. But the final step, identifying the two strikingly similar young men standing at opposite ends of the bar, had not been completed.

With Moody dead, the trail to the Ghost had disappeared. That was unless Stepka could pinpoint who the Ghost had hired to do the killings. If he failed, the Ghost would live up to his nickname and fade away. Forever lost, and forever unaccountable.

She knew she should wait for Stepka to get back to her, but doing so would make her crazy. She turned on her side and grabbed her phone.

'What?' Stepka said as he picked up.

'It's Petra.'

'Shouldn't you be asleep?'

'I want to know what you've learned.'

'I told you I'd call as soon as I had something,' he said.

'And when do you think that might be?'

'Twenty-four hours. Maybe forty-eight. Or it's possible I won't find out at all.'

'Twenty-four hours is too long,' she said, ignoring his other possibilities. 'We can't lose this opportunity. If you don't figure out who's been blocking our way, we're done. We *have* no other options.'

'As I said before, I'm doing everything I can.'

'You must have something. At least a hint of information.'

Stepka remained silent for several seconds. 'I've been able to narrow those potentially involved down to six groups.'

Petra straightened up. Six was a lot, but it was better than the dead end she was staring at.

'Who are they?'

'Petra, please. One more day and the information will be considerably more solid.'

'Mikhail and I are sitting here with nothing. No information. No idea where to go or who to talk to. If you don't give me something, then the

103

time we spend until you do will be completely wasted.'

'But what I have might be wrong. If so, your time would be wasted anyway.'

'But it's a chance,' she said. 'If you're right, it may give us the edge we need. And if you're wrong, we're no worse off.'

There was a pause, then, 'I don't have individual names, yet. But there is a pattern.'

'What pattern?'

'Of the six potential groups, one operates out of Prague, and one out of Paris. But the other four all work out of London.'

She let the new information sink in. 'And you're sure it's one of these groups?'

'I'm not sure about anything,' he said, irritated. 'I told you I have nothing solid.'

'Thank you. This helps. Let me know as soon as you have something more.'

'It won't be for a while, so go back to sleep.'

But she didn't go back to sleep. Instead she called Mikhail in his room, waking him up.

'Take a shower and get dressed,' she said.

'We're leaving?'

'Yes.'

'Where are we going?' he asked.

'London.'

★ ★ ★

The text from Wills said he'd arrive at the Grand Hyatt Hotel between twelve and twelve-thirty. So Quinn and Nate arrived a few minutes before eleven.

104

The hotel was at the corner of Forty-second Street and Lexington Avenue, midtown Manhattan, its black glass tower standing in stark contrast to the stone edifice of Grand Central Terminal next door.

Quinn and Nate entered through the revolving doors, staggering their entrance so that it didn't seem like they were together. An escalator took them up to the large open lobby. There, Nate headed toward check-in, while Quinn turned right toward the elevators at the rear of the room.

Though there were many people in the lobby, the size of the room made it seem almost empty. Here and there couples and small groups clustered together, while others sat on the couches and chairs reading or talking or just passing the time.

Each person in the room received either an X or a check in Quinn's mind. An X meant they could be ignored. A check meant follow-up might be required. By the time he reached the far end of the elevators, he had accumulated twenty-one Xs and two checks.

One of the checks was a woman standing alone off to the left. She was Caucasian, mid-thirties, and had dirty-blonde hair. She was dressed in a gray pantsuit and was holding a briefcase in her left hand. She also seemed to be trying very hard not to look at Quinn.

The second check was for a man seated on a chair near the elevators. He appeared to be around the same age as the woman, but was dressed more casually: dark green polo shirt and

105

blue jeans. What earned him the extra attention was that he had a look that screamed operative. Good shape, hair not too long and not too short, and eyes that took in everything without seeming to do so.

Quinn moved into the seating area and leaned against one of the circular pillars that held up the second-floor atrium. From this position, he could see both the man and the woman. After a few moments, the man picked up a newspaper and started to read. The woman held her position, still not looking at Quinn.

Wills's people?

It would make sense. If he were Wills, Quinn would have had people scouting the meet by now. Only with everything that had been going down, Quinn couldn't dismiss the possibility that one or both of them might be with the people who'd shown up at the Moody operation.

He pulled out his phone and brought up the text he'd received from Wills. He selected Reply, then wrote:

U send advance team to Hyatt? If yes, how many?

He touched Send, then glanced toward the far end of the lobby. He expected to see Nate, but there was no sign of his apprentice. As Quinn scanned the large room, his phone vibrated. He thought it would be a reply from Wills, but the text was from Nate.

Look up

Quinn glanced up at the atrium that ringed the lobby, and spotted Nate a second later standing a few feet back from the railing that stretched between the columns.

It was a good position. Great, considering that Quinn was stationed at the opposite corner, one floor down. Together they had the whole lobby covered.

Quinn texted Nate back:

Anything?

Nate's reply came twenty seconds later.

Man sitting near elevators w/paper. Woman at stairs south of you.

Nate had seen them, too. *Good.*

Quinn's phone buzzed again. Wills this time.

Leaving airport now. One person at hotel.

Quinn replied:

M/F?

Wills's answer came only a few seconds later:

M

The man reading the newspaper, then. So that meant the woman was an unknown.

Quinn strolled over to one of the empty seats, putting a little more distance between himself

107

and the woman. As he sat he called Nate.

'Hey,' Nate said.

'The man is with our friend.'

'And the woman?'

'Unknown. Perhaps not even interested in us.' Quinn paused for a moment. 'Stay on the line. I'm going to walk back to the bar. Let's see what she does.'

Quinn stood up, his phone still held against his ear. He smiled as if the person on the other end had said something amusing.

'Perhaps next time I'm in town,' he said, his voice loud enough for the woman to hear.

'I don't have to play this game, too, do I?' Nate asked. 'She can't hear me.'

Quinn began walking across the carpet. 'It'd be a big help to me,' he said.

'I'm sure it would . . . Wait, she just looked at you.'

'I appreciate that. For how long do you think?'

'Long enough for me to see that she's interested in you.'

Quinn left the carpet and stepped onto the marble tile. He held his position for a moment, pretending to listen.

'And now?' he asked.

Nate said, 'She just sneaked a second peek . . . now she's looking toward reception.'

'Glad to hear it.'

Quinn turned to his right and quickly moved up a short set of steps and into a hallway that cut along the eastern edge of the elevators and back to the bar where he was supposed to meet Wills. Within seconds, the lobby was out of sight.

'What's she doing?' Quinn asked, all pretense gone.

'She's still looking at the . . . hold on . . . She glanced back at where you were . . . Okay, she's looking around. Not hiding the fact, either.'

Quinn had a choice at the end of the hallway: either continue straight and enter the bar, or go left along another hallway directly behind the elevators. Along this new hallway were a set of public restrooms and several shops. Quinn turned left, heading for the men's room.

'She's on the move,' Nate said.

'Heading my way?'

'She doesn't seem quite sure where she wants to go. She started toward reception, then stopped . . . Walking toward the elevators now.'

Quinn stepped into the bathroom. It was a large facility with several stalls. A quick check revealed he was the only one present.

'If she comes anywhere near you, snap a photo,' Quinn said.

'Already got two, but profile only. If I can get something better, I will.'

'Position?'

'She's stopped at the bottom of the steps . . . Interesting. Our friend with the paper is also keeping tabs on her.'

Wills's man had probably spotted her before Quinn and Nate had arrived. He would no doubt be curious why the woman was interested in the guy his boss was supposed to meet.

'What's he doing?' Quinn asked.

'Just watching . . . Okay, the woman's coming your way . . . up the steps . . . and . . . there

'. . . she . . . goes. I can't see her anymore.'

'All right. Find a room we can use, then text me the number.'

'What's the plan?'

'Stow and go,' Quinn said.

14

Quinn donned a pair of thin, transparent gloves, then silently counted down from twenty. When he hit zero, he stepped out of the restroom.

The woman was ten feet away, heading toward the shops, her back to him. He walked up behind her, not hiding the sound of his steps. When she turned, her eyes went wide.

There was no question now. She'd definitely been looking for him.

'Hi,' he said.

She turned her head and started walking away.

Quinn reached out and grabbed her shoulder. 'Hold on.'

'Please, leave me alone,' she said, not even looking back. Her accent was British.

'Sorry. Not an option.'

'I'll scream.'

'And I'll kill you where you're standing.'

He could feel her tense under his palm. 'What do you want?' she asked.

He turned her around to face him. 'I believe *you're* the one looking for me. So what do *you* want?'

'I don't know what you're talking about. I need to — '

She tried to push past him, but he stopped her.

'I wouldn't do that.' He let his hand hover near the opening of his jacket. Sometimes the threat of a gun was all it took.

For several seconds she didn't move, then a barely perceptible nod.

'Great. We shouldn't have any problems.'

Quinn's phone vibrated in his pocket. With his other hand he retrieved it from his pocket, and glanced at the screen.

2467

Putting a hand on her arm, he said, 'Let's go.'

'Where?'

'Some place we can have a chat.'

'We can have a chat right here.'

'If we do, it'll be over very quickly, and you won't like the results.'

Her eyes moved side to side. 'Okay,' she whispered.

Quinn led the woman back to the elevators. While they waited for one to open, he said, 'If you cooperate, you'll be fine.'

'I won't give you any problems.'

Quinn smiled. 'Perfect.'

Over her shoulder, he could see Wills's man, still sitting in his chair, but now openly looking at him. Quinn gave him a quick nod, and the man returned the gesture.

One of the elevator doors opened, and Quinn ushered the woman inside, then pushed the button for 24.

As soon as the doors closed, he said, 'Give me your phone.'

She hesitated, then pulled a phone out of her suit pocket and handed it to him. It was a cheap pay-as-you-go model.

'Thank you,' he said, slipping it into his pocket. 'Now the briefcase.'

'I need this for work,' she said.

'Don't make me ask twice.'

She handed it to him.

'Do you have ID?' he asked.

'It's in the briefcase.'

'What should I call you?'

Another pause. 'Ann.'

'Are you sure?'

She nodded.

'Well, Ann, you're doing fine so far. You keep cooperating and you'll be okay.'

When they reached the twenty-fourth floor, Quinn led her down the hall and around the corner to room 2467.

'This is it,' he said. He could feel her tense again. 'Relax. If you cooperate like you said you would, then I promise I won't hurt you. And I always keep my promises.'

He rapped twice on the door. A second later Nate opened it and moved to the side so they could enter.

Quinn pointed at the bed. 'Why don't you sit there?' he said.

She walked over to the bed, but didn't sit down.

'You'll be more comfortable,' Quinn told her.

'I prefer to stand,' she replied.

He stared at her until she looked away. A moment later she sat.

Quinn placed her briefcase on the desk. It was the kind that had combination locks on each hasp. He pushed the release tabs, but the hinges didn't move.

'What's the combo?' he asked.

'You don't need to open it,' she said. 'There's nothing important inside.'

'What's the combo?'

Her lips pressed together for a moment, then she said, 'Zero-six-one.'

'For both sides?'

'Yes.'

He moved the case onto the bed beside her. 'Open it.'

If the briefcase was booby-trapped, she would either disarm it before opening the case or not open the case at all. And if she didn't know it, she'd soon find out.

She dialed in the combo and pushed on the tabs. With a *click* each latch popped open.

Quinn put the case back on the desk. 'Check it,' he said to Nate.

He then pulled out the cell phone the woman had given him. The call logs were empty. As was the contact list. There were no text messages, sent or received, and no pictures had been taken. Either she'd been deleting things as she was going along, or the phone had yet to be used.

He slipped it back into his pocket.

'Why were you following me?' he asked.

'I wasn't following you,' she said.

'Can I give you a piece of advice?'

She looked at him.

'Remember what I said about cooperating.' He smiled. 'Why were you following me?'

A pause, then, 'I made a mistake.'

'What mistake?'

'I should have said no.' The words were whispered, more to herself than to him.

Quinn felt a tap on his shoulder.

'Here,' Nate said, handing him a small booklet with a red cover, one very familiar to Quinn. In fact, he had a couple of them himself. A British passport.

He opened it to the information page. It had been issued a year earlier. The picture inside was of the woman sitting on the bed in front of him. The name listed was Annabel Taplin.

'Annabel or Ann?' he asked.

She looked at him, then away. 'Annabel.'

The corner of his mouth turned up as he looked back at the booklet. Her birth date put her age at thirty-two. Her birthplace was listed as Waltham Abbey. He checked for arrival and departure stamps. She'd made two round-trips from London to New York. First in May, and a second in August. Each time she stayed for less than two weeks before returning to the U.K. The final stamp denoted entry into the United States the previous evening.

'You'll want to see this, too,' Nate said.

He gave Quinn a business card.

WRIGHT BAINS SECURITIES
Annabel Taplin
Consultant

There was an address in London and a phone number.

The name of the company tugged at Quinn's

115

mind. Familiar, yet he couldn't place why.

He handed the card back to Nate, then leaned over. 'See what our contact can find out about this place. I think I've heard of it before.'

Nate nodded, then went into the bathroom to call Orlando, shutting the door behind him.

'Okay, Annabel. Why don't you tell me why you're in New York?'

'I'm here on business.'

'I'm your business?'

She took a second, then said, 'No. Not exactly.'

'Not exactly? That answer falls into the 'not cooperating' category. We had an agreement. But if you're going to break your end, I'm going to have to break mine.'

Her face was tense, her lips pressed tightly together. Then, as if someone had flicked an off switch, she slumped forward, her head falling into her hands.

'Oh, God,' she said as she began to cry.

It lasted only a few moments, then she wiped her eyes and looked up. Her mascara was smeared, creating a thick black outline on her lids.

'I was doing a favor, okay?' she said. 'Someone at work. They knew I was in New York and called me this morning. I was told to get that stupid phone.' She waved in the direction of Quinn's pocket. 'Then to come here and wait for you.'

'Only me?'

'Another man, too. They emailed me pictures of each of you.'

'The pictures weren't on your phone. Where are they?'

116

'On my computer,' she said, trying hard not to look at her briefcase. 'At my hotel.'

Quinn stepped over and looked inside the case. Besides a small stack of business cards, some pens, and two unused legal pads, there were also several folders. He picked them up.

'Those are confidential,' Annabel said.

Ignoring her, Quinn looked inside the first: letters, an unlabeled graph, and a report that looked of little interest. Most of the other folders contained similar documents. The second to last, though, contained printouts of three photos. The first was of David Wills, and the second of Quinn. The third was of a man Quinn didn't recognize. It was a headshot, the kind used not by actors, but by businessmen and politicians for PR purposes. The picture itself looked dated.

'Who is this?' Quinn said, holding up the man's photo.

'I don't know,' she said. 'They didn't give me any names. Just said that there was a chance that man might show up, too.'

'This shot's from at least twenty years ago. He'd be an old man now.'

She shrugged. 'I guess it was the only one they had.'

'You expect me to believe that?'

'I can tell you only what I know.'

Quinn returned the files to the briefcase, all but the one with the three pictures in it. That one he set on the dresser by itself.

'Once you spotted us, what were you supposed to do?' he asked.

'I was to wait until you were both here, then

117

make a phone call.'

'And after that?'

'After that I could leave.'

'What number were you supposed to call?'

She looked at him, then looked down, resigned. She took a clip out of her hair and handed it to him. On its back side was a local New York number. From the area code, he could tell it was a cell phone. Probably another disposable.

'Do you know whose number this is?' Quinn asked.

'I have no idea.'

'Not the person who asked you to do this?'

'Couldn't be. When he called this morning, he was in London.'

'And who is *he*?'

'Someone at work.'

'I'm looking for a name, Annabel.'

'I don't know his name,' she said.

'A man whose name you don't know asked you to do something you probably realized was dangerous, and you just said yes?'

'It wasn't the kind of request I could say no to.'

'Why not?'

The bathroom door opened, and Nate stepped out.

'You're not going to believe this,' he said.

But before he could go any further, Annabel said, 'Please, let me tell you.'

Quinn looked at her, curious. 'Tell me what?'

'It's about my company,' she said.

'Wright Bains Securities?' Quinn asked,

118

recalling the name from the business card.

'It's not what it seems.'

'Then, what is it?'

'Don't get me wrong. There are people there who do financial work.'

'But?' Quinn said.

She looked at Nate as if she was gauging whether he knew what she was going to say, and could modify her story if his knowledge was lacking. But Quinn had trained Nate well, and his apprentice's face betrayed nothing.

'I work for MI6,' she blurted out.

Quinn looked at Nate, and Nate nodded.

'Wright Bains is an MI6 front,' Nate said. 'Our contact didn't even need to check. Knew it the moment I said the name.'

That was why the name had been familiar.

'So you're MI6,' Quinn said.

'I'm a researcher. Strictly office work.'

'Then, what are you doing in New York?'

'We have meetings here sometimes. That's all.'

'I'm confused. Why were you in the lobby looking for me?'

'No one else was available. I was here, so they used me.'

'Does that happen often?'

She shook her head. 'Never.'

Quinn took a deep breath. He was having a hard time believing her story, but had no time to press her. He needed to warn Wills off and move the meeting someplace else.

'Secure her,' he said to Nate.

'What are you going to do?' Annabel asked.

'We're going to leave you here,' Quinn said.

119

Nate emptied one of the pillowcases, then used his pocketknife to cut it into long strips like Quinn had taught him.

'Tie her to the desk,' Quinn said.

'What?' Annabel asked.

'We can't have you leaving at the moment,' Quinn said. 'It's either that or knock you out.'

It took her only a second to make her choice. She moved over to where Nate was waiting and sat on the ground. He tied her hands and feet to the desk. It left her in an awkward position, but she'd be fine for an hour or two.

'Mouth?' Nate asked.

'Yes,' Quinn said. 'But not too tight.'

Annabel glared at Nate, but said nothing as he used two of the strips as a gag. While this was going on, Quinn removed the image of the unidentified man from the folder and snapped a photo of it on his camera phone, then put it back with the other two. He emailed the photo to Orlando with a short message: Need ID.

'All right, Annabel,' Quinn said. 'In a while I'll call the front desk and have them send someone up to release you. Until then, it would be best if you just relax. Understand?'

She nodded.

Quinn stood up and grabbed the folder with the pictures off the dresser. 'Next time someone asks you to do an errand like this, I'd advise you to say no.'

15

'Where are you?' Quinn asked, his phone tight to his ear.

He and Nate were on Lexington Avenue walking toward the side entrance to Grand Central Terminal.

'Still in the cab,' Wills said. 'The traffic is miserable, but I should be there in ten minutes.'

'No,' Quinn said. 'The Hyatt is off.'

'Problem?'

Quinn gave him the short version of what happened.

'Give me the phone number she was supposed to call,' Wills said. 'I'll have someone check it out.'

Quinn pulled out the hair clip, read the number to him, then said, 'If he hasn't left already, get your man out of there.'

'Right.' Wills paused. 'I still want to meet.'

'Give me an hour. I'll call back with a new location.' Quinn hung up.

'I think we're clean so far,' Nate told him. He'd been keeping tabs to make sure they weren't being followed. 'Stay on the street or take the subway?'

'Subway,' Quinn said. If they had picked up a tail, whomever it was would be easier to spot below ground than above.

Once inside they made their way through the labyrinth of Grand Central Terminal to the subway, then chose the uptown 4 train. As they stepped onto the platform, a train was just pulling in.

Nate raised an eyebrow, asking whether they should take it or wait for the next.

'This one,' Quinn said. 'We'll go two stops and get off.'

They spent the next forty minutes hopping trains, changing lines, and checking their back trail to make sure they were alone. When Quinn was satisfied, they resurfaced at 110th Street and began walking west.

At Columbus they turned south, walked on for a block, then stopped. Quinn scanned the neighborhood. *This will work*, he thought. There was little chance anyone would look for them in this part of town.

He pulled out his phone and called the Grand Hyatt first.

'Grand Hyatt Hotel, how may I direct your call?'

'I'm in 2465, and there's a terrible smell coming from next door, room 2467. Can you send someone up to check it out?'

'Absolutely, sir. We'll get someone up there right away.'

Quinn clicked off, then called Wills. 'There's a restaurant on Columbus,' he said, randomly choosing a place on the opposite side of the street. 'It's called Crêpes on Columbus, just south of 109th. Be there in thirty minutes.'

He didn't wait for a reply.

★ ★ ★

As Quinn and Nate entered the restaurant, a tall man with dark hair lightly sprinkled with gray greeted them with a warm welcome and a large smile.

'Just the two of you?' he asked.

'Three,' Quinn said. 'A friend will be here in a bit.'

The man started to lead them toward a table near the front, but Quinn stopped him.

'How about that one,' he said, pointing at one near the rear wall.

'Sure,' the man said. 'Wherever you'd like.'

'Thanks.'

The man showed Quinn and Nate to the table, then handed them menus. 'Can I bring you anything to drink?'

'Water,' Quinn said.

'Me too,' Nate said.

'You got it,' the man said. 'My name's Steve. If you need anything, just let me know.'

'Thanks,' Quinn said.

Twenty minutes later, as Quinn was working his way through a tiger shrimp and spinach crêpe, the restaurant door opened.

'Is it him?' Nate asked, his eyes on his own plate.

'Yes,' Quinn said.

Quinn had met David Wills in person twice in the past, once in London for a meet-and-greet five months earlier, and a second time in Chicago on a brief for another project. The Englishman was almost six feet tall and thin. His hair was a short but shaggy, fifty-fifty mix of gray and dark blond. Like on the two previous occasions, Wills was wearing his uniform — a dark suit, colored shirt, and expensive tie.

The Englishman scanned the dining area, then raised his hand a few inches when he saw Quinn.

'Welcome,' Steve said from behind the counter. 'I'll be right with you.'

'He's with us,' Quinn said.

'Great,' Steve said. 'I'll bring over a menu in a moment.'

Wills walked over and sat down across from Quinn, in the chair next to Nate.

'Nothing like a little excitement to get the day going, is there?' he said.

'I prefer dull,' Quinn said.

Wills looked at Nate.

'My colleague,' Quinn said.

'I assumed as much. Does he have a name?'

'Yes,' Quinn said.

When Quinn offered no more, Wills frowned, but said, 'The number you gave me went straight to voice-mail. A beep and that was it.'

'Could you trace it?'

'Still working on that,' Wills said. 'But I was able to confirm that a woman by the name of Annabel Taplin, fitting the description you gave me, does indeed work for Wright Bains.'

'And therefore MI6,' Quinn said.

'That would be the assumption.'

Quinn reached for the folder he'd taken from Annabel so he could show Wills the picture of the third man, but stopped as Steve approached the table and started to put a menu in front of Quinn's client.

Wills waved him off and pointed at Nate's

124

plate. 'I'll just have what he's having.'

'You got it.'

After they were alone again, Quinn pulled the picture out. 'Do you know who this is?'

'No. Should I?' the Englishman asked. The look on his face seemed to back up his words.

'It was in Ms. Taplin's briefcase along with pictures of you and me. She was told he might be joining us for our meeting.'

Wills's brow furrowed. 'Joining us? I have no idea who he is. Do you?'

'No.'

'Give it to me, I'll check it out.'

Quinn handed him the printed photo. 'Do you at least know why MI6 would be interested in our meeting?'

Wills hesitated a moment before answering. 'I'm dealing with that. Don't concern yourself.'

'I wouldn't be concerning myself if I hadn't had to get involved,' Quinn said.

'It was a miscommunication. They won't be bothering us anymore.'

'A miscommunication?'

Wills frowned. 'I won't go into it more than that.'

'All right. Fine,' Quinn said, sitting back.

'Tell me again about Maine,' Wills said.

Quinn gave him the same story he had on the phone. He paused for a moment when he was done, then said, 'Anything new about the shooter from your end?'

'Nothing.'

A possibility had been floating around Quinn's mind since the drive to New York. 'Any chance it

125

might have been a member of the ops team?'

'The team was cleared personally by me.'

'I did see Mercer there toward the end, though. He was out of position.'

Wills looked uncomfortable, but said, 'Mercer's clean, too. He's working for me directly.'

'Directly?'

'My eyes on the ground. He did the same in Los Angeles.'

'I never saw him there,' Quinn said. Of course, he hadn't seen anyone on the L.A. ops team.

'The Russian woman,' Wills said, changing the subject, 'you're sure she was in both L.A. and Maine?'

'One hundred percent.'

The look in Wills's eyes became guarded.

Quinn asked, 'She's been seen before, hasn't she?'

Wills reluctantly nodded. 'In the vicinity of liquidations in Hong Kong and Bangkok.'

'All part of this same project?'

'Yes.'

'Damn,' Nate said. 'How long is your list?'

Quinn looked at his apprentice, surprised. He'd been thinking the same thing, but knew to keep his mouth shut. *Still . . .*

'I'm sorry,' Nate said. 'None of our business.'

'That's right,' Wills said. 'It's not.'

The silence lasted only a second before Quinn decided it was time to push. 'I'm not so sure it's not becoming our business,' he said. He could feel the other two look at him. 'You obviously came here for a reason. We could have just talked on the phone.'

126

Wills looked toward the kitchen as if wondering where his food was. When he looked back, he said, 'I wanted to speak with you about Maine because you were an independent observer last night. I wanted to be sure the story Donovan told me was completely accurate. You blow a mission, you really want to play that down. And then there's L.A. You were there for both. So I felt a face-to-face would be best.'

'And?' Quinn said, knowing there was more.

Wills looked around the restaurant. 'You're sure this place is clean?'

'I haven't done a sweep,' Quinn said. 'But I never knew it existed until I spotted it less than an hour ago, and I know we weren't followed. If someone's listening in, it's because they followed you.'

Wills looked around the dining room again, then glanced at Nate.

'What?' Nate asked.

'Don't insult us,' Quinn said to Wills, knowing full well what the man was thinking.

Before the Englishman could respond, Steve arrived with his meal.

'Here you go,' he said as he set the plate in front of Wills. 'Roasted chicken crêpe with mango red pepper sauce.'

'Thank you,' Wills said.

'Anything else, gentlemen?'

Quinn shook his head. 'Think we're all good. Thanks.'

'Just give me a yell if you want anything.' He headed back to the counter.

'So what's it going to be?' Quinn asked. 'You

127

going to trust us? Or do we walk?'

Wills looked at his plate and said nothing.

'Let's go,' Quinn said to Nate. They both started to rise.

'Wait,' Wills said. 'I trust you. It's not that. It's . . . it's the terms of the job.'

Quinn scowled. 'Fine. Nate, find another table.'

Nate paused, a fork full of crêpe halfway to his mouth. 'Sure,' he said. He picked up his plate and headed toward a table near the front of the restaurant.

'Better?' Quinn said.

Wills relaxed. 'Yes. Thank you. I'm sorry I had to do that, but . . . well, you understand.'

After several seconds of awkward silence, Wills went on, 'The project I hired you for came through a small group at MI6.'

'Wait,' Quinn said. 'If you were working for MI6, why would they send someone to spy on our meeting?'

'First, like I said before, it was a miscommunication. My people in London have already straightened it out. Second, the job's not *for* MI6. Occasionally there are projects that come to them from someone outside the organization that would be problematic if they got involved. When that happens, one of the people they like to call is me. MI6 makes the introduction, then steps back into the shadows.'

Quinn nodded. It was a standard tactic. 'Then, who's your client?'

Wills paused for a half second, then said, 'They're not a big player in our world. Actually,

I've never had dealings with them before, so as far as I'm concerned, they are not a player at all.'

'I'm not sure I like the sound of that.'

'Remember, though they would deny it, this is MI6 approved.'

'So who is this client?' Quinn asked, knowing he was crossing way over the line with the question.

'A corporation, actually. My understanding is that they help out MI6 every now and again.'

'That's not an answer.'

'It's the best you're going to get.'

Quinn shrugged. It had been worth a try. 'What exactly is the gig, then?'

'This corporation deals with several classified technologies that the government deems necessary to keep both secret and under British control. I've been told a lot of money has been spent to ensure this. Unfortunately, two months ago, someone with access downloaded some extremely sensitive blueprints and technical specs to several flash memory cards. By the time alarms went off, the person had disappeared.'

'What kind of information?' Quinn asked.

'The kind of information North Korea would want to buy.'

What North Korea needed was food and help for its people. But what it wanted was weapons and power to annoy the West.

'Nuclear,' Quinn said. It was the only real answer.

Wills nodded. 'It was the design for a bomb. Portable. Lightweight. Easy to produce even with Pyongyang's limited resources. They would have

129

paid millions for the information.'

'Would have?' Nate said. 'They didn't get the cards?'

'No. That's what we've been doing.' Wills checked again to make sure no one was near. On the table in front of him, his untouched crêpe was growing cold. 'The head of security — '

'Does he have a name?' Quinn asked.

Wills thought for a moment. 'Call him Mr. B.'

'I assume there's a Mr. A.'

'There is.'

'Okay,' Quinn said. 'Just wondering.'

'Mr. B knew that finding the cards might involve methods his corporation was not capable of performing.'

'Why not?'

'They are a publicly traded organization. Shareholders frown on wet work. Mr. B talked to one of the company's contacts at MI6. The contact was concerned, but also smart enough to realize that knowledge of the leak needed to be kept to a small circle of people. That meant mounting an operation outside normal governmental channels.'

'You.'

'Yes, me,' Wills said. 'We were told that this was to be a terminate operation from the start, and that all members of the thief's network needed to be eliminated to prevent the potential release of the information. There was no telling which of them had copies. Our job was to isolate and eliminate. MI6 would then go in, do a search, and recover the cards and any copies that might have been made.'

130

'You weren't doing the search?' Quinn asked.

'We were hired to question each target, and only search their person before removing them. MI6 would do the rest.'

It wasn't a particularly unusual arrangement. A private group does the dirty work so that another agency can keep its hands clean. Quinn had been on similar projects in the past. The only unusual aspect was the involvement of a third organization, this corporation whose information had been stolen. Still, Quinn couldn't help thinking that the story was almost too pat. The feeling wasn't a strong one, just something that tickled at the back of his mind.

'Then who are these Russians?' he asked.

'We think they're part of a Georgian group fighting to rejoin Russia. In other words, terrorists who want to get their hands on a bomb. The big problem now is that they've been able to take one of the targets before we could get to them. If he had one of the disks on him, the information could be anywhere by now.'

'I can't imagine MI6 is happy about that.'

Wills paused. 'MI6 doesn't know yet.'

'You haven't told them?'

Wills shook his head.

'Could they suspect something went wrong? Maybe that's why they sent the watcher.'

'I told you, it was a miscommunication.' Wills's tone was less convincing than his words.

'So what are you doing about Moody?' Quinn asked.

'I have a team trying to track the Russians down. Find them and we find Moody.'

'Donovan?'

'No. Donovan and his team have split and gone to ground. I haven't talked to him since thirty minutes after the operation. If Moody's found, the new team will take care of him.'

'How many more names are on the list?' Quinn asked.

'Moody was the last,' Wills said.

Quinn raised his eyebrows. 'Last? Are you saying you came all the way over here to let me go? Or do you want me on standby for once they've taken care of Moody?'

'No,' Wills said. 'There's something else I need you to do. A related job.'

'What do you mean 'related'?'

'Mr. B asked if we could do a special project for the corporation on the side.'

Quinn's eyes narrowed with concern. If it was a project that involved him, it would mean someone was going to be killed. A few deaths of amoral thieves selling bomb plans to terrorists was one thing, but corporate murder? That would be going somewhere Quinn wasn't comfortable with.

Wills seemed to sense Quinn's reluctance. 'It's not what you think.'

'If it's not what I think, then you don't need a cleaner.'

'There *is* a body. It's in London. Hidden in a building that's about to be demolished.'

'Wait, what? Are you saying it's already there?'

Wills said nothing for a moment, then nodded. 'It's been there over twenty years.'

132

16

'I guess this isn't a surprise,' Nate said.

'Not really,' Quinn agreed.

They were still in Manhattan, standing across the street from a place called Molly Dryer's Delicatessen.

At the end of the meeting at the restaurant, Wills had asked Quinn to check out the address found on the dead man in the car outside Moody's house. The name on the license had been William Burke, but the address listed belonged to the deli.

'Hard sell, soft sell,' Quinn said, pointing to Nate first, then himself.

'Fine by me.'

Inside, a long buffet table served up everything from chow mein to Salisbury steak. Next to it another table specialized in salads. There were also shelves with chips and cookies and snacks next to glass-door cabinets filled with drinks. Beyond the buffet were dining tables and chairs ready for the next influx of customers.

A typical New York deli.

The employees manning the kitchen all looked Latin, while the two women at the registers looked Middle Eastern.

He grabbed a bottle of water and a bag of chips and headed for the checkout.

'Are you Molly?' he asked the woman who rang him up.

She gave him an odd look.

'Molly,' he repeated. 'The name on the sign?'

'Ah, right,' she said. She leaned toward him a few inches. 'There is no Molly. It's just a name my father picked out of a book. He said it sounded more American.'

Quinn laughed. 'He's right.'

At a signal from Quinn, Nate walked up.

'Excuse me,' Nate said.

The woman stopped herself in the middle of counting out Quinn's change and looked at him.

Nate smiled. 'I'm looking for a friend of mine. Says he comes here all time, so I thought you might know him. Bill Burke. Sometimes goes by William.'

The look on her face didn't change. 'Sorry. Don't know him.'

'You're sure?'

Again, she gave him the silent stare.

He raised a hand in the air. 'Okay, thanks anyway.'

As Nate walked away, Quinn said, 'Nate was a bit of a jerk, wasn't he?'

'I didn't notice.'

★   ★   ★

Quinn and Nate regrouped a block away.

'Like we thought, fake ID,' Nate said.

'You want these?' Quinn asked, holding up the chips.

'Are you kidding?' Nate said. 'Of course.' He snatched the bag from Quinn.

'Is there anything you won't eat?'

134

Nate smiled, but kept munching. When he was ready to pop another chip in his mouth, he paused long enough to ask, 'This new assignment, have you ever been asked to do anything like it before?'

'I had to remove a corpse from a cemetery once. It had been in the ground about two years.'

Nate gave him an odd look. 'Why would you have to do that?'

'I don't know,' Quinn said. 'Client never told me.'

'But why do you think . . . Never mind,' Nate said. 'The thing Mr. Wills wants us to do, doesn't it seem a little odd?'

'A little, maybe.'

'Couldn't they just go in and remove the body themselves?'

'I assume there's a reason they need us to do it,' Quinn said.

'But there can't be much left, can there? Bones, maybe some clothes?'

Quinn looked at him. 'What is it you really want to say?'

Nate stuffed a potato chip into his mouth. 'Okay, I know it's going to sound a little weird given what we deal with most of the time, but this kind of gives me the creeps.'

'The creeps.'

'Yeah. Come on. It doesn't make you feel a little odd?'

'No,' Quinn said. He started walking again.

Nate was a step behind him. 'Not even a little?'

'Not even a little.'

135

'Okay. Sorry I brought it up. It's just, you know, you always said to go by your gut.'

Nate stuffed another chip in his mouth.

Despite what he'd said to Nate, his gut was telling him pretty much the same thing. Only it wasn't the condition of the body that was bothering him. It was the whole nature of the project. For the first time in quite a while, he was starting to wonder if he was on the right side of things or not.

His phone vibrated, bringing a welcome diversion. It was Orlando.

'Hey,' he said. 'How's Garrett?'

'What? Oh, he's fine,' she said, seeming distracted. 'Okay, so I've got you on a 6:40 flight on Continental out of Newark.'

Quinn looked at Nate. 'Get a cab.'

'I could change it to the 9:45 if that'll work better,' Orlando said.

'No. Should be fine. Just need to pick up our bags and head over.' They'd left their luggage in the car they'd driven into the city. It was parked in a lot just off Broadway. 'I'll call you back if I think we're not going to make it. Have you found anything on that photo I sent you?'

'Not yet. The age might be a problem. But I'm running it through several databases.'

'Here we go,' Nate said as a taxi pulled to the curb. Quinn's apprentice climbed in.

'Our ride's here,' Quinn said into the phone. 'I'll check in with you before we leave. See if you've found out anything then.'

'Quinn,' she said.

The tone of her voice stopped him on the curb.

136

'What?'

'That problem I told you about before . . . '

'What about it?'

'It's worse than I thought.'

'Worse how?' he asked.

'Whoever's trying to find out about you knows what they're doing.' She paused. 'They found your name.'

'Which name?' The sounds of the cars and the people on the street disappeared. Even the October chill seemed to vanish.

'Your *real* name. Someone hacked into the Social Security Administration ninety minutes ago and looked you up.'

'I don't have a Social Security number.'

'You did once.'

'Yeah, but you got rid of that, didn't you?' he asked.

She hesitated. 'I buried it, but I wasn't able to delete it completely.'

'But you told me . . . '

'I told you I took care of it. Look, I'm sorry. I thought I had. No one should have been able to find it, but someone did.'

'Okay. All right. What — '

She cut him off. 'Ten minutes later I got half a dozen alarm messages from some improved trips I set up last night on things connected to your life before Quinn.'

'Where?' he asked.

'IRS, the Phoenix Police Department — '

'I know for a fact my record with the Phoenix PD was removed.' His tenure there had been short and long ago.

137

'*Your* file, yes. But you were cross-referenced on several others. I got what I could, but there were too many files to check. The tripwire at Phoenix did two things. Alerted me to the initial hack, then traced what the intruders were looking at. That's how I knew it was the same people as the other day. They accessed two files. A burglary and an attempted rape. In both cases you were one of the responding officers.'

'What the hell?'

'There's more,' Orlando said.

'Hey, you going to get in?' the cabbie yelled out at Quinn.

'Turn on the meter and give me a minute,' Quinn yelled back. Into the phone he said, 'What more?'

'They've also hacked into the record at School District 690,' Orlando said. 'That's the school district for Warroad, Minnesota.'

'Warroad?'

'You don't have a file there, either. There is no trace of you in their system. But the flag I have there worked the same as the one in Phoenix, so I know it was them.'

'Okay, so they checked, but I wasn't there. So that's good.'

She hesitated. 'Yeah. That's right. They didn't find your file. But they did find Liz's.'

Now it wasn't just the noises of New York that disappeared, but the ground Quinn was standing on, too.

'They didn't stop there, either,' Orlando said. 'They've traced her to Paris.'

In a flash, the whole world came rushing back.

138

He jumped into the cab and slammed the door closed behind.

'The bags,' he said to Nate.

Nate told the taxi driver where to go.

'Forget London,' Quinn said into the phone. 'We need to get to Paris.'

'That's the flight I booked you on,' Orlando told him.

Of course it was, he thought. She would have predicted his reaction, and anticipated the request. There was no one on the earth who knew him better than she did.

'My mother?' he whispered into the phone.

'They would have gotten her address off Liz's file.'

For one of the first times in his life, Quinn felt paralyzed. Should he go to his sister or his mother? Perhaps he was overreacting. Perhaps the hacker had only been after information. Perhaps there was no threat.

Perhaps, but Quinn knew he would be a fool to not assume the worst.

Everyone had their weaknesses. The most common was family. That's why most people in Quinn's business did all they could to hide their pasts. Some specialities, such as op agents and assassins, were more likely to see threats in this area. Cleaners, not so much. If they ever ran into trouble, they were more prone to a direct assault than someone trying to leverage the people in their lives. But that didn't mean Quinn didn't worry about this possibility. And now that worry had become a reality.

'I made a few calls,' Orlando said.

Quinn shook himself back into the here and now. 'Calls?'

'Steven Howard was in Chicago,' she said. 'He's on his way to Warroad to keep an eye on your mother now. Should be there sometime tonight. I've also rounded up Rickey Larson and Brent Nolan. They'll be there by noon tomorrow. And I'm going, too.'

Quinn could feel some of the tension in his shoulders ease. 'Thank you,' he said.

'What I need you to do is call her,' she said. 'Tell her you have a friend who needs a place to stay. Say he's working on a project, writing a book or something, and needs to go someplace quiet for a week or two. Tell her I'm going to bring him by. It'll let us get someone in the house with her.'

'Good,' Quinn said. He knew his mother wasn't going to like the idea, not this close to her husband's death, but she'd do it for Quinn.

'Once I get everything settled, I'll fly over to you.'

'You should stay with her.'

'They can handle things without me,' Orlando said. 'You're going to need me to help with the job in London.'

'Screw the London job. I'm not doing it.'

She paused a moment, then said, 'We'll talk about that when I see you.'

He was about to protest again, but realized it would be useless. She'd hung up.

17

Fall in Paris meant two things: cooler weather and fewer tourists. It wasn't that there were no tourists, it was just that their number was a fraction of what it was during the summer months. In August, the streets and monuments were overwhelmed by what seemed to be a torrent of refugees from the Tower of Babel. In October, it was more of a trickle.

When Quinn and Nate had gotten into the taxi, Quinn had asked the driver to turn up the heat. It was hovering around forty-four degrees Fahrenheit, several degrees colder than it had been in New York, and more than two dozen less than it was back in Los Angeles. To Quinn it was now officially too cold. The cabbie had fiddled with a few knobs, but from what Quinn could tell the temperature hadn't changed. He pulled his collar tight to his neck and looked out at the gray morning.

During the flight over he kept his eyes shut, hoping sleep would overtake him, but his mind only let him catch a moment here and there. By the time they landed, the only thing the attempt had been able to accomplish was to keep Nate from asking him questions. All his apprentice knew was that their destination had changed. Quinn had told him nothing else.

In the taxi, Nate tried again to find out what was going on. But Quinn cut him off with 'Not yet.' Yes, he was going to have to tell Nate something, but he just couldn't bring himself to do it. Not yet. The thing he was most focused on was that he was going to have to see his sister. And no matter which scenario he played out in his mind, none ended with Liz happy to see him.

He had toyed with the idea of not letting her know he was there at all. He and Nate could set up a perimeter surveillance that might work well enough. They could shadow her, bug her apartment when she was away, plant a GPS chip in her purse or shoes to keep track of her no matter where she went. It would be tricky, but not impossible. Still, relying on a blip on a screen was not a comforting idea.

He knew he was going to have to bite the bullet and approach her directly. That still didn't guarantee success. She might give him two minutes, or an hour. She might give him nothing, and then where would he be?

He would have to be careful in his approach, telling her just enough of the truth to get her cooperation. She already thought he was in international banking, so he could use that. Maybe he could tell her he was being targeted by a criminal organization that had a grudge with his bank. Maybe their problems were with Quinn specifically, and he feared the trouble might spread to her since she was in Europe.

Quinn frowned, then shook his head. The idea was ludicrous and convoluted. If it were true, why wouldn't the police be involved? That would be the first question out of Liz's mouth. She would poke holes in Quinn's story he wouldn't be able to plug fast enough.

He played a few more scenarios through his mind, but none proved any better. He needed something different, something believable. But what?

The cab stopped at the curb.

'Le Sorbonne,' the driver said.

On the other side of the intersection was the tan, stone, block-long Sorbonne, the world-renowned Paris university.

'*Merci*,' Quinn said as he handed the driver enough euros to cover the trip.

'Can you tell me what's going on now?' Nate asked once they were on the sidewalk.

Quinn stared at the Sorbonne for several seconds, knowing it was time. But how much to tell? *Everything*, a voice in his head said. Orlando's voice. 'Come on.'

They turned right at Rue des Écoles, walking on the opposite side of the street from the main entrance to the school. He eyed the people going in and out the front doors on the off chance Liz would be among them. No such luck. A short block down and to the right was a small park. Quinn led Nate inside.

The park was enclosed by an iron fence lined with bushes and trees that made it almost impossible for anyone on the outside to see in. Much of the vegetation was showing its fall colors. Scattered around the park were granite statues and a few benches.

In addition to Nate and Quinn, there were only three other people present. Two were reading books, while the third, an older gentleman,

143

seemed interested in some birds on the path. None were threats.

Quinn motioned to a bench in a deserted corner. They sat. It was over a minute, though, before he finally spoke. 'What I'm going to tell you goes no further than between you and me.'

'How's that different from anything else?'

'This isn't anything else. This isn't about a job.'

'Orlando?' Nate asked, unable to keep the worry from his voice.

'No. She's fine.'

'Okay. Then, what is it?'

Quinn stared at Nate, his face hard. 'I have your word, your blood oath, that you will never tell anyone what I'm about to tell you.'

'Of course you have my word. You shouldn't even have to ask that,' Nate said. 'What the hell is going on?'

Quinn took a moment, knowing he was about to break his most important taboo. 'My personal life may have been . . . compromised.'

It took a second, then Nate said, 'Oh, God. How far back?'

'All the way,' Quinn said.

Nate digested the information, then asked, 'Is that why we're in Paris and not London?'

Again, Quinn hesitated. He couldn't help it. It was a reflex he'd honed over many years. Finally, he nodded. 'You remember a couple of weeks ago, when I was out of town?'

'Sure.'

'I was attending my father's funeral.'

'I'm sorry,' Nate said. 'I had no idea.'

'How could you? I didn't tell you.'

'I really am sorry.'

'We weren't close,' Quinn said. 'Don't worry about it.'

'So the funeral has something to do with us being *here*?'

'Only in the sense that you need to know about it.'

Again, Nate looked confused.

'You're going to meet someone who was there, and if she mentions it I don't want you to be surprised.'

'All right. That makes sense. Who is it?'

'Her name is Liz,' Quinn said. 'She's . . . my sister.'

Nate stared at Quinn, surprised.

'She's studying at the Sorbonne,' Quinn explained. 'We're here because she might be in danger. I want to make sure that doesn't happen.' He paused. 'But to do that, I need your help.'

Nate didn't even hesitate. 'Whatever you need, I'm there.'

'Thanks.'

'Is there anyone else you're worried about?'

Quinn hesitated. Again, this was sacred ground. But he had no choice. 'My mother. Orlando's with her right now.'

'Whoa,' Nate said, shaking his head. It was a lot to take in. But like the professional he'd become, he seemed to quickly adjust and move on. 'What do you need me to do?'

'I'm not one hundred percent sure yet. Liz and I, we aren't exactly on the best of terms.'

'I sense a pattern. Does your mother hate you, too?'

Quinn shot him a withering look.

'I'm sorry,' Nate said. 'I shouldn't have said that.'

'It's complicated,' Quinn said. 'And no, my mother doesn't hate me.'

'Well, that'll save you some therapy at least . . . Sorry. Shouldn't have said that either.'

In the distance, the old man who had been watching the birds started walking down the path toward their bench. His gait was slow, almost a shuffle.

'Does your sister know what you do?' Nate asked.

'Of course not,' Quinn said. 'Wait. Does anyone in your past know what *you* do?'

'No.'

'I'm serious, Nate. Have you told *anyone* what you do? Have you even hinted about it?'

'No. No one.'

'You're sure?'

'Yes, I'm sure. And how did this suddenly become about me?'

Quinn leaned back, duly chastened. Nate was right. He'd momentarily channeled his anxiety into the possibility that his apprentice had screwed up.

'Liz thinks I'm in the international banking business. My mother thinks so, too.'

Nate had heard Quinn use the cover with other civilians in the past. 'At least you can use that to explain why you're in town.'

'Yeah,' Quinn said.

After a moment, Nate asked, 'What's Orlando setting up for your mom?'

Quinn explained the plan he and Orlando had worked out.

'When did you call your mom?'

'When we were waiting for the plane in Newark.'

'She go for it?' Nate asked.

'She didn't say no. Secretly, I think she's probably happy to have company. It's been less than a month since she lost her husband.'

The old man had advanced down the path, but was still out of earshot. Quinn gave him a glance, then turned back to Nate.

'So what's the plan?' Nate asked. 'Are we just going to keep an eye on her?'

'I'm not sure. I'm still trying to figure that out.'

'Do you know what Liz's living situation is?' Nate asked.

Quinn nodded.

'Does she have any roommates?'

'No.'

'So only a one-bedroom apartment.'

'Yes.'

'I assume she has a couch,' Nate said.

'Of course she has a couch.'

'Then why can't we do a variation on what Orlando's doing with your mom? You introduce me as a friend who needs a place to stay for a little while. I can crash on her couch and watch the inside. You can get someone to help you watch the perimeter. Done and done.'

The old man moved into hearing range, so Quinn and Nate fell silent.

Quinn used the quiet to think Nate's idea

147

through. Would it work? It would depend on whether Liz would even talk to him or not. Their less-than-quality time at their father's funeral tended to make him think the odds were against it. He tried to come up with another option, some other way of getting someone close to her for protection. But nothing came.

In front of them, the old man stopped on the path and stared in their direction.

'*C'est mon banc,*' the old man said.

'*Pardon?*' Nate asked.

'*C'est mon banc. Vous devez bouger,*' he said, waving his hands at them to get off the bench.

'*Je suis désolé. Nous ne savions pas,*' Nate apologized.

He and Quinn got up. Even before they started to walk away, the old man pushed past them and sat down.

'*C'est mon banc,*' he repeated.

'I guess he really likes that bench,' Nate said as he and Quinn walked toward the gate.

'He just wants to control his world,' Quinn said, painfully aware he was attempting to do the same thing.

'So what are we going to do?' Nate asked.

'Your idea is good. We'll work with that.'

'Okay,' Nate said. 'Then I guess there's one more thing I need to know.'

'What's that?' Quinn asked.

'What's your real name?'

Quinn tensed. It was the final box that he'd left closed. The one he had thought he would never have to open.

'It's Jake,' he said. 'Jake Oliver.'

18

Petra and Mikhail arrived in London at 9:15 p.m. Once in the terminal, Mikhail located a pay phone and made a quick call.

'It's all arranged,' he told Petra. 'An apartment in Bayswater.'

'Good,' was all Petra could manage to say. She didn't think she'd ever been as exhausted as she was at that moment.

They took the Underground into the city, and before they had even gone two stops, she was slumped in her seat, asleep. At Earl's Court, Mikhail woke her so they could switch trains, and woke her again when they reached Bayswater.

'Let me take your bag,' he said.

She yanked it away from his hand. 'I'm fine.'

Being Russian in London had its advantages. The city was teeming with their former countrymen. The Russian community was large, and very connected. The use of the apartment was courtesy of one of Mikhail's distant cousins. It was in a tired-looking building on the second floor. A fine layer of dust covered the floors and the windowsills. With the exception of two thin mattresses, a couple of plastic chairs, and a folding table, the place was empty.

Sleep was what Petra wanted, but she knew she needed to check in with Stepka first. So while Mikhail ran out to pick up some food, she called Moscow.

'Anything?' she asked.

'I've narrowed it down to three groups,' he said. 'All in London. But I think that's as far as I can get from here.'

'Who are they?' she asked.

'A group called CM8 run by a guy named Leon Currie. And another headed by an ops runner named David Wills.'

'And the third one?'

'That's kind of tricky.'

'What do you mean?'

'It appears to be associated with British intelligence.'

'Associated?'

'From what I've learned, it's a front for MI6. A business called Wright Bains Securities.'

MI6? Those were the last people she wanted to deal with.

'Do you have a name there?' she asked.

'No name yet.'

'See what you can dig up,' she said. 'We'll work on the others from this end.'

As she hung up, she felt a little better. They had a potential lead again. They just needed to figure out which of the three might be the connection to the Ghost.

'Finish it.' That's what Dombrovski had said the last time Petra had talked to him.

'I don't know if I can.'

'You're the smartest one of all of us.'

'No, I'm — '

'Yes, you are. You've been training for this moment for years. Your instincts are good. You've learned everything you need to carry this out.

150

The names, the photograph. It's the best lead we've ever had. Finish it, Petra. Finish it.'

Names, yes, but not *the* name. If she had that, finish it was exactly what she'd do. But she needed that damn name, the name the Ghost called himself now. Only so far all she had was a trail of useless bodies.

Petra looked at the picture again. Fourteen people, but only two who meant anything, the two young men standing at opposite ends of the bar. They almost looked like twins, but they weren't. The one on the right was the one she was looking for, but it was the one on the left who was the key. Learn his name and everything would fall into place. But his identity had been so thoroughly erased that only a small group of people had known who he was. A small group that had become a handful, then that handful had been reduced to . . . ? *How many? Three? Two?*

They had been so close with Moody. But in the end he, too, had given them nothing.

Petra lay down on the bed and pulled the thin blanket that had been left with the mattress over her shoulders. Tomorrow she had to be sharp. She needed to turn off her mind and *sleep*.

But so many things were still swirling inside. The Ghost. Dombrovski. Stepka.

And, of course, Andrei.

'I miss you,' she whispered. 'I miss you so much.'

19

Liz Oliver's apartment was located near the heart of the Latin Quarter, within walking distance of the Sorbonne. It was in one of the thousands of stone apartment buildings that lined Parisian streets. Solid, tasteful, and very European. It had been two years since Quinn had last been in the building.

The apartment had come as a free perk of Liz's scholarship. It was a far better place than what most students lived in. The letter from the foundation had explained the only requirement that came with the use of the apartment was that she could take on no roommates, the thinking being this would help her concentrate on her studies. Quinn had written the requirement himself, because, unknown to Liz, he *was* the foundation.

The ground level of the building housed a variety of shops: a shoe store, a used-book store, a small greengrocer, the prerequisite patisserie, and a café at the corner that even in the cool of fall had customers sitting at tables on the sidewalk. Above the businesses were five floors of apartments.

It being midmorning on a weekday, Quinn was all but certain his sister would not be home. He couldn't recall her exact schedule, but he knew that she was usually out of the building by 9 a.m. and, more often than not, didn't return until well after dark.

152

The residential entrance was a set of double wooden doors located between the shoe store and the greengrocer. Windows in the upper halves of each door looked in on an empty lobby. Mounted next to the door were a list of residents and an intercom. Liz's name was in the middle of the second column.

Quinn thought about pushing the one for her place, but decided against it. If she was home, it would be better if he knocked on her door than if he rang her on the intercom. *Harder to turn me away if we're face-to-face.* At least that's what he told himself.

'Someone's coming,' Nate whispered.

Quinn heard it, too. Footsteps, somewhere on the other side of the door. He peeked through the window, but saw no one, then motioned Nate to take a few steps back. Once they were far enough away, they began talking like two friends passing the time.

A few seconds later, the door swung open and an older woman stepped out. The moment she passed, Nate eased over and caught the door before it closed, then he and Quinn casually walked inside.

The lobby was fifteen feet wide by another twenty-five deep. It was clean, bright, and recently painted. There was a carpeted staircase to the right, an elevator just beyond it, and an opening near the back of the lobby that led to a rear hallway.

'Stairs or elevator?' Nate said.

'Stairs,' Quinn said. They started to climb.

'How far up?'

'One shy of the top.'

153

'How do you want to play this?'

'She should be in class, so she's probably not home. We'll keep it to a drive-by right now,' Quinn said. 'Besides, I think you need a shower and a change of clothes before you meet her.'

'Thanks, boss. That's sweet,' Nate said. 'You're not smelling so pleasant yourself.'

'Yeah, but she already hates me.'

★   ★   ★

The landing on Liz's floor opened into a carpeted hallway that led through the center of the building. On either side were the entrances to the apartments. Three doors per side, six apartments per floor. The apartments on the right looked out on the street, and those on the left faced whatever was behind the building. At the far end of the hallway, another door led to the emergency staircase.

'What's her number?' Nate asked.

'Twenty-one. Middle one on the right.'

Quinn glanced at Liz's door as they started to pass it, then stopped abruptly and knelt down. He moved in close, his attention on the door-knob and lock.

'What is it?' Nate asked.

Instead of answering, he pointed at the metal plate surrounding the lock. There was a scratch on it. To the trained eye it was like a neon sign.

Nate nodded. He wet his finger, then touched the carpet on the floor below the lock. When he brought it back up, Quinn could see two tiny metal shavings.

154

'Fresh,' Nate mouthed.

Perhaps Liz had caused the damage with her key, but Quinn didn't think so. The groove was too narrow, like it was made by a wire.

Or a pick.

The base of Quinn's neck began to tingle in apprehension.

He started to reach for the handle, but Nate touched him on the shoulder and shook his head. His apprentice then eased his backpack onto the floor and unzipped one of the sections just wide enough so he could reach in.

From inside, he pulled out two pairs of thin rubber gloves and handed one to Quinn.

Quinn donned the gloves, then tried to turn the knob. The door was unlocked.

'I'm going in,' he whispered. 'You stay here.'

Nate didn't look happy, but said nothing.

Painfully aware that neither of them was armed, Quinn pushed the door open a few inches, then paused to listen.

There was a sound from deep in the apartment. Quinn pointed at his ear, then at the opening, telling Nate someone was inside. Standing up, he pushed the door open several more inches and slipped through the gap.

A small entryway led into a living room. He eased to the end of the foyer and peered around the corner. The living room contained a mish-mash of furniture. A cloth-covered couch, a matching chair, an ornate coffee table, and two bookcases filled but not overstuffed.

Quinn glanced at the metal-framed windows, half covered by white sheer curtains. Through them he could see the building across the street.

Everything within his view looked normal. So normal, in fact, that he began to doubt himself. Perhaps Liz had made the sound. Perhaps there was another explanation for the scratch. Perhaps she had left her door unlocked by accident, or maybe she was expecting someone. Perhaps she was only seconds away from walking into the living room and seeing him standing there.

Then what?

Before he could retrace his steps, he heard a drawer being yanked out, then slammed back into place. It had come from the left, toward the bedroom.

Quinn slipped his backpack off his shoulders and placed it on the floor in the entryway. He motioned for Nate to come inside and wait by the door. Once his apprentice was in position, Quinn crossed the living room, stepping carefully so as not to cause any of the floorboards beneath the carpet to creak. If it was Liz in the bedroom, he could sneak back out. If it wasn't, he'd let his instincts take over.

At the hallway, he paused again. Like elsewhere in the apartment, the lights were off. Would his sister be moving around in the semidarkness?

The hallway was only five feet long. At the other end, an open door led into the bathroom. To the right, another door, also open, led to the bedroom.

From his position he could only see a narrow swath of the room, from the middle of the bed to the wall on the other side. It was dim, but not dark.

Another drawer yanked open.

Unconsciously, Quinn's hand moved toward where his gun would have been if he'd had one. He stopped himself halfway there, annoyed.

He scanned the surrounding area for anything he could use as a weapon. A paperweight, a letter opener, or even an ashtray — though he would have given Liz hell about that later if he'd found one. But he saw nothing he could use.

In the bedroom, the drawer moved back into place, this time with less force. Then the floor creaked. Once, twice, a third time, each wooden groan moving closer to the doorway.

Quinn pressed himself against the wall just inside the living room.

Another creak. This time in the hallway, not the bedroom.

He tensed, ready to move, but instead of heading toward the living room, the unseen person entered the bathroom.

A sudden splash of illumination spilled into the hall as the bathroom light came on. Quinn could hear the person going through the cabinet and drawers. Then there was the *thunk* of porcelain, and a second later the sound of water hitting water. From a distance.

Definitely not Liz.

The intruder was male.

Quinn moved into the hallway, anger bubbling just below the surface of his skin at this intrusion on his sister's life.

When he reached the bathroom, he peeked between the door and the jamb. Two feet on the other side was the back right shoulder of a large

157

man in a dark coat. Quinn estimated the guy was at least six foot three. His hair was covered by the kind of stocking cap favored by the reggae set from the seventies and eighties — loose and baggy, falling against the nape of his neck. The man was staring at the wall above the toilet in the time-honored tradition of males around the world.

The torrent of water began to slow, then finally stop. After a last push to clean out the pipes, the man bent down to zip himself up.

Without another thought, Quinn slammed the door into the man's back.

A pained grunt was followed by the sound of the porcelain lid to the toilet's water tank being jarred loose.

Quinn slammed again, harder.

Another grunt.

As he was about to go for a third time, the door smashed back into him, sending him flying against the door frame. His left arm flailed out, looking for something solid to hold on to, but found only the light switch and inadvertently flipped it off, plunging the room into darkness.

The intruder roared as he tried to get around the door. But the cramped space and his massive size slowed his efforts. When he finally shoved past it, Quinn unleashed a right hook to his jaw.

'Merde!' the man yelled.

Quinn hit him again, this time in the soft spot just below the ribs. The intruder doubled over, and Quinn grabbed him by the shoulders, pulling him out into the hall.

The man stumbled for a few feet, then fell to

158

his knees. Quinn jumped on his back, pushing him all the way to the ground, then began releasing punch after punch to the man's kidneys and ribs.

Suddenly someone grabbed his arm. It was Nate.

'We can't get any info out of him if you kill him,' Nate said.

Quinn held his position for a moment longer, breathing hard, then shoved the man between the shoulder blades and stood up.

'Search him,' he said, his teeth clenched.

'*Laissez-moi!*' the intruder yelled as Nate patted him down.

'Gun,' Nate said, his hand at the small of the man's back.

He removed the Glock pistol from the man's waistband and handed it to Quinn, then continued his search. There was a knife in the guy's boot, but that was it.

'ID?' Quinn asked.

'No wallet,' Nate said.

'*Qui êtes-vous?*' Quinn demanded, asking the man's identity.

'*Allez vous faire foutre.*'

Quinn didn't believe for a second his name was Go To Hell. '*Qui êtes-vous?*'

'*J'habite ici.*' I live here.

'Bullshit,' Quinn said, then shoved the barrel of the Glock into the base of the guy's head.

'Take it easy,' the intruder said in heavily accented English.

'One chance or I pull the trigger. What are you doing here?'

'Hey, no problem. I'll tell you. Okay? Someone asked me to look around this apartment,' the man said. 'So I look around. No reason to shoot me.'

Quinn leaned back, moving the gun from the man's neck.

'Keep your hands where I can see them and turn over,' he said. 'Slowly.'

Nate released the man's shoulders, then got to his feet.

As instructed, the man turned over and lay on his back.

The intruder had a dark beard, long and full, sticking a good five inches out from his face. Above the growth, his eyes were bright blue, and looked as surprised as Quinn felt.

'Julien?' Quinn said.

'Quinn?' the man asked.

20

'So who is she?' Julien de Coster asked.

They were sitting around one of the outside tables at the café below Liz's apartment building. Quinn had situated himself so that he could keep an eye on the entrance, but be shielded by Nate and Julien in case his sister suddenly showed up.

'The relative of a client,' Quinn said. Telling Nate the truth was one thing, broadcasting it to the rest of the world was something else entirely. 'He was concerned she might be in danger. Since I was in the area, he asked me to check on her.'

Julien sipped a coffee and narrowed his eyes. 'There's more, isn't there?'

'Of course there's more,' Quinn said. 'But you know there are things I can't tell you.'

'I understand,' Julien said, holding up a hand. 'Not my business.'

'Julien, I've always trusted you. You know that. But come on, you were *in* her apartment. I think it's safe to say we're working opposite sides on this thing.'

'If I'm on the other side from you, then I am obviously not where I should be.'

Quinn said nothing.

Julien took another sip. 'You can consider me off the job. But that doesn't mean someone won't come back and take my place.'

'I'm not trying to keep you from working,' Quinn said.

Julien scoffed. 'It was a throwaway job, anyway. Don't worry about it.'

Quinn put his hand around his cup, but didn't raise it. 'If that's the case, would you be interested in telling me what you were supposed to be doing?'

'I don't know,' Julien said. 'Backing out of the job is already not going to help my reputation, but you want me to sell out my employer? What is so important?'

'The girl's an innocent. Her only crime is being related to someone in our world. She doesn't deserve to be put in danger, and I'm here to make sure she isn't.'

Julien smiled. 'You are clever, my friend.' He reached into the pocket of his jacket and pulled out a four-by-six photograph, then laid it on the table so Quinn could see it. 'She has your eyes, you know. And your chin, too.'

Quinn had seen the same picture mounted in a frame on the piano at his mother's house. A happy Liz, smiling, and just about to board a plane to France.

'Part of my instructions was to find a photograph of the woman who lived there. This was in her bedroom.' Julien smiled. 'Your sister?'

Quinn looked up, his gaze boring into the Frenchman.

'D'accord,' Julien said, holding a hand up. 'I don't need to know.' He clapped Nate on the back. 'You have a very good boss here. He trusted me when it could have got him killed. I've always remembered that. That kind of trust is rare in our business, know what I mean?'

162

'I'd love to hear what happened,' Nate said.

Julien laughed again. 'I am not so easily fooled. That job was long ago, but even then we should never tell stories.'

Quinn barely heard any of this, his mind still trying to come to grips with the fact that the secret life he had created was on the verge of coming completely apart.

'Why were you in her apartment?' he asked.

Julien placed his arms on the table and leaned forward. 'Last night I got a phone call for a job. I was told it was a simple check-and-report. I was given a woman's name and an address. Nothing else. It's not the kind of work I usually take, but business for me has been slow lately. Perhaps you heard about my trouble in Bern?'

Quinn nodded. Julien had been caught during an exchange operation in the Swiss capital. Though he didn't know details, Quinn had heard secondhand that Julien had threatened to expose his employer if they didn't get him out. A threat like that would tend to put a hold on any future employment opportunities.

Julien seemed to deduce what Quinn was thinking. 'Don't believe all rumors.'

'I never do.'

'I didn't ask for anything,' Julien said. 'The people I worked for started that rumor to cover their own mistakes. It was their fault I was detained. But what could I do?'

Quinn was inclined to give Julien the benefit of the doubt. Making those kind of threats was not something he had an easy time seeing the big man doing.

'Last night,' Quinn said, trying to get Julien back on track, 'who called you?'

The Frenchman took another sip of coffee. 'A broker who has used me in the past.'

'A name, Julien.'

Julien shrugged. 'Charles Butler.'

'It sounds made up,' Nate said.

'It's the name he's always used. False? Probably. But the payment was sitting in my account this morning, so I didn't care.'

'American?'

'American. English. Sometimes it's hard for me to tell the difference.'

'What was the assignment?'

'They told me the name of the woman was Elizabeth Oliver. I was to check her apartment when she was out. They wanted a photograph and a list of contacts.' He picked up his coffee. 'That's not so easy these days. Everyone keeps their contacts on their phones and computers. I could find neither in the apartment.'

He lifted the cup to his mouth and finished it off.

'So you're saying you didn't find anything,' Quinn said.

'Just that,' Julien said, motioning toward the photo. 'I was about to leave when you shoved the door into my back. Really, Quinn. While I was taking a piss?'

'Can you think of a better time?'

Julien let out a deep, hearty laugh. 'Of course not. It was perfect. But how did you know I was inside?'

'You need to brush up on your lock-picking skills.'

'The scratch,' Julien said, nodding. 'I thought I

heard someone coming out of one of the other apartments and my pick slipped. It was sloppy.'

'Almost got you killed,' Quinn said.

Julien smiled broadly. 'How would you have gotten my body out?'

'I'd have found a way.'

'I believe that,' Julien said, laughing. 'Nate, did Quinn ever tell you about the removal I helped him with in Madrid?'

'I can't say that he has,' Nate said.

'Julien,' Quinn said, a warning in his voice.

'What? Who is going to care?' He turned to Nate. 'This is one I can tell. It was, what, eight years ago? The man who hired us is dead now. And besides, that conflict is over.'

'Hey, it's okay by me,' Nate said.

'This body, it got shoved in a basement storage cabinet at this restaurant near the Reina Sofia. Our job was to get it out. Only by the time we arrived, the staff was already there, getting ready for the day.'

'Enough,' Quinn said.

'Quinn knows we have very little time before someone discovers the body, so he says to me, 'How is your Spanish?' I tell him that my Spanish is fine. He then says, 'Good. You distract them while I carry the body out.' Distract them? How am I going to distract them? 'You'll think of something,' he says.

'So I give him five minutes. He sneaks in through the back. How? I don't know. Don't ask me. When the time is up, I pound on the front door. A waiter opens it, and tells me they're closed. Of course they are closed. 'Why else

165

would I be knocking,' I say to him. I tell him I left my phone there the night before, and I needed it right away for a business call. So he lets me in and goes to check.

'When he comes back, of course, he has no phone. I am ready for this, and I start to talk very loud. I accuse the man of stealing my phone, then say if it was not him, it must have been one of his coworkers. He assures me that no one would have done that, but I only get louder, then demand to talk to everyone who is there.'

'And that worked?' Nate asked.

'Of course it worked. Look at me. You think they'd want to make me mad?' Julien held his arms out and smiled. 'So when I have them all in the dining room, I begin yelling at everyone. Quinn hears this and knows it is time. He begins carrying the body up the stairs. Of course, this is the time my phone decides to ring in my pocket. Old girlfriend. We didn't last much longer after that. Now everyone is accusing me of lying. We all yell at one another.

'Quinn hears all this and realizes the cover is falling apart. He races the rest of the way up the stairs. As for me, I am desperately trying to keep everyone in the room. But the cook has had enough and heads back for the kitchen. I yell after him, trying to stop him, but no. So I run as fast as I can and reach the door just before he does. 'So you're the one who took my phone,' I say. He calls me a fool and a liar. 'Your phone is in your pocket. We all heard it,' he says. 'Now get out of my way!' Then he tries to push past me. But I am not so easy to push, I think. His friends, they come over and everyone is tugging and pushing. Finally someone comes in the front door and shouts, 'Hey, what's going on?'' Julien laughs. 'It's Quinn, of course. He looks at me and says, 'Come on. We've got to go.' Like he's my friend and has been looking for me. Well, I guess that was true, huh?' Julien clapped Quinn on the back. 'Thank God it was a clean kill. Broken neck, no blood. Otherwise it would have been messy, no?'

Quinn started to shake his head in resignation when he noticed a woman cross the street and approach the entrance to the apartment building.

'There she is,' he said.

Both Nate and Julien turned to look.

'Come on. Do either of you have any training at all?' Quinn asked.

But Liz hadn't noticed the attention. Her eyes were on her purse as she dug around inside. Draped over her other shoulder was a computer bag.

Once she disappeared inside, Julien let out an appreciative breath. 'How does someone like you get a good-looking sister like that?'

'I never said she was my sister,' Quinn said.

'True.'

'Look,' Quinn said. 'Seems to me you have a decision to make.'

Julien looked confused. 'What do you mean?'

'Your client is expecting you to report back.'

'Ah,' Julien said. 'Don't worry. I'll tell them I found nothing. Basically that's true.'

'They're going to ask you if you were at least able to confirm that she lives here, and were able to get a photo.'

'What would you like me to say?'

'You'd lie?'

'For you, yes. I don't spy on my . . . friend's *friend's* families. That's not right.'

Quinn couldn't help but smile. Thirty minutes ago he was punching the man in the face, and now Julien was offering to lie for him. 'You're a good man.'

'I am only good to people who are good to me.'

Quinn was silent for a moment. 'All right. Tell them that as far as you can tell, it's her apartment, but it appears like she might be out of town.'

'And the photo?'

'Tell them there wasn't any.'

'*D'accord,*' Julien said.

'They're going to ask you to keep an eye on the building,' Quinn said.

'And I'll tell them I'm not available.'

'No,' Quinn said. 'Tell them you'll do it.'

Julien raised an eyebrow. 'Why?'

'Think of it as free money.'

'I like the sound of free money.'

'Then you'll like the sound of double pay even more,' Quinn said.

Julien smiled. 'What do you have in mind?'

'While they will think you're working for them, in reality, you'll be working for me.'

★　★　★

They left Julien at the café and checked in to a small hotel near the Seine River. They took only one room. If things didn't go well at Liz's, they

168

could get a second one later.

They each took a shower, and changed their clothes before returning to the café. Julien was sitting at the same table. He had a newspaper now, and there was a plate with the remains of a sandwich in front of him.

'I could go for something to eat,' Nate said.

'Later,' Quinn told him. To Julien, he said, 'Status?'

'Unless she snuck out the back, she's still inside,' the Frenchman told him.

Quinn shook his head. 'No reason for her to do that. And no reason for us to waste any more time. Julien, check in with your client. Nate, you're with me.'

'That will take me only a few minutes,' Julien said. 'What after that?'

Quinn gave him the once-over. 'Get a haircut and a shave.'

Julien grinned. 'Now you ask the impossible.'

'Then maybe you can get us some hardware,' Quinn said. 'You know what I like. Nate'll take yours. So you'll need to replace that.'

'Why don't I bring you both nice new pieces? Nate will be happier.'

'My plan is better.'

Julien frowned. 'You want me to just pass it across the table?'

Nate picked up his backpack and handed it to him. Julien gave Nate a smirk, then unzipped the top. Once the gun was safely inside, he returned it to Nate.

'Yours I should have in an hour,' he said to Quinn.

169

'Good. You can take two. Is Shywawa still in business?'

'Of course.'

'Then that's where we'll meet.'

Julien pushed himself up from the table and thumped Nate on the back.

'Make sure you don't shoot Quinn's relative.' With a laugh, he took off down the street.

As Nate started to rise, Quinn reached out and touched his arm, stopping him.

'I can't have you screwing this up,' Quinn said.

'I'm not going to screw this up.'

Quinn closed his eyes for a second to focus his thoughts. 'I didn't mean that like it sounded.'

'Look. I get it. This isn't about a job. This is your family. This is about as personal as it can get. But I'm part of your team, Quinn. So that means it's just as personal for me.'

'Thanks.'

'Shall we do this?'

Quinn tried to think if there was anything else he needed to tell his apprentice beyond what he'd already filled him in on while they were at the hotel. 'Liz's anger toward me is deserved,' Quinn said. 'Don't judge her by that.'

'Judge her? Hell, if anything, I'm going to be sympathetic.'

'Let's go over your legend again,' Quinn said, ignoring Nate's attempt at humor.

With a sigh, Nate said, 'I'm a son of a colleague. Traveling around Europe for a few months before starting grad school in January.'

'What school?'

'UCLA.'

170

'In?'

'History. Just like my undergrad degree.'

'Go on.'

'Since you were in Paris on business, your colleague asked you to check on me. I arrived in town today, so I decided to hang with you for a few hours, secretly hoping for a free meal. Since we were close to your sister's apartment, you thought we should stop by. How's that?'

'How much do you know about me?'

'Very little. You've done business with my father. He works at Bank of America. I don't know which bank you work for, and I don't even know what you do. I hate the banking business, so don't pay much attention.'

Quinn nodded.

'Anything else you want to know?' Nate asked.

'What's your name?'

'Nate.'

Quinn's eyes opened wide.

'Relax,' Nate said, holding his hands up. 'My name's Andrew Cain. My father's Andrew also, so that would make me Junior, but I never use the Junior. My friends sometimes call me Andy. My really close friends call me A.'

Quinn raised an eyebrow. 'A?'

'Makes me sound cool.'

'Makes you sound stupid.'

'Matter of opinion.'

Quinn stood up. 'All right. Then let's go, A.'

'I said my close friends.'

171

21

Four minutes later Nate and Quinn stood at the door to Liz's apartment. From inside they could hear music.

Jazz? Quinn wondered.

He listened a moment longer.

Miles Davis. 'How Deep Is the Ocean.' One of Quinn's favorites.

'You all right?' Nate whispered.

As way of answer, Quinn raised his hand to knock on the door. But he hesitated, wondering again if this might be a mistake. Maybe a perimeter stakeout would be best. Liz could go on as she always did, completely unaware of his presence.

Or maybe I'm just making excuses.

He let his hand rap against the door three times, then took a step back.

There was no indication from inside that someone had heard him.

Quinn knocked again.

'Une minute, s'il vous plaît.' Liz's voice, distant.

'You ready?' Quinn whispered.

'I am. Are you?' Nate asked.

From beyond the door, he could hear the soft thud of feet on carpet, then the knob turned, and with little fanfare the door opened. Liz stood just inside, wearing the same clothes he'd seen her arrive home in. The friendly smile she initially greeted them with faltered.

'Jake?' she said, confused.

'Hi, Liz.'

She stared at him as if she wasn't sure he was there.

'Can we come in?'

For the first time she seemed to realize Quinn wasn't alone. She looked at Nate, then back at Quinn. Finally, she stepped aside so they could enter.

'What are you doing here?' she asked.

'I'm in town on business,' Quinn said. 'Thought I'd come by for a visit.'

Several silent seconds passed, then she said, 'Okay, you've visited. You can tell Mom you stopped by, saw my place, saw that I wasn't living in a shack. You can even tell her we had a nice talk if you want.'

She reached for the door.

'Liz, please,' Quinn said.

She stopped.

'Can't we just talk for a bit?' He smiled. 'That way I don't have to lie to Mom.'

Her shoulders rose as she took a deep breath, then she straightened up and ran a hand through her hair. She led them into the living room and nodded at the couch.

'Please sit,' she said. 'I've got some lemonade and some water.'

A good hostess even in adversity. That she had learned from their mother.

'Thank you,' Quinn said. 'Water would be nice.'

'It's sparkling,' she told him.

'That's fine.'

'What about your friend?' she asked.

'I'm sorry,' Quinn said. 'I should have introduced you. This is Andrew Cain. He's the son of someone I do work with. Andrew, this is my sister Liz.'

Nate stuck out a hand. 'It's nice to meet you.'

Liz barely touched his palm before she let go again. 'Water or lemonade?'

'Water too. Please,' he said.

Without another word, she headed into the kitchen. Quinn motioned for Nate to sit down. Liz came back and stopped short. Nate was sitting on the couch, and Quinn was on the chair.

After Liz handed out the waters, she moved to the window. She had opted for no drink and standing.

'Liz, sit down,' Quinn said. 'Join us.'

Again there was the deep breath. 'I'm fine here.'

'Liz.'

When she turned to her brother, the look on her face was not quite hatred, but close. She stood where she was for a second, then walked over and sat down on the couch as far from Nate as possible. She stared at the coffee table, while Quinn licked his lips and rubbed the fingers of one hand against the palm of another, neither saying anything.

Nate looked back and forth between them, then finally said, 'This is a great place. You been here long?'

Liz looked at him. 'Almost two years.'

174

'Swanky.'

'It's paid for by a scholarship,' she said, defensive.

'Nice.' Nate looked around. 'What are you studying?'

'I'm sorry. Who exactly are you?'

Quinn jumped in. 'I told you, he's the son of a colleague.'

'And why is he with you?'

'Hey,' Nate said. 'I didn't mean to upset you. This really is a nice place. And the way you've set it up, it's, you know, comfortable. I'm sorry. People tell me I sometimes come off a little abrasive.' He gave her a lopsided grin. 'Sometimes they're right.'

Liz seemed to relax. 'It's fine. And . . . thanks. People tell me I sometimes get a little defensive.'

Nate laughed. 'We're the perfect combination, then.'

That brought the hint of a smile to her lips. 'How long are you in town?' she asked her brother.

'A few days,' Quinn said.

'And then home?'

'Unless something else comes up.'

She nodded without feeling, but said nothing more.

'School,' Quinn said. 'How's it going?'

'Fine.'

'How much longer until you graduate?'

'Two more years.'

'Have you been able to — '

His cell phone buzzed in his pocket.

'I'm sorry,' he said as he pulled it out.

'Everything all right?' Nate asked. His tone was light.

'Yes. Sorry,' Quinn said. He accessed the log on his phone. 'Just a second.'

He could hear Liz let out a faint sigh, and imagined her rolling her eyes as he scrolled through his recent calls list.

There had been three additional calls to the one he'd just received. All had come from Wills. Checking the times, he was able to figure out the first had come during the initial encounter with Julien, while the other two sometime between then and when he'd returned to Liz's apartment. Missing one, okay. But more than that?

He knew the reason, of course. He'd been so focused on seeing his sister everything else had become background noise. *I'm losing focus.* Not good. Not good at all.

Just as he was about to slip the phone back into his pocket, it began to vibrate again, the same name on the display as before.

'I need to take this.'

'Sure,' Liz said, as if she'd expected as much.

He flipped the phone open, and said to Wills, 'Hold on.' He looked at his sister. 'Is there someplace private? It's a business call.'

'There's a bathroom at the end of the hall,' she said.

There's a bedroom down there, too, he thought. But she hadn't offered that up. It would have been too personal.

'Thanks,' he said, standing. 'I'll just be a few minutes.'

★ ★ ★

'You were supposed to be here this morning. Where the hell are you?' Wills asked.

'I had a personal matter to take care of,' Quinn said.

'You've already used up your personal matter allocation. I'm paying you to be here. Have you even left the States yet?'

'David, I know this is important. And I know you want it done right away. But this couldn't be helped. The body isn't going anywhere. A day or two delay shouldn't matter.'

'What are you talking about, delay? My client wants this done immediately. He's expecting me to tell him the removal is already in process.'

'Then tell him that. I'd need at least a day to scout the location before I could do the removal anyway,' Quinn said. 'One of my team members will be there by tomorrow morning to start the process. Okay?'

Whom that would be Quinn had no idea. Maybe he could get Orlando to reroute to London instead of coming to Paris. Or maybe he could hire someone local he'd worked with before. Whatever the case, he knew he could make it happen.

Wills was silent for a moment. Quinn could almost feel his client's anger emanating through the phone.

'This is not what I expected out of you,' Wills

177

said. 'I'm paying you a *lot* of money, and right now you're making me think I made a mistake.'

'You want your money back? Fine. I'll transfer a third back and we'll call it even. You can hire someone else.'

'A *refund*? I don't want a refund. I want you to get my goddamn job done!'

Quinn said nothing for a moment. 'I always get the job done. Always.'

'I need your assurance you will take care of this,' Wills said, his voice calmer.

'Isn't that what I just said?'

Wills remained silent.

'Okay, David. I *assure* you that this will be taken care of as quickly as possible. Tell your client your team is on it.'

'All right,' Wills said. 'But you had better not let me down.'

'I won't.'

For a second, Quinn thought Wills had hung up. Then the Englishman said, 'Sorry. I know you won't.' He paused. 'There's one bit of good news. Moody's body was found. Looks like he was killed when they were trying to drive away from the house.'

'What about the Russians?'

'No sign of them,' he said. 'Quinn, get here as soon as you can.'

'I will.'

Quinn hung up, then looked in the mirror and ran his hands across his face.

Professionally, he was in the wrong, and he knew it. He *should* have been in London by now, already having done at least one scout of the

178

building where the body was located.

He should have, but instead he was in Paris, two hundred miles away.

A job had been offered, and Quinn had agreed to do it. In his world, commitment, reliability, and trust were the true currencies. Without them, you quickly fell out of favor, and soon found yourself doing little check-and-reports like Julien just to stay afloat, or futilely scratching from the outside to get back in, or lying in an unmarked grave with a bullet in your skull because your unreliability came at a cost too high for your employer to ignore.

He eased the bathroom door open and stepped across the threshold, but then stopped. From down the hall, he could hear Liz and Nate. They were talking. Pleasantly.

In fact, they seemed almost friendly.

★ ★ ★

The minute Quinn stepped out of the living room, Nate said, 'About earlier, I apologize.'

Liz shook her head. 'It's okay. Don't worry about it.' She was more relaxed now that her brother was gone.

'So what are you studying? I mean, if you don't mind talking about it.' He was playing the disarming, interested male. A role he slid into naturally.

'It's fine to ask,' Liz said. 'I'm working on a doctorate from the Archaeology and Art History Department. Specifically, I'm interested in the influence of Flemish painters on French society

179

in the Renaissance period.' She gave him a sideways look. 'Did your brain just freeze? It happens to all my friends when I tell them that.'

'It might have. Painters like Jean Clouet, right?'

She stared at him, her surprise evident.

'I have a B.A. in history,' he said, smiling, 'and am working on a master's in European history at UCLA. Well, will be working on it when I go back to school in January.'

'You're kidding.'

'Okay, so maybe I won't be going back until next fall. But don't say anything to your brother. If he tells my dad, I'm screwed.'

From her throat came a sound that was half grunt, half laugh. 'You don't need to worry about that.'

Nate hesitated. 'Yeah, I got the impression you guys don't get along too well.' He paused. 'Sorry. I probably shouldn't have said that.'

'It's okay. It's not like we were hiding it. What are you doing with him, anyway?'

'My dad again. He found out your brother was in Paris, and he knew I was headed here. So he asked him to check on me. I'm only hanging out with him because he might buy me lunch, and if I play my cards right he might spring for dinner, too.' A sheepish smile. 'You know how it is. Student salary and all.'

'Totally get it,' she said. 'So you're traveling around?'

'Yeah. Doing the Europe thing. But wanted to come when it was quieter.'

'Where have you been so far?'

'Copenhagen, Berlin, Amsterdam, Brussels. And now here. Thought I'd hang around a week or so, then maybe head south for Spain.'

'I love Spain.'

'That's what everyone says,' Nate said. From down the hall, he thought he heard the bathroom door open. 'I'm thinking I want to hit Barcelona and Madrid for sure. Then maybe pop over to Portugal. I hear the coast is beautiful.'

'I still need to get there.' Liz's enthusiasm was genuine. She seemed caught up in the idea of his trip. 'When you're in Spain, you've got to check out the Al-hambra. You're planning on that, right?'

'Definitely. I'm visiting as many historic sites as possible.' He leaned toward her and said in a faux whisper, 'It's how I talked my dad into funding the trip. 'Seeing the actual locations will help me with my studies.''

She laughed. 'And he bought that?'

'I don't know if he did or not, but he pretended to. Funny thing is, it's kind of turned out to be true.'

'When did you get to Paris?' she asked.

'Just this morning. Your brother was waiting for me at Paris Nord. I was going to stay in Brussels a few more days, but my father wanted me to come here to meet Jake. He's paying the bills, so I said okay.'

'You're going to love Paris,' she said. 'History everywhere. You could spend months here and not see it all.'

'I can't afford to spend months,' Nate said. 'I think I can barely afford to spend a week. Kind of why I'm heading to Spain. I hear it's cheaper.'

'If you play it right, you can stretch your euro here. Are you staying in a hostel?'

'Don't know where I'm staying yet. Haven't had time to look.' Nate decided it was time to take a chance. 'Any recommendations?'

She looked like she was about to say something, but then stopped. She shook her head. 'I've always had a place here.'

He glanced around the apartment. 'Hey, no worries. I'm sure I'll find something.'

Again, she seemed to hesitate. 'Look,' she said. 'If you can't find anything you like, you can . . . uh . . . stay here.'

'Liz, you don't have to offer that.' It was Quinn. He'd entered the living room without either of them hearing him come in. In an instant, Liz's face tensed again.

'He's right,' Nate said. 'I really appreciate it, but I wouldn't want to impose.'

'Besides, you don't even know him,' Quinn said.

'I don't know a lot of people in my apartment right now, Jake.' That shut everyone up.

Nate stood. 'I think maybe I should leave. Find someplace to stay.'

'You've got a place to stay,' Liz said. 'That is if you don't mind sleeping on the couch.'

Nate glanced back and forth between her and Quinn, like he was caught in the middle of a situation he didn't know how to read.

'Are you sure?' he asked.

'Yes.'

'*I'm* not sure,' Quinn said. 'I think it's a bad idea.'

182

'Are you saying you don't trust him?' Liz asked.

'No, it's not that. I just don't think you should let someone you don't know stay with you.'

'I think I can make my own decisions,' she said. She looked at Nate. 'And I would be more than happy to have you stay here. Let me get you the spare key.'

She walked out of the room. As soon as she was gone, Nate caught Quinn's eye.

'Don't screw it up,' Quinn mouthed.

22

Julien was sitting at a table across from the bar inside Shywawa when Quinn arrived. There was an almost-empty glass of beer in front of the Frenchman, so Quinn ordered two more before taking a seat.

'*Merci,*' Julien said as Quinn handed him one of the glasses. Julien finished off the dregs of his first beer, then took a healthy swig of the new one. When he was finished, he asked, 'So where is your partner?'

'Getting settled in his temporary home.'

'You convinced her?'

Quinn lifted his glass and looked over the rim at his friend. 'I didn't. Nate did.'

'He is good, this partner of yours.'

Quinn smiled. 'He's not bad.' He took a drink. 'Did you talk to your client?'

Julien nodded, serious now. 'I told them she wasn't home. And, like you predicted, they want me to keep an eye out in case she comes back.'

'You took the job, of course.'

'Of course. Only they wanted something else, too.'

'What?' Quinn asked.

'They wanted me to keep an eye out for you.'

Quinn leaned back. 'What, exactly, did they say?'

'They said there's an operative named Jonathan Quinn who might show up. I was to let

184

them know if you did. When they asked if I knew you, I told them I had heard your name before, but had never met you. They emailed me a picture.'

Julien stuck his hand into his pocket and pulled out a cell phone. He pressed a few buttons, waited a moment, then turned the screen so Quinn could see.

The fact that it was a picture of Quinn wasn't the disturbing part. He'd expected that. What unnerved him was where and when the picture had been taken. It was from the lobby of the Grand Hyatt in New York the previous day. And from the angle, Quinn knew it could have only been shot by one person — Annabel Taplin.

'Son of a bitch,' Quinn said under his breath. 'I have to go to London. Tonight.'

'Why London?'

'This picture. It was taken by someone we identified as MI6. If they're the ones who hired you, then they have my answers. If I can neutralize the cause, then the problem will go away.'

'What do you need me to do?' Julien asked.

'Exactly what we talked about. You keep the perimeter watch on my sister. Nate will handle the inside. I'll text him to let him know I have to leave. But I'm counting on the two of you to keep her safe.'

'D'accord,' Julien said. 'What should I tell my client in the morning?'

'Tell them I'm not in Paris. That way you won't be lying.'

Julien grinned under his mountain man beard.

'And when they ask about your sister?'

'Tell them she didn't come home all night. Suggest that perhaps she has a boyfriend, and you'd be happy to track him down if they want. If they say yes, raise your rate.'

A deep laugh. 'You're good at this, my friend. Don't worry. I'll sell them the story.'

'Thank you. You don't know how much I appreciate this.'

Julien raised his glass in the air. 'To old friends, yes?'

Quinn raised his own. 'Yes.'

'And to screwing over those who try to do the same to us.'

Quinn smiled. 'I'll drink to that, too.'

★　★　★

Anton Nova was a surprisingly small man given his reputation. Petra had expected someone closer to six foot three than five-four. And fat, not thin.

His real name was Kirill Nikitov. Once part of the Moscow underworld, he'd been forced to leave the Russian capital seven years earlier due to a problem with someone higher in the organization. Since his exile to England, Nova had developed into the person you went to if you needed something from the evergrowing Russian community. His knowledge of the city, and of both the Russian emigrant population and the native English, was unparalleled. He was the kind of person most people made a point of avoiding unless absolutely necessary.

186

It had been Dombrovski who had told her that if she found herself in London, Nova could be trusted. There were other contacts in other places, too. They, like Nova, all had the same thing in common. They had all had their lives touched by the Ghost.

When she and Mikhail arrived at the pub in Piccadilly, they were directed to a large, silent man standing near a door at the back of the room. He ran a metal detecting wand over them, then performed a quick physical search. Satisfied, he opened the door and motioned for them to go through.

Inside they found Nova sitting at an otherwise empty round table. The only other person in the room was an unsmiling man standing along the wall by the door.

'Please. Sit,' Nova said, pointing at the two empty chairs at the table.

They did so.

'I had heard we had a couple of interesting visitors in town,' Nova said. 'What is it I can do for you?'

'We're looking for two people,' Petra said. 'Englishmen. We were hoping you could help us find them.'

'Have you tried the phone book?'

'These two are special,' she said. 'They wouldn't be in any phone book.'

Nova put a spoon into the bowl of soup that sat in front of him, then looked at Petra. 'I can guarantee you one thing. If you don't tell me their names, I can't help you.'

'One is named Leon Currie.'

Nova slurped the soup, then asked, 'And the other?'

'David Wills.'

Nova dropped the spoon onto the table, dabbed at the corners of his mouth with a linen napkin, then rested his arms on the edge of the table. 'I don't know if 'special' is the right word. 'Unusual,' perhaps.'

'Then, you know them?' she asked.

'Why would you be looking for these two men?'

'We have things we need to discuss with them.'

'What things?'

'Private things.'

Nova leaned back. 'If you want my help, then nothing is private from me.'

Mikhail touched Petra's arm. 'Tell him,' he whispered.

'Yes, please. Tell me,' Nova said.

Petra hesitated. Dombrovski *had* said Nova could be trusted. 'We need to talk to them because we think they can lead us to someone else,' she said.

Nova let out a little laugh and shook his head. 'Rurik, show our new friends out.'

The guard stepped out from the wall.

'The Ghost,' Petra said quickly. 'We're looking for the Ghost.'

Nova stared at her, his relaxed, superior attitude gone. 'The Ghost?'

'Yes.'

'Who sent you to me? Dombrovski?'

Petra nodded. 'We worked for him.'

'But no longer?'

She paused, then said, 'He's dead.'

'When?' Nova asked, surprised.

'Three weeks ago.'

'How did it happen?'

'The Ghost tracked him down,' she said, seeing no need to explain further.

Nova seemed lost in thought, then he shook his head incredulously. 'He tried to convince me when I was still in Moscow to help him, did he tell you that?'

Yes, she thought, but she remained silent.

'I told him what he was trying to do was impossible. No one would find the Ghost. No one knew who he was, or what he looked like. I told him for all we knew the Ghost was probably dead. That those he silenced were the only ones who could do anything now.' He locked eyes with Petra. 'Are you telling me I was wrong?'

She stared right back at him. 'How am I supposed to answer that?'

'Tell me the truth.'

'We don't know the truth yet,' she said. 'But we are close.'

'You know who the Ghost is?'

'We know his Russian name. Nikolai Palavin.'

'His *Russian* name? What do you mean?'

'We believe he fled Russia not long before Gorbachev gave up power.'

'So you think this Palavin is in London?' Nova asked. 'I have never heard of him.'

'We don't know where he is, but we think a person who does is here.'

'The men you asked about.'

'Yes,' Petra said.

Nova shook his head. 'If they do, why would they tell you?'

Petra thought of Dombrovski, and of Kolya, and of Luka, and of all those lost. 'Because we will make them.' She paused. 'Will you help us?'

Nova was silent for several seconds, then he smiled. 'I can tell you where they are, but you'll have to figure out how to get them to talk.'

'That's all we want.'

'There is a matter of payment,' Nova said.

'We were hoping you'd do this as a favor.'

The small man grunted a laugh. 'I don't even do favors for my family.'

'We don't have very much,' Petra said.

'I don't want your money.'

Petra was confused. 'Then, what?'

He leaned forward, the look on his face deadly serious. 'If you catch the Ghost, I want you to come back here, and I want you to tell me.'

'That's all?'

'That's enough.'

★   ★   ★

Nova had provided addresses and descriptions for both Currie and Wills. Mikhail went off to check out Wills, while Petra concentrated on Currie.

She had located the flat in Chelsea where Currie was supposed to be working, but after several hours she had not caught a glimpse of the man. It didn't help that dark clouds had moved over the city and let loose a steady, cold rain.

Mikhail wasn't having any better luck with Wills.

190

'There are lights on inside,' he said, 'but no one has come out. How long do we wait?'

'As long as we need to.'

But by ten-thirty that evening there had still been no sign of either man, and, reluctantly, Petra decided they should return to the apartment.

'Tomorrow we'll switch targets,' she said as she lay down on her mattress. 'That way we will both be familiar with the neighborhoods they live in.'

For a moment there was no response. Petra thought that Mikhail must already be asleep, but then he said in a low voice, 'Perhaps it will change our luck.'

She nodded in the dark. *Perhaps.*

23

The Eurostar left Paris Nord at 8:13 p.m. on its three-hour trip to London. As it emerged from the Chunnel — the tunnel under the English Channel — Quinn's phone vibrated. He had two text messages. Both coming while he'd been under the sea. The first was from Nate:

In for the night. All clear here.

Good, Quinn thought. One less thing for him to worry about at the moment.

The second was Orlando:

Have rerouted. Will arrive London in a.m.
Ck email 4 details.
This mean you've reconsidered the job 4 Wills?

Quinn had left her a message after Julien had shown him the photo, but he hadn't told her yet that he would be there, too. Hopefully, she'd see that as a pleasant surprise.

That she hadn't mentioned Quinn's mother meant she'd been able to get everything set up. Add that one to the worry-less list, too.

Outside, the half-moon was still low on the horizon, but it provided enough light for Quinn to make out the countryside. There was a quiet to the land, a sense that tomorrow would be very much like today, and yesterday, and the day before that.

While he couldn't pretend that even the simplest of lives had no complications, just for a second he longed for the sameness the people he was passing seemed to have, for the strength of continuity.

Of course he *had* had it once. When he was young. Only then he had chafed under the weight of small-town life. Back then he had longed for the anonymity that could only come when surrounded by millions of others. And truth be told, he knew that if he was to return to that quiet life now, he would once again go crazy. Maybe not at first, but in time.

'Where do you want to go most?' a seven-year-old Liz had asked her fifteen-year-old brother.

'Everywhere,' Jake replied.

'You have to pick just one. You made me pick one.'

He thought for a moment, then said, 'Pangaea.'

It was a name he'd read in a geography book. The name of the continent formed when all the continents were still together.

'Pangaea?' Her face crinkled in thought. 'Where's that?'

'I'll let you figure it out.'

'When you go there,' she said, suddenly serious, 'you'll always come home, right?'

Home to Liz meant Warroad, and the farm, and the way of life that was already crushing him. But home to Jake was going to be somewhere else entirely. Chicago, perhaps, or Miami.

Or even New York or Los Angeles. Places that had possibilities. Places that could act as hubs from which to explore the rest of the world.

'Yes,' he said to her. Not lying, not really.

Beyond the window of the train, the farmland was slowly being replaced by city. Soon he'd arrive in London.

He closed his eyes for a moment. So many lies he'd ended up telling. And what had they got him? His sister in peril. His mother hosting a man who was trained to kill in her guest room. Everything he'd worked to hide, exposed.

He blinked, then looked out the window again.

He'd made a promise long ago to always protect his family from harm. And no matter what it took, that was one promise he could never allow himself to break.

*   *   *

Like many places in London, Belgrave Road had once been a residential street that had, at some point in the past, been converted for business use. In this case, what had previously been five-story homes sitting side by side had been turned into a dozen or more small hotels.

Quinn chose one of the larger establishments, a place called the Silvain Hotel. He liked the fact that it was located on a corner, and since it was four homes wide, there would be plenty of exits if he found himself in need of a quick escape.

'May I help you?' The man at the front desk was of Indian descent, but his accent was pure British. His colleague, a blonde woman with fair

194

skin and an almost model-like angularity to her face, came off as either Nordic or Eastern European. She glanced up from her terminal, gave Quinn a quick smile, then returned to her work.

'I'm wondering if you have any rooms available?' Quinn asked.

'How long would you like to stay with us?'

'At least a week.'

The clerk smiled. Long-term guests were always good for business. 'Let me check.'

While he did, Quinn scanned the lobby. There was a comfortable seating area, and beyond it a small bar with a lounge that disappeared around the corner.

'We have two rooms to choose from,' the desk clerk said to Quinn.

'Excellent.'

'May I please have your name, sir?'

'Of course. James Shelby.'

'And you'll be with us for a week?'

'We'll start with that.'

★   ★   ★

His room was two floors up. It had a double bed that took up over half the available floor space, and a small but serviceable bathroom. Along the back wall a single window looked across a narrow alley hemmed in on the other side by a brick apartment building. Quinn raised the window, then stuck his head out into the cold night air and looked down.

Not as bad as he thought. A three-floor drop

might have been doable in a pinch, but there would have been too much chance of injury. Fortunately, the ground floor stuck out into the alley two stories below, making the drop more manageable.

He looked at his watch. It was late, almost eleven. He could pack it in for the night, but he still needed to figure out what he should do next. He needed to find out why MI6 would send someone to check out his sister's apartment. But how to do that?

The more he thought about it, the more his mind kept coming back to the same solution. David Wills. Wills had mentioned his connection with the British intelligence agency. He could be a way in. Quinn pulled out his phone and dialed.

'Hello?' Wills's voice was groggy.

'David, it's Quinn.'

There was a pause. 'What time is it?'

'Eleven,' Quinn said. 'Thought you'd still be up.'

'Hold on.' Movement on the other end, then, 'Okay. Is something wrong?'

'No. I'm in London,' Quinn said.

'I thought none of your team would be here until tomorrow.'

'I made a few schedule adjustments.'

'So you'll get started right away?'

'Already have,' Quinn said. A happy Wills would be more willing to help Quinn with his problem.

'Fantastic. I appreciate that.'

'Any luck IDing the man in that photo I gave you?'

'None,' Wills said, far too quickly.

Quinn's internal radar perked up, but now was not the time to pursue it. 'That's too bad. Listen, I was hoping you can help with something.'

'Any equipment or vehicles you want, just let me know.'

'Thanks. I will,' he said. 'But that's not the kind of help I'm talking about.'

'What is it, then?'

Again Quinn hesitated. Over the phone might not be the best way to do this. 'I'd like to meet.'

'Now?'

'If possible.'

Wills paused. 'It's not.'

'Because you're busy sleeping?'

'Do you want my help or not?'

'Yes, of course I do.'

'Then I'm sure whatever you need can wait until tomorrow.'

Though tomorrow seemed like a year away, Quinn reined in his impatience. 'Yeah, sure,' he said. 'In the morning.'

Silence on the other end.

'David?' Quinn said.

'I'm thinking.'

For several more seconds dead air filled the line.

'Nine a.m.,' Wills said. 'There's a park just north of Embankment Station. Sit on one of the benches and I'll find you.'

The line went dead.

At least the call with David had set things in motion. What it hadn't done was ease any of Quinn's concerns. Orlando could do that, but

197

she was already in the air on the way to him, so was unreachable. Nate? Not a good idea. If Liz was around, it would be hard to explain why her guest was getting phone calls from her brother.

But he needed to talk to somebody.

'*Oui?*' Julien's deep voice resonated through Quinn's phone.

'It's Quinn. Just checking in.'

'Good trip?'

'Uneventful. How are things there?'

'Uneventful.'

'You're watching the building?'

Quinn could hear Julien moving around on the other end. 'For another thirty minutes. Then I have a friend who will take over for me.'

'A friend? Someone you trust?'

'Of course it is someone I trust. Don't worry. He is just looking for people who don't belong. I have told him nothing else.'

Quinn didn't like it, but Julien couldn't keep watch twenty-four hours a day. 'Okay.'

'I get a little sleep and come back before our friends upstairs even wake up.'

'Any contact from your client?'

'No. I'll call them in the morning with an update. It's fun making up stories, you know. Easy money.'

'Just be careful,' Quinn said.

'If I was careful, I would have become a demolition expert like my brother.' Julien laughed.

'Might still be worth considering,' Quinn said. 'I'll call you in the morning.'

Quinn hung up satisfied that the situation in

Paris was under control, but no closer to falling sleep. He pulled his jacket on and headed back outside. He'd been hired for a job, so he might as well earn some of the money Wills was paying him.

★ ★ ★

According to the information Wills had given Quinn in New York, the body was located in the Alexander Grant Building in the financial district, not too far from the Lloyd's of London and the Swiss Re buildings, both modern landmarks of the city.

'This is good,' Quinn told the cabbie, a block from Lloyd's. As soon as they pulled to the curb, he paid the driver and got out.

This was the land of the briefcase and business suit, uniforms of daytime animals who, at near midnight, would be miles away, either tucked in bed or sitting at an after-hours bar. Any that did remain were the workaholics trying to impress a boss or the fearful trying not to lose their jobs. In both cases, they would be chained to their cubicles and offices.

Quinn found the Alexander Grant Building several streets away. He kept to the other side of the road and slowed his pace.

The information had claimed the Grant Building was due to be demolished. But one look at the place had Quinn wondering why it hadn't happened sooner. It was sitting on a corner lot, so the land was worth a considerable amount of money. But the building?

199

The best words he could come up with to describe it were 'unremarkable,' 'rundown,' and 'aging.' Eight floors of grimy stone. The kind of place a person could walk by every day for years and never notice. It was just there.

Scanning upward, he saw that most of the windows on the upper floors had been removed. *So the demolition's already under way,* he thought. *No wonder Wills's client is anxious to get the body removal started.*

But why did he need Quinn to do it? Any decent cleaner could handle the project with no problems. Didn't make a hell of a lot of sense. It was another question for Wills when they met up.

He was about to walk around the block when he saw a light flicker in the building. He stepped into a darkened doorway a few feet away and crouched down.

The main entrance to the Grant Building was at the midpoint of the ground floor. Two glass doors led into what had been a darkened lobby. Only now a flashlight beam was lighting up one of the walls. A moment later an overhead light came on, revealing a security guard at the far back of the room.

He walked up to the front door, unlocked it, then stepped through. Super cop he was not. Five foot eight, about twenty-five pounds overweight, and bored. He strolled along the front of the building to the three-foot gap between the Grant Building and its neighbor, then turned and walked back past the entrance and around the corner, disappearing from sight.

Quinn held his position, counting off the time in his head. It was just over four minutes before the guard reappeared. When he did, he was speaking into a walkie-talkie. Quinn couldn't make out the guard's words, but a tinny, overamplified voice responded through the receiver, ' . . . second floor . . . ' Quinn glanced up at the darkened windows, but saw nothing of interest.

The guard spoke again, then clipped the radio to his belt and finished his walk to the front door. A moment later he disappeared inside, turning the lobby light off as he passed. Quinn retrieved his phone, accessed the camera, and switched to night vision. He took several pictures, then used the zoom to check the street in both directions.

London was a city that lived under the camera's eye. Thousands of closed-circuit television cameras, CCTVs, were installed throughout the metropolis, where they passively watched everyone and everything. When people like Quinn worked in London, they had to take this citywide surveillance into consideration — altering appearances, doing nothing to attract attention, and, whenever possible, keeping real business to those dead zones with no coverage.

Occasionally, some of the quieter streets fell through the city's video net. Quinn was pleased to see the street the target building was on among them.

Minor good news, but good news nonetheless.

He settled in and waited for the guard to reappear so he could gauge the schedule of rounds. When the lobby light came back on, Quinn checked his watch. An hour and seven minutes.

Say an hour to an hour and a half between rounds. He watched as the door opened again and the man stepped outside. *Interesting.*

While the pattern was the same, the guard was not. This was a younger guy, probably early thirties, and in a bit better shape. *So there are at least two of them,* he thought. For an abandoned building this size, Quinn could see it go as high as three, but no more.

For the first time that evening, he could feel sleep hanging behind his eyes. As he had hoped, getting out and doing some work had helped him to relax. Now, maybe, he could get a few hours' rest before he met up with Wills.

When the guard disappeared around the side of the building, Quinn slipped out of his hiding place and returned down the street the way he'd come. At the end of the block, he took a look back at the building.

Easy.

Too easy.

24

Nate had assumed Liz would lose interest in him the moment Quinn was gone. And for a while she did disappear into the back of the apartment. When she finally came out, he was sure she was going to suggest it might actually be better if he did stay in a hostel, but instead, she said, 'I don't know about you, but I'm hungry. You up for some lunch?'

'Oh, don't go to any trouble for me,' Nate said. He was still sitting on the couch.

'Who's going to any trouble?' she asked as she walked over to the entryway, then opened a closet door. 'We'll pick up something on the way.'

Nate stood up slowly, confused. 'On the way where?'

She pulled out a coat. 'Nickel tour of Paris, of course. Unless you have something better to do.'

'Don't you have to go to school or something?'

'Done for the day. So are you coming or not?'

'I don't want to put you out.'

'God, are you always this difficult? Relax. Someone offers to show you Paris, you say yes.'

'Okay.' He smiled. 'Yes.'

He shot Julien a text update from the bathroom before they left, then bundled up and followed Liz out into the city.

She helped him to buy a Métro pass, then they took the train to Saint-Michel. A half block away was the Seine, and just on the other side was the

Île de la Cité and the Notre Dame Cathedral.

'You've come at a good time of year,' she said. 'Hardly any tourists.'

Nate nodded, then took a step toward the cathedral.

But Liz grabbed his arm and stopped him. 'Come on. Back on the Métro.'

'We're not going to go take a look inside?' he asked.

'You're here a week, right? I'm giving you the overview so you have an idea where things are and can come back when you want.'

Nate laughed. 'Overview, it is. Lead on.'

As they walked back to the Saint-Michel Métro station, Nate caught a glimpse of Julien standing in line at a patisserie. When the big man glanced at him, Nate said to Liz, 'Which way?'

'Over there.' She pointed at the Métro entrance. 'Same one we used before.'

'Right. Sorry, wasn't paying attention when we came out.'

He glanced quickly in Julien's direction. The Frenchman had gotten the message and was headed toward the subway.

It was the tour most locals would give to friends from out of town. The Louvre Museum, Montmartre and the Basilique du Sacré-Cœur, the Eiffel Tower, and finally the Arc de Triomphe and the Champs-Élysées. The only place they actually spent any time at was the Champs-Élysées. There they strolled down the famous street, looking at the shops and restaurants.

'How about a coffee or something?' Nate suggested. 'My treat.'

'You're on,' she said, smiling. She pulled him by the arm over to the nearest café.

A couple of hours earlier, the gesture might have been surprising, but now it seemed almost natural. She had been laughing easily at his jokes, teasing him whenever he attempted to pronounce the names on the street signs, and a few times glancing at him when she thought he wouldn't notice.

If nothing else, Nate decided, she was at least enjoying his company.

The café was one of those places that spilled out onto the sidewalk even in the fall. In deference to the weather, a cloth and plastic awning complete with front and side walls jutted out from the building, claiming a portion of concrete. Inside, heaters kept the customers warm.

A waiter looked over as they walked in. He was balding, with a close-cropped rim of dark hair. 'Deux?'

'Oui,' Liz said.

He pointed at a small round table. It had been set up in a row with several others. Each had two chairs, both on the same side of the table, so customers could watch people walk by.

Nate and Liz sat down, and soon the waiter returned, looking at them expectantly.

'You want some coffee, or something a little stronger?' Liz asked Nate.

'What are you having?'

'I was thinking about a glass of wine.'

'Sounds good to me.'

She ordered two glasses of Château Cos d'Estournel Saint-Estèphe Bordeaux.

205

'Anything else?' the waiter asked in English.

'*Non, c'est tout, merci,*' Liz said.

The waiter gave her a halfhearted smile, then left.

'I don't think he likes us,' Nate said.

'This part of town, they think Americans only really know English.'

'But you speak excellent French.'

She smiled. 'Thanks. I'd better. Three years in high school. Four years of undergrad. And two years here already. Oh, and I had a French boyfriend for a while, too.'

'In Paris?'

'No, back at Michigan State,' she said.

'What about now? No French boyfriend?'

She blurted out a laugh. 'Not with my schedule.'

'You can't be studying all the time,' he said.

'Wait until you start grad school. Then think what it would be like to write all your papers in two languages.'

'Seriously?'

'I think better in English, so it's easier to write that way first. Then I have to translate it, and make sure it reads correctly.'

'Sounds like a pain in the ass. I'd pay someone to do the translation for me.'

'That would mean I had extra money lying around.'

Nate realized he'd stumbled into an area he really hadn't meant to get into. Quinn had told him about the scholarship, but there was no way Andrew Cain would have that information. He decided to go with a more innocent approach. 'How much do they cost?'

She looked at him, one eyebrow raised. 'Why? You going to pay for it for me?'

He laughed. 'That would be a big no. I'm probably just as poor as you.'

'But your father sounds like he has a bit of cash.'

'He might, but I don't. He made it very clear as I was growing up that I wasn't getting any kind of free ride.'

'Good for him.'

Nate felt a sense of relief as the waiter approached with their drinks.

After that the conversation turned back to the safer topic of life in Paris.

Before they realized it, it was starting to get dark. At Liz's suggestion, they headed to the Latin Quarter to get some dinner.

The area was a maze of narrow cobbled streets closed off to most traffic and reserved, instead, for pedestrians. Along each road, restaurants and clubs vied for space and customers, some using touts and others lights and aromas.

Liz chose a cozy place that was about five times longer than it was wide. There they shared a cheese fondue and a bottle of wine.

By the time they got home it was after 9 p.m. Nate excused himself to use the bathroom, where he shot off two quick texts. Both were basically the same. To Quinn he wrote:

In for the night. All clear here.

And to Julien:

Done 4 today. Bed soon.

As Nate washed his hands, his phone buzzed once in his pocket. On the screen was a reply from Julien.

What? No late-night disco?

Nate texted back:

If you're up for it, I can suggest it.

A few seconds later, Julien responded:

Do it.

Nate smiled, then tapped in one last message:

Good night, Julien.

When he returned to the living room, he half expected Liz to have already gone to bed. But she was sitting on the couch, an open bottle of wine and two glasses on the coffee table in front of her.

He joined her, sitting near but not too close. She poured wine into both of the glasses, then raised hers.

'To your first night in Paris,' she said.

'To making a new friend,' he countered. They touched glasses, then each took a drink.

By now Nate was starting to feel the effects of the wine. He wasn't drunk, but he was less in control than he should have been. He was there on a job, he reminded himself. He'd have to nurse this glass for the rest of the evening.

'So what do you think of my brother?' Liz asked.

'He seems fine,' Nate replied, as naturally as he could. 'I didn't really spend that much time with him, and I've only met him once before. You know how it is, right, meeting a friend of your parents? What do you talk about?'

Liz smiled as she leaned back. She looked comfortable, totally relaxed. She raised her glass to her lips and took another drink.

'When I was a little girl, Jake was my hero. You know, one of those people who can do no wrong. I wanted to hang around him all the time. He was older, he didn't have to, but he let me anyway.'

Another dangerous topic, but for a moment Nate's curiosity won out over his caution. 'How much older?'

'Eight years.'

'That is quite a bit.'

'Eight years and seven months, actually.'

Nate instinctively knew the next question he should ask. 'Do you have any other brothers or sisters?'

She said nothing for a moment. 'We did.'

'Oh. I'm sorry,' Nate said. 'We can change the subject.'

'No, it's all right,' she said. 'We had a brother. Davey. He was in between us. But he died in a car accident when he was five, I think. I don't remember him.'

'Oh, God. I really am sorry.'

'I was in the accident, too. The whole family

was. You want to see my scar?'

She sat up suddenly, a little unsteady from the wine, and began working her fingers through her hair.

'It's okay,' Nate said. 'I believe you.'

'See?' she said.

She had created a part across her scalp that revealed a portion of a scar that looked like it ran for several inches.

'That must have hurt,' Nate said.

'I'm sure it did. I'm told there was a lot of blood.'

'Head wounds have a way of doing that.'

'Oh, really? And you know this how?'

He shrugged. 'Grew up watching *ER* on TV.'

She snickered, then let her hair fall down as she leaned back. 'I wasn't even two yet. This is the only proof I have that the accident even happened. Well, and Davey's grave, I guess.'

Nate tried to stop himself, but he couldn't. 'So what happened between you and Jake?'

'One night he just left,' she said. 'I was nine.'

That surprised Nate. 'He ran away from home?'

'Can you really call someone who leaves home at seventeen a runaway?' she asked. 'All I know is he was gone.'

'For how long?'

'The first time I saw him after that,' she said, 'was last month at our father's funeral.'

'Whoa,' Nate said. 'That's a long time.'

'The only reason I knew he wasn't dead was because he still keeps in contact with Mom. She asked me once if he'd ever been in touch with me. I lied and told her he had. Mom's always had this kind of defeated sense to her. I guess I just didn't want to add to it.'

'Look, you don't need to — '

'I thought I'd moved past him, forgotten about him. But then the funeral, and now here.' Her eyes started to glisten. 'He never called me. He never wrote. I don't understand why.'

Tears began to slide down her cheeks, then she took a big gulp of air and could no longer keep herself from sobbing.

Without even thinking, Nate reached out and pulled her into his arms, letting her bury her face in his shoulder. He rubbed her back, and every once in a while whispered, 'It's okay' or 'Just let it out.'

Then, when her crying subsided, she lay against him, her breaths fast at first, but gradually slowing down. After a while he thought she might have fallen asleep, but then she turned in his arms, and looked at him for a moment before pushing herself back up.

'More than you bargained for this evening, huh?' she asked as she wiped the last of her tears from her eyes.

He liked that she didn't apologize. 'You never know which way life is going to come at you. I find it better to let things happen than expect anything in particular.' He gave her a smile. 'At the risk of setting you off again, I'm wondering if you ever asked him what was up.'

She shrugged. 'Once.'

'And what did he say?'

'Nothing.'

'You mean he gave you the runaround?'

'No. I mean he said nothing. It was on the phone. He'd called to talk to Mom, but I happened to be home and had answered. So I decided I'd just ask him why he left. He was silent for a long time, and then he said, 'Can I talk to Mom, please.' That was it.'

'Maybe he had a good reason.'

'Yeah, well, if he did, I don't care anymore.' She drained the rest of her wine, then picked up the bottle. 'You want some more?' She looked at his glass. It was almost full. 'I guess not, huh?'

'I'm fine.'

She started to tip the bottle over her own glass, but stopped before any liquid spilled out.

'Maybe it would be better if we just call it a night,' she said. 'I've got class in the morning, and I'm sure you must be tired.'

'I'm doing okay,' Nate said. 'But it's up to you.'

She smiled, then started to stand, the bottle of wine still in her hand. When she straightened her knees, she swayed.

Nate jumped up and put out a hand to steady her.

'Thanks,' she said. 'I think I just proved another glass would have been a bad idea.'

'Why don't you give that to me?'

He took the bottle from her, then picked up the two glasses and carried them all into the kitchen. When he returned, Liz had moved the sheet, blanket, and pillow she'd set on the floor that afternoon onto the couch, and looked like she was about to make his bed.

'I can do that,' Nate said, rushing over.

She gave him a smirk. 'I'm not completely helpless.'

She tucked the sheet around the cushions, put the pillow at one end, then spread the blanket out.

'Thanks,' he said.

'My pleasure.'

'What time's your class in the morning?'

'Not until ten, thank God.'

'Mind if I come with you? Not to class, of course. But I've always wanted to see the Sorbonne.'

'Sure.' She leaned over and gave him a hug. 'Thanks for being a good guy, Andrew.'

'Eh . . . thanks? I guess.'

She laughed into his chest, then, as she pulled away, he felt her hesitate, her cheek only an inch away from his. He could sense tension building between them, a tension he unexpectedly welcomed.

She's Quinn's sister, a voice in his head said.

He closed his eyes and tried to regain control. Just as he was about to push her away, she pulled back.

'If we leave by nine-fifteen, we can pick up something to eat on the way,' she said.

'That sounds good.'

She walked over to the hallway, then looked back. 'I'm glad you decided to stay.'

He smiled. 'I'm glad you asked.'

She disappeared into her bedroom, but he continued to stare at the spot where she'd been. When he finally looked away, he pulled out his phone. As much as he hated thinking about work at the moment, there was one last text he had to send. He pulled up Julien's number, then typed:

Leaving 9:15 a.m. L has class at 10,
have talked her into letting me come along.
Will check in when I get up.

After hitting Send, he put his phone in his bag. Hopefully, Julien would get the hint and not reply. Right now all Nate wanted to do was pretend he was Andrew Cain, on vacation in Europe, and staying for a few days with an intriguing American girl in Paris.

And for a few seconds, right before he fell asleep, he actually believed it.

25

Quinn rose early the next morning. He took a quick shower, got dressed, then sat on the edge of the bed and checked his email.

One was from his mother, sent to a dummy address that forwarded the message through a series of sites before it showed up in Quinn's inbox.

Jake,

Just wanted to let you know your friend Steven is all settled in. He pretty much stays out of the way, but has been kind enough to ride into town with me when I have to go. Claire, unfortunately, was only able to stay a few hours. But while she was here she not only helped me sort through some of my mail, she also made a wonderful spaghetti dinner. I like her a lot, Jake.

Quinn smiled. He'd have to show Orlando that one.

I know you're busy, but I do hope you come again soon. This is your home, no matter how long you've been away.

I love you,
Mom

Quinn read the letter twice. He could feel the guilt of having stayed away so long pressing in on him again. The other important email was from Orlando. He checked the time/date stamp. It had been sent just before her text from the night before.

Hi Jakey,

Your mom's all set. I'm on a flight from Chicago to New York, and then New York to London. Should be landing at Heathrow around 9 a.m. Coming in on Kuwaiti Air. Let me know what you want me to do once I get in. I've found a flat in Soho that I've sub-let for two weeks. My sense is we won't even need a week, but I didn't want to have any problems.

Got a potential hit on that photo. Russian. Former KGB. Name: Nikolai Palavin. The information I found lists him as presumed dead. Maybe it's him, maybe not. Still have no idea why his picture would have been in the folder.

I'll call you once I land.

Love,
O

It was apparent Orlando had been talking a little too much about him with his mother. Jakey was a name he hadn't been called since he'd left home, and he'd had no intention of ever being called by it again.

At the moment, though, what troubled him

216

more was the ID of the man in the photo. Russian, like the woman who'd been showing up everywhere Quinn had been working. Maybe there was no connection, but he would be a fool to ignore the possibility.

He turned off his computer and stuck it in his bag. Since he'd be staying with Orlando that evening, he would take everything with him. But he wasn't going to check out. London was a big city, and it was always good to have an alternate safe haven.

Once he was ready, he donned his backpack and headed out for his meeting with Wills.

★   ★   ★

Petra and Mikhail were up and out of the apartment by 6 a.m. Thirty-seven minutes later, Petra was in position outside the building where David Wills supposedly worked. At 7:43, a man approached the front door. Unconsciously, Petra leaned forward as if those couple of inches would make the difference over the half a block that separated them. Based on the description Nova had given her, this guy was too short and too young to be Wills.

The man didn't knock at the door. Instead he pulled out a key and let himself in.

Petra kept her gaze glued on the entrance in case the man came back out.

Twenty-five minutes later, he did. Only he wasn't alone.

And there was no mistaking his companion.

David Wills.

217

As soon as Petra realized Wills and the other man were going to take a taxi, she moved to the curb to flag down one of her own. She didn't even let it stop before she pulled open the back door and jumped in.

'I'm with them,' she said, pointing at Wills's taxi in the distance. 'We need to keep up, I don't have the directions.'

The driver gave her a quick, knowing look, then took off in pursuit.

Maybe he thought she was a wife following her husband. That was fine by Petra. Whatever got him moving.

They drove for ten minutes, fighting traffic all the way. But her driver was a good one and never fell more than three cars behind Wills.

'Looks like they're getting out,' the cabbie said. 'Is here all right?'

Petra looked through the front window. They were nearing a busy corner.

'Where are we?' she asked.

'Oxford Circus, ma'am.'

Wills's cab was at the curb, the other man leaning in, paying the driver, while Wills waited on the sidewalk.

'This is fine here,' she said.

The cabbie pulled over. Petra threw some cash into the front seat, then scrambled out of the car.

It took her a moment to spot Wills again. His cab was gone, and he and the other man were walking down the sidewalk away from her. She increased her pace and closed the gap to within thirty feet. It was then that she saw a sign for the entrance to the Oxford Circus Underground station, and had a strong hunch that's where they were headed.

Using the crowd as cover, Petra moved around and in front of Wills, then descended the stairs to the station, praying she was right.

At the bottom, she made a beeline for the automatic ticket kiosk. Since she had no idea where they might be headed, she bought a ticket that would allow her to travel to any of the different zones, then looked back just in time to see Wills pass through a ticket gate.

She followed, once again using the crowd as her shield. She quickly realized that the man with Wills was the one to worry about. At random intervals he would look around like he was making sure they were going in the right direction, but in reality was no doubt checking for tails. Looking, in essence, for her.

She fell back as far as she could, a couple of times even letting them move out of sight for a moment. And so far, it had worked.

When it became apparent they were headed to the Bakerloo southbound platform, she fell back even more. Luck was with her. There were two women about her age heading in the same direction. Petra slipped in behind them, keeping the distance that separated them close enough so that it appeared they were all traveling together.

As she entered the platform it was all she could do not to look for Wills. It wasn't until the train arrived and she was moving forward with the crowd that she allowed herself to check. Wills was still there, entering the train one car down.

At Piccadilly Circus, then again at Charing Cross, she positioned herself at the doorway so she could see if the other two had gotten off. But they had stayed on until they reached the third stop. Embankment.

Embankment Station was much smaller than Oxford Circus, and soon they were all at ground level, exiting into the cold morning air. Wills and the other man stopped just outside, next to a flower shop, leaning close in conversation. Petra passed by as near as she could, but could hear nothing.

Ahead of her was a cobblestone street that had more pedestrians on it than cars, and on the corner opposite her was a Starbucks. She walked over and entered the coffee shop. Once the door was closed behind her, she looked back.

The other man was still there, but Wills was gone. She scanned the area and couldn't find him on the street, either. Had he gone back in to take the subway somewhere else?

No, there he is. He was just disappearing to the left of the flower shop, along a sidewalk that led between some bushes and trees. The small patch of wilderness stretched along the street from the station for dozens of yards.

The other man was still at the flower stall, but most of his attention was on the station. Petra pushed the door open and crossed the street to a path that led in the direction Wills had gone down. Within seconds the man at the flower stall was no longer in view.

On the other side of the bushes and trees, the

path led into a grassy park. Wills was walking slowly down one of the sidewalks, away from her.

Petra walked into the park and took the path parallel to the one Wills was on.

Ahead, he reached the point where the two paths intersected. Petra quickly glanced around. There were several benches lining the walkway. Most were empty, but the one nearest was occupied by a bundled-up woman reading a book. Petra hurried over to the next bench and sat just before Wills turned down the path in her direction. She could hardly believe her luck. She was never going to have a better opportunity to get him alone so they could talk than this.

She angled her head so she could see him in her peripheral vision, and watched as he continued forward for another twenty feet, then stopped.

Come on. Come on.

He checked his watch, so Petra did the same. It was ten minutes to nine. When she looked up again, Wills had resumed walking. Slowly though, like he was killing time.

As he drew near, she chanced a look out of the corner of her eye. He didn't appear to have noticed her at all.

Perfect.

⋆ ⋆ ⋆

Quinn made his way through the controlled chaos that was Victoria Station to the Underground entrance at the north end. He used a prepaid Oyster card to get through the gate, then, instead of heading to the platform for the

221

eastbound District and Circle lines — either of which would have taken him to Embankment Station two stops away — he headed to the Victoria Line northbound. This way he would arrive early via an indirect route. It was his standard-operating procedure.

The morning crowds were huge. It didn't matter which direction you were going, you couldn't help getting swallowed up in the mass of men and women making their way to work.

That suited Quinn just fine. More people meant he would be harder to follow. Still, he checked several times to make sure no one was behind him giving it a try.

A second train line later, he was exiting at Charing Cross, one stop shy of Embankment Station. From there he strolled down the cobbled street that led toward the park.

By Quinn's watch, there were fifteen minutes left before his meeting with Wills. Given what had happened at the last two job sites, and at the aborted meeting location in New York, Quinn expected Wills to have watchers already in place securing the site and keeping an eye out for trouble.

Straight ahead, at the far end of the street, Quinn could see the entrance to Embankment Station. On the left side, against the outer wall and near one of the paths into the park, was an outdoor flower shop. That's where Quinn spotted the first watcher.

It was the same man who'd been sitting in the lobby of the Grand Hyatt. He was wearing a suit that helped him blend in with the rest of the morning crowd, and was browsing the flowers with a watchful eye on the station exit.

Keeping a group of three businessmen between himself and Wills's man, Quinn approached the park, then ducked in through the northern entrance unseen.

The path led through a wide strip of bushes and trees that separated the park from the street. Quinn found a spot where he was out of view, but could still see into the park through the foliage.

He looked at his watch, then settled back against the concrete half-wall that separated the sidewalk from the bushes, content to wait until nine. But not thirty seconds after he'd adjusted his position, a man walking along the sidewalk at the far end of the park caught his attention.

Quinn pulled out his phone and switched on the zoom of his camera, training it on the man. It was Wills.

Early.

He watched as Wills continued down the path, killing time. Quinn was just about to go out and meet him when he noticed a woman sitting on one of the benches. She was trying very hard not to look at Wills. Just as the Englishman passed her, she did glance up. Quinn could see her face.

She had a look that seemed almost . . . *predatory.*

26

Where was the backup? Quinn wondered. Had Wills thought the meet was safe enough to bring only the man he'd left out by the entrance?

Quinn brought up Wills's number on his phone and called his client. He could hear the line ringing, but Wills continued undisturbed down the path.

Could he not have his phone?

But then Wills paused and reached into his jacket. When his hand reappeared, it was holding his cell.

He looked at the display.

★ ★ ★

Just a few more seconds, Petra told herself.

Wills had just passed her position. A couple more feet and she could get behind him before he'd even realize it. From that position she'd be in control.

She tensed her legs, ready to push herself up.

Then abruptly Wills stopped.

Petra remained on the bench, waiting for him to start walking again. But instead he pulled a phone out of his pocket, checked the screen, then raised it to his ear.

'Quinn? Are you — '

As soon as Wills lifted the phone to his ear, Quinn could see the woman start to rise off her bench.

'Quinn? Are you — '

'Watch out,' Quinn said, cutting Wills off. 'Behind you.'

* * *

Petra sensed movement to her left.

She turned and saw the woman who had been sitting on the other bench jump up and start running toward Wills.

No! she thought.

* * *

Quinn watched as Wills ducked to the right and moved off the path through a gap between two of the benches.

The woman raced after him, in her hand a suppressor-enhanced pistol.

Wills had turned toward her and, from under his jacket, was pulling out his own weapon, bringing it to bear on the woman.

But then Quinn saw him hesitate.

The cause was a second woman right in the fire zone.

And she seemed . . . familiar.

Son of a bitch, he thought. *It's the Russian.*

He glanced back to where he'd last seen Wills, but the Englishman had slipped down behind the row of benches, out of view.

His attacker moved quickly toward the gap

Wills had passed through, then pulled the trigger on her gun.

Thup.

One of the benches exploded in a spray of wood chunks and splinters.

The attacker rushed through the gap, seeking a clear shot at her target. But as she did the Russian threw something at her. A bag.

It hit the attacker's hands just as she was pulling the trigger, ripping the gun from her grip, sending it flying. Before she could even react, the Russian rammed into her, shoulder first, carrying her through the gap and down onto the grass.

Where's Wills? Quinn thought. *And where the hell is his backup?*

The Englishman had yet to reappear from behind the bench. Now would be the perfect opportunity to make a move, but Wills didn't seem to be taking it.

Screw it.

Quinn pushed himself out from his hiding spot and sprinted into the park. As he neared the benches, he could see the attacker trying to pull herself from the Russian's grasp, her eyes searching for her gun. The Russian hit her in the face, then twice hard in the gut.

Quinn jagged to his left through the gap in the benches, then pulled to a quick stop. Now he knew why Wills hadn't made his move.

Quinn's client was lying on the grass, blood all over his neck and shirt. His gun lay several feet away.

Quinn knelt beside him. The bullet had

entered Wills's neck just left of his windpipe. By the angle of entry, Quinn was willing to bet it had also hit Wills's spinal cord. He wasn't dead, but he soon would be.

Quinn picked up the gun, then leaned down next to Wills's face. The Englishman's eyes were half closed and unfocused, but he seemed to realize someone was there.

'Just relax,' Quinn said.

'Quinn?' Wills's voice raspy.

'Everything's all right.'

Quinn heard footsteps walking toward him. Without looking up, he raised Wills's gun.

'Close enough,' he said.

The footsteps halted.

Quinn glanced over and wasn't surprised to see it was the Russian. He also wasn't surprised to see the other woman's gun in her hand, pointed at him.

'Are you here to take his body away, too?' she asked.

Wills coughed. Blood was coming out of his mouth, but his gaze was still on Quinn. He tried to say something. Quinn couldn't make it out, so he leaned closer.

'Care . . . ful,' Wills said.

'David, do you know who's responsible for this?'

Wills coughed again.

'It's okay. Don't force it.'

Wills coughed again, then looked at Quinn as if he was begging for help.

Another wet breath.

Then . . . nothing.

David Wills was dead. And if he knew the woman who'd killed him or who she worked for, he'd taken that information with him.

Quinn stood up, his gun still pointed at the Russian. Behind her he could see the other woman, the attacker, sprawled out on the grass, her dead eyes staring up at the sky.

'Who are you?' he demanded.

'Who are *you?*' she countered.

In the distance, he could hear sirens heading in their direction.

The Russian lowered her gun and motioned behind her. 'You were with her, weren't you? She is probably one of Palavin's dogs, and you work for Palavin, too.'

Palavin? That was the name Orlando had mentioned. He hesitated before he spoke. 'I don't work for anyone by that name. But if he's responsible for David's death, then maybe you're the one who works for him.'

The look on her face was utter shock. 'What? Of course not. I'm trying to find him. But you know him, don't you? You must know where he is. Tell me! You have to tell me!'

He could hear the sirens getting louder. As much as he would have liked to place his gun against this woman's head and find out what she knew, there was no time to pursue it now. He tucked Wills's gun under his jacket and turned to leave.

'Wait. If you know where he is, please tell me,' the woman pleaded. 'I need to know.'

He kept walking, but the woman didn't give up.

'Leave me alone,' he said.

'Your name's Quinn, right?' she asked. She glanced back over her shoulder to where Wills's body lay. 'I heard him call you that. I need your help, Quinn. I need to find Palavin.'

'I can't help you.'

She started to point her gun at him. But he reached out and yanked it from her hand before she even knew what was happening, then shoved her to the ground.

'Get the hell away from me,' he told her.

'I can't,' she said, pushing herself up and rushing to catch him. 'You're the only lead I have left.' They reached the section of bushes and trees that separated the park from the street. 'I'm not leaving until you help me.'

Quinn stopped and turned to her. 'I'm not your lead. I'm not anyone's lead. I can't help you. You need to get away from me right now, or I'll — '

'Or you'll kill me?' she asked, cutting him off. 'Then go ahead and kill me.'

Who the hell is this woman?

He stared at her for a moment, then walked down the path toward the street.

The sirens were very near now, and all instincts told Quinn to run the other way. But he knew that the easiest escape route was often toward the police, not away. At least initially. If he could get past them before they'd set up a perimeter, then he'd be in the clear. Most of their focus would be in the direction Quinn had come from, not behind them.

But his biggest problem wasn't the police. It

was the Russian woman. She was still shadowing him, matching him step for step. Then, as he stepped out of the park and onto the street outside Embankment Station, he momentarily forgot about the police and the woman.

What had been a typical busy morning had turned into a madhouse. Instead of several dozen people, there were now several hundred. They were gathered in groups, some small and some large. The biggest of which was near the entrance to the station. At the other end of the street, two police cars and an ambulance were trying to make their way through the crowd, but traveling slowly to avoid hitting anyone. Policemen tried to direct a pathway for an ambulance to drive, pushing people out of its way.

Quinn headed toward the group at the station, tried to blend in. Without even looking, he knew the Russian had pulled in tight behind him.

The crowd had formed a large circle with an open area in the center. A couple of police officers on foot were running toward the gathering.

'Get back!' one of officers shouted, trying to clear a path.

'A little late, if you ask me,' a man near Quinn muttered.

'What happened?' Quinn asked.

'Someone got shot,' he said, nodding toward the clear area in the center of the crowd.

Quinn thanked the man, then worked his way to the front of the crowd.

There was a body on the ground, blood pooling around his torso. Quinn couldn't see the man's face, but he didn't have to. He recognized the hair and the clothes.

It was the man who had been watching the station exit, the man who had been in the lobby of the Grand Hyatt in New York.

Wills's man.

Quinn looked over his shoulder. The crowd had begun to separate him from the Russian woman. He stepped forward into the clear area and jumped over the dead man's body.

'Hey!' an officer yelled as he emerged into the center of the circle. 'You can't do that.'

'Sorry,' Quinn said.

Behind him, he could hear the Russian woman fighting through the throng of gawkers. 'Excuse me . . . Please let me pass.'

Quinn was only feet from the entrance to Embankment Station.

The woman, having guessed his intent, had given up trying to follow him directly, and was heading back out of the crowd. The second she took her eyes off him, Quinn crouched down next to a rubbish can, out of sight. Using the receptacle as cover, he angled himself so that he could see the entrance to the Underground station.

A few seconds later, he watched the Russian rush inside. The moment she disappeared, he stood up and started moving clockwise around the crowd. As he did, he spotted a man getting into a cab just under the train bridge.

It was Mercer. No mistake.

Wills had said Mercer was working for him. *So was he Wills's second watcher?* Quinn wondered. Perhaps he had been on the outer perimeter, then had come back to check on his colleague and found him dead in front of the station. If Quinn were in Mercer's shoes, he would have gotten the hell out of there, too. In fact, he did need to get the hell out of there, right now.

As soon as he cleared the crowd, he headed up the cobbled street back toward Charing Cross. At the end of the block, he tucked himself in between two souvenir kiosks and checked to see if the Russian had followed him. She hadn't.

Instead of using the Underground, he walked toward Piccadilly Circus. No matter what the weather or the time of day, there was always a crowd there. He could blend in and take the tube to anywhere from there. A few blocks away, his phone vibrated. He checked the caller ID, then pressed Accept.

'I'm in London,' Orlando said. 'You got my email, right?'

'I got it.'

She paused. 'Is something wrong?'

'Where's the flat you rented?'

'Quinn, what's wrong?'

'I'd rather tell you in person.'

'You're here?'

'Yeah.'

She rattled off an address on Charlotte Street in Soho. 'You know where that is?'

'I know the area,' he said. He was only a ten-minute walk away.

'Okay, then I'll see you soon.'

'Not soon enough.'

27

'Wills is dead?' Mikhail sounded like he almost expected it.

'Killed right in front of me,' Petra said into her phone. 'I tried to stop the shooter, but she got him before I could.'

'Who was she?'

'I don't know,' she said. 'But it doesn't matter. We need to concentrate on finding Quinn.' Petra had heard Wills speak the name into his phone. Then she had heard him rasp it again when the body snatcher, Quinn, had tried to comfort the dying man.

'Who is Quinn?'

'The body snatcher,' she said. 'The one I saw in Los Angeles. He was there, too. When I spoke the Ghost's name, I could tell he had heard it before. He *knows*, Mikhail. We just need to find him, and convince him to tell us.'

'But where would we look? If he wants to stay lost, he sounds like the kind of man who can do it. Today might have been our only chance.' He paused. 'You had him, Petra.'

'I know,' she whispered.

Mikhail took a deep breath. 'I didn't mean — '

'It's okay. I *should* have done more.'

'No. You did what you could. I couldn't have done any better. But the question is still, what do we do now?'

Neither of them said anything for several seconds.

233

'What about Stepka?' Mikhail said. 'We have a name now. Maybe he can help.'

'I've already given him Quinn's name and description,' she said. 'I guess the only thing we can do is wait. Let's meet back at the apartment.'

'Okay.' The defeat in Mikhail's voice was palpable.

'We're almost there,' she reassured him. 'We know Quinn has information that will help. We'll be able to see this through to the end.'

'Perhaps.' Mikhail didn't sound as optimistic.

'We're going to find the Ghost, Mikhail. We're going to make him pay for what he did.'

* * *

Petra kept scanning the crowds the entire way back to Bayswater. She knew she was hoping for the impossible, but if there was even the smallest of chances that she'd spot Quinn, she couldn't afford to relax.

But he wasn't on any of the trains, nor the platforms, nor the streets. The only thing she could hold on to was the fact that he was in the city.

Mikhail had not yet arrived when she got back to the apartment. So she checked in with Stepka.

'In the right circles, your new friend is something of a legend,' Stepka told her.

'How so?'

'First, we should make sure we're talking about the same person. Do you have your computer?'

'Yes,' she said, glancing at the bag that held her laptop.

'I've sent you a picture.'

234

Petra switched her phone to speaker mode, retrieved her computer, and booted it up. She then opened the browser and logged on to her email. Stepka's message was in her inbox. She opened the attached picture. It wasn't a photograph, but a drawing. It looked very much, but not exactly, like Quinn.

'What is this?' she asked.

'A police sketch from New York City. The man in the drawing was wanted for a murder earlier this year.'

'They were looking for Quinn?'

'They stopped searching for him when another suspect turned up. The question is, is he the same man you're looking for?'

She looked at the picture again. 'It's not quite right, but yes, this is him.'

'Okay, then this is what I've got,' he said.

She heard a key slip into the lock on the front door. 'Hold on.' She waited for Mikhail to enter, then said, 'Stepka dug up information about Quinn.' She pointed at the computer screen where the drawing was still up. While Mikhail took a look, she told Stepka to go on.

'The man's name is Jonathan Quinn. He's a freelance cleaner, not associated with a specific organization. His reputation is stellar. He gets the job done. My contacts could not recommend him higher. Says he has a bit of an ethical streak, so if he doesn't think you're on the up-and-up, he'll refuse the job.'

'Then, why would he be working on the jobs in Los Angeles and Maine?'

'Every job has many angles. What's ethical to

one may not be ethical to another.'

'Or maybe he's been lied to.'

'Also a possibility. But you should know my contact did say that Quinn is not one to mess with. He's not above leaving a body for someone else to clean up.'

Petra let it all sink in for a moment. 'Anything else?'

'That's not enough?'

'No, it's fine. Thank you.' She hung up the phone.

'We can print out copies of the sketch,' Mikhail said. 'Then we can make the rounds and see if any of our people have seen him.'

'Good idea,' she said, nodding.

She felt like they were clinging to their last bit of hope. But at least it *was* hope.

28

Charlotte Street was in one of those quaint London neighborhoods that made tourists wish they lived in the city. Its centerpiece was the Charlotte Street Hotel. Combining an older London façade with a contemporary, warm interior, the hotel was an upscale place that didn't make you feel like you had to be wearing a tuxedo just to use the elevator. Quinn had been inside once before. Not as a guest. On a job. And though he had had little time to look around, what he saw of the place as he removed a body from an upstairs suite had impressed him.

Quinn spent thirty minutes walking the rest of the street, checking alternative routes in and out, and reacquainting himself with the neighborhood. Besides the hotel, Charlotte Street was lined with four- and five-story buildings with offices and flats on the upper floors, restaurants and shops on the ground level.

Cars were parked in most of the available spots, but actual traffic was light due to the way this part of Soho was laid out. Charlotte Street was a one-way road ending at Percy Street, where traffic that needed to continue south would have to go west first, then turn left on Rathbone Place. To make things even more confusing, the northern section of Rathbone took a jog to the west before heading north again and paralleling Charlotte. Quinn considered the

237

complicated layout an asset; in his business, the more escape options, the better.

Once he was satisfied, he sat at a table outside a coffee shop a half block away. He'd ordered a cup of the house blend, black, but he had yet to take a sip when the cab carrying Orlando arrived.

As she got out, she subtly scanned the neighborhood, then pulled her bag out of the back seat and tipped the cabbie. The moment he drove off, she retrieved her cell phone. Quinn's own phone was sitting on the table. He picked it up just as it started to ring.

'You here?' she asked.

'Just having a coffee down the street.'

'Caffè Nero?' As always, she had researched where she was going. Quinn guessed she probably knew the names of *all* the businesses in the area.

'Like you didn't know that already.'

'I have no idea what you're talking about.' She picked up her bag with her free hand. 'Bring me a latte.'

★ ★ ★

The flat was on the second floor. The door was open a crack, so Quinn nudged it with his hip and stepped across the threshold. Orlando stood just inside, looking fresh despite the transatlantic flight. Her black hair was pulled back in a ponytail, and she was wearing a pair of glasses, rectangular in shape and framed in blood-red plastic.

238

She looked at him for a moment, then reached up and touched his face.

The warmth of her skin temporarily pushed away all thoughts of Wills's death, of the Russian woman, of the danger facing both his sister and his mother. He leaned forward and kissed her with more love and tenderness than he'd ever felt for anyone else in his life.

She moved into him, her body pressing against his, letting him know she was there, that she loved him, too.

'Come inside,' she whispered. 'Unless you want to give the neighbors a show.'

He smiled again, then stepped into the apartment, Orlando closing the door behind him.

'Is that my coffee?' she asked.

Quinn had almost forgotten he'd been holding the cup. But even as he'd been hugging her, he'd kept it upright, spilling nothing.

'Thanks,' she said as he handed it to her.

She raised it to her mouth, testing its temperature. When she seemed satisfied, she took a drink. As she did, Quinn plopped down on a chair in the living room and took a look around.

Besides the utilitarian armchair he was in, there was a well-worn couch, two cloth-covered cubes that served as either ottomans or coffee tables, and a shelving unit with a TV and various knickknacks spread around. As far as exits, other than the front door, there were two: a hallway to the left, and a doorway leading to a small kitchen on the right.

'You want to tell me what's going on?' Orlando asked.

He did another scan of the room.

She sat on the couch. 'You're stalling.'

'I'm not stalling. I'm trying to get my thoughts in order.'

'You've had thirty minutes to get them in order while you waited for me.'

'Wills is dead.'

Ever the pro, there was no change in her expression. 'What happened?'

'Shot. This morning.'

'You know this for sure?'

'I was kneeling next to him when he died.' He told her about the assassin, Wills's attempted last words, and finally the Russian.

'That's not all,' he said.

'There's more?'

'She mentioned the name Palavin,' he said. 'She thought I knew where he was, and demanded I tell her.'

'Did she say why she was looking for him?'

Quinn shook his head. 'I didn't have a lot of time to press the point. But I don't think she wanted to use the information to drop in for tea. She doesn't like him. And by 'not like' I meant she seems to hate him.' He paused. 'I know I told you to put him on the back burner, but maybe you should see what else you can find out about him.'

'Absolutely.'

'There was something else,' Quinn said. 'Mercer was there, too. He was getting into a cab on the street near where Wills's man had been shot.'

'Mercer? The guy from Maine?'

'According to Wills, Mercer was working directly for him. He'd also been on the Los Angeles gig. He must have been part of Wills's protection.'

'Didn't do a very good job,' she said.

'No, he didn't.'

She mulled it over, then said, 'What about the woman? You sure you lost her? No chance she followed you here?'

Quinn frowned. It was a question he'd often asked, usually of Nate. 'No one followed me.'

'Let's step back. Why were you meeting with Wills in the first place?'

There was so much she'd missed while she'd been getting Quinn's mom settled, then flying to Europe. Quinn explained to her what had happened in Paris, and about the photo Julien had shown him that had to have been taken by Annabel Taplin.

'That's why I came to London,' he said. 'Last night I arranged a face-to-face with Wills for this morning so I could ask for his help. I thought he could use his contacts to get me in touch with the right people at MI6. We were supposed to meet at the park.'

'Do you think you were a target, too?'

'No. He was killed several minutes before the time we'd agreed to meet.'

'The Russian woman? You think she was the one who wanted him dead?'

'She tried to *stop* the hit. Almost succeeded, too. She seemed even more upset with Wills's death than I was.'

Orlando's brow wrinkled in the way it did

when she was trying to figure something out. But when she let out an exasperated expulsion of air, Quinn knew she had no more answers than he did.

'Mom emailed me,' he said, trying to lighten the mood. 'I take it everything went well.'

'It did,' she said. 'She took to Steven right away. I think the only thing we have to worry about is if he eats so much he's too lethargic to notice anything.'

Quinn surprised himself by laughing a little. 'I know my mother. That's actually a possibility. Larson and Nolan?'

'They're in position outside the farm, ready to move if your mom goes out. They're taking shifts so that the house is watched around the clock.'

'Thank you,' he said. The words seemed inadequate.

She looked at him for a moment, smiling, then she pulled out her computer and booted it up. 'I take it Nate and Julien are keeping a watch on Liz's place?'

'Better than that. Nate's actually staying with her.'

'*Staying* with her?'

'I stepped out of the room for a few minutes, and by the time I came back, he had her asking him if he wanted to sleep on her couch.'

'Really?' she said, her eyebrow raised.

'Really.'

'Good for him. Told you he's almost ready.'

'He is.'

She gave Quinn a mischievous smile. 'What if he doesn't stay on the couch?'

'That is *not* an option.'

'Why not? They're close enough in age, and your sister's cute, and smart, too. What's she studying again?'

'I don't even want to think about this.'

'Art history, wasn't it? Didn't Nate study history in school? Seems like there'd be some common ground there.'

'Stop it,' Quinn said.

'You're no fun,' she said, scowling.

Her computer chimed. She looked down at her screen, then clicked on something.

'It's a message from Romy,' she said. Romy specialized in information gathering and worked out of Eastern Europe. 'She says someone's been asking about you.'

'The same person who was looking into my background?'

She shook her head. 'I'm not sure. It was a direct inquiry, asking about you by name.' Orlando looked up. 'She says the guy doing the asking is a Russian based out of Moscow.'

'He have a name?'

'Goes by Stepka.'

'Never heard of him. You?'

'No.'

'He's in Moscow now?'

'Apparently.'

'Do we have someone there who can pay him a visit?'

'I think I can arrange that.'

'Do it. And if he — ' His phone vibrated, stopping him.

But there was no name on his display, only

243

BLOCKED. He held it out to Orlando.

'I thought the software update you gave me was supposed to decode blocked numbers.'

'It is.' She frowned. 'Give it to me.'

He handed her the phone. Without punching the Accept button, she accessed the virtual keypad and began typing. When the vibrating ceased, she looked up. 'The program should have been able to figure it out.'

'Maybe you need to start thinking about writing an update.'

'Go to hell,' she said, but Quinn knew as soon as she had a little free time, updating was exactly what she'd do.

As Orlando handed the phone back to him, it buzzed again, indicating a voice message. Quinn pushed the button to play the message, and switched it to speaker so they could both hear.

Nothing at first, then a voice: male, older, with an accent that seemed almost English, but not quite. 'I will call you back in ten minutes. Please do answer your phone.'

Quinn played the message again.

'Do you recognize him?' Orlando asked.

'No.'

She then held out her hand. 'Give it to me again.'

As she began scrolling through different displays, Quinn asked, 'What are you doing?'

She frowned at him. 'The software I installed, which you've already pointed out needs an update, includes the ability to record both sides of a conversation. I just haven't activated it yet.'

'And why not?'

'We talk a lot. The last thing I need is for you to record one of our conversations, then throw something I say back in my face.' She tapped the screen one more time, then sat back. 'Okay, it's ready.'

'Does your phone have this capability?'

'Of course.'

'And it's active, I assume.'

She smiled.

He took the phone from her. 'I want you to keep this function active on *my* phone.'

'We'll see.'

Precisely ten minutes after the first call, Quinn's phone began to vibrate again.

'Do I need to do anything?' Quinn asked.

'Just hit Accept. It records automatically.'

Quinn did as she instructed, then raised the phone to his ear. 'Hello?'

'Is this Mr. Quinn?' It was the same voice from the message.

'Who is this?'

'What are your plans in regards to the project you are doing for David Wills?'

Quinn paused. 'I don't know any David Wills.'

Orlando looked at him, the brow over her left eye arched.

'We both know that's not true,' the caller said.

'You have five seconds to tell me who you are, or I'm hanging up.'

Nothing for three seconds, then, 'Have you read *A Burnt-Out Case* lately?'

Quinn said nothing. He also didn't hang up.

Some organizations created code phrases for when the legitimacy of a third party needed to be established. *A Burnt-Out Case* was the one given to Quinn by Wills when they first started working together.

'Do I have your attention now?' the man asked.

'Who are you?' Quinn said.

'You can call me Mr. Smith. The job you are doing for David Wills is actually for me. I'm his client.'

'Hang on for a moment,' Quinn said. He punched the Hold key and looked at Orlando. 'It's the client. The one with the body in the wall.'

'You're kidding.'

'He knows Wills's code phrase.'

'What does he want?'

'Wondering the same thing myself.' Quinn took the call off hold. 'Mr. Smith. You may be David's client, but you're not mine. He's the one who hired me, so he's the one I work for.'

'I see no distinction between the fact that David hired you and I hired him.'

'I do.'

'Please, Mr. Quinn,' the caller said, his tone now conciliatory. 'I'm not trying to go around David's back. You see, certain circumstances have arisen that have made it necessary for me to contact you directly.'

'What circumstances?'

'I'm sorry to say David is dead,' Mr. Smith said.

'Dead?' Quinn said, acting surprised.

'Apparently he was shot.'

'When?'

246

'This morning.'

'By whom?'

'I don't know, Mr. Quinn. Do you?'

'I have no idea,' Quinn said. Could this guy really have found out about Wills's death already? It was plausible. Mercer, if he was indeed working for Wills, would have informed Wills's organization, and then they might have begun notifying clients to assure them that current operations were not compromised. Plausible, but the timeline was tight.

'I thought as much, but it is good to hear. The reason I'm calling you is to make sure you're planning on completing the job. You've already been paid, and nicely, I might add. I only ask that once you have the package in your possession, you consider calling me. I would like to dispose of it myself. But if you are not comfortable with that, I understand. Fair?'

'Yeah, see, that's not the way it works. First I verify what you're telling me about Wills is true. If it is, then I immediately remove myself, putting as much distance between me and anyone connected with Wills as possible. Including you. So if your information's good, you'll have to find someone else. I'm done.'

Dead air for a moment, then, 'What?'

'Done,' Quinn said. 'No longer on the job.'

'You've been hired for the task. I expect you to carry it out. Mr. Quinn, maybe we should meet in person. We can discuss this — '

'There's nothing to discuss. Per my standard agreement, in the case that my client is killed, I can terminate my involvement at my discretion.

You can be sure I'll be exercising that clause.'

'Mr. Quinn, that is not an opt — '

Quinn disconnected the call.

'Are you sure that was such a good idea?' Orlando asked.

Quinn's phone began to vibrate again. BLOCKED on the display.

He pushed the button rejecting the call.

'We have more important things to worry about than a body in a wall,' Quinn said. 'We're off.'

29

A vibration.

Without even opening his eyes, Nate reached out and grabbed his bag off the floor. Back in college the vibration of a phone wouldn't have even caused him to stir in his sleep. But now, no matter how deep he was under, it immediately woke him.

The room was still dark, the only illumination seeping in coming from the streetlights outside. Nate activated his phone, then squinted at the sudden brightness of the screen. Once his pupils adjusted, he could see he'd received a text message from Julien.

All quiet out front. Let me know when you're up.

Nate looked at the clock at the top corner of the display. 5:07 a.m. He tapped out a reply:

Up now, thanks to you.

Julien texted back:

You're welcome.

There was no use trying to go back to sleep. Nate knew from experience it wouldn't come. His mind was already alert. He turned off the no-longer-needed alarm he'd set for 6 a.m., then

249

put his phone down and swung his legs off the couch.

He listened for any other noise in the apartment, but all was quiet. Liz apparently didn't have friends who texted her at five in the morning. Making as little noise as possible, he crossed the living room to the entry.

After Liz had gone to bed, he had braced one of her dining room chairs under the handle of the front door for added security. The last thing he wanted was for her to see it there, so he picked it up and carried it back to where he'd found it.

He thumbed through some of Liz's magazines, then perused the books on her shelves, before deeming it late enough to take a shower. By 6:20, he was dressed and ready for the day. He began to make bets with himself on when he would hear Liz get up. The winning time turned out to be 7:37 a.m. But it was almost an hour later before she joined him in the living room.

She was wearing dark jeans, a white sweater, a pair of brown boots, and had wrapped a multi-colored scarf around her neck. After what had happened the previous night, Nate had been anxious about the moment they would see each other again. As she looked at him, he thought, *Here it comes.* The I've-been-thinking-it-might-be-better-if-you-stay-in-a-hostel speech. Or the listen-last-night-I-drank-a-little-too-much-so-if-I-led-you-to-think-anything-I'm-sorry line followed by the hostel speech.

'Good morning,' she said, a hint of a smile.

'*Bonjour*,' Nate said.

250

'Aha. Nice. You work on that all night?'

'As a matter of fact I did. Didn't sleep at all.'

'Well, it sounds like it paid off.' She stared through him. *Now, for sure*, he thought. *I'm so kicked out*. 'I've been thinking . . . '

He suppressed a laugh.

'What's so funny?' she asked.

He shook his head. 'Nothing. Sorry.'

Her eyes narrowed as if she was assessing him anew, but then she smiled. 'I've been thinking that I really don't want to go to class this morning. So, why don't we grab some breakfast, then visit one of those places we just looked at from the outside yesterday. Maybe the Louvre? Take in the *Mona Lisa*? How's that sound?'

He was stunned into momentary silence. That was definitely not the hostel speech.

'No?' she said.

'Ah, no. I mean, yes,' he said. 'That sounds great. But I don't want to mess you up at school.'

'If I thought it was going to mess me up, I wouldn't do it.'

'Okay. Sure. I'd love it.' He stood up and met her at the entrance hall.

'Besides,' she said as she pulled her jacket out of the closet, 'I'd have probably taken the day off whether you were here or not.'

'I feel so special.'

'Thought you'd like that.'

'Hold on,' he said. 'I should hit the bathroom first.'

'Make it quick. I'm hungry.'

In the bathroom, he took a moment to

refocus, then texted the new plan to Julien. Before he left, he looked at himself in the mirror.

'She's Quinn's sister,' he said. 'Don't screw this up.'

The only problem was, he wasn't sure if the Nate who was looking back at him was listening.

★   ★   ★

They spent over an hour and a half at a café a few blocks away. Then followed that up by browsing through a couple of bookstores in the neighborhood, looking for a book Liz wanted for her dissertation. It wasn't until they visited their fourth bookstore that they found it.

'Thanks for letting me take care of this,' she said as they exited the store. 'You mind if we drop it off at my place before we head out?'

'Are you kidding? I'd be furious.' He smiled and held up his hands. 'You're in charge today. I'm just happily along for the ride. I mean, I'm in Paris for God's sake.'

She raised an eyebrow. 'I'm in charge?'

'Within reason.'

'Hmmm.'

A light rain began to fall. They raced down the sidewalk and ducked under the cover of the entryway. While she unlocked the door, Nate glanced back just in time to see Julien slip under the awning of the café. He was talking tensely into his phone.

'After you,' Liz said, holding the door open.

They ducked inside, then rode the elevator up to Liz's floor.

'Maybe we should just stay in,' Nate said once they were back in the apartment.

She gave him an odd look. 'You're not going to let a little rain stop you, are you?'

'It's not just rain. It's cold rain.'

'We won't be outside that much. Besides, it's a perfect day for the museum.'

While Liz was in her room, Nate went into the bathroom, once again using the time to text Julien.

Everything ok?

There was no immediate response.

As he was washing up, he heard a noise from down the hall. A double bang, like someone slamming pots down on a counter.

He dried his hands, then stepped out of the bathroom.

There were voices coming from near the entrance. Liz's and a man's.

He ran toward the entryway.

'I already told you. There is no Nate here.' Liz's voice. She was speaking in French.

'I'm sorry, not Nate,' the other voice said, also in French. 'Em . . . Andrew. I need to talk to Andrew.'

'Andrew?'

As Nate turned into the foyer, he saw Liz standing next to the partially open doorway. On the other side was Julien.

The second Julien saw him, the Frenchman pushed the door all the way open and stepped across the threshold. In English, he said, 'I need to talk to you now!'

'You can't come in here! Get out! Now!'

'What's going on?' Nate asked Julien.

'Do you know this guy?' Liz asked.

'Yeah.' Nate instantly switched out of back-packing-college-student mode and into that of highly trained operative. 'He's a friend. Do you mind if he comes in for a minute?'

Liz eyed the massive Julien, then looked back to Nate. 'You can talk to him in the hallway. I don't feel comfortable with him in my apartment.'

'We don't have time for this,' Julien said. He took a step further into the apartment, then shut the front door.

'What do you think you're doing?' Liz yelled. 'Get out!'

But the Frenchman had turned his attention to Nate. 'We have to get her out of here. Now.'

'I'm calling the police.' Liz started for the living room, but Nate grabbed her waist and stopped her. 'What are you doing?' she shrieked. 'Let me go!'

'No police,' Nate said.

A look of terror crossed her face. 'Oh, God. You've been fooling me, haven't you? You've just been waiting for your friend to get here, and now what? Are you going to rape me, is that it?'

'Relax. We're not going to hurt you.'

Liz wrenched herself free from Nate's grasp and pushed herself against the wall. Since she wasn't going for the phone, he let her be for the moment.

To Julien, Nate said, 'What happened?'

254

'I just received a call from my client. He has three men in the city on their way over here right now. They said they checked with her school and know that she's in the city. I couldn't hide her from them any longer. I had to tell them she just got back. As soon as the others arrive, we are to take her to someplace quiet.'

Liz's eyes grew wide.

'Nate, we have no more than fifteen minutes.'

Nate grimaced, then turned and took a step toward Quinn's sister. 'You need to listen to me. We're here to help you, not hurt you.'

She stared at him for a moment, then pushed herself off the wall and tried to run into the living room. Nate grabbed her again, lifting her off her feet, then all but carried her to the couch and set her down.

'Leave me alone! Leave me alone!' she said, striking at him wildly with her hands.

'Liz, please. Stop.' He was able to finally grab her wrists, and pushed them down into her lap.

'Who are you?' she asked.

'Your life's in danger. Do you understand? Some people who want to harm you are on their way here right now.'

'No. No. You're lying,' she said, shaking her head. 'You're just saying that to get me out of the building, then you'll . . . you'll . . . '

Nate needed to calm her down, and fast. 'I think you should talk to your — ' He looked at Julien. The Frenchman already thought he knew the truth, but as far as Nate knew, Quinn had never confirmed it. *To hell with it*, he thought. Quinn could be pissed at him later. 'Your brother.'

She stopped struggling, confused. 'My brother?'

'I work for him.' Nate said.

'You *work* for Jake?'

'Yes.'

'I thought you said you'd only met him once before.'

Nate took a deep breath. 'I lied.'

Her eyes flicked to Julien, then back to Nate. 'Who's Nate?'

Nate took a deep breath. 'I am.'

'But . . . what about . . . you said your name was Andrew.'

'Liz, we need to get you out of here.'

'Why would my brother want you here?'

'To protect you.'

'Protect me?'

'He knew you were in danger.'

'I don't believe that for a second.' She started pushing against him again.

'Julien. Get Quinn on the phone.'

'Who the hell is Quinn?' Liz asked.

He looked at her. 'Your brother.'

Nate knew it was all coming at her too fast. He could almost see her mind overloading.

Dammit, he thought. This was not the way this should have gone.

'Quinn? It's Julien. We have a problem.' Nate listened as the Frenchman described their situation to Quinn.

When he was finished, Nate said, 'It would be great if he would talk to her.'

Julien relayed the request, then walked over to the couch and tried to hold the phone up to Liz's ear. But she moved her head away, twisting

256

it and turning it so Julien couldn't get the phone in place.

'It's just a trick,' she said. 'It's not him.'

'Use the speaker,' Nate said.

Julien touched the screen of his phone, then said, 'Quinn?'

'I'm here.'

Liz froze.

'Quinn,' Nate said, 'we need to get Liz out, but she's not cooperating. We've got five minutes tops before we run into a potential overlap. Could you please convince her we're not here to hurt her?'

'Liz,' Quinn said, 'you need to listen to them. They have to get you out of there now.'

'I don't know who you are, but you're not my brother,' she said.

Quinn took a moment before responding. 'When we were out on the lake after we flipped, and I grabbed ahold of you, remember?'

'Shut up!' she yelled. 'Shut up!'

'I whispered something in your ear.'

'Please stop,' she said, only this time some of the fight was missing from her voice.

'I said it over and over. Do you remember? I said, 'I'll never let anything hurt you.''

Liz's hands began to shake. 'Jake?'

'My friends are there to keep you safe. You need to listen to them, and do exactly what they say. Can you do that?'

'Jake, what's going on?'

'We'll talk about that later. I promise. Right now you have to get out of your apartment.'

'I . . . I don't understand.'

257

'Someone is on their way to your place right now. If they get there before you leave, they will kill my friends and take you. They very likely will kill you, too. You have to leave now.'

'Kill us? Why would they — '

'Liz! You're running out of time. Once my friends get you someplace safe, I'll explain everything to you.'

The stunned look on her face turned defiant.

'Why should I believe you?' she said. 'You haven't cared about me for twenty years.'

'Liz! You can hate me all you want, but you still need to get the hell out of there. Please, listen to Andrew.'

'Ah, yeah,' Nate said. 'About that. She already knows my name.'

'I don't care what she knows! You all need to leave right now!'

Julien's phone beeped.

'What's that?' Quinn asked.

Julien looked at the display. 'It's them. I think they're here.'

30

Julien turned off the speakerphone function, then switched to the incoming call.

'*Oui?* . . . There's a café at the corner,' Julien said, switching to English. 'I'll meet you there in five minutes.' The Frenchman listened. 'Because I'm checking her floor right now . . . No, it's better that we meet there. I can give you the layout.' He glanced at Liz. 'Yes, she was alone last I checked . . . I'll be right there. Four minutes now.'

Julien switched the call back to Quinn and reengaged the speaker.

'They're outside,' he said. 'We have five, maybe six minutes before they become suspicious.'

'Then get moving, and don't call me until you're someplace safe,' Quinn said.

The phone went dead.

'All right, come on,' Nate said.

He grabbed his backpack and slung it over his shoulders, but Liz didn't move. He put his hand on her arm and yanked her to her feet. 'Come on. We don't have any more time.'

'Is there really someone downstairs who wants to hurt me?'

'Yes,' Nate said, leading her toward the door.

'Wait. How long are we going to be gone?'

'I don't know.'

She tried to pull her arm out of his grasp. 'I

need some clothes.'

He gripped her harder. He didn't want to hurt her, but at the moment it was better than delaying their departure. 'We can buy what we need. Now let's go.'

'My purse at least,' she said.

It was on a small table along the back wall of the living room. Nate steered their course so she could grab it, then hurried her out of the apartment.

As they ran down the corridor, Nate said, 'There's got to be a back way out of the building. Where is it?'

Liz didn't seem to hear him.

'Liz.' He gave her a gentle shake. 'You need to help us. Back exit. Where?'

'There's a door to the alley. But you can only get to it through the lobby.'

'That's what I was afraid of,' Nate said.

'Stairs, yes?' Julien asked as they neared the end of the hallway.

'Stairs,' Nate said.

Julien raced down, agile for such a large man. On his own, Nate would have been able to keep up with him, but he knew if he let go of Liz she'd fall back, so he slowed his pace and kept a hand on her.

When they reached the final flight, they found Julien three risers from the bottom standing rock still.

'What is it?' Nate whispered.

'I saw someone through the window outside.'

'Did he see you?'

'He was turned the other way.'

'One of them?'

'I'm not sure.'

Could be anyone, Nate thought. But Quinn had taught him to always assume the worst. He looked at Liz. 'Which way to the alley door?'

'It's across from the elevator at the back of the lobby,' she said. 'There's a hallway that leads to the exit.'

They would have to cross through the center of the lobby. If someone looked through the window while they did, they'd be spotted.

'I'll check,' Nate said.

The men outside might have descriptions of both Liz and Julien, but they would have no idea who Nate was.

'Stay with Julien,' he said as he let go of her arm.

He moved around Julien and entered the lobby. Then, as if he'd done it a million times before, he strolled toward the entrance of the rear hallway. He was only a few feet from it when someone rapped against the window on the front door.

'*Monsieur, s'il vous plaît. Pouvez-vous me laisser entrer?*' The voice was male, most likely the same person Julien had seen.

Not even flinching, Nate continued on as if he hadn't heard a thing.

'*Monsieur? S'il vous plaît.*'

The rapping on the glass didn't stop until Nate disappeared into the back hallway.

That's a problem, he thought.

He looked at his watch. Julien was due at the café in one minute.

261

'Julien,' he whispered as loud as he dared.

'*Oui?*'

'You're going to have to go out and pretend like everything is okay. You need to get that guy away from the door long enough so I can get Liz out the back.'

'*D'accord,*' Julien said. 'I'll do what I can.'

Nate angled himself so he could see as much of the lobby as possible without coming into view of the door. Fifteen seconds passed, but the Frenchman hadn't appeared.

'Julien. Now would be good.'

Ten more seconds went by before Julien emerged from the staircase. The Frenchman stutter-stepped, glanced back over his shoulder in the direction he'd just come, then recovered and headed to the door.

He whispered something, but Nate couldn't make it out.

As Julien opened the door, the man who'd been standing there backed up a few steps. He looked at Julien, and they exchanged a few words. As this was happening Julien let the door close behind him, then moved in front of the window to block the view.

Nate sprinted across the lobby and turned onto the stairs. 'Come on, we — '

He didn't finish, because no one was there to hear him.

★   ★   ★

Quinn looked stunned as he disconnected the call from Julien.

Orlando already had her own phone up to her ear. 'Steven? I know it's early there. But there's been an escalation. What's your situation? . . . Have the others seen anything unusual? . . . Okay, I'll hold.' She moved the cell away from her mouth and looked back at Quinn. 'Everything's quiet at your mother's house. He's calling Rickey to see if he's seen anything.' She suddenly swung the phone back. 'Yeah, I'm here . . . Okay . . . good.' To Quinn, she said, 'Everything's quiet.'

'Let me talk to him,' he said.

Orlando handed him the phone.

'Steven? It's Quinn. We have reason to believe that someone might make a move on my mother at any time. I need you to get her out of there.'

'Okay, sure,' Steven Howard said. 'Anyplace specific?'

Quinn thought for a moment. 'If they do come looking and see that she's gone, they'll think she headed to either Winnipeg or Minneapolis.' They were the two closest cities of any size, and would be obvious destinations. 'Go west into North Dakota. Stay on Highway 2. When you reach Montana, find a motel somewhere out of the way. Use precautions.'

'Got it,' Howard said.

'I should probably talk to my mom,' Quinn said. 'I'm going to have to wake her.'

Quinn looked at his watch, then did a quick calculation. It was 4:27 a.m. in Minnesota.

'Do it,' he said. First he had to convince his sister, and now his mother. This was a day he never saw coming.

On the other end, he could hear Howard

moving through the house. There was a gentle knock. 'Mrs. Oliver?' A pause. 'Mrs. Oliver, are you awake?' Then in a whispered voice, 'She's coming.'

The creak of a door opening, the same creak Quinn had heard a few weeks before when he'd been there for his father's funeral.

'Steven? Is something wrong?' Dorothy Oliver said, her voice muffled.

'It's your son,' Howard said. 'He needs to talk to you.'

'Jake?'

'Yes.'

'Jake. Is everything all right?' His mother's voice was now clear and unimpeded.

'Mom, I need you to do something for me.'

'Of course.'

'I need you to leave the house. Steven will — '

'What?' she said. 'Why?'

'Please, Mom. I need you to trust me, and not ask any questions.'

She was silent for a moment, then said, 'I trust you, honey. But you can't wake me in the middle of the night and tell me I have to leave my house without telling me why.'

He hesitated, but knew he had to tell her something. 'There are some people . . . people who might use you to get to me. They may be on the way to the farm right now.'

'What are you talking about? What people?'

'Mom, we can talk more later. Right now I need you to do whatever Steven asks. He has a couple of friends who will be there in a few minutes to help. They're going to watch over you.'

'Jake, are you in some kind of trouble?'

'I won't be if you do what I've asked.'

'Okay,' she said. 'If that's what you need me to do.'

'That's what I need you to do.'

'Then fine, honey. I'll do what Steven tells me to do.'

'Thank you, Mom,' Quinn said, relieved. 'Please put him back on.'

'I love you, Jake.'

'I love you, too, Mom.'

When Howard was back on the line, Quinn said, 'Text me every hour, and call me if *anything* even slightly unusual happens.'

'You got it.'

'Keep her safe, Steven.'

'I will.'

Quinn hung up. Orlando was sitting on the floor in front of the couch, her computer in her lap.

'I can get us on a flight to Paris leaving in an hour and a half,' she said. 'That should give us plenty of time to get to the airport.' When Quinn didn't respond right away, she looked up. 'Yes or no?'

He took a deep breath, trying to quell his anger and frustration. He wanted to take out whoever was trying to harm his sister with his own hands. But he let the moment pass in silence, and tried to rein in his emotions. As much as he wanted to say yes, he knew it was more important for him to stay here and find the source of the problem than to go rushing off to Paris to act as a bodyguard. He shook his head. 'Nate and Julien can handle it for now. The only

265

way to really stop this is to get to the one calling the shots.'

'And who would that be?'

'The guy I just quit on.'

Not sixty minutes after Quinn said he was not going to finish the project, a move was being made on his family. In Quinn's world, the obvious wasn't always right, but there were times it just couldn't be ignored.

Orlando turned her laptop so Quinn could see the screen. On it was a hybrid map/satellite image of a city street. A single glowing blue dot pulsed over a building.

'Your sister's street in Paris,' Orlando explained.

The blue dot, then, would be Nate's position. Orlando had implanted chips in both Quinn's and Nate's phones that would allow her to track them even if the SIM cards had been removed.

'They're still in Liz's building,' he said. 'They need to be out of there already!'

He started to raise his phone, but Orlando reached out and put a hand over his. 'Don't.'

Quinn glared at her, fire in his eyes.

'If you call him now, he's not going to answer. And even if he did, you'd only delay them more.'

It took every ounce of will he had to lower his hand.

★ ★ ★

Nate raced up the stairs to the landing of the first floor.

'Liz,' he said, raising his voice as loud as he dared. 'Liz. Where are you?'

266

She wasn't on the landing. He looked down the central corridor, but didn't see her there either. He took two steps in to make sure there was no place she could hide. There wasn't.

He returned to the landing, listened for a second to make sure Julien and the others hadn't come in yet, then headed up the stairs, searching the second and third floors.

As he neared Liz's floor, he heard the lobby door open far below. It wasn't loud, but it was unmistakable. He increased his speed.

When he reached the fourth floor landing, he could hear breathing. Rapid, but low, like someone trying to keep from being heard. Then, as he stepped into the hallway, he saw her.

She was pressed against the door to her apartment, trying in vain to find the right key to the lock. Her purse was at her feet, her wallet half in, half out. Nate guessed she'd dropped the bag when she found her keys, no longer concerned about anything but getting into the false safety of her own apartment.

He ran over to her and grabbed her wrist just as the key began to turn.

'Let me go,' she said.

'Liz, we have to get out of here.'

'Let me go. I'll be fine inside. I won't let them in.'

'They'll still get in.'

'I won't let them!'

Nate pulled the key out of the lock, then swept up her purse and handed it to her.

'Hold this,' he said.

Out of reflex, she did. He then lifted her over

his shoulder in more or less a fireman's hold.

'Put me down,' she said.

'If you keep talking, they'll kill us,' he said.

Just then the door to apartment 25, two down from Liz's place, opened. An old woman stuck her head out.

'*Qu'est-ce que vous faites?*' she asked.

'*Rien. Tout va bien. Rentrez à l'intérieur,*' Nate said, reassuring her there was nothing going on she needed to be concerned about.

'You speak French, too?' Liz said.

'A little.'

The woman looked at them for a moment longer, then closed her door.

Nate, with Liz still over his shoulder, began moving toward the stairs.

'What else did you lie to me about?' Liz asked.

'Not as much as you might think,' Nate said between breaths.

He could hear the elevator moving. Up or down, he didn't know, but it didn't matter. The next time the door opened on this floor, Julien's pseudo colleagues would be behind it.

He turned for the stairs, but he couldn't carry her down, so he lowered her to her feet.

'You have to do everything I tell you or this won't go well. Understand?' He was using his best no-bullshit voice.

She nodded. He could see in her eyes that maybe she was finally getting it.

'We go down. Quickly but quietly.'

But before they had even gone one step, Nate heard someone on the stairs several floors below heading up.

'Dammit,' he said. 'Back down the hall.'

She followed him without question this time. Behind them, he could hear the elevator stop for several seconds, then start up again. Then he noticed the doorway at the far end of the hall.

'What's that?' Nate asked. He was pointing at the door.

'Emergency stairway. An alarm sounds when you open it.'

The alarm was a problem, but not as much of a problem as getting shot in the hallway.

The door to apartment 25 opened again, and the old woman stepped into the hallway.

'*Si vous n'arrêtez pas, je vais appeler la police!*'

Nate veered toward her and pushed Liz through the open door.

'*Vous ne pouvez pas rentrer ici!*' the woman protested, trying to block the way.

'*Je suis désolé,*' Nate apologized. '*S'il vous plaît, rentrez à l'intérieur.*'

The woman didn't move.

Liz reached out and pulled the woman by the shoulder back inside the apartment. 'Madame Gerard, *s'il vous plaît.*'

Nate looked at Liz. 'Shut the door, and don't answer it unless you know it's me.'

'Where are you going?' she asked.

'To distract them.'

'But you'll be back?'

He flashed a quick smile. 'As soon as I can. Promise me you'll stay here.'

'I'll stay,' she said.

He turned and headed straight for the emergency stairway. He could hear the elevator behind him start to slow down. It would only be a few seconds before the doors opened and the others spilled out.

Nate checked to make sure Liz and Madame Gerard were safely inside, then he threw open the door. An alarm began to wail as he raced down the stairwell.

Come on, he thought. *Come on*.

He banged against the wall on the second floor landing and kept heading down. When he reached the first floor, he finally heard footsteps on the stairs above him.

With a sense of relief, he raced to the ground floor, then burst out the exit onto the sidewalk.

Forty-five seconds later Julien and two other men ran out the door. By then Nate was across the street, leaning against the opposite building like he'd been there all day.

31

The rain was steady and cold by the time Nate felt it was safe to return to the apartment building for Liz. Back on the street with no umbrella, they were both getting soaked, but if it bothered Liz, she didn't say anything. She just held on to his hand and followed as close behind him as she could.

He kept them moving in a westward direction, changing streets at random and always checking to make sure no one was following them. At Rue Duguay-Trouin they went left, then veered onto Rue Huysmans. The streets here were residential stone buildings not unlike the one Liz lived in. When they reached the corner of Rue Notre Dame des Champs and Rue de Rennes, Nate guided Liz under the awning of a patisserie, thinking it was safe enough to take a short rest.

'Are you okay?' he asked.

'Fine,' she said, but her trembling jaw revealed the truth.

They needed to get out of the rain and dry off, fast. He looked through the window into the patisserie. Definitely dry, and probably warm, too. But Nate was hesitant to slow their progress. At the moment, putting as much distance as possible between themselves and the apartment building was their number one goal.

A taxi? Not the best option. A cabbie might remember them. Steal a car? Even in the rain,

271

they might be noticed. Then Nate spotted an entrance to the Métro across the street. He'd avoided the stations closer to Liz's place, but they were far enough away now that the risk was minimized, and with the way Liz was shivering, he knew they had little choice.

'This way,' he said, then led her over to the stairs and down into the station.

He could feel her trembling under his arm. Whether it was from the cold or from fear, he couldn't be sure. He guided her over to a map on the wall and said, 'We need to get as far away from this part of town as possible. So I need you to tell me which way we should go.'

'Okay,' she said, her voice weak. 'We're here.' She pointed to a station called Saint-Placide. 'Only one line. The four.'

Nate examined the map. South wouldn't get them very far.

'Looks like we should go north,' he said.

'If we go all the way to Gare du Nord, we'll have lots of choices of where we can go from there.'

'Perfect. You're doing great.'

She smiled weakly. Within five minutes they were settled on a northbound train, as far from the other passengers as possible. With nothing to do for the first time since Julien had pounded on Liz's door, Nate pulled out his cell phone to check it. As he looked at the display, he realized there was something he should have done before they'd even left Liz's apartment.

'Did you bring your phone?' he asked.

'My phone?'

'Yes. Do you have it?'

'It's in my purse.'

'Let me see it.'

She furrowed her brow.

'Please,' he insisted.

Liz opened her purse and hunted around until she found her phone, then reluctantly handed it to him. Immediately, he popped open the back and removed the battery and SIM card.

'What are you doing?' she asked.

'You can get a new one later,' he said as he slipped the pieces into his jacket pocket. 'This one goes in the trash.'

'Why?'

'Because they can track us using your phone even if it's off.'

'You have a phone.'

'Mine's special. Can't be tracked.'

He looked back at his cell. Two text messages, both asking the same thing.

The first was from Julien:

Are you safe?

Nate wrote a one-word reply:

Yes

But when he tried to send it, it failed. He had no signal on the train.

The second message was from Quinn:

Update

Nate typed out an answer, knowing he'd have to wait to send.

Got her out. Looking for place to lay low.
Julien working diversion.

'What are you doing?' Liz asked.

'Responding to your brother,' he said. 'He wants to know what's going on.'

She hesitated, then asked, 'You really work for him?'

'Yes.'

'And that other guy, he works for my brother, too?'

'Sometimes, I guess,' Nate said.

'You guess?'

'Yesterday was the first time I met him.'

She was quiet for a while. 'What exactly is it my brother does?'

'I think maybe he should answer that one.'

'But he's not here. You are.'

Nate had no response for that, so he kept his mouth shut.

They rode in silence, stopping at several stations before Liz suddenly sat straight up. 'My mother. If people were coming after me, do you think someone might go after her also?'

'We have people watching her, too. She'll be fine.'

'She can't run like me,' Liz said. 'If they get close, she won't be able to get away.'

'Your brother won't let that happen.'

'He let that happen with me,' she snapped.

Several of the passengers at the other end of

the car looked over. But they soon returned to their own worlds when it was apparent a yelling match wasn't about to break out.

After several seconds of silence, Liz whispered, 'Sorry.'

'Don't be,' Nate said. 'I'd be mad, too.'

'I need to ask you something.'

Nate gave her a sideways glance. 'Isn't that what you've been doing?'

That drew out just the barest of smiles on her face.

'Is Jake a criminal?'

Nate had to catch himself from laughing. 'No,' he said. 'Well, I guess it depends on how you look at things. Some people might think so. But no, he's no criminal.'

'That's not exactly a clear answer.'

Nate thought for a moment, then said, 'Your brother is one of the most honorable people I know. If he gives someone his word, he doesn't break it. I'd trust him with my life any day of the week.' Nate paused for a moment. 'He's not the easiest person to get to know. And he doesn't have a lot of close friends. But that's not because he's not a good person. He is. He cares more than he ever shows. He's just . . . Quinn.'

'There's that name again. Quinn.'

'It's his name now.'

'Jake Oliver wasn't good enough for him?'

'In our world it's safer to create a new identity. Hell, until just before I met you, I didn't know him by anything *but* Quinn.'

She scrutinized him again. 'So you're saying your name really isn't even Nate?'

275

He smiled. 'It depends.'

'On what?'

'On if we're talking about before or after I started working for your brother.'

Just then the train began to slow as they pulled in to a new station. Nate looked out the window. A sign on the wall said *Gare du Nord*.

'Our stop,' he said.

He stood up and walked toward the door.

★　★　★

'Movement,' Orlando said.

She was at the dining room table, her laptop in front of her. Quinn moved in behind her. The image on the screen showed the blue dot representing Nate's phone moving west from Liz's apartment. But was Liz with him? For that matter, had they been taken or were they still free?

Quinn pulled out his phone.

'You still shouldn't call him,' Orlando said.

'I'm not calling. I'm texting.'

Orlando rolled her eyes as he brought up the virtual keyboard and tapped in one word.

Update

He hit Send. If he didn't hear back within the next thirty minutes, they'd go to Paris whether it was a bad idea or not.

Orlando's phone began to ring. She looked at the display, then at Quinn. 'It's Scott Bethel.' Bethel was the person in Moscow she'd asked to follow up on the Stepka lead. She hit Accept. 'Hold on, Scott. I'm putting you on speaker.'

She set the phone down next to her computer and touched the screen.

'Okay,' she said. 'What have you learned?'

'I found this Stepka guy in an apartment full of high-end computer gear,' Bethel said. 'Didn't want to talk at first. But he's the soft type.'

'Did you hurt him?' Quinn asked.

'Didn't have to,' Bethel said. 'I don't think he goes out much.' Bethel's specialty was getting in and out of places unseen. Though he wasn't large like Julien, he was solid, and could be intimidating if he wanted to.

'Where is he now?'

'Sitting in front of me.'

'What?'

'I'm in his apartment. We just had a nice little talk. But I thought you might want to hear directly from him what he had to say.'

'I'd love to.'

'Let me put him on speaker.' There was a bit of static, then Bethel said in a voice more distant than before, 'All right, Stepka. Why don't you tell my friend what you just told me?'

Silence.

'Stepka. My name is Quinn. Jonathan Quinn. I believe you were doing a little research on me. I'd like to know why.'

More silence.

'So you're not going to talk to my friend?' Bethel asked. 'Maybe this will change your mind.'

There was a loud crash and the sound of

something breaking into several pieces.

'No, don't!' a voice yelled. English with a Russian accent. Stepka.

'What was that?' Quinn asked.

'This kid's got more computer equipment jammed in here than most IT departments I've seen. Well, a little less than he had a moment ago.' Bethel paused. 'How about we try this monitor now?'

'No! No, I will talk.'

'Then talk.'

'Mr. Quinn. I . . . I was only checking on you because . . . because you have been getting in our way.'

'In your way of what?' Quinn asked.

'Our search for the Ghost.'

'The Ghost?'

'His real name is Palavin. Former KGB. A butcher.'

That jibed with both what Orlando had uncovered and what the Russian woman had claimed. 'Why are you looking for him?'

'We want to . . . talk with him.'

'Talk with him? Really? I get the feeling you want to do more than that.'

Stepka said nothing.

'All right,' Quinn said. 'Tell me about the woman.'

'What woman?'

'The woman who is here searching for him.'

'Petra,' Stepka said. 'She is the team leader.'

'How many in her team?'

'Now? Just two. She and a man named Mikhail.'

278

'Why is she interested in me?'

'You have information that will help us find Palavin.'

'I have no such information.'

'Of course you have,' Stepka said. 'You've been working for him. We need what you know. Petra will find you. She will — '

'Take him off speaker, Scott,' Quinn said. He shared a look with Orlando.

There was a faint click, then Bethel said, 'Okay, it's just me.'

'Put him on ice for right now. Someplace no one can find him for a few days. I'll let you know when you can release him. But don't hurt him. Feed him and give him a place to sleep.'

'I can do that.'

'Good,' Quinn said. 'We'll be in touch.'

As soon as he hung up, Orlando said, 'What do you think?'

'If Palavin really was Wills's client, then that might explain why Annabel Taplin had his picture with mine. But even then, whatever these Russians are up to could mess things up for us. My family's safety comes first. I'm not going to allow them to get in my way.' He paused. 'What we really need to do is have a little chat with Ms. Taplin. Can you find out if she's returned to London yet?'

Orlando smiled. 'I can do that.'

32

Petra visited restaurants and grocery stores and hotels and massage parlors and whatever else she could find that was owned and operated by Russian expats. At first, when they realized she was also Russian, they were friendly enough. But when she showed the drawing of Quinn and started asking more questions, they became wary. Some refused to give her any more answers, while others kept their responses to one or two words.

She knew the look in their eyes well. She'd borne it herself more times than she could remember. It was the fear and suspicion that came with having grown up in the former Soviet Union.

She returned to the apartment just before 9 p.m., unsuccessful and completely drained.

'Mikhail?' she called out.

There was no response.

She sat down at the table and tried calling Stepka, but he didn't answer. So she left a message, folded her arms, and lay her head down, intending to rest her eyes for a moment.

The sound of a key turning in the lock of the front door made her snap back up. The side of her mouth was damp, and she realized she'd fallen asleep. She glanced at her watch, surprised to see a half hour had passed.

She rubbed her face as she turned toward the

door. That's when she got her second surprise. It wasn't Mikhail. It was a young woman.

She was beautiful. Long blonde hair that had been clipped in place so that it flowed down her back, bright blue eyes behind a fashionable pair of semi-rimless glasses, and a trim but appropriately rounded figure that would go unnoticed by no one.

'Who are you?' Petra asked, rising from her chair.

An instant later Mikhail entered behind the woman. 'Please,' he said to the girl in Russian, motioning toward the table. 'Sit down.' The woman looked at him uncertainly, so he smiled and pointed again. 'Please.'

Once she'd sat, Mikhail signaled for Petra to join him near the door.

'Who is she?' Petra whispered.

'Her name is Natalia,' he said. 'She recognized the picture.'

Petra's eyes widened as she glanced at the girl.

'I was checking a couple of Russian-run hotels in the West End,' Mikhail went on.

'She saw him in a hotel?' Petra asked.

'Well, yes, but not the one I found her in. She works at two different places. Where I met her, and another in Belgravia called the Silvain Hotel. It's not owned by Russians, but they employ several of our people.'

'So she saw him there?'

Mikhail led Petra to the table, then said to Natalia, 'Tell her what you told me.'

The girl looked nervous. 'A man like the one in the picture arrived at our hotel last night.'

'The Silvain,' Mikhail clarified.

'Yes.'

'Describe him,' Petra said.

Natalia bit her lip, then closed her eyes for a moment. 'Brown hair, dark and cut short above his ears. I don't know age, probably less than forty.'

'Height? Weight?'

'Maybe five foot ten. Normal weight. In shape.'

'Did you at least get his name?'

'The last name he used was Shelby. The first name I don't remember. I wasn't the one who checked him in, so I didn't look at his passport.'

Shelby? The name meant nothing to Petra. 'Did he arrive alone?'

'Yes.'

'And you're sure he looked like the man in the drawing.'

'Very close,' Natalia said. 'Please, I need to leave. I'm supposed to be at work by ten, so I'm already going to be late.'

'Where are you working tonight?' Petra asked.

'The Silvain.'

Petra looked at Mikhail. 'What do you think?'

'It's worth checking.'

She nodded. It's what she'd been thinking, too. To Natalia, she said, 'Did you see him leave this morning yet?'

'No, but my shift was over at seven a.m. Can I go now?'

'We'll all go,' Petra grabbed the girl by the arm and started to pull her up. 'Come on. We don't want you to be late.'

Despite her reluctance, Natalia proved more than adequate. Not only did she supply Petra and Mikhail with all the information the hotel had on James Shelby, she also learned from one of her colleagues that Mr. Shelby had left the hotel around 8 a.m. that morning and had not returned.

To top it off, Natalia made a copy of the keycard to Mr. Shelby's room.

Petra and Mikhail had waited down the street, out of sight, while all this had gone on. When Natalia showed up with the information *and* the key, Petra paid her the two hundred pounds she had promised her.

'And our rooms?' Petra asked.

'Two,' Natalia said quickly. 'In the same part of the hotel as Mr. Shelby, but one floor up. I've put them on hold, but you'll have to check in at the desk.'

'Of course.' Petra handed Natalia an extra fifty for her efforts. 'Thank you for your help.'

The girl tried to smile, then said, 'I must go now.'

'If we need anything else, we'll let you know,' Petra said.

It didn't seem to be what Natalia wanted to hear, but she tried to smile, then retreated back to the Silvain.

'How do you want to do this?' Mikhail asked.

'You check us in,' Petra said. 'I'll have a look at Mr. Shelby's room.'

Petra entered the Silvain and walked purposefully past the front desk toward the lounge. In the narrow corridor beyond, she found the elevator, and beside it a stairway. She rode the elevator up to the floor Shelby's room was on, then followed the numbers on the doors until she reached the right one.

Leaning close, she listened. There was dead silence on the other side. She pulled out the duplicate keycard and held it to the lock.

There was a gentle click, and she slipped inside.

The room was dark, not quite pitch black, but close enough. 'Housekeeping,' she said, her voice barely above a whisper. She stepped to the end of the entryway and peeked into the room. The bed was made and empty. She stepped around the corner and nudged open the door to the bathroom. It was even darker inside than the rest of the room, and equally as unoccupied.

As expected, Mr. Shelby was still out.

She pulled a penlight from her pocket. The first thing she checked was the small wardrobe cabinet next to the window. Empty. That wasn't necessarily unusual. Many people preferred leaving their belongings in their suitcases when they traveled. Of course, that should have meant there was a suitcase in the room. There wasn't. In fact, there were no bags of any kind.

Petra frowned.

According to his registration form, Mr. Shelby had reserved the room for an entire week. So then, where was his luggage?

She moved into the bathroom. Towels folded and ready for use, fresh bottles of shampoo and conditioner, but no personal items whatsoever.

284

She touched the sink near the drain. Bone dry. The same went for the shower.

Back in the bedroom, she located the wastebasket. Also empty.

The room wasn't being used at all, but why? The only reason she could come up with was that he was using it as a safe location, in case it was needed later.

The question now was, would Mr. Shelby come back?

33

'I don't think she's going to show,' Quinn said.

Orlando touched him on his thigh. 'Let's give it another hour. If we don't see her by then, we'll come back in the morning.'

Quinn grimaced, but didn't get up. He knew she was right. It was just that he was having a hard time reining in his impatience. Something that seldom happened.

They were sitting by the front window of the Queen Anne Pub. From there, they had a direct view of the office building across the street where Wright Bains Securities was located. It was six stories of glass, steel, and stone, surrounded on three sides by similar generic, soul-sucking structures. The kind of place a secret division of MI6 would choose. There were two ways in: a glass door main entrance at the center of the building, and a less-flashy steel door off to the left. From Quinn and Orlando's position, they could see both.

With Wills dead, Taplin was Quinn's best chance at getting information. His biggest fear had been that she was still in New York. But Orlando was able to learn that a U.K. citizen named Annabel Taplin had returned to London the night before. Which meant there was a very good chance she had returned to work that morning.

When they got there, it was already lunchtime.

Quinn had hoped they might spot her going out to eat with some of her colleagues, but no luck. And, as the afternoon turned to evening with no sign of Annabel among those heading home for the day, he began to wonder if she had come in at all.

Orlando picked up the cup of coffee she'd been drinking and took another sip. Quinn, who had been nursing the same beer for over an hour, reached for his glass, but then decided against it. Instead, he pushed his chair back and stood up.

'Toilet,' he said, walking away.

'Thanks for the information,' Orlando called after him.

He headed across the pub and down a small hallway to the public toilets. He didn't really need to use them; he just couldn't stand sitting around any longer.

The men's room was a single stall and one urinal. Tucked in behind the door was a sink with a mirror above it. It had obviously become a tradition to put stickers on the walls and mirror, most touting bands.

Quinn turned on the cold water, then wiped some of it across his face. He felt the need to do something. Anything. This waiting was killing him. Usually he could be on a stakeout for days before he'd feel the need to get things moving. But never before had it been his own family who was being threatened.

He stared at himself in an open spot on the mirror between a sticker for the Arctic Monkeys and a throw-back for Stiff Little Fingers, but didn't like what was looking back. There was something in his eyes that he had never seen.

Fear.

He couldn't deny it. It was staring right back at him.

Fear that he wasn't in control of what was going on. Fear that he wouldn't be able to make the problem go away. And most of all, fear that because he'd put his family in the line of fire, something would happen to them.

He had to make this right. And once he did, he could never again assume that Liz and his mother were safe. For so long he'd been able to keep their existence a secret, but that secret was gone now, gone forever.

Quinn grabbed a towel and dried his face. What all this meant about his future was something he was going to have to deal with once he'd taken care of his current nightmare. He was nowhere near in the right frame of mind to think about it now.

His phone began to vibrate. It was Nate.

Finally.

He hit Accept, then headed back into the pub.

'Where are you?' he asked.

'We're safe,' Nate said. 'We found a room near — '

'Hold on,' Quinn said, cutting him off.

Orlando was no longer sitting down. She was standing near the door, waving him to hurry over. He took the phone from this ear, then pushed his way through the growing crowd.

'What is it?' he asked.

'The woman on the sidewalk across the street.

288

About thirty feet left of the main entrance. Is that her?'

Quinn followed her gaze. Though the sun had gone down, the streetlamps provided more than enough light to see.

'It's her,' he said. 'Go.'

Orlando headed out of the pub.

'Sorry,' he said into the phone. '*Where are you?*'

'A small hotel near Sacré Coeur.'

Outside the pub, Quinn could see Orlando cross the street and fall in about a half block behind Annabel. The MI6 woman had no idea who Orlando was, so the plan they had worked out was for Orlando to follow her, and Quinn to follow Orlando a couple of blocks back, using the GPS tracker in his phone. That way there would be no chance Taplin would spot him.

'Did they check your ID?'

'Of course not,' Nate said, his tone a little pissed off. 'We wouldn't be here if they did.'

Quinn grimaced. That was basic training stuff. A dumb question to ask, but his objectivity was a little blurred at the moment. 'How's Liz?'

There was a pause, then when Nate spoke again his voice was lower. 'She's a little freaked out. But that's understandable. I'm actually surprised she's still functioning at all . . . She *has* been asking a lot of questions.'

'What kind of questions?'

'About you. About what you do . . . what I do.'

'What have you told her?'

'I said that she needs to ask you.'

That was something else he was going to have

289

to deal with, Quinn realized. Liz was going to want to know what was going on. His mother, too, for that matter. 'You did the right thing,' he said as he started for the door.

'What if she keeps pushing?'

'Tell her what you already told her.'

'I'm not sure if that's going to be enough.'

Quinn stepped outside. Orlando was no longer in sight. He started down the sidewalk in the direction he had seen her go. 'Is she giving you trouble?'

'Not yet,' Nate said. 'But I can see it coming. Don't forget, she *is* your sister. She's not stupid.'

No, she wasn't stupid. 'Then use your best judgment. Tell her what you need to tell her, but nothing more.'

'I'm not going to lie to her. I need her to cooperate with me, and she won't if she thinks I'm just handing her another line.'

'Okay. No lies,' he said.

'Thanks.'

Quinn stopped as he neared the end of the block. There was no way to know which direction Orlando and Annabel had gone. He was going to have to use the tracker on his phone. 'I want you to get her out of Paris,' Quinn said.

'I thought you might. Where do you want us to go?'

Good question. What Quinn really wanted was for her to be close, but London might be just as dangerous for her as Paris. Still . . .

'Bring her to England. Don't take the Chunnel. Get a car and drive to Belgium. You can get a ferry in Ostend. We'll get some rush

290

docs for her. I think Orlando knows someone there who can probably do them for you tonight. I'll have her let you know where and when to pick them up. Then I want you out of Paris by morning.'

'I'll make sure we're up early and moving.'

'And Nate . . . '

'I know. Take care of Liz.'

Quinn hesitated. 'Yes. But also yourself.'

★ ★ ★

After almost losing them in the Underground, Quinn caught up to Orlando not far from Russell Square Station.

'She went in there,' Orlando said, nodding down the street at a tan, three-story brick structure that had been designed to look like a series of row houses.

'Apartments?' Quinn asked.

'Yes. The index next to the front door lists twenty-four residents.'

'Must go back a little ways. Doesn't look like that many from here.'

'Unfortunately, yes. I was hoping I'd see a light go on in one of the rooms when she went in.' She shook her head. 'Nothing.'

'What about her name? Isn't she listed?'

'There's no Taplin.'

'Do you think she might have spotted you, and used this place to throw you off?'

'I wondered about that,' Orlando said. 'But I don't think so. She was exhausted, even fell asleep for a few minutes on the train. I don't think she noticed much of anything.'

'Could have been faking it,' Quinn suggested.

'She wasn't.'

Quinn looked back down the street. 'Well, we can't go door-to-door.'

'Yeah. Bad idea.'

'And if she was that tired, she's probably in for the evening.'

'I'd agree with that, too.'

Quinn turned to her, his eyes narrowed. 'Then, what do *you* think we should do?'

She took another look at the building, then said, 'Nothing's going to happen tonight. Let's come back early tomorrow and pick her up when she leaves for work.'

Quinn frowned.

'You could use some sleep yourself,' she said.

'I'm fine.'

'No. You're not.'

He stared at the building a moment longer, knowing she was right but wishing there was more he could do. He rubbed a hand across his eyes. The weight of it all seemed to be increasing every second.

'You're not alone,' Orlando said softly as she put an arm around him. 'This is our family in trouble, not just yours. And if we want to help them, we need to be sharp.'

He opened his eyes and looked at her, saying nothing.

'Okay?' she asked.

He said nothing for a moment, then he nodded once. 'Okay.'

34

'I know,' Nate said. 'Take care of Liz.'

Quinn hesitated. 'Yes. But also yourself.'

Then the line went dead.

Nate stared at his cell. His boss didn't sound quite like the Quinn he knew. But, of course, Quinn had never been in a situation like this before. Nate had no idea how he would handle it if it was happening to him.

'What's wrong?'

Liz was standing in the doorway to the tiny bathroom. She wore a baggy T-shirt they'd purchased that afternoon and was drying her hair with one of the thin hotel towels.

Nate slipped his cell into this pocket. 'Everything's fine.'

'Were you on the phone?'

He hesitated. *No lies.* 'Yes. I was talking to Quinn.'

'I don't think I'm ever going to get used to that name.'

'I could try to call him Jake if that helps.'

'That would be just as odd for you. Call him Quinn.' She let out a humorless laugh, then said 'Quinn' again as if she was trying it out.

She shook her head, and rubbed the towel across her hair one last time before tossing it on the floor in the corner.

The room was barely big enough for the full-size bed that dominated it. There was no dresser, no desk, no table, no chairs. Just the bed. But the clerk downstairs had taken cash and had asked no questions, so the room was perfect.

'How was the water?'

'Started hot,' she said, then added, 'but more lukewarm by the end.'

'No worries. I'm fine with lukewarm.'

The truth was he was glad she'd used up the hot water. The rain had stopped around four, so by the time they found the hotel their clothes were no longer soaking wet, only damp. But Liz had continued to shiver.

That would be ironic, Nate thought. *Save her from whoever it was who was trying to kill her, only for her to die of pneumonia.*

They did an awkward dance around the end of the bed. His hand accidently brushed against her stomach, but she showed no signs of noticing. Nate entered the bathroom and shut the door behind him. He put the lid down on the toilet, then sat down so he could remove his prosthetic leg. As he did, he could feel his stump sigh in relief.

Even on the most strenuous jobs with Quinn, he'd seldom had to push his leg as much as he had escaping with Liz. So it wasn't surprising that his thigh muscles ached.

There was a knock at the bathroom door.

'I'm sorry,' Liz said from the other side. 'I meant to grab my jeans so I could dry them on the heater.'

'Hold on,' Nate said.

He spotted them on the floor, picked them up, then opened the door just enough to slip them through.

'Thanks,' she said, then added, 'My purse is in there, too.'

The smile she gave him made him forget for a moment about the pain in his leg.

'Sure,' he said.

He found her purse and gave it to her.

'Anything else?'

'No,' she said, again with the smile. 'Enjoy your shower. Maybe it's hot by now.'

As he closed the door he couldn't help thinking that maybe he needed a cold shower more than a hot one. What he got was the lukewarm one he'd said earlier would be okay, but turned out to be as unsatisfying as it sounded. He spent the whole time alternating between praying to the water gods for hot and trying not to think about Liz. He was unsuccessful on both fronts.

Oh, no, he thought as the realization struck him. He'd been so focused on getting Liz to safety, he hadn't thought about their sleeping arrangements. They were going to have to share a bed.

What if he reached out and put an arm around her in his sleep? How would she react to that? Perhaps he should suggest that he sleep on the top of the covers while she slept beneath. That would put a nice, physical barrier between them, and lessen the chance that Quinn would kill him and drop his body in the middle of the ocean later.

When he finished showering, he dried off and pulled on a T-shirt and clean pair of boxer briefs from his backpack.

He was still thinking about the potential pitfalls of who slept where as he opened the door and hopped into the bedroom. 'Do you have a side of the bed you prefer?'

Liz was sitting at the end of the mattress, holding a small brush in midair, but she was staring at Nate, a look of confusion on her face.

'What happened?' she stuttered.

'I'm sorry?'

'Your . . . your leg.'

His brow furrowed momentarily, then he realized he'd never said anything about his missing leg. *Like that would have been an easy topic to bring up.* 'I was . . . in an . . . ' *No lies.* 'I got hit by a car.'

'Oh, my God. When?'

'A little over a year ago.'

'But you were running today.'

'Prosthetics have come a long way,' Nate said, echoing one of his doctors.

She moved around the bed to get a better look.

'Does it hurt?'

'Just sore. Like anyone would be after the day we had.' Perhaps not like anyone, but it was more the truth stretched than a lie.

'Do you want to sit down?' She moved out of his way so he could get to the bed.

'I'm not an invalid,' he said.

'I didn't mean to — I'm sorry.'

'Hey, it's okay.' He pivoted around, then sat on the bed and smiled at her. 'Thanks.'

She sat next to him.

'Were you in the car when it happened?'

'I'd rather not talk about it,' he said. 'You didn't answer my question. Which side of the bed do you want?'

She was silent for several seconds. 'This happened because you were working for my brother, didn't it?'

'Liz, please. I don't want to get into — '

'What is he?' she asked. 'An assassin? Is that what it is? He kills people for a living?'

'No,' he said, knowing he was walking a fine line. 'That's not his job.'

'Then, what is it? What could he do that would make those men come after me? That would cause you to lose your leg?'

'I really think this is something you should hear from him.'

'He's. Not. Here,' she said. 'And I need to know. I want to understand.'

He thought for a moment, then took each of her hands in his. She didn't fight it. 'I'm not going to tell you everything,' Nate said. 'I don't think that's my place.'

She started to pull away, but he held on.

'I will, however, try to tell you what I can. Okay?'

She bit her lower lip, then nodded. 'Okay.'

'Your brother doesn't work for a bank.'

Liz snorted. Then they both laughed.

'He's also not an assassin. He's hired by certain agencies and governments to provide a very specific service.'

'He's a spy?'

Nate tilted his head to the side as he raised his shoulders a few inches. 'Not exactly. But I think it would be fair to say that's the world that he plays in.'

'So he doesn't kill people,' she said.

'That's not what he's hired to do.'

'Then, what *does* he do?'

Nate hesitated. 'That's where I'm going to have to stop.'

She looked away. 'And you? What do you do?'

'I'm his apprentice.'

'His apprentice?'

'He's been training me to be — ' He paused. 'To do what he does.'

The corner of her mouth rose. 'I almost got it out of you, didn't I?'

'Almost.'

'I don't mean to sound ungrateful or anything, but he left his apprentice to take care of me? If he was really concerned, wouldn't he have stayed himself?'

'Three things,' Nate said. 'One, thanks for the confidence.' He smiled so she'd know he was giving her a hard time. 'Two, I've been his apprentice for several years now. I know what I'm doing. And three, I've never seen him act the way he has since he found out you might be in danger. He's usually one of the most calm, patient people I know. At the moment, he's scared and pissed. And the only reason he's not here now is because he's trying to find the source to stop this.' He paused. 'Liz, I don't know exactly what happened between the two of you, but I can tell you one thing. I don't think he cares for anyone more than he cares for you.'

He'd expected her to laugh that idea off, but

she remained silent, her gaze fixed on a point on the floor in front of the bathroom.

'Look, we should get some sleep while we can,' he said. 'I'm probably going to have to run out for a little while at some point between now and the morning.'

She looked scared again. 'Why?'

'I need to pick up something that will help us get someplace safe. It won't be for long.'

'Out of Paris?'

Nate nodded. 'We need to leave town as soon as we can. So we'll get up pretty early.'

'What are you getting?'

Keeping the promise to himself, he said, 'A false ID for you. So we can travel anonymously.'

'Are you kidding?'

'Not kidding at all.'

She was silent for a moment. 'Then where are we going?'

'Someplace safe.'

'That's the best you can do?'

'For now.'

She thought for a moment, then nodded.

'Good,' Nate said, pushing himself off the bed. 'Now pick a side. I'll be right out.'

'Where are you going?'

He hopped to the bathroom door. 'Forgot to brush my teeth.'

Once inside, he shut the door and turned on the water. He then picked his pants up off the floor and got his phone out of the front pocket. He shot off a quick text to Julien.

Status?

While he was waiting, he decided to go ahead and brush his teeth again, anyway. *No lies.*

His phone vibrated. Julien had responded.

> Active search still on. R u safe?

Nate typed:

> Safe. But need car. Can u help?

Twenty seconds later, from Julien:

> Think so. When?

Nate thought for a moment, then texted:

> 5:30 a.m.

It was almost a minute before Julien responded.

> Ok. Will text meeting place once arranged.

Nate sent a confirmation, then put the phone back in his pants pocket. When he opened the door, the bedroom was dark. He flipped off the bathroom light, but he'd seen enough to know Liz had taken the far side of the bed. She had also folded back the covers on his side so he could get in.

'I was thinking,' he said. 'I mean if it makes you feel more comfortable, I could sleep on top of the blankets.'

'You'd get too cold,' she said.

'It's fine. I can put on some of my clothes.'

'No,' she said. 'Please just get in.'

He stood by the bed, paralyzed.

'Nate, please,' she said. It was the first time she'd called him by that name. 'It's okay.'

He lay down on his back and pulled the covers over him. He and Liz weren't touching, but he could feel her warmth only inches away. He could also sense that her eyes were open. He was about to tell her to go to sleep, but she spoke first.

'Tell me that I have nothing to be worried about, and it will all be okay.'

'It *will* all be okay,' he said. 'I'll make sure of it.'

Silence.

'Why are they coming after me?'

'They think they can control Quinn if they have you.'

'But they can't?'

'No.'

'He'd just let them have me?'

'That's not what I meant,' Nate said. 'They wouldn't be able to control him, because if they did somehow take you he would come after them and get you back. And if that happened, they wouldn't know what hit them.'

'He could do that?'

'Yes.'

More silence, then the rustling of blankets as Liz turned on her side toward the window.

'I'm sorry I lied to you,' he said. 'We weren't sure if there was going to be any trouble, so it seemed best to — '

'It's okay. I get it,' she said.

301

Nate hesitated, then said, 'We should get some sleep.'

She didn't say anything, but he thought she nodded her head.

'It's all going to be okay,' he said as he instinctively reached out and put a hand on her shoulder. 'Just try to sleep.'

Her left hand touched his. He thought she was going to push his off, but she grabbed it instead, pulling it around her so that he was hugging her. As if it were a single movement, they moved closer together, her back pressing against his chest.

She seemed about to say something, but her voice remained silent. He, too, opened his mouth to speak, but no words came.

After a few minutes, he could feel her body begin to relax. He thought she had fallen asleep, so he started to pull his arm into a more comfortable position. As he did, his hand brushed against her breast.

Before he could pull it away, she turned under his arm until she was facing him. She looked at him, her eyes soft. The fear was still there, but there was something more, too.

He leaned forward, his lips finding hers.

As her left leg slipped over the stump of his right, she hesitated. But it was only a second, and after that it didn't seem to matter to her that he wasn't whole.

35

The 2 a.m. pickup went off without a hitch. Nate had slept for just over an hour and a half before he got up and made his way to the trash can on Rue de Rivoli across from the Jardin des Tuileries. Just as arranged, inside he found Liz's false documents wrapped in a paper bag, stuffed halfway down.

Nate had been afraid when he returned he wouldn't be able to fall back asleep. But within a minute of closing his eyes, he was out.

At 4:30 a.m. he woke again, courtesy, as it so often was, of the alarm on his phone. Liz was draped across him, her head on his chest, her legs intertwined with his.

He started to stroke her hair, then stopped, suddenly realizing what he was doing. *I should have slept on the floor. Or the bathroom. Hell, I should have taken a second room.* His hand started moving again, lifting strands of hair from her face.

Her eyelids parted and she looked at him.

'Time to get up?' she asked.

'Almost,' he said.

'What are you doing?'

'Your hair fell on my hand.'

She smiled, then pulled herself onto him.

'You probably shouldn't do that,' he said.

'You want me to stop?'

In his mind, he said, *Yes*, but in the real

world, he slid a hand behind her head and pulled her mouth to his.

When they had made love before falling asleep, there had been an urgency to it, a want and desire that possessed them both. This time their motions started slower, as if they wanted to remember every second. But then the intensity overtook them, and by the time they finished, Nate now on top, they were both drenched in sweat.

Nate held on to her for a few moments. 'We're already late.'

'Just a little longer.'

'I want to.'

'Then do it.'

'Julien is going to meet us with a car at five-thirty,' he said.

'When did you arrange that?' she asked.

'Last night.'

'Sneaky,' she said. 'What time is it now?'

He looked at his watch. 'Crap,' he said.

'What?'

'It's almost five. We need to move.'

'Once more,' she whispered. 'He'll wait. And we might not get another chance for a while.'

She slipped her hand between his legs and moved her lips to his ear.

Yeah, he thought. *Julien can wait.*

★ ★ ★

By the time Nate and Liz left the hotel, it was already twenty minutes after five. There was no way they were going to make it on time. Nate pulled out his phone and sent Julien a quick text:

304

Outside, it took a few minutes longer than he'd hoped to find a taxi, but once they did, traffic was light, so it wasn't long before the driver dropped them off near the entrance to the Sully-Morland Métro station on Boulevard Henri IV. As soon as the cab left, Nate pointed at the station entrance.

'Wait down there,' he told Liz, then handed her a piece of paper. 'That's your brother's number. Give me fifteen minutes. If I'm not back, find a pay phone and call him.'

'What do you mean, if you're not back? Why wouldn't you come back?'

'It's just in case. Don't worry, I'll be back.'

'Then I don't need this.'

She held the paper out to him, but Nate insisted. 'Just keep it. For me, okay?'

She didn't look happy, but slipped the paper into the pocket of her jeans. Once she'd descended the stairs, he walked to the end of the small cobblestone square and turned onto Rue de Sully. Julien's message had said he'd be parked somewhere along the northeast side.

Rue de Sully was a one-way street with empty cars lining each side, narrowing the useable space to a one-car lane down the middle. Keeping to the opposite side of the road, Nate searched the parked cars for the silhouette of a man sitting behind the wheel. But the further he went without seeing anyone, the more concerned he became. Had Julien already left?

He glanced at his watch. The deadline he'd

given Liz was already a third of the way gone. Either he found Julien in the next few minutes, or he turned around and figured out some other way to get them out of town.

Empty, empty, empty, he noted as he continued to check each car. *Where the hell are you?*

He was almost ready to give up when he spotted Julien six cars ahead on the other side. At least he thought it was Julien. The silhouette sitting behind the wheel of the beat-up blue Peugeot looked right, but all Nate could see was the back of the man's head and his shoulders.

Still pretending to be out on an early morning stroll, he didn't cross the street until he was three cars past Julien's position. As he did he allowed himself a quick glance back at the Peugeot. Definitely Julien. But, he realized, something was wrong. The Frenchman was in the exact same position he'd been when Nate first spotted him.

Nate turned down the sidewalk so that he would pass the Peugeot. As he neared, he could see that both of Julien's eyes were closed. For a split second he thought that the Frenchman had fallen asleep. But another step closer brought something else into view.

A dark, damp stain surrounding a hole in the middle of Julien's shirt. *Not asleep.*

Nate's mind screamed at him to run, but his pace didn't falter. He knew showing no reaction was the only thing that might save him. He'd only gone about five car lengths when he heard footsteps on the sidewalk behind him. He searched the road ahead, thinking there would be others coming from that direction, boxing him in. He pulled out his phone, accessed the keyboard, and began typing.

The steps behind him increased their pace. He counted three separate sets.

'*Pardon, monsieur,*' a voice called out.

Nate was almost done. Only two more words.

'*Monsieur,*' a second voice, more forceful than the first.

Nate looked over his shoulder, his face displaying the appropriate mix of caution and uncertainty. The three men were only twenty feet away. Two were about the same size as Nate, while the third was a few inches shorter. Nate had seen them all before. He'd watched from across the street as they'd come rushing out of Liz's apartment building with Julien the previous afternoon.

'*Oui?*' he said.

'*Parlez-vous anglais?*' one of the tall ones asked.

'*Un peu . . .* a little,' Nate said, hoping his accent was convincing.

'You're French?'

'Of course.'

'You live around here?'

'*Pourquoi?* Eh, why? Are you lost?'

The one doing the talking smiled, while the other two stared at Nate. 'Not lost,' he said. 'And I'm willing to bet you're not from around here either.'

'*Je ne comprends pas,*' Nate said.

'I think you do.' The talker looked at the other tall one. 'What did Julien call him? Nat? No, it was — '

Before he could finish, Nate's foot slammed into the man's stomach. The talker flew backward on his ass, doubling over as he lay on the sidewalk.

The other two were quick to respond, but not quick enough. Even as he was kicking, Nate had switched his phone to his left hand and had reached under his jacket with his right, grabbing the Glock he'd gotten from Julien.

The short one was pulling his own gun free, so Nate shot him first. The second guy didn't even try for his gun. Instead he rushed forward before Nate could aim at him.

They crashed to the sidewalk, the attacker landing on top of Nate and nearly knocking the breath out of him.

The man reached for the gun, gripping Nate's wrist with one hand and going for the barrel with the other. Nate rolled to his left and threw the guy's weight off him. A movement beyond the man caught Nate's attention. It was the first guy, the talker. He was pushing himself to his feet, a pistol already in his hand.

The guy on the ground didn't see this, so Nate let the man twist his arm until the barrel was pointed at his partner. Nate pulled the trigger. The bullet hit the talker just below the neck, dropping him to the sidewalk in a heap.

The shot, having gone off less than a foot from the ear of the guy struggling with Nate, stunned him. Nate wrenched his hand free and pushed himself away along the ground. As the man clawed at his jacket, going for his own weapon, Nate shot him in the chest.

Three dead, and enough gunfire to wake up several blocks' worth of potential witnesses.

Nate scrambled to his feet.

He spotted his phone and picked it up, but it was immediately apparent he would never be able to use it again. The display screen was smashed in and the frame was bent. Not wanting to leave it behind for the police to find, he stuffed it in his pocket, then began running down the street.

There were no sirens yet, but they'd be coming, and soon.

Nate headed back toward the Peugeot. As he passed it, he realized there weren't three dead. There were four. 'I'm sorry, Julien,' he whispered.

He ran as fast as his one and a half legs could carry him, circling around the neighborhood so that he'd approach the Métro station from the opposite direction. Ahead he could see the police had already arrived at the crime scene, the flashing lights of their cars reflecting along the buildings down Rue de Sully.

Nate again looked at his watch. He was ten minutes late. If Liz had done as he'd asked, she should have already called Quinn, and he would have told her to get the hell out of there.

He was just about to descend the stairs when she called out to him. 'Nate!'

She was across Boulevard Henri IV, standing near the entrance to a small park. He waited for a break in the traffic, then jogged over to her.

'Why are you still here?' he asked.

His tone made her pull back a couple of

309

inches. 'I didn't know — ' Her voice faltered.

'Did you call Quinn?'

'No,' she whispered.

'Why not?'

'I heard the gunshots. I thought they'd killed you. I didn't know what to do.'

He pulled her to him, wrapping his arms around her. She resisted only a second, then grabbed him tightly. She'd been as concerned about him as he'd been about her.

'It's okay. I'm fine,' he said. 'But we need to get out of here.'

'Those *were* shots, right?'

'Yes,' he said.

'They tried to kill you?'

'They didn't try hard enough.'

'Will they come after us?'

'Not those guys,' he said.

'No?'

He knew she didn't really want to know the truth, so he just shook his head, and he guided her away.

36

'We should have heard from them by now,' Quinn said.

He and Orlando were at opposite ends of the street, watching Annabel Taplin's apartment building. They had their comm gear on, so were in constant contact.

'You told him to get Liz out of town, so that's what he's doing,' Orlando said. 'He'll call in as soon as he can.'

'I know, I know.'

A large vapor cloud formed in front of his face as he let out a breath. The weather had taken a decidedly colder turn that morning, and even with a muffler wrapped around his neck and the collar of his jacket flipped up, Quinn was freezing.

'We should have just staked out her office again,' Quinn said. It was almost 8 a.m. and so far no sign of Annabel. Perhaps the building *had* been a ruse.

'Why don't you go grab some coffee,' Orlando told him. 'I can watch things here.'

'I'm fine. I'm just . . . '

'Annoying me?'

'Sorry. I'm fine.'

'Keep it up and I'm sending you home.'

Seven minutes later, movement in front of the building made him forget the fact he was losing feeling in his cheeks. 'Is that her?'

Orlando was positioned closer. 'It's her.'

'Finally,' he said. 'I'm heading for the station.'

They had made the assumption that Annabel would use the Russell Square Underground station like she had the night before. Quinn headed there first, while Orlando kept Annabel in sight in case she went somewhere else.

If Annabel stuck to her script and did a reverse of her trip home, she would go one stop to Holborn, then switch to the Central Line. So Quinn went straight to the platform and found a spot against the wall halfway down, blending into the rush-hour crowd.

He glanced up at the display screen hanging from the ceiling. The next train was due in three minutes, with another five minutes later. He then turned so he could see the platform entrance, and waited.

Annabel arrived just as the sound of the first train began rumbling through the tunnel. She walked through the crowd, passing within five feet of Quinn, before stopping, her eyes never straying in his direction.

Orlando showed up a few seconds later. She eased her way through the other commuters and into position directly behind Annabel. The train whooshed into the station with a sudden roar, and the waiting commuters acknowledged the arrival by pushing themselves closer together.

As the train slowed to a stop, there was a pause, then the doors slid open. As one, the crowd lurched forward. Annabel entered the car and grabbed ahold of one of the poles. She turned back toward the door just as Quinn entered.

He didn't even try to hide.

The look on her face was at first blank, then confused, as if she recognized him but wasn't sure from where. Then, almost as quickly, her eyes went wide.

Quinn raised a finger to his lips as he reached out with his other hand and grabbed the same pole she was holding on to.

Her eyes darted around. 'You're fine where you are,' Orlando whispered into her ear. She was beside Annabel, pressing up against her.

Annabel looked at her, then glanced down at where their bodies made contact. Quinn knew she was feeling the barrel of Orlando's hairbrush against her ribs. An adequate substitute for a concealed gun under the circumstances, though ultimately less lethal.

'Hello, Annabel,' Quinn said.

'What do you want?'

'We'll get to that when we're alone.'

'I'm not going anywhere with you.'

'You're not?' He gave Orlando a quick glance, and she shoved the barrel of her faux gun hard into Annabel's ribs. 'Next time I tell her to pull the trigger.'

'What?' Annabel said, a nervous smile on her lips. 'You wouldn't.'

He stared at her, his face completely blank. 'Try me.'

Her smile faded quickly.

'I suggest you keep quiet and do exactly what we say,' Quinn told her. 'Understood?'

Annabel started to speak, but Quinn shook his head and raised his finger back to his mouth. So

313

she stopped, then nodded.

'Good,' he said. 'My associate is going to stay right next to you like she's your best friend. Okay?'

Another nod.

'See? Not so bad.'

As the train pulled in to Holborn, Annabel tensed.

'Hold tight,' Orlando said. 'You won't be getting off here today.'

'What do you want? I don't know — ' Annabel grimaced as Orlando jabbed her abdomen again.

Quinn leaned close, his mouth an inch from her ear. 'Don't test me.'

'Sorry,' she whispered.

They rode in silence all the way to Green Park. There, with Orlando tight to Annabel's side, they navigated the warrens of the station until they reached the southbound platform for the Victoria Line.

'I could make a scene right now. There are cameras everywhere. You'd never be able to get away.'

'Perhaps,' Quinn said. 'But you'd be on the ground bleeding out, so you'd never know if we did or we didn't, would you?'

She bit her lower lip. 'You're not going to hurt me.'

'Who said anything about hurt?'

Orlando snickered. 'Give me your phone.'

Annabel hesitated, then pulled a cell phone out of the pocket of her overcoat and handed it to Orlando. Unlike the cell she'd been carrying in New York, this was a sophisticated model that must have cost someone a bundle. Orlando turned it off and dropped it into the trash.

When the train arrived, Annabel boarded without protest. This time they rode only two stops, exiting at Pimlico, then rode the escalators up from deep below the city. As they did, Quinn's phone vibrated, indicating a voicemail. He pulled it out, but had to wait until they reached the top before the signal strength was strong enough to check it.

'Quinn, it's Nate. First, Liz is fine. Second, we'll be in London at nine-thirty. I know you told me to use a less direct route, but something happened this morning and I felt the sooner we got there, the better. We're on the Eurostar and have already passed through the Chunnel. And before you ask, yes, I got the papers Orlando arranged, so no one knows we're on the train.' He paused. 'Quinn, Julien's dead. I'll give you the details later. What I need to know now is what you want me to do once we arrive.'

The message ended.

'What's wrong?' Orlando asked.

Quinn had stopped near the entrance to the station.

'Quinn?' she asked.

He glanced at Annabel, then turned to Orlando. 'There's been . . . a complication.'

Orlando looked concerned. 'Did something happen to . . . ?'

'They're both fine.'

'Then, what?'

'Julien.'

She raised an eyebrow in question.

He knew he didn't have to say anything. His expression was answer enough.

'Where are they?' she asked.

Quinn looked at his watch. It was just after nine. 'They'll be here in thirty. We'll need to split up.'

She nodded. 'Don't worry. I can take care of our friend here.'

'I'll be back soon.'

'Wait. You might want to show me where I'm supposed to take her first,' Orlando said.

'Right.' God, where was his head? 'It's not far.' He led them out of the station and down Lupus Street to the corner of Belgrave Road. 'There. Two blocks up on the left. The Silvain Hotel.' He reached into his pocket and pulled out the plastic keycard he'd been carrying for two days now, and handed it to her.

Quinn locked eyes with Annabel. 'You're going to go with my friend. Despite her size, she's a hell of a lot meaner than I am. If you're even thinking you might be able to make a break, you should reconsider. She'll kill you without hesitating. Understand?'

'Yes.' Annabel's voice was a dry croak.

'Good. She's going to ask you some questions. Do yourself a favor and answer them. If you don't, you're going to have to deal with me.'

Annabel nodded.

'I won't be long,' he told Orlando, then he ran back toward the Underground station.

37

It was a Saturday afternoon when everything changed forever.

Quinn was seventeen, and for as long as he could remember he wanted to see more than the farms and the woods of northern Minnesota. He wanted to be someplace where there were people, lots and lots of people. There was a whole world out there, a world he could reach only through the books he read. And as interesting as reading about everywhere else was, it wasn't enough. He wanted to experience it all with his own senses.

His closest friend was probably Liz, only nine at the time. Sure, there were a couple of kids he hung out with sometimes, but their dreams weren't the same as his. They thought about taking over their parents' farms, or hitting it rich at the Indian casino, or playing hockey all winter long. It wasn't that he thought his dreams were better, just different.

Liz was the only one who would listen to him without giving him that funny, you're-crazy look. He would tell her about Istanbul and Tokyo and Mecca and Prague. He would describe as best he could the mountains in Nepal, the caste system of India, the carnival celebrations in Rio de Janeiro, and the Grand Canyon in Arizona. He would show her the world atlas that he'd let no one else see, a cheap, cardboard-covered booklet with continental maps and ones of a few of the larger countries. On each he had marked in blue the places he wanted to go, circling in red those that were first priority.

Liz would listen intently, her face often reflecting his own excitement. But the place that she had fallen in love with just from his descriptions was Paris. That last summer before he left home, he read to her the whole of Victor Hugo's *Les Misérables*. Liz had cried when Éponine was shot, then cried again when Jean Valjean died.

'I don't ever want to see anyone I love die,' she had said. 'Not Mom or Dad. Not you.'

'Everyone dies someday, Liz.'

'I don't want to see it. I never want to see it.'

The end of one life and the start of another began with an argument Jake had with his father about something he could no longer remember. His relationship with his father was strained, often formal, and most times nonexistent. At least, that's how the teenage Jake perceived it. Looking back . . . well, looking back, who knew? They didn't fight often, but when they did, Jake would be so agitated it sometimes took days for him to calm down. One of the things he did to help was take a long hike in the woods. He was about to do just that when Liz had found him and reminded him about his promise to take her fishing.

So he did. And that had been the mistake.

They'd borrowed the boat from a friend in town, and gone out on the Lake of the Woods. It was a vast body of water, the kind where if you were in the middle, you'd lose sight of shore. On a map it was easy to find. It filled most of the little bump at the top of Minnesota that jutted into Canada.

The boat was a twelve-foot aluminum V-hull with a 9.9-horsepower outboard motor, more than enough power for the lightweight vessel.

Liz tried to engage him several times, but Jake just wasn't interested in talking. So after a while she gave up, and the only sounds came from the lapping of the water against the hull, and the whiz of their reels as they cast out their lines.

But the argument from that morning was still heavy on Jake's mind, and he had no patience for sitting in an aluminum tub. After an hour that seemed like a year, he said, 'Reel it in. We're done.'

'But . . . but we've just started,' Liz said.

'We've been here long enough.'

'You promised me!'

'Yeah,' he said. 'And I kept it. We're going home. I have things to do.'

He never snapped at her, but he had then. He knew it was wrong at the time, but he was just too worked up to worry about it.

He got his line in first, and stared at her until she secured hers, but he didn't wait for her to put her pole down before he started the engine and turned the boat for the harbor. He quickly took the motor up to full speed, pushing the small, light boat at quite a clip across the lake.

Liz gripped the edge of the hull. 'Slow down!'

But the speed helped release some of the tension that had been burning away at Jake since the fight, so he paid her no attention.

'Jake! Please! You're scaring me.'

'We're fine,' he started to say.

But he only got the first word out before Liz shrieked.

The next thing he knew, they were airborne, the boat twisting sideways as it first rose, then fell sharply back toward the lake. Jake, thrown free, hit the water hard, then skimmed across the top before going under.

When he poked his head back up, he was surprised by the silence. He swiveled his head around from side to side. The boat was capsized about twenty feet to his left. Floating behind it was the cooler Liz had brought along, Jake's fishing pole, the empty fish bucket, and the bright orange life vest Jake had not been wearing.

'Liz!' he yelled.

He didn't see her. He whipped around in a full three-sixty, but she wasn't there.

'Liz!'

Unlike Jake, she had been wearing her life vest, so she should have been visible.

'Liz! Where are you?'

He swam toward the boat, worried she was trapped underneath. He dove down under the side of the hull, then came up inside the boat in a small pocket of air. No Liz.

Desperate, he swam out again and took another look around.

'Liz!'

There was something floating about fifty feet back in the direction they'd come. It was long, and low in the water.

'Oh, God. No.'

Jake put his head down and began swimming as fast as he could.

Please be all right. Please be all right.

But the image that kept coming to him was that of his brother, Davey's, lifeless body lying in the back of their car, and his father's voice, 'I said *enough*!'

Please be all right.

He didn't look up until he was only five feet away.

'Liz! Liz!'

He reached out and put a hand on the body. Only it wasn't a body at all.

It was the trunk of a tree. This must have been what they had hit. If he had been going slower, he would have seen it and steered the boat around it. If he'd listened to his sister, they'd still be on their way to the marina now.

Jake threw an arm over the log, panting. *What have I done?*

As the full weight of the crash began to descend on him, he realized how cold the water was. Perhaps that was a blessing. He would die out here, too, and not have to face his parents, his father.

'Jake!'

Jake's head snapped up. The voice was distant, weak. He looked in the direction from which it had come, but saw nothing.

'Jake!'

The boat. It was somewhere over by the boat.

He pushed off the log and began swimming again, all thoughts of the cold temporarily forgotten. As he neared the upside-down vessel, he stopped for a moment and yelled, 'Liz!'

321

'Jake!' The voice was beyond the boat, but much closer now.

He swam around the end.

'Jake! Over here.'

Another thirty feet beyond the boat was a rectangle of bright orange. A life vest. Liz.

When he reached her, she grabbed on to him, and they both went under for a moment. Jake pulled her loose, then told her, 'Just hold on to my hand. I'll pull you over to the boat.'

'I thought you were dead,' she said as they moved through the cold water.

'Of course I'm not dead.' He forced a smile. 'I'd never do that to you.'

When they reached the boat, Jake tried to flip it back over, but was too weak, so he grabbed on and used it as a float. He tucked Liz up against his chest, his other arm around her.

'I'm scared,' she said, her voice shaking with cold.

'Don't be scared. I'm here. I'll never let anything hurt you again.'

She was silent for a moment. 'Promise . . . '

'Promise. I'll never let anything hurt you again.' Then he repeated it, and repeated it again, and again, and again.

He didn't even hear the other boat approach, two fishermen who had seen the crash from a distance and had come to help.

Exposure kept them in the hospital, Jake for a day and Liz for two. By the time she got home, he was gone.

The day he'd come home from the hospital, Jake had found his father in the barn. He knew this moment was coming. He might have been able to avoid it for a little longer, but in reality he couldn't do that. He had made his decision and needed to act now. His father looked up at him, then back at whatever it was he was working on without saying a word. Jake wished his father would just yell at him, show some kind of reaction, but ever since the accident, his father hadn't even spoken to him.

'I'm sorry,' Jake said because he could suddenly think of nothing better to say. He took a step closer to the bench. 'It was my fault.'

A grunt.

When Jake didn't say anything else, his father finally set down the wrench he was holding and looked at his stepson. 'What are you expecting from me?' he asked. 'Forgiveness? You're going to have to wait a hell of a long time.'

'No,' Jake said. 'I don't expect that. I . . . I just came to say . . . '

'What? That you didn't mean to almost kill my daughter? That you didn't mean to kill . . . ' He turned back to the bench. 'Just leave me alone. Just go.'

Jake didn't move. 'That's what I wanted to tell you. I'm going.'

'Good.'

'No. I mean I'm leaving.'

His father looked at him again, but said nothing.

'I'm not coming back.'

The stare continued, then a nod. 'I think maybe that would be for the best. Have you told your mother?'

'I'm going to leave her a note.'

His father grimaced, but he didn't argue the point.

'I'll . . . I'll call Liz in a week or so,' Jake said, 'and explain it to her.'

'Explain what to her, Jake?' His father shook his head. 'I think it's better if you just leave her alone. You've already taken a brother from her, and nearly drowned her. I think it's best if you let her live her own life now. She doesn't need you.'

Jake left the barn without another word, and did exactly that.

38

They decided to watch the hotel room in shifts, Mikhail going first. Petra, in the meantime, would pick up where they'd left off with the Russian immigrant community. She wanted to check something first, so she gave the cabbie the name of the street Wills's office was on. There was the chance someone the Englishman had worked with might still be around. If so, Petra thought she might be able to isolate them and find out if he knew how to find Quinn or, even better, the Ghost.

But as the taxi drove by the building, she realized that she was out of luck.

'At the corner all right, ma'am?' her driver asked, the taxi already slowing.

'No,' Petra said. 'I've changed my mind. Take me to Oxford Circus.'

The cab picked up speed. If the driver was at all curious about the change in direction, he didn't look it.

Standing outside the entrance to Wills's building were three uniformed police officers and a group of several men in well-cut suits, talking in a tight circle. Wills's death had generated a strong response. And if Quinn was even close to being as smart as she thought he was, he wouldn't be within ten blocks of the building.

Another dead end.

Her phone buzzed.

'Hello?' she said.

'Get back to the hotel,' Mikhail said.

'Why? What happened?'

'Someone's in the room.'

Petra put her hand over the phone, then leaned toward the front of the cab. 'Forget Oxford Circus,' she said. 'Belgrave Road. The Silvain Hotel.'

★   ★   ★

Petra met Mikhail as she neared the elevators at the Silvain. 'Two women. They're in the room now,' he said.

'You're sure?'

'There are only two ways out. The elevator or these stairs. I've been keeping tabs on both. I also did a walk-by five minutes ago and could hear voices inside.'

'No sign of Quinn?'

'None.'

Petra considered their options. 'Let's keep up the surveillance. We don't make a move until Quinn shows up.'

'What if he doesn't?'

'He will.'

He looked at her, concern in his eyes. 'Petra. Shelby still might not be Quinn.'

She frowned, then sighed. 'All right. If he's not here in a few hours, we'll reassess.' She paused. 'Let's take a look at his floor again. Then I'll relieve you for a while.'

Mikhail led her up the staircase. At the landing, he opened the door just wide enough to peek into the hall. Petra could feel him tense.

'What?' she asked.

'The door to the room is open a few inches,' he said.

'Do you think they're gone?'

'We would have heard them or seen them,' Mikhail said, but he didn't sound confident. 'Stay here.'

'What are you going to do?'

'Just walk by and check if I can see anything.'

She put a hand on his arm. 'I don't know if that's such a good idea.'

'It'll be fine. I'll go all the way to the other end, wait for a few minutes, then come back. I'll just be somebody who's staying on this floor.'

She released him. Mikhail opened the door wide enough to slip into the hallway. Petra caught the door before it closed all the way, and peered through the crack as he walked away from her. The door to the room was still partially open, like someone had gone through it but hadn't made sure to close it.

Five feet.

Four.

Three.

Two.

All was quiet.

Mikhail neared the door. As he turned his head to take a quick look, it whipped open.

He jerked back in surprise as a tiny, dark-haired woman rushed out and rammed her head into his abdomen. He flew into the wall opposite the door and slipped to the floor.

The woman leaned over him, her fist drawn

back ready to deliver another blow. Without a thought, Petra raced into the hallway, pointing her pistol at Mikhail's attacker.

'Don't touch him,' she said in English.

The woman froze.

'Take a step back.'

The woman did as Petra commanded. Only she didn't stop with one. Three quick steps took her back inside her room.

Petra sprinted for the door, jamming her foot in the closing gap, then she tried to shove it inward with her shoulder. The door didn't budge as the women worked against each other. Suddenly Mikhail was at Petra's side, adding his weight to hers.

Combined they were too much, and the door began to inch inward. All at once the force on the other side disappeared, and the door swung open with a bang. The woman had given up trying to keep them out, and was sprinting across the room toward the window.

Petra rushed forward, gun first. 'Don't try it,' she said.

The woman froze.

As Petra took another step forward she could hear Mikhail close the door behind her. 'We only want to talk, but if you go through that window, you're dead. Now turn around. Slowly.'

The woman did.

She was Asian, though which specific nationality Petra couldn't tell. She couldn't have been much more than five feet tall, and if she had an ounce of fat on her, Petra would have been surprised.

'Where's your partner?' Petra asked.

The woman looked unsure of what she meant. 'My partner?' Her accent was American.

'The person you arrived with,' Petra said.

The woman seemed to consider her answer, like she was calculating the odds of what response would best favor her. She then pointed at the closed bathroom door to Petra's right. 'She's in there.'

Petra moved to a spot near the wall where she could see both the woman and the bathroom door. 'Sit down,' she ordered the woman.

The woman shrugged and sat on the edge of the bed.

Petra shot a glance at Mikhail and nodded at the bathroom. 'Check it,' she told him in Russian. When she looked back, the woman on the bed was staring at her, a curious look on her face. 'What?'

'I didn't say anything,' the woman said.

Mikhail approached the door, stopping against the wall just shy of the jamb. It was hinged on the other side and would open into the room.

After a brief hesitation, he reached out with his free hand, pushed the levered handle down, then gave it a jerk. As the door swung open, he fell back against the wall, his gun trained toward the opening.

Though there was no light on inside, enough spilled in from the bedroom so that Petra could see someone hunched low a few feet inside.

'Come out,' Petra said.

The other woman remained where she was.

'You don't want us to drag you out,' Petra said.

The woman swayed back and forth a few times, but still made no move to exit.

'Out now!'

The woman on the bed smiled as she shook her head once. 'She can't.'

'Why not?'

'See for yourself.'

'Mikhail,' Petra said, nodding at the open doorway.

Mikhail leaned forward so he could see inside. 'What . . . ?' The question was barely audible, meant for himself, but it concerned Petra. Something was not right.

She watched as he stepped into the bathroom, his gun falling to his side.

'Careful,' Petra snapped.

'It's okay,' he said without turning around.

Mikhail flipped the bathroom light on, but his body blocked Petra's view. He leaned forward for several seconds, then with a grunt stood back up. Now Petra could see the woman's head.

What in God's name?

The woman was wearing a gag. As Mikhail pulled her into the main room, Petra saw that, in addition, her hands were tied behind her back.

'You want me to take the gag off?' Mikhail asked Petra.

Petra looked at the Asian woman. 'Who is she?'

'Like you'd believe me if I told you,' the woman said.

'Take it off,' Petra told Mikhail.

As soon as the gag was off, the woman coughed, then drew in a deep breath. 'Thank you,' she croaked.

330

'Who are you?' Petra asked.

There was another fit of coughing.

'Your name.'

'Can you untie my hands?' the woman asked. 'I think I've lost feeling in them.'

The Asian woman rolled her eyes.

'What is your name?' Petra said, growing annoyed.

'Annabel,' she said.

'Annabel what?'

'Why do you need to know that?'

'Put the gag back on,' Petra ordered.

Mikhail raised the cloth back to Annabel's face.

'No. Wait,' Annabel said. 'Taplin. My last name's Taplin.'

Mikhail paused, glancing at Petra.

'I didn't say stop.'

Annabel's eyes widened as Mikhail tied the gag back over her mouth.

'Perhaps you'd like to tell us your name,' Petra said to the Asian woman.

Instead of answering, the woman stared at Petra, a knowing smile on her face. 'You're the one who was in Maine, aren't you?' she said.

Petra tensed.

'And in Los Angeles, too. Right?'

Los Angeles? Except for the watcher on the street, Petra didn't think she'd been seen in Los Angeles.

'Who are you?' Petra asked.

'I might ask you the same question.'

Petra paused for a moment. There was something about this woman she liked. She got a serious no-bullshit vibe from her. 'We are looking for someone we think you might work with.'

'And who would that be?'

'A man named Jonathan Quinn.'

'And I'm supposed to know him?'

'I know you do. You wouldn't have known where I've been, otherwise.' Petra hesitated. 'We need to talk to him.'

The woman smirked. 'That's all? Just a little chat?'

'Just talk.'

'Not kill him like you killed David Wills yesterday?'

'We didn't kill Wills,' Petra said.

'You were there.'

'If I could have talked to him, I wouldn't be looking for your friend now. But he was dead before I had a chance.'

'So you moved on to Quinn.'

'I have no one left.' Petra knew she sounded desperate, but she didn't care.

The woman stared curiously at her for a moment. Petra almost felt like she saw sympathy in her eyes. Then the woman looked past Petra, toward the front door.

Petra turned her head to see what the woman had seen. Mikhail was keeping an eye on the other woman, but otherwise there was nothing —

Her gun was suddenly wrenched from her hand. She started to turn back around, but before she could she was flying backward into Mikhail. They both fell to the floor, Petra on top.

'Gun,' the woman said.

She was standing over them, Petra's weapon in her hand pointing at Petra's chest.

'Slowly,' the woman said. Mikhail's gun flew up over his leg and landed on the floor near the woman's feet.

Not taking her eyes off them, the woman crouched down and picked it up, then stood again. 'Now, what exactly is it you want to talk to Quinn about?'

39

When Quinn arrived at St. Pancras station, the inbound Eurostar was already disembarking. Hundreds of passengers were spilling out the doors from the passport control area into the main concourse and mixing with the hundreds of others making their way to and from the domestic trains, or passing through on their way to the Underground at the far end. Barely controlled chaos. If Nate had stuck to his training, he and Liz would have blended in with the departing crowd, being neither the first nor the last to leave. And sure enough, when the exiting crowd was at its height, Nate and Liz appeared.

The look on Nate's face was all business as he surveyed their new surroundings, while Liz looked tense and tired. Quinn also noticed something else. Not only were they holding hands, but Liz's other hand was wrapped around Nate's forearm, keeping him close.

Nate made eye contact with his boss a moment later, but kept walking into the station with no acknowledgment.

Quinn let them pass, and continued to scan the crowd to see if anyone was interested in them. When he was confident their arrival had been unobserved, he joined the flow of exiting passengers.

A minute later he came up to Nate on the side opposite his sister.

'Here,' he whispered as he slipped two Oyster cards into Nate's hand. 'Underground. Piccadilly Line. Southbound.' He then picked up his pace and disappeared back into the crowd before his sister noticed him.

The waiting crowd on the Piccadilly southbound platform was large but off its rush-hour high. When Nate and Liz arrived, Quinn stayed visible just long enough for Nate to spot him, then he took a step back out of sight.

As soon as the next train eased to a stop, Quinn wormed his way through the other travelers and entered the opposite end of the same car Nate and Liz had stepped onto. Again he caught his apprentice's eye. He held two fingers against the support pole, indicating they were only going two stops. At Holborn, Quinn made his way to the westbound Central Line, making sure that Nate never lost sight of him. From there it was a one-stop ride to Tottenham Court Road, then back outside into the gloomy morning.

Quinn waited, tucked into a shallow recess, until Nate and Liz exited, then he moved beside them and said, 'This way.'

'Jake?' Liz said.

'Let's not talk here.'

'How did you know this was where we were going?'

'Liz, please. Just a few minutes more,' he said, then led them to the apartment Orlando had rented on Charlotte Street.

The moment they were inside and the door was closed, Liz said, 'Can we talk here? Or am I

335

still supposed to stay quiet?'

'I'm sorry,' Quinn said. 'We had to be careful. We couldn't risk anyone overhearing us.'

'What the hell is going on?' she asked.

'Everything's all right now,' Nate said. He reached out to touch her on the arm, but this time she pulled away.

'All right? Are you kidding me?' She looked at her brother. 'Have you gotten yourself into some kind of trouble? Is that what's going on?'

'We don't have time for this right now,' Quinn said. 'I have to get back to Orlando.'

'Orlando? Florida?'

Quinn shook his head. 'Not the city. Claire.'

'Claire?' Liz said, surprised. 'Your girlfriend? She's mixed up in this, too?'

'We work together.'

'So she's not your girlfriend?'

'No, she is,' Quinn said. 'But we also work — Never mind. That isn't important.' He was being drawn into a conversation he neither had time for nor wanted. 'I needed to make sure you were safe. And now that you are, I have to go make sure you stay that way.'

'Safe? I had men searching through my apartment building for me. Nate got shot at. Julien's dead, for God's sake. I even had to come here using a fake passport. Where's the 'safe' in any of that?'

'Listen to me,' Quinn said. 'No one can get to you here. No one knows about this place except the three of us and Orlando.'

'You mean Claire,' Liz said, defiant.

'She prefers 'Orlando.''

336

''Claire' is actually kind of nice,' Nate said.

'Shut up, Nate,' Quinn said.

'Don't tell him to shut up,' Liz said.

Quinn took a deep breath and tried to say calm. 'Liz, please. We can talk about all this later.'

'So you can tell me another lie? No thanks, Jake. You can live in whatever kind of world you've created. I don't care. I don't care if we never talk again. I don't need you. I'm getting out of here.'

She started to turn toward the door, but he grabbed her by the arms. She tried to pull away, but he held on.

'I'm trying to protect you.'

'Like you've protected me all these years since you left home?' she yelled, tears welling in her eyes. 'I just want you to disappear. I don't need you.'

Quinn closed his eyes for a second, then looked at her again. 'Until I make sure the threat is over, you need to stay here. After that, I promise, you never have to deal with me again.'

She stared at him, her shoulders moving up and down with each breath. 'Fine,' she said. She tried to pull away again, but he didn't let go. 'Do you mind?'

'You'll stay in this apartment until I tell you you can go?' he asked.

'I already said I would.'

'Even if we have to leave you here alone sometimes?'

Her eyes darted away from his. 'Sure.'

'Liz, I'm serious. I might need Nate, and that

337

means you'll be here by yourself. But if you think you can use it as an opportunity to sneak out, then our deal is off, and you'll never be rid of me. You understand?'

They stared at each other for several seconds. 'I understand,' she finally said. 'I assume it's okay if I use the bathroom, or is that off-limits, too?'

He let go of her arms. 'Down the hallway,' he said, pointing behind him.

She brushed past him and disappeared into the hallway. Once he heard the bathroom door shut, he turned to Nate.

'Don't you ever do that again,' he said.

'What?' Nate asked.

'Get between me and my sister.'

'I was just trying to lighten the mood. I thought you were going to rip each other apart.'

'I don't care what you were trying to do. Your job is to make sure Liz is safe, and that's all!'

Nate's eyes narrowed, his face hardening. 'That's exactly what I've been doing!' Tension filled the space between them for another moment, then, in a calmer voice, Nate asked, 'Do you want to know what happened this morning?'

'Yes. Of course,' Quinn said. 'What happened?'

Nate told him about the failed meeting with Julien and the subsequent encounter with the men Julien had been pretending to work with.

'How much does Liz know?' Quinn asked, shooting a glance toward the hallway, expecting his sister to reappear at any second.

'Only that Julien is dead, and that there were some gunshots. She doesn't know I killed them.

338

Not for sure, anyway.'

'About me, I mean.'

'She knows you don't work in banking. And that I work for you. She asked a lot of questions, but I told her she would have to get details from you.'

'Okay. Good,' Quinn said. It was the best he could hope for. 'Any other problems after your encounter this morning?'

Nate shook his head.

'I need to get back to Orlando,' Quinn said. 'You stay here for now.'

'Have you found out who sent the men to Paris?'

'Not yet. But we've got a pretty good idea who he is.' He looked around the room like he'd set something down and couldn't remember where it was. 'There's no food in the kitchen. You'll have to go out and get some. But only you. Liz isn't to leave.'

'Got it.'

'I'll check in later.'

'Okay.'

Quinn took a few steps toward the front door, then stopped and looked back in the direction of the bathroom. Liz still hadn't come out.

He started to open his mouth, then paused, and turned back to the front door. 'Call me if there's a problem.'

He pulled the door open and left.

40

'Where are you?' Orlando asked.

'I just got off the subway,' Quinn said into his phone. 'I should be back to you in five.'

'All right. I'll prop the door open. But knock once before you walk in.'

Quinn was instantly alert. 'What's going on?'

'You'll see when you get here.'

He hesitated, then said, 'Orlando. How are things?' It was their code phrase. If she didn't answer correctly, he'd know she was not in control of her situation.

'Things are things,' she said.

The I'm-okay response. He relaxed.

'But . . . ' She stopped. 'Just hurry up.'

Quinn made it to the Silvain Hotel in two minutes and all but ran up the stairs to his room. The door was propped open by the deadbolt.

He knocked once.

'Come on in,' Orlando said.

The first thing he saw as he pushed the door open was Orlando standing in front of the television. She'd been armed only with a hairbrush when he'd left her, but now she was holding a gun in each hand, and was facing the bed.

'Welcome to the party,' she said.

Quinn engaged the deadbolt on the door, then walked the rest of the way into the room.

There were two other people present. A middle-aged man with dark hair was sitting on the bed, leaning against the headboard. And in the chair squeezed between the left side of the bed and the far wall sat a woman. But not just any woman.

The Russian.

Neither was tied up, but with Orlando covering each of them with a gun, they weren't going anywhere.

'Okay,' Quinn said. 'This is interesting.'

'You think?' Orlando handed him one of the guns. 'They showed up not long after I got here with Annabel.'

'Where is she?'

'In the bathroom.'

Quinn glanced at the closed bathroom door.

'She's not using it,' Orlando said. 'She's tied up.'

Quinn looked back at the bed. 'So they knew you were here.'

'They were watching the room. I caught a glimpse of the guy when we arrived. He made me a little suspicious, so I slipped my hose camera under the door for a look. I saw him peeking out of the stairwell every so often. He was definitely interested in us, so I decided to see if he wanted to come for a visit. The woman was a bonus.'

'What have they told you?'

'Not much. And once I got their guns . . . '

'Remind me to ask you how you did that later.'

' . . . they pretty much stopped talking.'

'I would have thought the opposite.'

'Me too,' she said. 'The guy's Mikhail. And the woman's — '

'Petra,' Quinn said.

The Russian woman's mouth all but dropped open in surprise.

'What did she say before she shut up?' he asked.

'Pretty much the same thing she told you at the park. That she's been looking for you. That she wants to talk to you. Blah, blah, blah. That was it, though.'

'Okay, Petra,' Quinn said, taking a step toward the woman. 'Why is it we keep running into each other?'

'How do you know who I am?' she asked.

'We know because we're good at what we do,' he said, then stared at her for a moment. 'My patience level is a bit low, so I'd advise you to answer my question.'

She hesitated, then said, 'We don't want to hurt you.'

Quinn glanced at the gun in his hand, then looked back at her. 'Good to know.'

'I mean, you don't need to point those at us,' she explained.

'Thanks for the suggestion, but why don't you convince us first.'

'Okay. I understand. I would do the same.'

'You would, would you?'

'If I felt it was necessary.'

Quinn smiled, as if amused. 'How did you know I'd be here?'

'We only thought that you had been here. We waited on the chance you'd come back.'

'Why would you think it was me?'

'We . . . we had a picture of you we could

342

show around,' she said. 'A drawing.' She started to reach into her pocket.

'No, no, no,' Orlando said, raising her gun a few inches and reminding the Russian she was still in the line of fire. Petra put her hands back into her lap.

Orlando moved around the bed and reached into the woman's pocket. She pulled out a piece of paper, then unfolded it.

'This was never my favorite picture of you,' she said, holding it up so Quinn could see.

It was the police sketch that had run in all the New York papers earlier that summer. First reports had said that the man in the drawing was a suspected killer, something that was later retracted and forgotten.

Mostly forgotten, Quinn thought.

'You lied to me before, didn't you? You do work for Palavin,' he said.

He'd wanted to provoke a response, perhaps a little tic, or a look in her eye that would either confirm or deny what they had learned from Stepka. What he got instead was a volcano.

Petra's face scrunched up in a snarl as her cheeks and forehead turned red. Her fingers seemed to dig into the arms of the chair, and she leaned forward like she was going to jump up. Mikhail, too, had become tense and angry. He said something to Petra in Russian that dripped with disgust.

'I told you, we do *not* work for Palavin,' Petra said, barely able to get the words out through her clenched teeth.

'You are connected to him somehow.'

Mikhail again said something in Russian.

'That's not working for us,' Orlando said. 'English only.'

'Or what?' Mikhail asked.

'Or we kill you,' Quinn said.

Mikhail glared in defiance, but said nothing more.

'We don't work for him,' Petra spat. 'We are trying to find him.'

'Why?' Quinn asked.

'He must answer for what's he's done.'

Quinn's eyes narrowed. 'So you're here to kill him.'

'No,' she said. 'We will take him home and put him on trial.'

'I was told you are terrorists. Are you telling me you work for the Russian government?'

'I said nothing about our government.'

'So you are terrorists?'

'No!' she yelled. 'The only one who caused any terror is Palavin.'

The room was silent for a moment, then Orlando said, 'A private trial, then.'

Petra bowed her head a fraction of an inch, but said nothing.

'And after you'll kill him,' Quinn said.

'Why not?' Mikhail said. 'He is responsible for so much — ' He stopped himself.

'He's responsible for so much what?' Quinn asked. 'Why do you want him?'

'Why don't you tell *us* why *you* are working for Palavin?' Petra said, looking directly at Quinn.

'Who said I was?'

'It appeared that way to me in Los Angeles. Apparently you were in Maine, too, though I was a little too busy to see you. You were working for Palavin both those times.'

'I was working for David Wills. Emphasis on *was*. Once he was dead, I was out.'

'Semantics,' Petra said. 'Wills was obviously hired by Palavin. So in effect you were working for him.'

'Why obvious?'

'Because the Ghost knew we were trying to track him down, and hired Wills to systematically kill all the people who would have led us to him. Ironic that Wills would also become the last victim.'

'The Ghost. That's your pet name for Palavin, isn't it?'

She said nothing.

'You know for a fact Wills was killed by Palavin?'

She hesitated. 'I told you, it's obvious.'

Quinn said nothing. He suspected she was right, but wasn't going to accept it only on her word.

'Show him the picture,' Mikhail urged her.

Petra nodded, then started to lift one side of her jacket.

'Careful,' Orlando told her.

'I'm only taking a photograph out of my pocket,' Petra explained.

She pulled the picture out of her pocket. It was large, maybe eight by ten, and folded in half. She opened it and set it on the bed.

'Sit back,' Quinn told her once she was done.

345

As soon as she was leaning back, he picked up the photo.

It was a color picture faded in a way that made it seem several decades old. By the hair and clothing styles of the fourteen people captured in the image, Quinn guessed it had probably been taken in the late 1950s or early 1960s.

Those photographed were scattered around what looked like a small restaurant, either sitting at one of the two tables, or standing along the bar at the back. With the exception of a middle-aged man off to the side, the rest appeared to be in their late teens or early twenties.

'What is this?' he asked.

'May I show you?' Petra started to push herself up out of the chair.

'Stay,' Quinn told her. He held his gun out to Orlando. As soon as she took it, he knelt by Petra's chair and held the photo out so they both could see it.

'In Los Angeles, what was the name of the man whose body you took out of the warehouse?'

'You know I can't tell you that.'

'Ryan Winters, correct?' She pointed at the photo. 'There. Ryan Winters.'

Though the Winters Quinn had seen was much older, there was definitely a resemblance. He shot Orlando a look.

'At the other table. The one sitting in back. You know him, too. Kenneth Moody.'

The skin at the back of Quinn's neck began to tingle.

346

'The man sitting with him is David Thomas,' she said. 'Missing and most likely dead.' She paused. 'Behind Thomas, Freddy Chang. Dead. The woman next to Winters, Stacy McKitrick. Dead. The two women at the bar, Alicia Anderson and Sara Hirschy. Both dead.' She looked at Quinn. 'All of them murdered or presumed murdered. Most within the last six weeks. The only exceptions are the two men at either end of the bar, and the older man near the door.'

Quinn took a closer look at the two men at the bar. *They look like brothers*, he thought. If one's hair hadn't been darker and wavier than the other's, Quinn would have thought they could almost be twins.

'The photo was taken in 1964 in Hong Kong. A youth meeting.'

'Youth meeting?' Quinn said. That was a term he hadn't heard used since his days back in Warroad. 'You mean like church?'

'A political youth meeting,' Petra said. 'The kind you wouldn't advertise in a British colony in the mid-sixties. Or anywhere in the West for that matter.'

'A Communist Party meeting.'

She nodded. 'Exactly. There were hundreds of these kinds of groups all around the world at that time. I think the Soviets thought these would be the catalysts for revolutions, and since the groups were Russian backed, the USSR would be able to control the eventual outcome. But most weren't more than opportunities to complain and argue.' She looked back at the photo. 'This group called itself the Young Leninists.'

Quinn shrugged. 'The Cold War is ancient history.'

'In this case, not so ancient.' Petra paused. 'The older man at the door was named Yuri Kabulov. KGB.'

Quinn took a look at the man. 'If he's alive, he must be over one hundred now.'

'Kabulov died of a state-sanctioned heart attack in 1973. It is the dark-haired one at the bar we are really looking for.'

Quinn took a good look at the wavy-haired boy. It wasn't hard to imagine the man he would become. Quinn had actually seen him as an adult. The third photo in the folder from Annabel Taplin's briefcase. 'Palavin,' he said. 'Your Ghost.'

Petra smiled without humor. 'A name of convenience.'

'How did he get involved with a youth group in Hong Kong?'

'The first question is really, how did *Kabulov* get involved with them?' she said. 'He generally didn't deal with these groups. His specialty was coordinating agent infiltration into enemy governments. At the height of his career, it was said he had dozens placed throughout Western Europe.'

'Okay. So why was he there?'

She pointed first at the Ghost, then at the straight-haired boy who looked like him.

'Are they brothers?' Quinn asked.

Petra shook her head. 'Not brothers. Not even related. Palavin was born in Moscow, and was actually twenty-three when this was taken. All we know about the other one is that he was born in London, but lived most of his life in Hong Kong. If we knew his name, we wouldn't have been looking for you.'

'Why not?'

'Because in 1988, the Ghost,' she said, her finger hovering over the wavy-haired youth on the right, 'became this man.' She moved her finger to his doppelgänger.

41

'How did Palavin steal someone else's identity?' Quinn asked.

Petra looked back at the photograph. 'The look-alike came to the attention of Kabulov in the early 1960s through a KGB agent named Glinka working in Hong Kong,' she said. 'Glinka had met Palavin on a previous trip to Moscow, and noticed the resemblance between the two men.'

Quinn nodded.

'Kabulov was always looking for infiltration opportunities,' she went on. 'He investigated, and agreed with Glinka. He arranged for Palavin to be transferred to Hong Kong and to be assigned as Russian youth advisor to the Young Leninists. Palavin's real job, though, was to get close to the young man, get to know him and his habits.'

'So the Ghost could eventually assume the other man's identity,' Quinn said.

'Exactly,' she said, nodding. 'It was Kabulov's ultimate plan, the piece that would be the crown jewel of his career. In his mind, once the Ghost had become the Englishman, he would return to the U.K. and begin a rapidly advancing career within the British government.'

'But things didn't work out that way,' Quinn said, making an educated guess.

'No. Kabulov became involved in a series of

failures, and was eventually declared an enemy of the party, and disposed of. Palavin, on the other hand, had been smart. He had taken a position in Moscow while waiting for the day Kabulov would decide it was time for him to become the Englishman. It was a job that obviously fed the sadist inside him. He became an internal security officer based out of Lubyanka Prison, and built his reputation within the party. He was able to use that to shield himself from Kabulov's downfall.'

'If Kabulov died, what happened to his plan?' Quinn asked.

'It died with him. The only one who knew about the Englishman other than the Ghost was Glinka, and he had become a loyal member of the Ghost's inner circle. For Palavin, assuming the Englishman's identity transitioned from being a potential career as a British mole to a potential escape valve, just in case things went south for him like they had for Kabulov. It was perfect. If things *did* go bad, here was a new identity with a real-life history.'

'So he just left his look-alike in Hong Kong? Hoping he'd be around if ever needed?'

She smiled without humor. 'Palavin was smarter than that. He recruited the Englishman, telling him he would be an agent for the Soviet Union, with Palavin as his handler, of course. Only he wasn't an agent for anyone but the Ghost. It was a way to put the man on ice for as long as needed. Palavin would send him here and there, carrying packages that the man was told were top secret messages, or keeping tabs on

351

people who really had no intelligence value at all. Palavin thought of everything, even setting him up with a woman who he probably thought cared about him. It wasn't long before the Ghost controlled him completely.

'Palavin continued his work in Moscow, honing his craft and becoming a master at extracting confessions. A KGB star. Most of those he interviewed never saw the outside of Lubyanka again. Their voices silenced, never to be heard by the people who loved them again.' She paused. 'If you had been working for him, Mr. Quinn, you would have been kept very busy.'

Quinn ignored the comment. 'What drove him to take on the Englishman's identity?'

'By the late eighties, he realized the Soviet Union was heading for disaster. We all did. Only he had a way out, and decided to take advantage of it before it all crashed down. With the body count he'd amassed, he had to know if he stayed his own life would be in danger.

'In 1988, he ordered his double to return to London. It was the first time the Englishman had been in the U.K. since he'd been a child, and what family he had there, he'd lost contact with long ago. The important thing for Palavin was that the U.K. Border Agency recorded the Englishman's entry back into the country from Hong Kong.'

She fell silent.

'And then?' Quinn asked.

'Palavin killed him, and *became* him. At that point, Nikolai Palavin disappeared.' She paused. 'Like a ghost.'

'How do you know all this?'

Petra exchanged a look with Mikhail. He started to say something in Russian, but then stopped, and said in English, 'What will it hurt?'

She nodded in agreement, then turned back to Quinn. 'A man named Dombrovski brought us together. Mikhail, myself, and the others back in Moscow who have helped us, we all suffered at the hands of the Ghost. Some of us were victims who survived his interrogations. But most of us lost relatives and loved ones to his methods.' She looked at her partner. 'Mikhail's brother, tortured then killed. Kolya, our friend who died in Maine, lost his parents. Others in our group, too, lost brothers, sisters, whole families. All taken from us, silenced by the Ghost.'

Mikhail took up the story. 'Dombrovski had been a KGB doctor, but he had made the mistake of helping one of Palavin's victims. The Ghost then tortured him, keeping him from death only because he was KGB. Though several years in a labor camp in Norilsk probably felt like death. When Dombrovski returned to Moscow, he found that his wife and his son were dead. More victims of the Ghost. But at the time, the only thing he could do was remember. It wasn't until the Soviet Union dissolved that he saw his chance. He tried to locate Palavin to bring him to justice, but it was too late. Palavin had disappeared.'

'Obviously, your friend didn't let that stop him,' Quinn said.

'Of course not,' Petra said. 'Dombrovski knew he needed help, so he reached out to other

353

victims and family members. He made sure those of us who were most dedicated got the best training possible. Mikhail and myself spent over two years learning what we could from a former army intelligence officer who had lost a cousin to the Ghost. But all the training wasn't getting us any closer to finding Palavin. For years there was no trace of him. Some thought that he was dead. But not Dombrovski, and not me. Then, seven weeks ago, we finally caught a break. Dombrovski learned Glinka was still alive and living in Moscow. He's the one who told us what had happened to the Ghost. And he's the one who told us about the picture.'

'I thought you said he was loyal to Palavin.'

'He was, even to the end. But we . . . *encouraged* him to be helpful. He told us most of the names of the Young Leninists. But he never gave up the Englishman's name.'

'So you used the same tactics that the Ghost used?'

'No,' she said, her teeth clenched. 'The Ghost tortured for no reason. We are trying to bring justice to the dead.'

'Distinction noted,' Quinn said.

She waved him off like it didn't matter. 'We set out to try and find one of the others in the photo Glinka had identified, hoping they could give us the name of Palavin's twin. But we had barely left Moscow when Palavin learned of Glinka's betrayal, then used his contacts to track Dombrovski down.' She fell silent.

'His people forced Dombrovski to tell them about you. Am I right?' Quinn asked.

She looked at him, her eyes hard. 'Dombrovski was old, frail. But he told them nothing of us!'

'How do you know that? You weren't in the room.'

Mikhail sat forward. 'You are right. We weren't there. That's why we had taken the precautions Dombrovski himself had trained us to use when we set out on our mission, including using multiple IDs as we traveled. We didn't realize it, but that was a potential weak point. You see, Dombrovski knew who created them for us. He could have given Palavin that information. Yes, he told the Ghost's men we were out here looking for him, but he didn't give them the name of who had provided us with our documents. If he had, we wouldn't be here talking to you now. Dombrovski kept that secret to the end.'

'So not knowing exactly who you were, Palavin starting eliminating the others from the photograph?'

'Unfortunately for us, yes,' Petra said. 'Don't you see? You're our last hope. Do you know the name of the Englishman? Do you have some way of getting ahold of him?'

Quinn stared at her for a moment, then stood up without saying anything. He put the group photo in his pocket and crossed over to Orlando.

'Please,' Petra said. 'We've told you everything. We're so close. Just a little help is all we ask.'

'Why not go to the Russian government? Get them to help you?'

'Our government has more than its share of old KGB still in it,' she scoffed. 'His old comrades would block any attempt to bring him home. Even if they didn't, the government would not want him back, because of the embarrassment he could cause. Many in our country have moved on. They'd rather forget the past than deal with it. Mikhail and I and the others who have helped us knew long ago if we wanted justice we would have to obtain it on our own.'

Quinn frowned to himself. 'Give us a moment,' he told Petra, then motioned for Orlando to follow him to the edge of the entryway.

'I think she's telling the truth,' Orlando said.

'Yeah, I think so, too,' he said, then glanced at the bathroom. 'Keep an eye on things out here for a few minutes.'

She smiled. 'Be my pleasure.'

As Quinn stepped over to the bathroom door, Petra spoke up again. 'Do you know how to reach the Ghost? Are you going to help us? Please, tell me.'

He grabbed the handle of the door. 'I'll let you know in a minute.'

★   ★   ★

Annabel's eyes grew wide as Quinn stepped into the bathroom. He flipped on the light and pulled the door closed behind him.

She was sitting on the toilet, her mouth gagged, her hands and feet tied.

'Hope you didn't think we forgot about you,' he said.

He turned on the water and filled one of the

356

glasses on the counter. When he was done, he set it down and stepped over to the MI6 agent.

'I'm going to take the gag off,' he said. 'If you utter one syllable that is not an answer to one of my questions, I guarantee you will regret it. Is that clear?'

She nodded.

'I'm deadly serious. Any slip and you will never see the outside of this room again.'

She nodded again.

He reached behind her head and untied the gag. She coughed as it fell from her mouth. Quinn picked up the glass of water and held it in front of her.

'Take a sip.'

Her first attempt ended in another fit of coughing. The second time, she managed to get some down.

'Better?' he asked after a moment.

'Yes,' she said, her voice strained. 'People are going to be looking for me. You should let me go now.'

'That's a slip, Annabel. I'll let this first one go, but that's it. Are we clear?'

She took a breath. 'Yes.'

He set the glass down on the sink and crouched in front of her. 'I believe you played me.'

Her brow furrowed. 'What do you mean?'

He pulled out his phone and accessed the picture of him at the Grand Hyatt. 'Recognize it? It's from the last time we met.'

She looked at the phone, then back at Quinn, confused.

'Didn't expect me to see this, did you?' He

357

smiled. 'You took it, then sent it to someone who is trying to harm someone I love.'

'I didn't . . . I . . . I . . .'

Quinn raised the gag so she could see it. 'You're very close to that second offense.'

She fell silent.

'You took this photo.'

'Yes.'

'Who did you send it to?'

'My office.'

'Okay, we can go with that for a moment. Who did they send it to?'

She shook her head. 'I don't know.'

Quinn moved the gag toward her mouth.

'I'm telling the truth,' she said quickly. 'I don't know. I didn't realize they'd sent it to anyone.'

Quinn pulled the photo Petra had showed him out of his pocket, unfolded it, then held it out so Annabel could see.

Her reaction was uncensored surprise.

'I take it you've seen this before,' he said. He then accessed the headshot of Palavin on his phone and held it up for her to see. 'And I know you remember this photo. If I remember correctly, you said you were told this man might show up at the meeting I was having with Wills, but you didn't know who he was.' He paused, but she remained silent. 'That was a lie, wasn't it? You did know him.' He paused. 'He looks a hell of a lot like an older version of this kid, don't you think?' He used the phone to point to the young Palavin in the group shot.

Her gaze moved from one image to the other, then to Quinn's face.

'You're not a low-level analyst, are you?' he said.

'Why would I have lied about that?' she asked.

'Because you wanted me to think you didn't know what was going on. You wanted me to figure out the connections myself, and leave MI6 out of it.' The pieces had fallen together for him as Petra had told her story. 'You planted that picture in your briefcase. That's why you were at the Hyatt in the first place, to somehow get me that folder. You hoped once I had it I'd try to find out who the man was. And then maybe I'd dig a little deeper to see why he was so important.'

'I don't know what you're — '

'Palavin,' Quinn said. 'That's the man's name. He's also known as the Ghost. Or did you not know that either?'

She did know it. He could see it in her eyes.

'You were trying to push me in a direction,' he went on. 'And it worked. Only better than you thought, because I also figured out what you were doing. Now, Annabel, this is what I need from you. First, I know Wills's client was Palavin, but I want you to confirm that for me.'

A slight hesitation, then an even-slighter nod.

'Good. Second, David told me the job was passed to him through MI6. It was through your division at Wright Bains, correct?'

Another nod, this time with a sense of resignation.

'Through you directly?'

She stared at Quinn for several seconds. 'Yes,' she whispered.

'Mighty important task for a low-level analyst.'

'I'm a case officer.'

'Field cases?'

She shook her head. 'My department is tasked with handling defectors and other sensitive foreign nationals living in the U.K.'

'Like Palavin,' he said.

She nodded.

'Well, isn't that interesting. Did he come to you or did you go to him?'

'It was all before my time.'

'That's not very helpful,' he said. 'I'd be happy to turn you over to my two other guests. I'm sure they'd love to get ahold of someone who worked directly with the Ghost.'

'It's not like that!'

'Then enlighten me.'

'You don't understand. I'm good at my job. I love doing work that helps protect my country. But this . . . ' She paused. 'This wasn't right.'

Quinn waited for her to go on.

'When Robb contacted — '

'Robb?' Quinn asked, not recognizing the name.

'That's what he goes by now. Trevor Robb.'

The name Petra was so desperate to know, Quinn thought. 'Go on.'

'When . . . *Palavin* contacted us, I had to look up his file just to know who he was. Former KGB. Arrived U.K. in 1988. According to the report, he'd already established himself as Trevor Robb, but he'd left Moscow in a hurry and had arrived with only limited funds.'

'So he came to you for money, is that it?'

'Yes. He agreed to share what he knew in exchange for enough cash to make him wealthy, and the promise that we would provide whatever protection he deemed necessary for the remainder of his life.'

'That's a pretty steep price.'

'Apparently his information more than compensated for his demands at the time.'

'But not now,' Quinn said.

'He hasn't been an active asset for us for many years. I understand he still tries to keep his fingers in things, but nothing we would be interested in. Then we heard from him a little over a month ago that his life was in danger, and that we were bound by our agreement to protect him. He was an inactive client I inherited from previous case officers, so it fell to me to arrange what he wanted. I talked with his representative, who laid out their plan, and instantly I knew it was something MI6 couldn't touch. I took it to my superiors, thinking they'd instruct me to tell Mr. Robb to go to hell. But they didn't. They agreed we shouldn't be directly involved, but they felt it was important we stick to the deal. There are British interests at stake. It was decided that we would pass it on to one of our contractors, giving them a story that they would find plausible.'

'David Wills, and suitcase bombs for North Korea?' Quinn said.

'You've figured a lot out.'

Another connection surfaced in Quinn's head. 'Did you set him up with a computer information specialist, too? Someone to dig into the histories of those working for him?'

She looked away. 'That . . . that we kept in-house. One of our top hackers was assigned to the project.'

Quinn stared at her in disbelief. 'You're telling me your little group there at MI6 is responsible for the danger my . . . people are facing?'

'Whatever Palavin's done with the information is all on him,' she said quickly. 'We had no idea what he wanted it for.'

'No idea?' he yelled. 'That does *not* absolve you!'

'Hey, everything all right in there?' Orlando asked through the door.

'Fine,' Quinn shot back. He locked eyes with Annabel. 'If anything happens to them, *anything*, then I will kill you myself. That's not a threat, nor a promise. That's a fact.'

She sucked in a nervous breath, but said nothing.

Quinn allowed himself a moment to calm down, then said, 'Once you passed the job onto Wills, why didn't you just let it go then?'

Her lips trembled slightly as she spoke. 'This wasn't something that was furthering national security. It was eating me up. When I found out Palavin had planted a man on Wills's teams, I knew I had to do something.'

'Wait. Planted?'

'A man named Mercer.'

'Mercer? David said Mercer was his man.'

'Cover story. Mercer's mission, as I later found out, was to not only make sure the targets were neutralized, but also to liquidate the strike teams after each mission. Donovan and his men, they're all dead now. The same is true for Freeman in Los Angeles and the people he was working with.'

'What?' Quinn said, shocked. 'They're all dead?'

Annabel looked at the floor, then nodded.

Quinn was silent for several seconds as he let it all soak in. Finally, he said, 'Mercer was at the park after Wills was killed. My Russian friends in there think that Palavin was responsible. Are they right?'

She nodded. 'We're almost positive. The dead woman in the park is a freelancer Palavin has been in contact with before. We think she'd been hired to tie up loose ends.'

Quinn shook his head. 'Then why didn't she wait until I showed up? I'm a loose end, too.'

'You showed up?'

'He was in the park to meet me.'

She stared at him. 'We didn't know that, and Palavin probably didn't know that either. If he did, he would surely have had her wait.'

If Wills hadn't told anyone who he was meeting at the park, Quinn thought, only that he was going there . . .

Then it hit him. Mercer.

Wills had undoubtedly used him for security. Except instead of watching Wills's back, Mercer had let Palavin know the plan.

Then he realized something else. The body removal from the Alexander Grant Building, the job most anyone could do, now he understood why Palavin wanted him to do it. It was meant to be Quinn's last job. Once he turned the remains over, he would be eliminated, too.

'If Palavin's so afraid of being uncovered, why doesn't he disappear again?'

'Disappear? You don't understand him at all. He spent decades preparing his post-Soviet Union identity, and even more decades living it. He's not going to give up the life he created that easily. And with the support of his agreement with British intelligence, his ego is large enough that he feels he doesn't have to, that he can rid himself of the problem with several well-placed bullets.' She shook her head. 'He's a monster. All these people he killed in Moscow, we should have never helped him cover that up.'

'Spare me your guilt.' He paused for a moment, then said, 'So I'm the only one left on the Ghost's removal list.'

'Not after he finds out what I've done to help you.'

'You, Ms. Taplin, already have plenty of blood on your hands. Being on his list is the least of your problems. But if you're interested in staying alive and seeing what karma has in store for you in the future, then I suggest you continue being helpful.'

★ ★ ★

Ten minutes later, Quinn reentered the bedroom. This time he left the door open.

He looked at Petra. 'To answer your question, I'll help under one condition.'

She looked surprised. 'Anything you want.'

'This is non-negotiable.'

364

A hint of caution entered her voice. 'What is your condition?'

'I'm in charge,' he said. 'Because I'm going after him no matter what, and unless you're with me, you're in my way.'

'Only if you promise we take him alive.'

He frowned. 'I can't make that promise.'

Petra said nothing for several seconds. Then she nodded. 'All right.'

42

'Nothing cute,' Quinn said. 'keep to the script.'

He and Annabel were the only ones left in his room at the Silvain. Orlando had gone upstairs with Petra and Mikhail into one of their rooms to arrange for the extra help Quinn's plan would need. Petra had said she knew someone who could provide the men, but Quinn didn't trust her enough yet to make the contact on her own.

'Don't worry,' Annabel said. 'I know what to do.'

He held his phone out to her. It was attached via wire to his laptop. Orlando had started a program that would make the call look like it was coming from a cell phone inside the Wright Bains building.

She dialed a number, then held the phone up to her ear.

'Fedor? It's Annabel Taplin. I need to speak with Trevor . . . Well, where is he? . . . No, I can talk to you . . . It's my understanding that your project with Wills wasn't completed . . . Because it's my job to know, that's why . . . Thirty minutes ago, while one of my agents was cleaning Wills's office, a call came in from someone who'd been working for Wills. They transferred it to me . . . Someone who was working on *your* project. He said that he got a call yesterday asking him to stay on the job, but he had no way of knowing if he could trust the

366

caller or not . . . ' She glanced at Quinn and nodded. 'Then, you know who I'm talking about . . . Quinn. That's right . . . I convinced him that your call was legitimate. He told me he's willing to finish the job . . . Correct. Just tell your boss to call him again and everything should be fine.'

She listened for a moment longer, then hung up.

'Did he buy it?' Quinn asked.

'He had no reason not to. At least not my part of it. He may think you were feeding me a line, but I'm supposed to be on his side.'

'How long do you think before they call back?'

Taplin shrugged. 'Fifteen minutes. Thirty tops.'

'Then we wait.'

★ ★ ★

Trevor Robb. That was the name of the light-haired Englishman who'd had the unfortunate luck of sharing a physical similarity to a Russian psychopath. His life had only been a placeholder for the day the Ghost would take it over. Over two decades dead, his was the body the man now using the name Trevor Robb wanted Quinn to remove.

'According to the file, the Ghost rented several offices in the basement of a building in the financial district,' Annabel had told Quinn in the bathroom before he had reemerged.

'The Alexander Grant Building,' Quinn said.

'Wills told you?'

Quinn nodded.

'Then you know it's pretty rundown. In 1988 it wasn't much better. After the real Robb returned to the U.K., he was instructed to go straight there. Palavin was waiting for him. He killed Robb there, then entombed the body in a small closet, walling him inside. Apparently, Palavin planned it as a temporary solution. When he came to MI6 to sell what he knew, he expected that we would remove the body for him. But my predecessors told him we wanted no part of it. They were afraid that he might kill others in the future and expect us to help again.'

'You mean like he's doing right now?'

She squirmed uncomfortably. 'At some point Palavin decided that the risk of leaving the body in the wall was less than attempting to get it out on his own. Ironically, MI6 realized that even though we had told him no, there was always a chance that if the body was found it might blow back on us. It took a couple of years, but it was finally decided to have the body removed. Only we didn't want Palavin to know, so we made sure the closet tomb looked the same.'

'Then, the body he wants me to remove isn't even there?' Quinn said.

'Not for almost two decades.'

★ ★ ★

The return call came twelve minutes after Annabel's conversation with Fedor.

'Hello?' Quinn said.

'Mr. Quinn?' It was the same voice that had

368

called him not long after Wills had been gunned down.

'Yes.'

'We spoke yesterday,' Palavin said. 'I was told you would be expecting my call.'

'I appreciate you getting back to me.'

'Perhaps we should put yesterday's conversation behind us. It was a very stressful day for everyone.'

'I think that's a good idea.' Quinn gave it a beat, then said, 'Do you still need your project completed?'

'As a matter of fact, I do. Can I assume you're willing to reconsider?'

'I've had a conversation that leads me to believe you're on the level. So I'll do your job, but my fee has just gone up.'

There was a pause. 'Gone up how much?'

'A hundred and twenty thousand. U.S.'

Quinn could hear the other man clicking his tongue against the roof of his mouth. 'You have me in a difficult position. And I don't appreciate people trying to take advantage of me.'

'I'm not taking advantage. I'm just being practical. With Wills's murder, the risks have increased.'

More silence. 'I'll give you eighty.'

'I'll go as low as a hundred thousand, but any lower and I walk.'

'Fine, Mr. Quinn. One hundred thousand. I'm not happy about it, but I guess I can understand. I'll wire it to you as soon as the job is done.'

'You'll wire it to me now.'

Palavin took a deep breath. 'Very well.'

369

Quinn gave him the account number, then said, 'To confirm, you want the package removed and delivered to you, correct?'

'Correct. I will give you a place and a time where my associate will meet you once you let me know when you will be in possession of . . . it.'

'It'll be tonight,' Quinn said.

'Tonight?' The Ghost sounded surprised.

'I already did the preliminary work before yesterday's events. We're ready to go. I anticipate having the package ready for you before midnight.'

'That's excellent,' the Ghost said. 'We will call you this evening with the drop-off location.'

'Perfect.'

Quinn disconnected the call.

'So?' Annabel asked. 'Did *he* believe *you*?'

'Everyone believes in greed,' Quinn replied.

43

'Hungry?' Nate asked, standing in the doorway.

Liz was lying on the bed, curled in on herself, her eyes staring at the wall.

'What's going to happen to me?' she asked. 'Am I going to have to live on the run like this forever? And what's going to happen to Mom? Is she going to have to give up her home? She's too old for this.'

'You shouldn't worry about any of that right now. Your brother is going to take care of things.'

She turned to him. 'How can I not worry?'

He wasn't sure what to tell her. He certainly didn't have an answer. So he said, 'Let me get you something to eat.'

'I just want to sleep.'

He nodded. 'Sure. Okay, I'll come back later.'

As he started to turn away, she said, 'No. Lie with me. I think that'll help.'

He smiled. 'That I can do. Just let me put the food away first.'

'Promise?'

'I promise.'

In the kitchen, he gathered the meats, cheeses, and vegetables he'd set out to make sandwiches, and returned them to the refrigerator. He then got a glass and filled it with water.

He was carrying it across the living room when someone knocked on the front door.

He stopped and looked toward the entry, but

371

made no other move.

Another knock. Not pounding, and not a polite tap. Something in between.

Nate remained still, listening. But the exterior hallway was carpeted and the door was thick, so he picked up nothing.

Just as the visitor knocked for a third time, Liz stepped out of the bedroom.

'What's that — '

Nate held a finger to his mouth, quieting her, then motioned for her to go back into the bedroom. She complied with the first part, but not the second.

Five seconds passed, then ten. If there was to be a fourth knock, it should come within the next fifteen seconds. But those silently came and went.

Though still uneasy, he smiled, and held out the glass. 'Thought you might be — '

With a loud crash, the front door splintered inward, flying open.

Nate dropped the glass and raced forward. Grabbing Liz, he carried her into the bedroom, where he dropped her back to her feet, then slammed the door closed.

'Help me,' he said, as he began to push the meager dresser in front of the door. Liz quickly joined him.

Once it was in place, Nate raced to the window and threw it open. The drop was two floors. Ankle-breaking height, especially if you didn't know what you were doing.

He glanced back, then pulled a sheet off the bed.

'Tie this end around your waist,' he said. 'Tight.'

'What are you going to do?' she asked, grabbing the end of the sheet and looping it around her body.

'It's too far for you to jump, so I'm going to lower you enough so you can drop down without getting hurt.'

'What about you?'

'Don't worry, I'll be right behind you.'

They could hear people running in the apartment.

'Come on. We don't have time.'

Someone slammed into the bedroom door.

'Climb out,' he said. 'I'll lower you as far as I can, then let go.'

'You're not going to make it!'

'Don't worry about me. Just get down, and get the hell out of here. I'll find you later.'

'Where?'

'Westminster Abbey.' It was the first place he could think of.

Another slam. This time the door cracked.

'Please, Liz.'

She looked reluctant, but climbed over the sill. Nate held tightly to the end of the sheet as he lowered her as fast as he dared.

A third slam toppled the dresser.

'Stop!' someone shouted.

Nate didn't even look back, he just kept lowering Liz. Only a few more feet and it would be enough.

'He's letting her down into the alley,' the voice behind him said.

'Roger.'

Nate tensed. The second voice wasn't from someone in the room with him. It had come over a radio.

Movement at the end of the alley caught his attention. He looked over and saw two men running toward the back of the apartment building. There was no other exit. Liz was trapped. A second later someone grabbed Nate by the shoulder and pushed him to the side. Nate held tight on to the sheet, unwilling to let it go.

'She's far enough down that the fall won't kill her,' the man at the window said.

'You can let go now,' another voice said, this one behind Nate.

Nate's fingers dug into the sheet.

'Let it go!'

The man at the window shoved Nate, spinning him around. There were two men standing in the middle of the room, both with guns pointed at him.

'Let. It. Go!' one of them said.

'Not a chance,' Nate told him.

He saw the muzzle flash, and felt the impact, but he never heard the gun go off.

★   ★   ★

At 6 p.m. Quinn and Orlando stopped for a quick bite at the Iron Duke in Victoria Station. All the pieces of the plan were in place. There was no question in Quinn's mind whether they would succeed or not. They had to. The survival of his family depended on it.

374

At 6:14 his phone rang.

BLOCKED.

It was time.

He let it ring four times before he answered. 'Hello?'

'Good evening, Mr. Quinn,' Palavin said.

'Been waiting to hear from you.'

'Is everything still on schedule?'

'Yes. Everything's fine. You have the location for me?'

'My assistant will be calling you with that information later,' Palavin said.

Quinn tensed, not liking the deviation from what he expected. He stood up and walked to a less-populated section of the pub, 'So you're just calling to make sure everything is fine?'

'Not exactly. I'm calling to ensure you know how important it is that you stay on track.'

'Everything *is* on track.'

Orlando walked up, her backpack over her shoulders, Quinn's in her hand.

'That's good to hear. But sometimes I find that extra incentive doesn't hurt.'

'What incentive?' Quinn said.

'I think maybe we should stop playing games with each other,' Palavin said. 'You've known for at least a day now that I've had an interest in making sure you finished what I hired you for. If you didn't, you wouldn't have tried to hide your sister from me.'

Quinn froze.

'What is it?' Orlando mouthed.

But Quinn could only shake his head, his eyes wide.

'I do appreciate that you brought her to London. It makes my job easier.'

'I don't know what you're talking about. I don't have a sister.'

'Oh, my God,' Orlando whispered.

She walked away from him, pulling her phone out of her pocket.

'I can let you talk to her if you'd like.'

Quinn looked over at Orlando. She had her phone to her ear, but shook her head. Nate wasn't answering.

'What do you want?'

'What I've wanted from the beginning. For you to finish the job you were hired to do.'

Quinn's grip tightened on his phone. 'You don't need my sister to make that happen. I'm already doing the job.'

'Perhaps it would have been unnecessary before, but once you knew I was trying to find her, how could I trust you were being honest with me? Now that I actually have Elizabeth, I think maybe we can see eye to eye. You bring me the body, and I will let her go.'

'I want to talk to her,' Quinn said.

'Naturally. I wouldn't expect you to believe me if you didn't.'

'Just put her on!'

The phone fell silent for a moment. The next thing Quinn heard was heavy breathing.

'Liz?'

'Jake? God, Jake. Help.'

'Are you hurt?'

'Just bruised.'

'That's it?'

'So far.'

He then asked the question he'd avoided with Palavin. 'What about Nate?'

She sobbed. 'They shot him. They — '

There was the sound of movement. 'I think you've talked enough,' Palavin said. 'We'll call later with the location.'

Palavin hung up.

Quinn grabbed Orlando by the shoulder. 'Come on,' he said, pushing her toward the exit back into the station.

'What happened?' Orlando asked.

'Nate,' he said, then started sprinting for the entrance to the Underground.

★   ★   ★

There were half a dozen police cars parked on Charlotte Street. A large area in front of the apartment building had been cordoned off. As with all crime scenes, a small crowd had gathered around the outside of the police zone.

Quinn and Orlando approached a couple standing just off to the side.

'What happened?' Quinn asked, trying to sound curious but unconcerned.

The woman glanced over. 'We heard a man was shot,' she said.

'Really?' Orlando said. 'In this neighborhood? Was he badly hurt?'

The woman shook her head. 'Don't know. We've only been here a few minutes.'

'Thanks,' Quinn said.

They walked over to the sidewalk on the other

side of the street. There was a waiter standing next to an empty outside table in front of an Indian restaurant. He was looking toward a group of police gathered beyond the police line. The restaurant itself was empty.

'Someone got shot? Did I hear that right?' Quinn asked.

'Yes. Apparently.'

'Did you hear it happen?'

'No,' he said. 'But I saw people running out of the building. Then one of the neighbors came out yelling about gunfire.'

'Just the one person hit?'

'As far as I know,' the man said. 'An ambulance took him away ten minutes ago.'

'Unbelievable,' Orlando said. 'I wonder what happened.'

The man shrugged. 'Drugs probably. Isn't that what it always is?' He turned and walked back into the restaurant.

Orlando pulled out her phone and began typing. While she did, Quinn guided them toward Tottenham Court Road.

'The closest medical facility is University College Hospital,' Orlando said.

'Is that where they took him?' Quinn asked.

'I don't know yet.' She pressed a button on the phone, then held it up to her ear. 'Yes, hello,' she said, using a remarkably good British accent. 'This is Chief Inspector Owens. I'm checking on the status of a man who would have been brought there within the last thirty minutes . . . Yes, I'll hold.'

They had reached Tottenham Court Road.

'Taxi or foot?' Quinn asked.

'Foot for now,' she said, then pointed toward the north. 'That way.'

They darted through traffic to the other side of the street.

'I'm here,' Orlando said as they reached the sidewalk. 'Yes, I'm involved with the investigation on Charlotte Street. It was my understanding that the victim was brought to your hospital. Is that not right? . . . Oh, good. He *is* there . . . And his condition? . . . No, I understand. Thank you.'

She disconnected the call.

'He's there, but she had no information on his status.'

'How the hell did Palavin know?' Quinn asked.

'A spotter at the train station?' she suggested.

'I would have seen them.'

'Did Liz still have her phone?' They both knew if she did, it would have been a simple matter for someone with the right resources to track it.

'Nate got rid of it in Paris,' he told her.

'A homing device in her clothes?'

'The only one who could have put one there was Julien. And there's no way he did.'

'So how?' she asked. 'They were spotted somewhere? That seems pretty random. Palavin wouldn't have known where they were headed after Paris, and I doubt he had the resources to — '

'The passport,' Quinn said.

'What?'

'The passport you arranged for them to pick up in Paris before they left. Did you have your

379

contact install a GPS clip?'

'Of course. In case we needed to track them.'

Quinn looked at her without saying anything, the suggestion that the GPS IDs might have been compromised clear on his face.

'Not possible,' she said. 'I've used Michael Loge many times. He wouldn't give that information away.'

'For the right amount of cash, some people will give anything away.'

Orlando drifted off for a second, then brought her phone up and made a call. It was soon apparent the person on the other end wasn't answering. She frowned, accessed another number, and called it.

'Christophe, it's Orlando,' she said. 'I'm trying to get ahold of Michael, but he's not answering. Have you heard — ' She paused, listening. 'When? . . . How did it — No, no. It's okay. *Merci.*' She hung up.

'What?' Quinn asked.

'Loge is dead. Shot, two hours ago.'

★   ★   ★

They found a small area off the main lobby of University College Hospital's Accident and Emergency Department. There were gray plastic chairs along one wall, all empty at the moment. Orlando sat down and pulled her laptop out of her backpack. Once she was up and running, it took her less than a minute to hack into the hospital's computer system.

'Can you get us inside?' Quinn asked.

380

Orlando shook her head. 'It wouldn't matter. He's in surgery.'

Quinn felt a sudden rush of relief. 'Then he's still alive. Does it say where he was hit?'

She studied the screen. 'The chest,' she said. 'Upper left side.'

Not his heart, though, Quinn thought. If that had been where he'd been hit, Nate would have been in the morgue, not surgery.

Orlando looked at her laptop a moment longer, then closed it and stuffed it back in her bag. 'I'll make a few calls. Make sure he gets the help he needs. The only other thing we can do is wait.'

Quinn stood up. 'No. No waiting.'

'Stick to the plan?'

'Yes.'

'We'll have to modify it,' she said.

'Not much.'

She stood up and slipped her hand into his. 'Then, we'd better get to work.'

44

At 9:15 p.m. the night guard appeared from around the corner of the Alexander Grant Building on his exterior rounds.

'East side. Street's clear,' Mikhail said over the receiver in Quinn's ear.

'West side. Same.' Petra this time.

Quinn and Orlando were standing in the same alcove Quinn had hidden in on his initial stakeout two nights prior. They were decked out in gray janitorial uniforms, matching light utility jackets, and black caps. Each had a backpack slung over their shoulder.

Once the guard had passed their position, Quinn gave Orlando a nod.

Silently she crossed the street and moved in behind the guard. The first indication he gave that he knew anyone was there was when Orlando's hand slapped down a chloroform-soaked washcloth over his mouth and nose. He started to struggle, but that lasted only a few seconds before he lost consciousness.

Quinn crossed the street as Orlando eased the man to the ground.

'Target down,' he said.

Quinn reached into the inner pocket of his jacket and pulled out one of the syringes Petra had procured from her contact, a man named Nova. He knelt down beside the guard and stuck the needle into the man's arm. He gave the rent-a-cop only half a dose. There was no need to keep the guy knocked out all night.

Orlando had already appropriated the guard's security badge and ring of keys, so together they pulled him into the narrow gap at the end of the building.

'Target secured,' Quinn said. 'Proceeding to stage two.'

Based on his previous visit, there were, at most, only two more guards inside. Odds were pretty good any remaining personnel would be in whatever room served as their office, watching TV or taking a nap.

Quinn took the lead as they approached the lobby door. Though there were no lights on inside, the residual illumination from the streetlamps was enough to confirm that the lobby was empty.

Orlando checked the lock, then looked at the guard's key ring and selected one of the keys. It went in a little rough, but turned when she twisted it. She pulled the door open, and let Quinn in first, then followed.

'Inside,' Quinn said. 'Street check.'

'Clear,' Petra said.

'Clear,' Mikhail said.

Only they all knew the street wasn't completely clear. They had spotted Palavin's watcher in a car two blocks away when they first arrived, and soon after discovered a new camera trained on the Alexander Grant Building. Palavin's, of course.

Quinn walked to the middle of the lobby, then looked left and right down the hallways that ran off in each direction. There were a few lights on in each, like someone had disconnected all but the absolute minimum needed to see. From Quinn's experience, security offices were usually set up close to the front entrance. But he got no sense of anyone nearby.

Orlando raised an eyebrow, silently asking him, *Which way?*

Before he could answer, the unmistakable sound of a toilet flushing cut through the silence. It was to their left, muffled and distant, like it might be all the way at the other end.

Staying in the lobby, Quinn and Orlando moved to opposite sides of the hallway entrance, shielding themselves against the wall.

Water running now, then off. Silence for a few seconds, then the sound of a door opening.

Orlando peeked around the edge. When she looked back, she held up one finger, then used her hands to indicate a wide man of average height.

There was the *thud-thud-thud* of the man's footsteps as he drew closer.

Quinn watched Orlando pull the chloroformed rag from her pocket. He hoped it was still potent enough to work on the new guard if they needed it. He tensed, ready to grab the man, but the steps stopped fifteen feet shy of the lobby.

A door opened for a few seconds, then closed again. After, silence descended on the hallway.

Quinn and Orlando shared a look, but they both knew to give it a few seconds before checking. When they finally did, as expected, the hallway was empty.

As they stepped out of the lobby and into the corridor, Quinn pointed at a door on the side nearest him. 'That one,' he whispered.

Orlando nodded her agreement.

Together, they approached the door, then stopped to listen. From inside came the sound of a TV. Someone was flipping through the channels and finally settled on a station. Quinn tried to tune the TV out and listen for anything else. But the only voices were those filtered through the television's speakers.

He looked at Orlando and held up one finger, then pointed at himself. He would take care of the guard. He didn't have to tell her that her job was to make sure there wasn't anyone else.

Once Orlando handed him the chloroformed cloth, he took a few steps away, then whispered into the radio mic on his collar, 'Going for target two.'

He placed his hand on the knob and gave it a slight turn. Unlocked.

He glanced at Orlando, and she nodded, indicating she was ready. He took a deep breath, turned the handle all the way, and pushed the door open.

The guard was alone, sitting on an old cloth couch. By the time he looked up, Quinn was already halfway across the room.

'Who the hell — ?'

Quinn raced the rest of the way and knocked the rising guard back onto the couch. He then dove forward, shoving the cloth over the man's face. Unfortunately, the chloroform didn't work as quickly on the larger man as it had on his partner outside.

The guard tried to grab at Quinn's arm and

move the cloth away, but Quinn held tight. The man then changed tactics and shoved at Quinn's torso while turning his own body.

'What . . . are you . . . trying . . . ? Who . . . ?'

The guard attempted to push himself up and away, but slipped, the chloroform finally beginning to take effect.

Quinn jumped off the couch, then removed another one of the syringes from his pocket. As the guard rolled onto his side, Quinn plunged the needle into the largest target available, giving the man a full dose.

The guard tried to swing his arm at Quinn, but missed miserably and rolled completely off the couch onto the floor. He made a feeble attempt to get up, then collapsed, slipping into dreamland.

Panting, Quinn looked over at Orlando. She was leaning against the wall, not too far from the door, a playful smile on her face.

'Thanks for the help,' he said.

She snorted. 'Hey, you're the one who said you had him.'

He stared blankly at her, then said into his mic, 'Target two secured.'

For the next five minutes Quinn searched the rest of the building in case there was more security, while Orlando headed down to the basement to assess the situation there. After he confirmed there were no more than the two men they'd already dealt with, Quinn headed back downstairs.

When he hit the lobby, he told his new Russian friends, 'Give us thirty minutes, then bring the van into position.'

'Roger,' Mikhail replied.

The basement level was a mess. The long central hallway was littered with boxes and damaged office furniture. Off the corridor were doors every twenty feet. Most were open, revealing equally trashed rooms.

'Where are you?' he called out.

'Down here.' Orlando's voice came from the far end of the hall.

Quinn worked his way around the scattered debris until he reached the room she was in. It was a fair guess that in the eighties the basement rooms had all been used as offices, but they had sometime since been turned into storage areas. The room that had once been rented by the Ghost was full of near-empty wooden shelving units.

Orlando was standing off to the right, in front of a unit against the wall. She'd already cleared a lot of debris out of the way.

'This should be it,' she said.

Quinn immediately saw what Palavin had done, or rather, what MI6 had redone. The room was in the corner of the building. The wall on the right seemed to be about a meter further into the room than it needed to be. Plenty of space for a walled-off closet.

'Looks right to me.'

She grabbed the wooden shelf. 'Help me with this?'

Together they started to pull the bookshelf away from the wall. The rusty screws that had been holding it in place easily gave way. Once the

387

area was clear, Quinn set his backpack on the floor and removed a two-foot-long wrecking bar that was strapped to the outside. Though it was unlikely that Palavin's watcher would check inside the building after they left, they couldn't take any chances. They needed to make it look authentic.

Quinn began swinging at the wall, and five minutes later he had a hole wide enough for the job he was supposed to be doing. As expected, there was nothing inside.

While he took a moment to catch his breath, Orlando staged the scene by propping some of the debris against the wall and making it look like something had been removed from inside. Once she was done, Quinn helped her push the shelving unit back in place. That was part of the show, too. Since the building wasn't long for life, there would have been no need for Quinn to repatch the wall like the one MI6 had done. Covering it up with the shelves so that it wouldn't draw the attention of security was all that was required.

That done, Orlando pulled two heavy-duty plastic-fiber bags out of her backpack, while Quinn scanned the room for the last things they needed to complete the illusion. He found some old chairs in the corner and used the wrecking bar to create several chunks of wood about the same size as human bones.

'What do you think?' he asked Orlando.

She glanced at his handiwork. 'Perfect.'

★ ★ ★

388

'Pulling up now,' Petra announced.

Quinn and Orlando, each carrying one of the plastic bags that now ostensibly contained the remains of Trevor Robb, stepped from the hallway into the front lobby. Through the glass doors, they could see the van stop at the curb. Painted on the side was the business name *Halvorsen Cleaning Services*.

'Street?' Quinn asked.

'Clear,' Petra said.

Orlando went first, with Quinn right behind her. As soon as they cleared the building, the side door on the van swung open. Mikhail was standing several feet inside so that he wouldn't be seen. They wanted Palavin's surveillance to think there were only three people on the job.

'Here,' Orlando said, setting her bag just inside so Mikhail could grab it.

As soon as he did, she ran over to where they'd left the first guard to return his keys and badge. Quinn waited until she came back, then they both climbed inside, and he slammed the door closed.

'Go,' Quinn said.

Petra took her foot off the brake, and they were off. Mikhail, sitting in the back with Quinn and Orlando, was talking to someone in Russian on his phone. After a moment he moved it away from his face.

'Is he moving?' Quinn asked.

'Yes,' Mikhail said.

'Following us or checking out the building?'

'Following us.'

Quinn nodded. 'Good.'

389

So their work in the basement had been unnecessary. That was fine. The energy he'd expended had worked off any rough edges he felt. What was left now was focus.

Clear, lethal focus.

45

Ten minutes had passed since they'd left the financial district when Quinn's phone rang. The caller ID read BLOCKED.

'Here we go,' he said.

He pushed Accept.

'Hello?'

'Mr. Quinn?'

'Who is this?' Quinn asked.

'My name is Fedor.'

'Sorry, I'm talking to only your boss.'

Quinn could hear Fedor start to say something, but he disconnected the call before he could hear what it was.

It took only ten seconds for the phone to ring again.

'Mr. Quinn,' Fedor said, 'I'm calling to give you instructions for — '

'I talk to your boss or I talk to no one.'

'Wait!'

'Tell him if he wants Trevor Robb's body,' Quinn said, 'he'd better be the one on the other end when my phone rings again.' He hung up again.

No one said anything for several moments.

Finally, Orlando looked over at Petra. 'You never told us what he did to you.'

'I'm sorry?'

'The Ghost. You said he hurt all of you in one way or another. What did he do to you?'

Petra looked uneasy.

'If it's too personal,' Orlando said, 'you don't have to answer.'

'No,' Petra said. 'It's just hard to talk about.' A wan smile crossed her lips. 'His name was Andrei. I was twenty-three, and he was twenty-five. We'd been married a year and a half when the Ghost's men came for him. He did nothing wrong, other than want a better future for our children.'

'How many did you have?' she asked.

She shook her head. 'None. We were going to have two. A boy and a girl. That's what we talked about. But the Ghost took them from me before they could even be conceived. Someone in our building overheard Andrei saying something they took to be subversive and turned him in. What, I never knew.'

Once more, silence descended on the car.

After nearly a minute, Quinn said, 'I think we've waited long enough.'

He called the number Annabel had given him, and almost immediately Fedor answered.

'Is he ready to talk to me now?' Quinn asked.

'How did you get this number?' Fedor stammered.

'Seriously? That's what you're worried about? Do you know what I do for a living? Put your boss on.'

The line went silent for half a minute, then Palavin came on. 'Mr. Quinn?'

'Yes.'

'You have a problem talking to my assistant?'

'I don't have a problem talking to him,' Quinn

392

said. 'I just don't have any reason to. This business is between you and me.'

'You have something for me?'

'If you mean do I have the body you sent me after, yeah, I have Trevor Robb right here.'

Palavin's response was quick and casual. 'Robb? Is that supposed to mean something to me? Because, Mr. Quinn, it doesn't.'

'That's interesting,' Quinn said. 'It's the name I found on the ID tucked under the sole of his shoe.'

'His shoe?'

'Yes. Looks like he put it there in case something happened to him. Guess it's a good thing he did.'

Neither of them said a thing for several seconds.

'What is it you want?' Palavin said.

Quinn smiled at Orlando and nodded.

'I assume you still want his body,' Quinn said. 'If you don't, I'm pretty sure I can think of some alternate places to leave it. Only, I'd probably have to leave an explanation, too.'

'Do I have to remind you about your sister?'

Despite himself, Quinn tensed. But he refrained from responding.

'This is completely unnecessary,' Palavin said, trying to sound conciliatory. 'We were calling you with the drop-off location.'

'No.'

'No?'

'That's not the way it's going to work.'

'What are you talking about?'

'We're doing this my way,' Quinn said. 'Step

one. You're allowed one car. One. And in that car will be one of your men, my sister, and you. No more.'

'You can't be serious. I might as well kill her now.'

'And I'll turn over Trevor Robb to someone who will be more than happy to find out the backstory on this guy.'

'You mean you'd risk your sister's life on some unknown interest in this dead person?'

'No,' Quinn said. 'You're not seeing this clearly. You're the one taking the risk. As long as I have the body, you won't do anything to my sister.'

'What makes you think that?'

'Because according to my sources in British intelligence, Trevor Robb is still alive and well. And around your age.'

Silence.

'This can go very simply,' Quinn said. 'What you have for what I have. No problems. Be in your car *with* my sister in ten minutes. I will call you back.'

He hung up.

'Are your people in position?' Quinn asked Mikhail.

'Yes.'

'Tell them it won't be long now.' He looked at Orlando. 'How about you? All ready?'

'Absolutely.'

He turned to Petra. 'Time to lose the tail just long enough to drop Orlando off.'

★ ★ ★

394

Five minutes after Orlando had left the van, Quinn called the Ghost back.

'Are you in your car?' he asked.

'Of course.'

'Is my sister with you?'

'She's here.'

'Let me talk to her.'

'No,' the Ghost said. 'You can't talk to her until our business is done.'

It was an empty threat, and they both knew it. 'Put her on or our business is already done.'

'Jake?' Liz said a moment later.

'Liz. It's going to be all right. It'll all be over very soon. Tell me, how many people in the car, including you?'

She paused. 'Four.'

'Four including you?'

'Yes.'

Quinn's eyes narrowed. 'Just stay strong and I'll make sure everything is all right.'

'I'll try,' she said.

Palavin came back on. 'That's enough. So where do you want us to go?'

'My instructions were one man, my sister, and you. No more.'

'Well, that's just too bad, isn't it?'

Quinn was silent for several moments. 'Fine,' he said. 'Should I assume, then, that you have other cars following behind somewhere? Ready to move in if necessary?'

The Ghost said, 'Of course not. Just my two men and me. I want this over.'

'That makes two of us. Waterloo Station. Fifteen minutes.'

'Fifteen minutes is not enough — '

'Fifteen minutes,' Quinn repeated, then turned his phone completely off.

★   ★   ★

They headed first south across the Thames River, then west toward Waterloo Station, the sound of raindrops thumping against the roof of the van. Per Quinn's instructions, Petra made sure not to shake their tail. He knew as long as the person behind them had them in sight, the Ghost would still think he had the upper hand.

'Anything?' he asked Mikhail.

'Not yet,' the Russian said, his phone held firmly to his ear.

'Does your friend speak English?'

'Of course.'

'Put him on speaker.'

Mikhail said something in Russian into the phone, then pushed a button and lowered it into his lap. 'Can you hear me?' he said in English.

'*Da*,' a voice said on the other end. 'A little noisy but I can hear you.'

'Nova, right?' Quinn said.

'Yes,' Nova said.

'This is Quinn. I appreciate your assistance.'

'Not necessary. The Ghost is no friend of mine.'

'He should be arriving soon,' Quinn said.

Nova was in a car near Waterloo. 'Good. I have men all around the station. The moment they see him, I'll know.'

'It's important that he doesn't realize he's been spotted.'

396

'We understand,' Nova said.

'We'll keep you on speaker. Let us know the moment there's a change.'

'I will.'

Quinn pushed himself off the floor and shuffled into the front passenger seat. The rain was steady, but not hard, the windshield wipers more than a match for the storm so far. Quinn looked at the GPS device mounted on the dash, but it only showed a closeup of the road they were on. 'Our friends?'

She glanced into her side-view mirror. 'Still there.'

'Okay. Let's do a little zigzagging.'

'Zigzag?'

'Take a few turns. Left-right?'

'Ah, yes. No problem.'

'But don't lose them. Just make it look like we're being cautious, and keep our basic direction the same. We want them to still think we're headed for Waterloo.'

'Hold on,' she said, grinning.

Quinn grabbed the dash as Petra took the next turn, then leaned over enough so he could see the side mirror out her window. Nothing for several seconds, then a set of headlights made the turn behind them.

'Palavin's men?' Quinn asked.

Petra gave the mirror a quick glance. 'Yes.'

'Okay. Take the next turn. My guess is once we do, they'll start to wonder if we know they're there, and they'll halve the distance between us.'

She turned again, and just as Quinn predicted, they were only a half block down when the trailing car showed up again.

'Keep it straight for a few blocks,' he said.

After several seconds of silence, Quinn looked over at Petra. 'I'm sorry.'

'For what?'

He paused. 'For Andrei.'

They sat in silence, both watching the road ahead. Suddenly Nova's voice echoed over the speaker-phone.

Quinn looked back at Mikhail. 'What did he say?'

'Possible sighting,' Mikhail said.

Quinn glanced at the GPS unit. Waterloo Station was only a few blocks away now.

'Make it like you're heading toward the station, but keep a block or two between it and us. If you have to, go all the way around. When I give you the word, break off and head toward point two.'

She nodded.

Quinn then made his way back to Mikhail, but remained in a standing crouch.

'Nova?' he said.

'I'm here,' Nova replied.

'Tell me exactly what your people saw.'

'A dark blue Mercedes. S600. Very nice.'

'How many inside?'

'Windows are tinted, so could only see the driver and a man in the passenger seat.'

'What makes you think it's them?' Quinn asked.

'They circled the station once, then pulled off onto Spur Road and parked at the curb. No one's gotten out.'

'Any following cars?'

'Yes,' Nova said. 'Two so far. A black Audi and a silver Mercedes. Four people in each.'

Counting the car behind the van and the Ghost's sedan, the total rose to fifteen people.

'There could be more, but two cars sounds about right,' Quinn said. Then in a voice loud enough for the whole van to hear, he said, 'Time for the next phase. Is everyone ready?'

'Yes,' Petra said.

'Give my people two minutes to get to their cars,' Nova said.

'All right,' Quinn told them. 'Two minutes and I make the call.'

46

'Let me speak to my sister,' Quinn said.

'Where are you?' the Ghost asked.

'Let me speak to my sister.'

'You already spoke to her.'

'And you could have dumped her since then. Let me speak to her, or we abort.'

The phone exchanged hands.

'I'm here,' she said, strain still in her voice, but a little calmer than the last time.

'Still okay?'

'Yes.'

'Good. It won't be long.'

'All right,' she said. 'Jake, what about Nate? Is he — '

Quinn could hear the phone moving again.

'I'm at Waterloo,' the Ghost said. 'Bring me the package now and you can have her back. Then we can both move on.'

Quinn's phone vibrated, indicating a text, but he ignored it for the moment.

'Step two,' he told the Ghost. 'Head toward Victoria Station. I'll call you in five minutes with further instructions.'

'That is unaccep — '

Quinn disconnected the call, then looked at the screen. The text was from Orlando.

Arrived point 3. All clear.

Quinn sent her a quick message back.

Did you check on Nate?

While he waited for her reply, he leaned toward Mikhail's phone. 'Anything?'

'The Mercedes is moving,' Nova reported. 'Hold on.'

Quinn heard Nova speaking in Russian. There was a muffled reply that sounded like it was coming over another phone. When he came back on, he said, 'It's heading west toward Westminster Bridge.'

'That's him,' Quinn said.

Nova said something in Russian again. Quinn looked at Mikhail, his eyebrows raised.

'He's checking on the backup cars,' Mikhail said.

Good. That was going to be Quinn's next question.

Fifteen seconds of nothing, then Nova said, 'Have positions on the Audi and the other Mercedes, too. The Audi looks like it's hanging back to cover the Ghost's car, while the Mercedes is racing ahead.'

'Any sign of anyone else?' Quinn asked.

'None,' Nova said. 'Should we drop the hammer?'

'Soon,' Quinn said.

His phone vibrated again.

Still alive

★ ★ ★

The rain had increased, soaking the road and chasing most people off the streets.

'Now,' Quinn said to Petra as they passed Victoria Station.

Ahead, the light was changing. Petra pressed the accelerator to the floor, then swerved the van around a car that was slowing for the light, and raced through the intersection.

'Did they make it?' Quinn asked.

Petra looked in the mirror. 'No. There were too many cars between us.'

'Lose them,' he said.

Petra took the next right, then went several blocks before taking a left onto a quieter residential street. As she continued to work her way through the neighborhood, Quinn kept checking to see if the other car had returned, but it hadn't.

'Where's our tail?' Quinn asked.

Mikhail spoke Russian into the phone, then looked back at Quinn. 'They've gone south. Back toward the river.'

Quinn smiled. 'And Palavin?'

Mikhail spoke into his phone again, then said to Quinn, 'Nearing Victoria.'

'Take us to point three,' Quinn told Petra. He then called Palavin.

'We're here,' Palavin said. 'We'll park on the north side. You'll have three minutes to find us, or the deal is off and your sister is dead.'

'I think you misunderstood me. We're not meeting at Victoria Station,' Quinn told him.

'I'm done playing your games. Come get her and give me my property.'

402

'Step three. You should write this down. Fifty-one point seven — '

'What the hell is this?' the Ghost said.

'Figure it out,' Quinn told him, then gave him the rest of the GPS coordinates. 'You should be able to get there in an hour. I'll give you fifty minutes. And if you do anything to my sister, I will expose you, Mr. *Robb*, and you'll be spending your last years in prison for murder.'

He hung up the phone.

'Well?' he asked Mikhail.

The Russian was sitting across from him, listening to his own phone. 'They're still at Victoria,' he told Quinn. 'Wait . . . they are on the move again . . . ' There was a pause of several seconds. 'Heading . . . toward . . . point three.' Mikhail said something in Russian, then to Quinn, 'Definitely heading toward point three.'

'Okay,' Quinn said. 'It looks like we're on.'

47

The house was twenty miles northeast of the city, outside Chelmsford, near a little town called Sandon. It was down a rural road lined with fields and the occasional home. The house belonged to a Dr. Ryan O'Sullivan and his Russian wife, Ilya, both friends of Nova's. When Quinn had scouted it with Orlando and Petra that afternoon, his only question had been where the doctor and his family were.

'Nova says the husband and wife are out of the country at a medical convention, and that the children are away at boarding schools in Ireland,' Petra told him.

'Any chance someone will show up unexpectedly?' Orlando asked.

'He says zero.'

Quinn took another look around. 'All right. This will do.'

At the front of the property was a small pond that served as home to a pair of black swans. Quinn had seen them that afternoon, but the only movement on the water now was the frenetic dappling caused by the rain from the storm.

The house at the back of the property was two stories in front with two single-story wings that ran further back on each side. Though Nova had supplied a key, Quinn had no intention of entering. Their business would be dealt with out front, between the house and the pond.

The closest neighbors were a good four acres away to either side, separated by rows of trees and brush. Behind the house, nothing but a tree-ringed field.

When they arrived, Orlando was waiting for them. Her job had been to make sure no one had shown up.

Petra parked the van in front of the house, visible from the road, then Quinn and the two Russians joined Orlando under the carport on the south end of the house.

'How is he?' he asked Orlando, still thinking about Nate.

'Not great, but he's hanging in there.'

Quinn took a deep breath. In all his years in the business, he had never been seriously shot or lost a limb. In Nate's short time, he'd experienced both. And, Quinn realized, both times had been on projects that were Quinn initiated. Which meant there was no way to rationalize either injury as just being part of the job.

They were Quinn's fault. He was responsible.

Orlando placed a hand on his back. 'He's a fighter,' she said. 'He's going to be fine.'

If he makes it through the night, Quinn thought.

Something buzzed nearby.

Mikhail pulled his phone out of his pocket. He listened for a moment, then said, 'Five minutes away.'

Quinn nodded. 'Tell Nova to drop the hammer now.'

While Mikhail passed on the instructions, Quinn turned to Petra and Orlando.

'We should get into position,' he said.

405

Petra and Mikhail headed off to the right, past the van. Orlando gave Quinn's hand a squeeze, then ran along the edge of the driveway opposite the pond.

Three minutes later, Quinn saw headlights in the distance down Meyers Lane. They were proceeding slowly. He moved out from the cover of the carport to a spot in the middle of the driveway a dozen feet away from the van, then turned so he faced the road, and waited as the rain soaked his head and jacket.

A large tree at the northeast corner of the property momentarily obscured the car, then it reappeared along the road just on the other side of the pond. Even with the stormy conditions, Quinn could see it was a Mercedes sedan. It slowed to a near stop fifteen feet shy of the driveway's entrance, then began crawling forward, finally turning onto the driveway. When it stopped again, it was two car lengths away from Quinn.

Quinn's phone vibrated in his pocket. He pulled it out knowing what would be on the display: BLOCKED.

He accepted the call and held the phone up to his ear, but said nothing.

'You weren't alone. Where are the others?'

'What others?' Quinn asked.

'You think I didn't have you watched? Where are they?'

Quinn raised his arm. A second later Petra and Mikhail stepped out from around the van.

'Show me your weapons,' Palavin said.

'That's not necessary,' Quinn told him.

'Show them or your sister is dead.'

406

'How do I know you didn't kill her already?'

There was the sound of a slap, then Quinn could hear Liz yelp. 'Your weapons,' Palavin repeated.

Quinn pulled a pistol out of his jacket, and held it out so those in the car could see it.

'Drop it on the ground.'

Quinn did so.

'Now your friends.'

Quinn paused, then turned and nodded at Petra and Mikhail. They repeated Quinn's actions, their pistols joining his in the mud.

'Happy?' Quinn asked.

'Where is the package?' Palavin said.

'In the van.'

'Get it.'

Quinn walked over to the van. As he reached for the door Palavin said, 'Tell me now if there is anyone inside.'

'Other than Trevor Robb?' Quinn asked. When Palavin didn't respond, Quinn said, 'No one.'

'Open it.'

Quinn opened the door. The two bags he and Orlando had carried out of the Grant Building were visible just inside.

'That's him?' the Ghost asked.

'What's left,' Quinn said.

'Bring the bags over and set them beside the car on the driver's side.'

'Let my sister out first,' Quinn said.

'I don't think so.'

'Look. The bags are right here. If you really had someone watching me, then you know these are the same bags I brought out of the building.'

'I know nothing of the kind,' Palavin said.

'You've had plenty of time to replace what was inside with anything. Bring the bags over.'

'The deal was an exchange. That means we both get something at the same time.'

Quinn heard movement on the other end, then Palavin's voice, muffled and unintelligible.

The two front doors opened, and the driver and the front passenger got out. The driver was about Quinn's height, and at least fifty years old. Quinn had never seen him before.

The passenger was different, though. Quinn knew exactly who he was.

'Hello, Mercer,' Quinn said.

Mercer sneered at Quinn.

The driver opened the rear passenger door and leaned inside. When he stood back up, he had Liz with him. She looked scared.

'Now the bags,' the Ghost said over the phone.

Quinn slipped the phone into his pocket, then pulled the bags out of the van and walked them over to the car.

On the road in front of the property, two cars appeared — a Mercedes and an Audi. A moment later they turned down the driveway.

'What is this?' Quinn yelled.

The rear passenger door on the other side of the S600 opened, and an elderly man climbed out. There was no mistaking his face. He was the older version of the wavy-haired twin in the Young Leninist photo, and the middle-aged man from the headshot in Annabel Taplin's folder.

The murderer.

The faux Trevor Robb.

The Ghost.

He was smiling an ugly smile.

'I'm afraid this was a career-ending job from the beginning. For a last assignment, I'm sure it wasn't as satisfying as you would have hoped, and for that I apologize.'

The Mercedes and the Audi pulled to a stop behind the Ghost's car.

'What are you talking about?' Quinn asked, wiping the water from his face.

'You know about the people I've had removed. You obviously know about the late Mr. Robb. I'm afraid you are too dangerous to me alive. I can't have that.'

'So you're just going to kill me?' Quinn said.

'You and your new friends,' Palavin said, glancing back toward Petra and Mikhail. He smiled. 'Yes. I know who you are. Dombrovski's puppets. Mercer was kind enough to take photos of each of you in Maine before he killed your friend.' He looked back at Quinn. 'So kind of you to team up with them. Makes things so much more neat and easy.' He then said something in Russian.

Mikhail spat several words back.

Palavin laughed, then said in English, 'A fool's quest to think you could best me.'

'So you and your two men there are planning to take on all of us?' Quinn asked.

'Me and my two men?' He waved toward the two cars behind his. 'There's far more than just the three of us.'

'If that were true, shouldn't there be a third car? I mean, in addition to the two cars that were shadowing you, didn't you have another one following me?'

Palavin cocked his head, his eyes narrowing. 'So you had your own surveillance,' he said. 'So what? My third car is just down the road, making sure we're not disturbed.'

'No,' Quinn said. 'It's not.'

Even from this distance, he could see doubt flash across Palavin's face. He stepped toward the Mercedes.

'Stop,' Palavin ordered. His gaze flicked to the man standing with Liz. 'Fedor!'

The man raised a gun to Liz's head.

'She's dead if you come any closer,' Palavin said.

'I don't think so,' Quinn said.

The *thup* of a bullet passing through a suppressor was all but drowned out by the rain. Fedor collapsing to the ground dead, though, was impossible to miss.

Liz, jerking in surprise, let out a disbelieving shriek as she looked down at Palavin's driver.

'Get down!' Quinn yelled at her.

On the left side of the car, Mercer drew his own gun. But before he could aim, Quinn dove to his right, his hand reaching out for the pistol Fedor had dropped. As his fingers curled around the grip, a bullet pierced the air a few inches above his back.

Quinn rolled forward so he was against the car, out of Mercer's direct line of sight.

The rain muffled a lot of the other sounds, but Quinn could still hear the doors of the Audi and other Mercedes opening further down the driveway.

'Kill them all!' Palavin yelled.

410

'Give it up, Quinn. You don't have a chance,' Mercer demanded as he popped out from around the end of the car, his gun trained on the place he thought Quinn would be.

But Quinn had used the noise of the rain as cover and had moved along the front of the car, stopping a few inches shy of the corner. When Mercer came into view, Quinn was much closer than the other man expected.

'I don't think so,' Quinn said as he pulled the trigger.

Mercer twisted to his right just enough so that the bullet caught him in his shoulder instead of his heart. He yelled out in pain and fell to the ground, his gun landing with a thud on the wet gravel a few feet away. Still in survival mode, he tried to grab at it, but Quinn kicked it out of reach.

'You keep moving like that, you're going to bleed to death,' Quinn said, pointing the gun at him.

'What are you waiting for?' Palavin shouted toward the backup cars from his crouched position behind the car door. 'Take them out!'

The sound of weapons being drawn and slides being pulled back could be heard by everyone, even in the rain. But no triggers were pulled.

Quinn moved around the door until he could see the Ghost, then pointed his gun at him. 'I'm sorry,' he said, acting embarrassed. 'Did you think those were *your* men in those cars?'

The blood drained from the Ghost's face as he turned to look behind him.

There were eight men, each with guns trained

on the former KGB agent. On Quinn's earlier command, Nova and his men had 'dropped the hammer' on the Ghost's backup cars, then procured the vehicles for themselves.

Orlando stepped out from the bushes near the pond, adding a ninth gun to the mix.

Quinn motioned for her to get Liz, then he pulled Palavin to his feet.

'You can't kill me,' Palavin said. 'I'm under the protection of MI6. If anything happens to me, they'll hunt you down and make you pay.'

'Really? That's what you're counting on? Some tenuous, outdated relationship with British intelligence?' Quinn smiled, then leaned in close. 'Who do you think gave me your phone number? MI6 is done with you.'

Palavin's face turned red. 'You won't kill me and you know it.'

Behind him, Quinn could hear two sets of footsteps approaching on the wet driveway.

'You're right. I won't. I don't need to.' He glanced over his shoulder. Petra and Mikhail were now standing behind him. 'My friends here might have other ideas, though.'

Petra said something in Russian, and though Quinn wouldn't have thought it was possible, Palavin went even paler.

'You can't leave me with them,' the old man said.

'Is it Ghost? Or Mr. Ghost?' Quinn asked.

The old man could only stare at Quinn, his lip trembling.

'Well, Mr. Ghost. No one *ever* messes with my family or my friends and lives to talk about it.'

48

'I have people who are going to be looking for me.' Mercer said as he was being led toward the van, his shoulder patched up enough to stop the bleeding.

'We both know that's not true,' Quinn said. 'No one cares about you. And even if someone did, they'd never find you.'

'What the hell does that mean?'

'It means you're going on a trip.'

'What trip?'

Quinn turned to Petra.

'I'm very pleased to meet the man who killed my friend,' she said to Mercer.

'Now, wait a minute. Hold on. I was only doing — '

'Enough,' Petra told him. She motioned to Mikhail, and he slipped a gag over Mercer's mouth. 'You'll be coming with us. We have a boat waiting that will take us home to Russia. It's beautiful there, but you probably won't be able to see much. We've already planned on one trial for your employer.' She nodded toward the van, where they had already loaded the Ghost. 'It won't be much trouble to have two. You can speak all you want then.'

Once he was loaded inside the van and the doors were shut, Mikhail held out his hand to Quinn. 'I never thought this day would come,' he said. 'Thank you.'

Quinn shook it and said, 'Be safe.'

Petra was not interested in handshakes. Instead, she wrapped her arms around Quinn. 'We would have never succeeded without you.'

'I hope this puts some of your demons to rest,' he said.

'Some,' she admitted as she let him go. 'But it will never bring Andrei back. It will never bring any of them back.'

A few moments later, Petra, Mikhail, and a contingent of Nova's men set off in the van for a boat moored at Ramsgate Harbour on the coast. From there it would be a nice, slow cruise to St. Petersburg.

★   ★   ★

Quinn and Orlando took Liz to a suite Orlando had prearranged at the Crowne Plaza. Quinn promised to take her to see Nate if she promised not to try and leave while he ran a final errand. Once she agreed, he and Orlando returned to the Silvain Hotel.

Annabel Taplin was standing by the window when they arrived.

After Quinn asked the guard Nova had provided to step outside, Annabel said, 'What happened?'

'The Ghost is no longer your problem,' Quinn said.

'Good. That's good,' she said, though she still looked uneasy. 'Can I go now?'

'Soon enough.'

'What's the problem?'

'No problem,' Quinn said. 'I just want to make sure we're in sync on a couple of things.'

She narrowed her eyes. 'What things?'

'First, I have a colleague who is in critical condition at University College Hospital. You will have him transferred to a private facility as soon as he can be moved. There he is to be provided with unparalleled medical care. His own physician, his own nurses, anything and anyone he needs. The incident he was involved in will be covered up. I don't care how, but neither he nor any of us are to be involved. Is that clear?'

She thought for a moment, then said, 'I can do that.'

'You *will* do that,' Quinn said.

'Yes. I will do it.'

'Second, no matter what kind of internal mess our business with Palavin creates for you and MI6, absolutely *none* of it will blow back on me or my team. Not now. Not ever.'

'I don't know — '

'These are the conditions of your release,' Quinn reminded her.

'It'll take some work . . . but . . . but I'll get it done. Can I go now?'

'Not until our Russian friends are out of the country. Consider it a precaution.' Quinn glanced at his watch. 'Another two hours should do it. If you, at any point, feel the need to renege on our agreement, know this. Palavin is still alive. My friends have him, and, therefore, his entire story, including his close relationship with the British government through MI6. If even part of one of my conditions is not fulfilled, that

415

story, with your name featuring prominently, will be front-page news around the world.'

She looked stunned.

'Do you understand?'

She nodded. 'I understand.'

'Do you agree to the terms?'

'I agree.'

★ ★ ★

Annabel Taplin kept her word. Nate was moved late the next day to a secure private hospital. No questions were asked. The shooting was covered up as a drug deal gone bad, and soon forgotten.

Liz spent all her time by Nate's side, holding his hand, reacting to every sign of movement whether real or imaginary, and even sleeping in the chair beside his bed. Because of this, Quinn kept his own visits to a minimum, spending more time in the visitors' lounge or with the doctors than with his ailing apprentice.

The good news was that his mother was back home, and safe. He had spoken to her briefly and promised to visit soon.

'I trust you, sweetie,' she'd said. 'If you say it was necessary, it was necessary. And if you don't want to tell me, I don't need to know.'

'I love you, Mom.'

The distressing news was that for three days Nate was touch and go. Finally, on the fourth day, he began to show signs of recovery. His lung was damaged, and that was something that might cause him problems later in his life. But the doctor emphasized Nate's youth, saying

416

there was a good chance he would have few lasting effects from the injury.

The scar, though, would always be there.

'You're doing it again,' Orlando said.

'What?' Quinn asked.

They were alone in the waiting room.

'Blaming yourself.'

'I don't want to talk about this right now,' he said.

'Then, what do you want to talk about?' she asked.

'Vacation.'

She gave him an odd look.

'I think we should go away. You, me, and Garrett. A nice long trip someplace warm.'

'Garrett's in school,' she reminded him.

'There's no way he can take a little time off?'

'That's not how it works and you know it,' she said.

'We need to get away soon, or I'm going to go crazy.'

'You get another gig you can dive into and you'll be fine.'

Quinn wasn't so sure about that, but he said nothing. The future was not something particularly clear to him at the moment.

Orlando must have sensed something, because she said, 'How about Christmas? He'll have two weeks off then.'

A little over two months away. Not soon enough, but he knew there was little he could do about it. 'Sure,' he said.

They sat in silence for several minutes.

'You know, you're going to have to go in and

417

talk to her at some point,' Orlando said.

He shook his head. 'She doesn't want to talk to me.'

'She wants to talk to you more than anything in the world.'

Smiling without feeling, he said, 'She wants Nate to get better more than anything, I think.'

'She can want both.'

He stared at the floor, unsure.

'If you don't do it for yourself, or even for her, you need to do it for Nate. He nearly sacrificed his life to save her. He did that for you.'

Quinn rubbed his hands across his face. 'I know,' he whispered.

'So make it right,' Orlando said.

She got up and walked out of the room.

Make it right. For the third time in his life, he was responsible for nearly getting his sister killed. *Make it right?* He should just walk away, like he did before. That would make it right, wouldn't it?

But ten minutes later, he found himself standing in front of Nate's door, not sure how he got there. He remembered getting up. He remembered walking down the hall. But he didn't remember choosing to do either.

Make it right, he thought, breaking the trance.

He placed his palm against the door and pushed, hoping that for some reason it would be locked. But it swung inward.

He took a step forward. And then another.

His sister was there, her chair pulled up next to Nate's bed, his hand in hers. It was as if she hadn't heard Quinn come in. Then, finally, she seemed to sense that she was no longer alone, and turned to see who it was, her face blank.

Quinn hesitated a moment, then took the last step into the room, and let the door swing shut behind him.

ACKNOWLEDGMENTS

I'll try to keep this brief this time. All the usual circus clowns did superb work keeping me on track, helping me out of holes, and generally moving me forward. Thank you Tasha Alexander, Rob Browne, and Sophie Littlefield. Special recognition and thanks for head clown Bill Cameron for being the perfect sounding board/story compass. And to Tammy Sparks for keeping me from sounding like an idiot.

In addition, special thanks to all the wonderful folks at Preface in the United Kingdom for taking me into your arms and being the most wonderful hosts while I stumbled around London researching this book: Rosie de Courcy, Ben Wright, Nicola Taplin, Trevor Dolby, and the rest of the crew. Thank you!

Big thank-you to the folks at the Novel Café for providing a great environment to spend countless hours writing, and for keeping me well fed.

And to K, of course. You were a big part of this one. Thank you.

Finally, to my editors Danielle Perez and Randall Klein, to Nita Taublib, and to my agent Anne Hawkins. Thank you all for everything you've done to support and help me with this book.

Oh, one last thing. I blame all errors on software glitches. Yeah, that's it. Software glitches.

We do hope that you have enjoyed reading
this large print book.

Did you know that all of our titles
are available for purchase?

We publish a wide range of high quality
large print books including:
Romances, Mysteries, Classics
General Fiction
Non Fiction and Westerns

Special interest titles available in
large print are:
The Little Oxford Dictionary
Music Book
Song Book
Hymn Book
Service Book

Also available from us courtesy of
Oxford University Press:
Young Readers' Dictionary
(large print edition)
Young Readers' Thesaurus
(large print edition)

For further information or a free
brochure, please contact us at:
Ulverscroft Large Print Books Ltd.,
The Green, Bradgate Road, Anstey,
Leicester, LE7 7FU, England.
Tel: (00 44) 0116 236 4325
Fax: (00 44) 0116 234 0205

Other titles published by
The House of Ulverscroft:

THE UNWANTED

Brett Battles

The meeting place was carefully chosen: an abandoned church in rural Ireland just after dark. For Jonathan Quinn — a freelance operative and professional 'cleaner' — the job was only to observe. If his clean-up skills were needed, it would mean things had gone horribly wrong. But an assassin hidden in a tree assured just that. Suddenly Quinn had four dead bodies to dispose of and one astounding clue — to a mystery that was about to spin wildly out of control . . .

THE DECEIVED

Brett Battles

Jonathan Quinn is a professional 'cleaner': he disposes of bodies and ties up loose ends; he doesn't get his hands dirty; he doesn't ask questions. But when Quinn is hired to vanish all traces of Steven Markoff, a rare friend in his line of work, all that has to change. Determined to avenge Markoff, Quinn embarks on a trail that snakes from the corridors of power in Washington to the bustling streets of Singapore, along with his quick-witted apprentice Nate, and the brilliant, beautiful Orlando. But events spiral dangerously out of control. The pace quickens as the bullets get closer . . . and to trust is to be deceived . . .

THE CLEANER

Brett Battles

Jonathan Quinn is a freelance espionage operative with a take-no-prisoners style and the heart of a loner. His job? Professional 'cleaner'. Nothing too violent, just disposing of bodies, doing a little erasing of uncomfortable evidence if necessary. When Quinn has to investigate a suspicious case of arson, it seems simple enough. But when a dead body turns up where it doesn't belong — and Quinn's handlers at 'the Office' fall strangely silent — he knows he's in over his head. With only a handful of clues, Quinn dives for cover, struggling to find out why someone wants him dead — and if it's linked to a larger attempt to wipe out the Office.